Dedicated to Jan, Órla and Cíara Murphy,
and all Young Samurai fans who have fought
for this final chapter!

CONTENTS

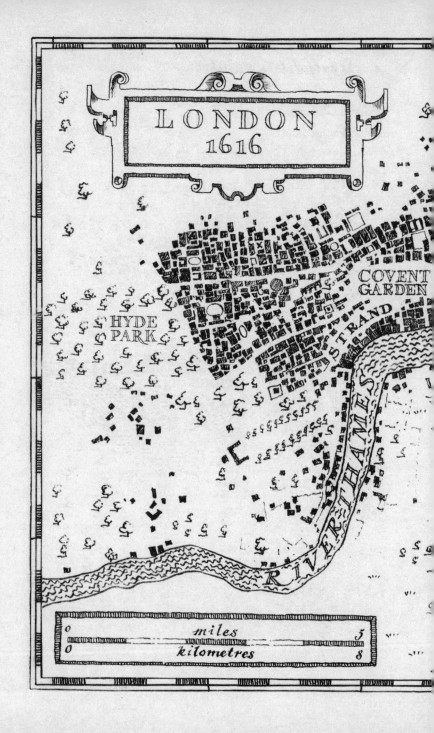

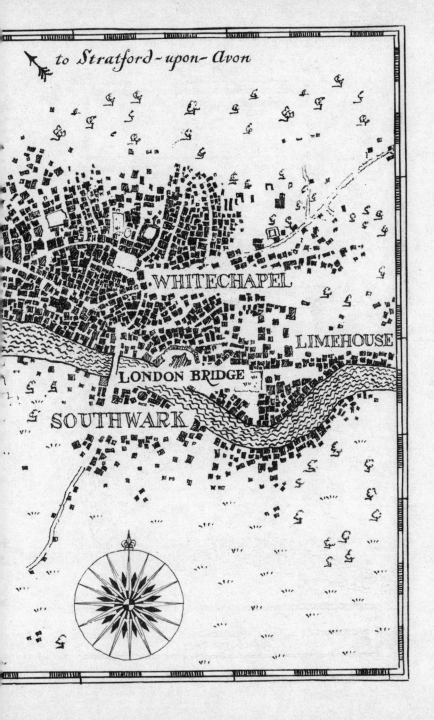

to Stratford-upon-Avon

WHITECHAPEL

LIMEHOUSE

LONDON BRIDGE

SOUTHWARK

PROLOGUE
GHOST SHIP

Hole Haven, England, autumn 1616

The galleon ship slid through the sea mist, a phantom in the darkness, her sails rippling like shrouds. Entering the Thames Estuary, the vessel maintained her steady silent course. From the shoreline, keen eyes followed her progress.

'Smugglers?' grunted the nightwatchman, a gaunt-faced fellow with a pinched nose underlined by a pencil-thin moustache. He pulled his cloak tightly round his skinny frame to ward off the night's chill.

The customs officer, a portly gentleman with reddened cheeks, lowered his spyglass. 'I don't see any boats waitin' to greet her. She looks to be a trading vessel, though: the *Salamander*, 'ccording to her bow. Yet she's sailin' far too close to shore to be headed for London.'

A bearded, heavyset constable stood beside them on the sandbank, his cudgel tapping lightly against his leg. As the three-masted ship loomed out of the mist towards them, his deep-set eyes widened slightly. '*Fie!* If the captain don't change tack soon, she's going to run aground!'

The three men watched the galleon glide past, eerie and ominous as a monster of the deep. A little further along the shore – just as the constable had predicted – the boat's keel ploughed into the soft silt of the estuary's bank and the ship shuddered to a halt. The three men exchanged an uneasy look, then took off down the beach. Their feet squelching in the sodden sand, they approached the galleon. The vessel lay still and bloated as a beached whale.

'Ahoy there!' cried the customs officer, craning his neck towards the upper deck.

But there was no reply, only the creak of timbers, the loose flap of a sail and the lapping of water against the hull.

The watchman swallowed uneasily. 'Shouldn't we call for the militia?'

The customs officer sneered. 'And incur the wrath of Sir Francis for waking him at this ungodly hour? No, we investigate further before disturbing the Lord Lieutenant from his bed.' He gestured towards a loose rigging rope dangling over the side of the ship. 'Go and look, constable.'

Hooking his cudgel to his belt, the constable waded through the water, then hauled himself up the barnacled planking and over the gunwale. All remained ominously silent. The watchman pulled the collar of his cloak even tighter, the chill in his bones not from the sea mist but from the galleon's sinister arrival. As they waited for the constable's return, the customs officer's feet began to sink into the silt.

'What's keeping him?' he muttered, tugging a leather boot free and irritably kicking off the sludge.

Another minute or so passed. Then the constable's bearded

face appeared. 'All clear,' he called, and dropped down a rope ladder for them.

Splashing through the frigid sea, they caught hold of the ladder and clambered aboard. The upper deck was deserted. No lanterns were lit. Not a soul in sight.

The customs officer glanced sidelong at the constable. 'Where's her crew, then?'

The constable shrugged. 'Below decks maybe.'

Cautiously the men approached the main hatch. The customs officer silently beckoned to the constable to open it. With a squeal of hinges, the hatch was heaved back. A set of wooden steps led down into the ship's black belly.

'Light,' ordered the customs officer.

The watchman lit a lantern and passed it to him. The gloom fled the flames, and the customs officer gasped as the lower deck revealed itself. A sailor lay slumped against a wall, his head bent forward as if in sleep. But it was the sleep of the dead. A large black rat that had been gnawing on the man's fingers scuttled away as soon as the lamplight hit it.

The watchman's sunken cheeks became even more hollow. 'You think she's a *plague* ship?'

Taking a handkerchief from his pocket, the customs officer covered his mouth and descended the steps to inspect the corpse. He set aside the lantern, its orange flame warping the sailor's waxen face.

'No sign of black spots on him.' The customs officer drew his dagger from its sheath and prodded the body with the tip of the blade. The sailor's head lolled unnaturally to one side.

'Looks like his neck is broken,' said the constable, tightening his grip on the cudgel.

3

'Perhaps he fell down the stairs?' the watchman suggested hopefully.

'Perhaps,' murmured the customs officer, sheathing his dagger and picking up the lantern. 'Let's see if we can find the rest of the crew.'

Reluctantly the watchman followed the constable down the steps. He kept close to the pool of lamplight as his eyes flitted towards every nook and cranny of the lower deck. Shapes took form, then melted back into the shadows: wooden barrels stacked five high . . . piles of cotton cloth . . . rolls of expensive silk . . . hessian sacks of grain . . . a pair of gleaming black eyes –

The watchman let out a startled cry, causing the customs officer to turn sharply. '*What?*' he snapped.

'Someone's there!' the watchman whispered, pointing a trembling finger into the inky darkness.

The customs officer directed his lantern at a gap between two barrels. 'I see no one.'

'I tell ye, a pair of eyes was watching us.'

Raising his cudgel, the constable stalked forward to investigate. As he approached the barrels, there was a *hiss* and a black shape bolted from the shadows. The constable brought his cudgel down but stopped short as a furred creature shot between his legs.

'It's just the ship's cat!' the constable snorted, lowering his cudgel.

The customs officer scowled at the watchman, then turned away with a shake of the head and resumed the search.

'It *wasn't* the ship's cat,' the watchman insisted. 'The eyes were human . . . or else demon!'

'Pull yourself together, man,' muttered the constable as he shouldered past.

Ignoring the watchman's protests, they headed deeper below deck where they discovered the galleon to be laden with exotic spices from the Far East: clove, nutmeg and mace. A king's ransom in cargo, destined for the London docks. But still no sign of the crew. The ship groaned as the hull shifted with the incoming tide.

'Strange,' remarked the customs officer, completing their sweep of the lowest deck. 'Her crew must be *somewhere* aboard.'

'Let's try the hold,' suggested the constable.

As the three men headed towards the ladder that descended into the ship's bowels, a flicker of movement caught the watchman's eye. 'Over there!'

The customs officer swivelled round, the lantern light casting a yellow wave through the darkness. But there was no one to be seen.

'Call yourself a watchman?' sneered the customs officer. 'You're jumping at shadows!'

'B-believe me, I saw a shadow *move*,' replied the watchman, his breathing now panicky and shallow. 'This is a ghost ship! We should leave. *Right now.*'

The customs officer raised a bushy eyebrow. 'A *ghost* ship? I didn't take you to be such a superstitious fellow. Get a grip of yourself! There's no –'

His rebuke was cut short by a clatter as the constable's cudgel rolled across the wooden planks and stopped at his feet. The two men glanced down at the weapon before peering nervously into the gloom for its owner.

The watchman's eyes were as round as two full moons. '*Where's the constable gone?*'

The customs officer held up his lantern, pivoting slowly to reveal yet more barrels, grain sacks and piles of cloth . . . but no constable. 'Samuel?' he called. 'You playin' games?'

Then the lamplight fell upon an open hatch. Through it, the customs officer could see body upon body piled like ballast in the hold. Their cold dead eyes stared blankly at him. The missing crew!

The customs officer stumbled away. His heart hammering in his chest, he spun back towards the watchman – only to see a black limb reach out and drag his companion away. The darkness appeared to swallow him whole, not even giving him a chance to scream. Dropping the lantern in horror, the customs officer fumbled for his dagger. But his sheath was empty. A moment later, the missing blade was pressed against his neck, the razor-sharp steel cutting into his skin and drawing a bead of blood. A shadow materialized in front of him, silhouetted against the guttering flame of the discarded lantern. Only a pair of demon-black eyes were visible.

'Is this England?' hissed the shadow, its accent strange and sinister.

The customs officer nodded, terror taking his tongue. The shadow held a piece of paper before his face. Upon it was a hand-drawn portrait of a young man with straggly straw-blond hair and ocean-blue eyes.

'You know him?' asked the shadow.

The customs officer shook his head. 'W-w-who is he?'

'Jack Fletcher, the *gaijin* samurai.'

The customs officer frowned. 'I never heard of him.'

'Pity.'

The dagger was drawn sharply across the customs officer's throat and he collapsed in a spluttering heap. As his blood spilled over the wooden deck and flowed into the hold, three more shadows emerged from the darkness. On their leader's command, they swiftly and silently made their way to the galleon's upper deck. Then, vaulting over the side and down the ladder, all four ninjas disappeared into the night.

1

AN ENGLISH WELCOME

London, England, autumn 1616

'Welcome to England!' said Jack, spreading his arms wide with pride.

He stood on the prow of the *Hosiander*, the Dutch trading ship that had provided him passage back from the Japans. Before him, in all its glory and majesty, lay the great city of London. An awe-inspiring vista of peaked roofs, church spires and palace towers. Beneath them, a sprawling mass of houses, inns, markets and shops stretched almost as far as the eye could see – further than Jack could ever recall. And from its centre, rising like a great monolith to dominate the skyline, stood the immense Gothic tower of St Paul's Cathedral.

Yet it was London Bridge that truly took his breath away. He'd forgotten just how magnificent and impressive it was. Built upon huge starlings – low pillars of boat-shaped stone – the twenty arches spanned the mighty River Thames from the Great Stone Gate on the southern bank to the New Stone Gate on the north. Eight hundred feet long, sixty feet high and almost thirty feet wide, the bridge towered over the waterway. And along its length, like frosting on top of a cake, was a tier of spectacular buildings, shops and fancy residences, some as many as six or seven storeys high.

The bridge was far more than just a bridge: it was a symbol of London's strength and power.

Jack turned to Akiko and Yori, who stood beside him on the deck. 'So what do you think?' he asked in English.

His two friends gazed around them, wide-eyed and open-mouthed, speechless at the sight. Jack was pleased at their reaction. After so many years of him talking about England and all its splendour, they were finally getting to see it with their own eyes. During his imposed stay in Japan, he'd been introduced by Akiko to the many glittering jewels of her country: from its ancient Buddhist temples and golden palaces to its paradisal gardens and snow-capped mountains, and from the cherry blossoms in spring to the maple leaves in autumn. Now *his* country would have its turn.

The *Hosiander* changed tack as she eased through the river traffic into port. She was greeted by a cacophony of boats creaking, sailors heckling one another and seagulls shrieking overhead. The waterway was bustling with hundreds of ferries, boats, trading ships and galleons. It seemed everyone was seeking to make their fortune in the burgeoning city and simply finding a place to dock was a challenge. The north bank bristled with quays and wharves, but each harboured such a flotilla of vessels that the riverside was transformed into a thick forest of masts and sails.

'Look at all the swans!' Akiko remarked, gazing in astonishment at the flocks of regal white birds dotting the water like snowflakes.

Jack smiled warmly at her wonderment. Akiko's love of nature was just one of the many things he admired about her, along with her kindness, her steely resolve and her skill with a bow. Like a *katana* wrapped in silk, she was slim, elegant and razor sharp.

'What's that?' asked Yori, peering over the gunwale. Standing on tiptoe, he pointed at the formidable drum-towered castle commanding the river's north bank.

'The Tower of London,' replied Jack.

'We *must* go there!' Yori said enthusiastically, his eyes widening.

Jack glanced ruefully at his dear friend. 'I don't think we'd wish to visit there willingly. It's a prison for traitors.'

'Oh . . .' said Yori, his eager expression deflating like a balloon. 'Perhaps another castle then.'

As the *Hosiander* docked at Somers Quay, they were met by the grim sight of four men hanging by their necks from a gibbet, their feet dangling in the water, their eyes pecked out by crows.

Akiko and Yori exchanged an anxious look, but Jack attempted a reassuring smile. 'They're probably pirates. Don't worry – *we'll* receive a far friendlier reception.'

With the gangway lowered, Jack led the way down on to the wharf and planted his feet on English soil for the first time in seven years. 'Home at last!' he exclaimed, his heart bursting with joy at being back in his own country.

Yori tottered down the gangplank after him, using his *shakujō* staff to keep his balance as he adjusted to the sudden stillness of dry land. Akiko joined him too and immediately wrinkled her nose. 'What's that *smell?*'

Jack drew in a deep breath . . . and almost gagged. The city air was putrid and stagnant compared to the fresh breeze of the open ocean. A strong waft of pitch from the shipyards in Wapping mingled with the stench of countless middens, piled high with human waste, in the streets. To make matters worse, the reek of boiling vats of urine, for making alum, blended with the putrid fumes of the leather tanneries to concoct a stink so bad that it turned all their stomachs. After so many years away, Jack had forgotten how foul-smelling daily life was in London.

'I think it might be what Jack is standing in,' said Yori, pointing his *shakujō* staff at the noxious pile surrounding Jack's feet.

Akiko grimaced. 'Ah, horse sh–'

'Yes,' Jack cut in, 'quite right.' The long twelve-month voyage back to England had given Akiko and Yori the opportunity to learn English and both were now fluent – although Jack considered some of the words the sailors had taught Akiko improper for a lady.

'I guess . . . only the reddest rose grows in the most fertile soil!' said Yori jovially as Jack scraped the muck from his sandals, his face reddening at his undignified arrival on English shores.

'Oi, I like your skirt!'

Jack glanced up to see a burly dockhand, flanked by two other young brutish lads. They wore shirts and breeches and had a rough unkempt look born of a hard life lugging cargo.

'It's not a skirt – it's a *hakama*,' Jack corrected, standing up straight and allowing the full length of his black wide-pleated trousers to show.

The dockhand smirked. 'Looks like a skirt to me.'

Jack bristled, his hand coming to rest on his samurai sword. Unabashed, the dockhand now eyed Yori in his saffron robes and over-sized straw-bowl hat. 'And what are you supposed to be?'

Yori frowned. 'I'm not supposed to be anything. I'm a monk.'

'You look like a mushroom!' the dockhand said with a snort.

His two friends laughed raucously. Then the dockhand's eyes fell upon Akiko in her shimmering silk kimono, her long dark hair straight as an arrow down her back. ''Ello, and what do we 'ave 'ere?' He swaggered up to her. 'You're a precious piece of cargo.'

'Don't you dare touch her!' warned Jack.

The dockhand shot him a sidelong look as he took hold of Akiko's hand and drew her to him. 'Why? What are you going to do about it?'

'Nothing,' Jack replied coolly. 'It's what Akiko will do to you.'

All of a sudden, the dockhand's eyes flared wide in shock and pain as Akiko twisted his arm into a *nikyo* wrist lock. The lad dropped to his knees, gasping in agony.

'*Help me!*' he cried to the others.

Fists clenched, the two other boys rushed to attack, but Yori stepped aside to let them pass and nonchalantly stuck out his ringed staff, catching one of them by the ankle.

'Oops!' said Yori, watching his victim tumble over the quayside and into the water. The boy was swiftly followed by his friend, as Jack grabbed the second boy by the lapel of his shirt and executed *seoi-nage*, the shoulder throw, sending him sailing through the air and into the Thames with a splash.

The dockhand remained on his knees, confounded by Akiko's apparently miraculous strength. Jack knew it was all in the technique. He strode up to the ill-mannered dockhand and took over *nikyo* from Akiko.

'Show some respect to our guests,' said Jack. 'In Japan, it is polite to bow.'

He applied more pressure to the wrist lock, and the dockhand, grimacing with pain, lowered his head until his face was buried in the pile of horse dung. Akiko raised an eyebrow at Jack. 'I think he's learnt his manners now.'

Reluctantly Jack let the dockhand go and the lad slunk away, spluttering and retching. After throwing a line to the two boys still floundering in the water, Yori approached Jack with a wry smile.

'What a warm welcome to England!'

2

CHEAPSIDE

'I see you're making friends already,' said Captain Spilbergen, striding down the gangplank on to the quay. As tall and sturdy as a mast, the Dutch captain cut a fine figure in his brown leather jacket, black breeches and white linen shirt with its stiff lace ruff. In emulation of Sir Walter Raleigh, he sported a trimmed beard and thin moustache of light auburn hair.

'Here,' he said, handing Jack a heavy purse. 'Your share of the cargo's profits.'

Jack held up a hand in protest. 'You've done more than enough bringing me home.'

Captain Spilbergen laughed off the suggestion. 'Nonsense! You and your *rutter* cut a whole *year* off our route and saved me a fortune in supplies and wages.' He thrust the purse into Jack's hands.

Gratefully accepting the money, Jack put the purse into his pack beside a dark oilskin-bound book. This was the precious *rutter* that he'd battled to keep safe and in his possession during his long years in Japan. His father's navigational logbook was one of the few accurate *rutters* in existence and it had helped Jack guide Captain Spilbergen's small fleet of ships across the oceans and through the North-East Passage – the fabled shortcut between Europe and the Far East. This knowledge alone made the *rutter* invaluable. But its value went beyond safe navigation and secret trading routes. For Jack, the *rutter* was his last link to his father.

'Are you sure you won't stay aboard as a permanent member of my crew?' continued the captain. 'I could do with a fine pilot like you.' His keen eyes scanned the ships in dock. 'In fact, Captain Kroeger could damn well do with you too! Where the hell's the *Salamander* got to?'

'Thank you for the offer, Captain,' replied Jack, 'but I have to find my sister. It's been seven years. Jess must think I'm dead!' – *like our father*, he thought with a sudden stab of sadness. While he longed to be reunited with his sister, Jack dreaded having to tell her that their father had been killed by a ninja – the cruel and ruthless assassin Dragon Eye. The only comfort he could offer her was that Dragon Eye was dead too. Justice had been served when Jack's friend Yamato had sacrificed himself to save Jack and Akiko from the ninjas during the battle of Osaka Castle.

'Well, it's been good sailing with you,' said the captain, laying a callused hand on Jack's shoulder. 'I wish you luck in your quest. Remember, you've always got a place aboard my ship.' Then he turned to Akiko and Yori. 'The same goes for you. I expect you'll be seeking passage back to the Japans at some point?'

Akiko bowed. 'That's very kind of you, Captain, but my fate is bound with Jack's.'

A deep warmth filled Jack's heart. He knew he'd asked

a great deal of her – and Yori – to cross half the known world to join him in England. Yori had readily agreed in order to expand his horizons, Akiko because of her love and loyalty for him, enshrined in their vow: *Forever bound to one another*. But following their encounter with the dockhands, Jack imagined his friends' initial impression of his fellow countrymen wasn't that high. So he saw it as his duty to guide and protect them in his own homeland, just as they had done for him in Japan – not that Akiko needed protecting!

'And you, Yori?' asked the captain.

'A journey is best measured in friends rather than miles, Captain,' replied Yori. He glanced over at the two bedraggled and fuming dockhands clambering back on to the quayside. 'Since we've yet to make friends here, we may stay a while!'

Captain Spilbergen laughed. 'Well, if you're looking for somewhere to lodge, I can recommend the Mermaid Inn in Cheapside.' With that, he bid them farewell, then reboarded his ship.

Noticing a number of dockhands gathering at the end of the quay, one with a smear of horse dung still visible on his cheek, Jack turned to his friends and clapped his hands. 'Come on, let's go and find my sister!' he urged, picking up Akiko's pack and handing it to her, along with her bamboo bow and quiver of hawk-feather arrows.

'Can we perhaps freshen up first?' Akiko asked as Jack ferried them swiftly along the wharf and through the muttering crowd of longshoremen. 'I'd *really* like a bath before I'm introduced.'

'Of course,' said Jack, not slowing his pace until they were clear of Somers Quay. No stranger to Japanese customs, he was well aware of how important cleanliness was to Akiko. And after a year at sea he too could do with a long soak, a decent meal and a good night's rest. As eager as he was to see Jess, he wanted to appear at his best for their reunion. Besides, after seven years, one more day wouldn't make that much difference. 'Let's head to Cheapside.'

Leaving the docks behind, they entered the city and wended their way through the backstreets, Jack guiding them by memory. But London wasn't *exactly* how he remembered it. In his head the city had been a gleaming jewel – but now he was confronted with a grim and desperate scene. Overhanging houses cramped the narrow alleyways and cast the lanes into permanent shadow. The stink they'd first smelt on their arrival intensified in the listless air to eye-watering potency. And most of the busy thoroughfares were little more than rivers of clay and mud, with only the main routes laid with gravel. People pushed rudely past amid a hubbub of noise and chaos, the calls of hawkers selling their wares competing with the yells of the city criers delivering news and public announcements. Starving beggars in filthy rags filled the street corners and gangs of young vagrants loitered in darkened passageways like packs of wild dogs. From the ship, London had appeared the heavenly dream he'd held on to for so many years. But up close the city was a hellish nightmare.

'People actually live here?' asked Akiko, gazing round in astonishment at the dire conditions.

Jack nodded. 'London's the place to be!' he said heartily, not wishing to admit his disappointment. Either the city had changed remarkably in his absence or his memory of it had been softened by the years.

A casement window overhead suddenly opened and there was a cry of 'Look out below!'

Pedestrians scattered as a chamber pot was emptied and a pile of human excrement splatted on the ground at their feet. Only Akiko's nimbleness prevented her from being covered in the muck. She stared aghast at Jack. 'I thought you said London was *civilized*!'

'It is,' he assured her, keenly aware that his home capital was not comparing favourably with the cleanliness and order of Kyoto's city streets. 'We're just in one of the poorer parts, that's all.'

Then, as if to prove his point, the alley opened out on to a wide paved street lined with splendid five-storey buildings, their timbers brightly painted and crystal-clear glass glinting in all the windows. Gentlemen and ladies, dressed in their finery, strolled up and down the thoroughfare. They browsed round the goldsmiths' shops and through the latest fashions in the milliners', the newest titles in the booksellers' and the gleaming goblets and bowls in the glass-sellers' stores. There was even a row of handsome houses decorated in real gold leaf.

'See?' said Jack, relieved to find the London of his dreams.

Akiko nodded appreciatively. 'Yes, far more civilized.'

Yori, with a wry smile, said, 'I guess, like the plume of a peacock, London is far finer in front than from behind.'

Cheapside, the widest street in the city, was a bustling hive of activity. Horse-drawn coaches rattled along the paving. Women with baskets on their heads called out, 'Hot pudding pies, hot!' while others bearing trugs of herbs cried out, 'Rosemary and bays!' Water carriers and servants queued up to fill their pails at the large stone fountain of the

Great Conduit. And at the far west end of the street a great throng of housewives, maids and travellers perused the timber-covered market stalls in such numbers that the street overflowed like a churning river.

'I've never seen anything like it,' Akiko gasped, her wonder and respect of the city growing.

Jack puffed out his chest a little. 'I told you London is the centre of the world!'

The shoppers parted as the three of them passed through the busy market, and Jack realized they must make quite a sight. While many Londoners were used to foreigners, few would have encountered Japanese people before – or their fashions. Akiko drew many an eye in her red-and-gold silk kimono, her *yumi* bow strapped across her back; and Yori was a curiosity in his plain yellow monk's robes and oversized straw hat, his Buddhist ringed staff jingling with each step.

But that was nothing compared to Jack in his black *haori* jacket and *hakama* trousers, his *daishō* of a *katana* and *wakizashi* swords on his hip.

Conscious that, as an Englishman, his Japanese garb was drawing unnecessary attention, Jack said, 'I think I'll invest in some new clothes.' He stopped beside a market stall selling long, thigh-length shirts.

'Good day, sirrah!' greeted the trader, a short fat man with cheeks as red as apples. 'You've come to the right place. I've the finest cambric shirts in the whole market!'

Jack remembered his father once telling him that 'cloth is class' and, with a full purse in his pack, he decided to treat himself to the finest clothes money could buy. He found a couple of shirts that fitted him, then moved on to a stall

20

selling breeches and waistcoats. Half an hour of shopping later, Jack was quite laden down with two cambric shirts, damask breeches, a velvet waistcoat and doublet, calico netherstocks and a pair of knee-length black leather boots.

'Are they *all* for you to wear?' asked Yori, staring agog at the array of clothes.

'Fashion has moved on in England since I was last here,' Jack replied, carefully folding them into his pack. 'Have you seen something you need?' he asked them, offering his purse.

Yori politely declined. 'All I need is my robe and sandals,' he said cheerily.

Akiko, eyeing a pile of stiff bodices and heavy skirts, said, 'I'm fine with my kimonos, thank you, Jack.' She gazed around at the countless stalls in the market. 'I never imagined such a wealth of goods. It's quite unbelievable.'

'There's nothing in the world that you can't buy here in London,' said Jack proudly, shouldering his now-heavy pack. 'Right, time for a bath and a hearty meal.' He looked up and down the street for their lodgings.

A girl in a plain brown smock, her straw-blonde hair left loose and long, was leaning beside a water fountain in the centre of the market, watching them curiously. 'You lost?' she asked.

'Do you know where the Mermaid Inn is?' said Jack.

The girl offered a bright smile. 'Follow me!'

As they trailed along behind, Akiko touched Jack's arm. 'Londoners are certainly friendly folk.'

'I'm glad you think so,' replied Jack, comforted by both her words and her touch. 'I was worried those dockhands had put you off England for good.'

'Not at all,' said Akiko, smiling. 'As Sensei Yamada might say, one rotten apple doesn't spoil the whole tree.'

The girl led them across the road and into the backstreets, and the crowds thinned out as they left the market behind. Checking they were still following, she beckoned them on through a gateway. Then, as she ducked into a dank and dirty alley, Jack questioned, 'Are you *sure* this is the right way?'

'Absolutely!' rasped a deep and unsavoury voice from the shadows.

3

VAGABOND

Out of a dark doorway stepped a man with glinting mud-brown eyes, a raggedy beard and a black-toothed grin. He wore a battered feathered hat, cocked at an angle, and he had a large hole in his right ear, burnt straight through the gristle – the mark of a vagabond.

'My sparrow 'ere,' he said, nodding at the girl whose sweet smile had now soured to a sharp look of cunning, 'she says you're lost.'

Jack glanced over his shoulder, but the gateway behind had been filled with the bear-like bulk of a man who was all straggly hair and rippling muscle. 'Looks like we are now,' Jack replied, realizing their way out was blocked.

A gaunt, rat-faced lad scurried out of a side alley. 'First time in London?' he enquired, nonchalantly swinging a heavy spiked stick.

They were surrounded.

'As it happens, yes,' Yori replied genially, then bowed low, 'and it's an honour to meet such noble folk as yourselves.'

His polite gesture took the vagabond and his gang off guard. They stared in astonishment at the little monk, before the vagabond snorted a laugh. '*Noble?* I ain't been called that before!'

'Nah,' agreed the girl, smirking, 'but you have been called a no—'

The vagabond shot her a fierce look. 'Shut it!'

The girl shrugged. 'Just saying. These travellers look *very* noble to me.' And, reaching out, she fingered the soft silk of Akiko's kimono. 'These are some fine glad rags. Wouldn't mind trying them on myself. Let's swap!'

Akiko tugged her kimono away and studied the girl's dull brown smock. 'I don't think the colour of your dress would suit me as well as it does you,' she replied with a courteous smile.

'I wasn't asking,' snapped the girl. 'I was *telling*!' She made a grab for Akiko's sleeve, but Akiko deftly evaded her lunge. As the girl overbalanced, Akiko gave her a subtle nudge and the girl ended up in a heap on the ground. Springing back to her feet, she spat at Akiko like an alley cat, her mouth twisting into a snarl.

'Steady now, Tabby!' warned the vagabond. 'It seems like we got off on the wrong foot with these strangers.' He bowed with a flourish of his hat. 'My name's Porter. It's a delight to meet you . . . in particular this good lady.'

He gently took Akiko's hand in his, raising it to his lips as if to place a kiss on it . . . before licking his rough tongue across her smooth skin. With a grimace, Akiko snatched her hand back.

'You rogue!' Jack went to draw his sword but was engulfed in the colossal arms of the bear-man.

Porter tutted. 'Quick to her defence, aren't you?' He

smirked, then his eyes alighted upon the *katana*. 'Why, that's a fancy-looking sword. Must be worth a pretty penny. What else you got?'

Jack struggled in the bear-man's grip, helpless as a trussed-up chicken. Akiko made a move to free him, but the girl drew a butcher's knife and held it to her throat. At the same time, the rat-faced lad backed Yori up against the wall with the spiked stick.

'Enough of the small talk,' said Porter. 'Hand over your purse.'

'What purse?' said Jack, playing for time as he tried to figure out a way to escape.

Porter rolled his eyes. 'The one my sparrow saw you flauntin' in the market.'

'It's in his pack,' said the girl.

Porter grabbed Jack's bag and yanked it off him. 'It's heavy!' he declared, avarice shining in his eyes. 'Perhaps we can help lighten your load.' Rifling through the bag, Porter found the oilskin *rutter* and let out a disappointed groan. 'Aww . . . it's just a book.'

He tossed it aside, where it landed in the mud. Jack gritted his teeth against the anger rising in him. If only the vagabond knew just how valuable that *rutter* was, he wouldn't have discarded it so readily. Indeed, other men had been willing to *kill* just to get their hands on it.

'We've struck gold!' Porter suddenly cried, fishing Jack's purse out and jangling the heavy weight of coins.

Enough is enough, thought Jack. He exchanged a look with Akiko and Yori, then smiled.

'What you grinning for?' demanded Porter.

'Isn't it like that line in Shakespeare's *Othello*? "The robbed that smiles steals something from the thief"?'

'Never seen one of his dumb plays. What's that supposed to mean anyway?'

'Perhaps I can explain,' replied Yori. He took a deep lungful of air, then shouted '*YAH!*' at the lad pinning him against the wall. The cry echoed loudly through the alley, half-deafening them all.

'No use callin' for help, little monk,' laughed Porter. 'No one in London hears or cares.'

But the lad with the stick suddenly slumped to his knees as if all the wind had been knocked out of him.

'Get up, you wimp!' snapped the girl irritably.

'*I can't . . .*' he gasped, clutching his stomach. His face had turned pale with a combination of pain and confusion. But Jack knew exactly what had happened. Yori was an expert at *kiai-jutsu*, the art of the *kiai*. The vibrational energy of his shout had momentarily paralysed the boy, its power hitting him as hard as a punch to the gut.

'For heaven's sake!' said the girl, booting him in the rear. 'Get up!'

In that moment of distraction, Akiko grabbed the girl's wrist and twisted the butcher's knife away from her throat. The girl squealed as Akiko over-rotated the joint, pushing the bones to breaking point. She had no choice but to drop her weapon and was driven to the ground.

Meanwhile, his arms still pinned, Jack used the bear-man's iron grip to his advantage. Lifting up his legs, he double-kicked Porter in the face, cracking the vagabond's nose and sending him reeling backwards into the mud.

26

But the bear-man was another matter. He began to crush Jack like a walnut. Jack fought for breath as his ribs were compressed and, in a desperate attempt to free himself, he flung his head back to strike his captor on the chin. But it had no more effect than a light slap to the face. Growling in annoyance, the bear-man flexed his muscles and tightened his grip. It felt to Jack as if his chest was imploding. His head pounded and his vision misted . . .

All of a sudden the pressure disappeared and Jack felt the air rush back into his lungs. Akiko had struck a *kyusho* point in the bear-man's upper arm, sending a shockwave of pain through his radial nerve and forcing him to loosen his hold on Jack. At the same time, Yori targeted the tip of his staff at another nerve point on his foot. Howling in agony, the bear-man dropped Jack and began hopping around like an enraged rabbit.

'I . . . had . . . him,' Jack protested, as Yori helped him to his feet.

'Of course you did,' his friend replied with a wry grin. 'He would've tired *eventually* of crushing you!'

Jack picked up the *rutter*, wiped it clean and stuffed it back into his pack. Then turning to the bloody-nosed Porter, he snatched his purse out of the vagabond's hand. 'I'll have that back too,' he said. And, with that, Jack led his friends out of the alley.

Porter, left fuming in the mud, flicked the blood from his broken nose. He drew a dagger and growled, 'Get up, you lot. Quick, shake yourselves! After them!' And the gang gave chase.

Jack, Akiko and Yori dashed through the gateway and

back through the warren of alleys and side streets, before bursting out into Cheapside market.

'We'll lose them in the crowd,' said Jack.

But their Japanese attire meant they didn't exactly blend in and Porter and his gang were soon upon them.

'No one makes a fool out of me!' snarled Porter, slashing at Jack with his dagger.

Hemmed in by the glut of shoppers, Jack barely managed to evade the rusty blade. He unsheathed his *katana* in one swift movement. The gleam of steel caught people's attention and the crowd scattered in panic. Porter, glancing at his own dagger and comparing its undersized blade with Jack's, hesitated – but the lad with the nail-studded stick didn't. He swung his weapon viciously at Yori, who dived aside at the very last second. The stick smashed into a fruit stall behind. As apples, oranges and lemons splattered everywhere, the girl thrust at Akiko with her butcher's knife, while the bear-man lumbered in, fists flailing.

A bell started ringing urgently across the market and several men in wide-brimmed hats carrying pikes rushed to contain the violence.

'City constables!' yelled the girl, splitting from the scene like a scalded cat. The lad fled too. But Porter wasn't so quick. He was seized by two constables. Another pair tried to contain the bear-man with their pikes, giving Jack, Akiko and Yori the chance to slip away into the crowd. As they pushed through the throng, Jack spotted the iron-tipped pikes of more constables heading in their direction but, keeping low, he steered his friends away. Eventually they came to the corner of Bread Street and stopped to catch their breath under a lavishly painted wooden sign of a woman with a fish's tail.

'In here!' cried Jack, and they dived inside the Mermaid Inn.

4

GIVING THE LIE

Jack pressed himself against the wood-panelled wall, alongside Yori and Akiko, and peered out of the leaded window. Outside the inn, the marketplace was in a commotion, as constables barged through the crowd searching for their quarry. A washerwoman in an apron pointed in the tavern's direction and Jack's breath caught in his throat. There was nowhere left to run.

'Why don't we give ourselves up?' suggested Yori. 'After all, we were attacked first.'

'There's no guarantee they'll see it that way,' Jack replied as three pike-bearing men strode purposefully towards the inn. 'It would be Porter's word against ours and we're strangers in this city.'

'*You're* not,' observed Akiko.

Jack glanced down at his Japanese robes. 'I feel like it, though,' he said, as he considered their welcome so far.

The constables were almost at the door and Jack's hand instinctively reached for his *katana*. But instead of entering, the men filed past and disappeared down Bread Street. Jack let out a long sigh of relief, resting his head against the glass.

'Are you 'ere to drink or just stare out me window?' said a gruff female voice.

Jack turned round. The inn was gloomy, lit only by guttering candlelight. The stink of tobacco hung in the air, wreaths of smoke swirling like mist up to the rafters. Groups of men and women, rich and poor, clustered round heavy wooden tables piled high with tankards of beer. A burly ale-wife with an ample bosom and arms like a docker's stood behind the counter. She squinted at them with hostile suspicion.

'We're seeking lodgings,' said Jack, offering his most charming smile. 'Your establishment comes highly recommended.'

The woman's stern face didn't crack. 'You got the means to pay?'

'Of course,' said Jack, confidently striding up to the bar. 'Your finest room please, and dinner for three.'

'And a hot bath,' added Akiko.

The ale-wife blinked. 'A *bath*?'

'Yes,' said Akiko eagerly. 'A *hot* bath.'

The ale-wife eyed her dubiously. 'Are you sure that's wise? You don't want to catch anything.'

Akiko frowned. 'What could I catch? Washing *cleanses* the body.'

Shaking her head in astonishment, the ale-wife snorted. 'Huh! Foreigners!' Then she turned to Jack. 'That'll be sixpence for room and board. Plus another threepence for the bath.'

Jack baulked at the price but nonetheless paid over the coins from his purse. The sight of hard cash seemed to soften the woman, but only for a moment. 'BOY!' she bellowed, and a runt of a lad came scuttling out. 'Take our young guests' bags up to their room, put fresh sheets on the bed and stoke up the fire to heat the water.'

The boy furrowed his brow. 'What for?'

'A bath,' said the ale-wife, rolling her eyes.

'*What?*' he moaned, his shoulders slumping. 'I'll be to and fro from the conduit all afternoon!'

'Then you'd best get moving!' snapped the ale-wife. With a put-upon sigh, the boy went to take Jack and Akiko's packs, but Jack hesitated. He was nervous about handing over his precious belongings, in particular the *rutter*. Noticing his reluctance, the ale-wife said, 'Have no fear. There ain't no thievery in my inn. You have my word.'

Judging by the size of the woman and her brusque manner, Jack believed her. He relinquished his pack, although still somewhat reluctantly, and declared, 'We'll have three mugs of small beer too, while we wait for our food.'

After plonking three tankards on the bar, the ale-wife disappeared to the back of the inn. Jack, Akiko and Yori took a table in the corner.

'What's wrong with the water here?' asked Akiko. 'That landlady didn't much like my request for a bath.'

'Nothing,' replied Jack, conscious that the English weren't so regular with their bathing habits as the Japanese – once a year being thought quite enough. 'But you wouldn't want to drink it. It'd make you sick. Anyway,' he said, raising his tankard, 'here's to coming back home!' And they all clinked mugs.

Jack took a long swig from his tankard, savouring the distinctive malty taste familiar from his early childhood, small beer being the staple drink of all English folk, young and old. Akiko sipped hers and Yori ventured a gulp. A second later he gagged and stuffed a fist in his mouth, his face going green.

'Are you all right?' asked Jack.

'*F-f-fine*,' Yori spluttered, setting aside his tankard. 'I guess . . . English beer is an acquired taste.'

Jack laughed. 'You'll get used to it! It's safer than drinking the water, I assure you. And don't worry – there's barely any alcohol in it.' He thought of all the strange food and drinks he'd encountered in Japan – small beer was nothing compared to raw fish, fermented beans, pickled salt plums, rice wine and even *green* tea!

The ale-wife waddled over and dumped three steaming plates on the table, along with a handful of knives and spoons. 'Beef and kidney pie,' she grunted.

Akiko examined the cutlery. 'Do you have *hashi*?' she asked.

The ale-wife puffed out her lips. 'I certainly hope not,' she retorted. 'It sounds painful!' With that, she strode off, her large chest heaving with mirth.

Jack grinned at Akiko. 'No chopsticks here, I'm afraid. Now it's your turn to learn my customs,' he said, picking up his knife, cutting open the pie and scooping out the thick gravy and meat with his spoon.

Yori followed suit, while Akiko delicately sliced a cut in the pastry, sniffed the aroma tentatively, then took a mouthful and slowly chewed.

'Well, what do you think?' asked Jack, devouring his own pie.

Akiko managed a weak smile. 'Very . . . delicious.'

But Jack could tell by her forced swallow that, just like English beer, English food might be an acquired taste too.

They were finishing their meal when raucous laughter burst from a table nearby. Three gentlemen, merry on ale, were glancing in their direction and making comments loud enough to be overheard. One of them, a fellow with a tight crop of copper-red hair and a preened moustache, and wearing a lace ruff so broad and stiff that it looked like his head was on a plate, remarked, 'I thought the Globe Theatre was across the river. These players must have forgotten the way back to the stage!'

He sniggered at his own humour. His companions joined in too.

'With such wit, sir, *you* should be on the stage,' said his portly friend, whose flushed cheeks were almost as plum-red as his lavish velvet waistcoat.

'Too right,' agreed the other man, snorting a laugh and quaffing from his tankard. Tall and thin with long lank hair like combed flax, he peered down his hooked beak of a nose at his friend. 'You could be Mercutio in *Romeo and Juliet*.'

The red-haired fellow grinned beneath his curled moustache. 'And those three over there could play the fools in *A Midsummer Night's Dream*. The lad could be Bottom; the monk could be Flute the bellows-mender (he lacks a beard and he's already wearing a dress!); and the China woman, she could –'

'Akiko is Japanese,' Jack interrupted sharply, his patience at an end. 'And a samurai. So show some respect.'

'A *what*?' smirked the moustachioed gentleman.

Jack narrowed his eyes. 'A samurai. A warrior of the military class in Japan. Like our English knights.'

Dismissing Akiko's slight frame with a single look, the man raised an incredulous eyebrow, then turned to his friends. 'A *girl* knight! Pull the other one, eh?'

The whole group fell about laughing.

'These folk aren't from the theatre, that's for sure,' chuckled the portly red-faced man. 'They're mad! Must've escaped from Bedlam.'

'Or else had one too many ales!' guffawed the hook-nosed fellow, raising his own tankard to his lips again.

By now, other drinkers in the tavern had fallen silent, their attention drawn by the boisterous laughter. Incensed that he and his friends were being ridiculed so publicly, Jack rose from his seat. But Akiko laid a hand on his arm. 'Ignore them,' she urged. 'We've had enough trouble for one day.'

Jack fumed. The gentlemen's behaviour was unacceptable. Yet again his fellow countrymen had let him down. This wasn't the impression he wanted Akiko and Yori to have of England. Nonetheless he retook his seat, but not before the moustachioed man had spotted the *katana* and *wakizashi* on his hip.

'What's that you're bearing?' he demanded.

'My *daishō*,' Jack replied tersely.

The man frowned suspiciously. 'Look like swords to me. And in London no one may carry a sword unless he's been knighted.' He swivelled slightly in his chair to reveal a long slim rapier attached to his own belt.

'And who might you be?' asked Jack, unperturbed.

'Sir Toby Nashe. And you?'

'Jack Fletcher.'

'No "Sir"?' He eyed Jack disdainfully. 'Then you must relinquish your swords, for you are no knight.'

Jack stiffened. 'I will do no such thing.'

Sir Toby got to his feet, planting his hands on his hips. 'You have no choice. It is the law of this land.'

Jack shook his head. 'I've been bestowed the rank of *hatamoto* by the Regent of Japan. I am a samurai. So I've the right to carry a sword. Two, in fact.' Jack now stood so the full length of his *katana* and *wakizashi* could be clearly seen, their black lacquered *sayas* gleaming in the muted candlelight.

'That title holds no status here in England,' answered Sir Toby. 'Hand over your swords.'

'No,' said Jack, squaring up to him. There was no way on earth he'd surrender his weapons to a stranger!

A tense silence descended on the inn. Everyone was watching the stand-off, some still with their tankards of beer half-raised to their lips.

'Jack . . .' intervened Yori timidly, 'perhaps our room is ready now.'

His eyes still locked on Sir Toby's, Jack slowly nodded. 'Yes, I've had enough of the poor company in this tavern. Let's retire to our quarters.'

'Don't walk away from me! We're not finished,' shouted Sir Toby, stamping his foot like an impetuous child.

Jack continued to follow Akiko and Yori in the direction of the stairs. But Sir Toby rushed forward to block his path. 'Hand over your swords *now*!'

'On whose authority?' Jack challenged.

'The King's.'

It was Jack's turn to laugh. '*You* don't speak for the King.'

Sir Toby's face went livid. 'You dare to mock me? I have connections with His Majesty, don't you know!'

'Oh yes? Well, I know the Emperor of Japan,' said Jack, pushing past.

Suppressed laughter rippled through the inn. Sir Toby bristled, his moustache quivering on his upper lip. 'Are you giving me the lie?'

Jack glanced over his shoulder at the pompous man and shrugged. 'If you say you know the King, you know the King.' Then he turned and headed towards the stairs.

But he'd barely put his foot on the first step when he heard Sir Toby call out, 'You have offended my honour, sirrah! I challenge you to a duel!'

5

A MATTER OF HONOUR

'Are all your fellow countrymen so quick to anger?' asked Akiko as they were frogmarched through the city gates to the open space of Moorfields, a knot of curious onlookers trailing in their wake. 'Everyone we've met so far wishes to insult us, rob us or kill us!'

'Now you know how I felt in Japan!' Jack muttered irritably.

Akiko winced and fell silent. Jack immediately felt bad. He knew he'd been rude to her and that his tone had been harsh. But the imminent prospect of the duel, which would further delay his reunion with Jess, had combined with his utter dismay at the hostile welcome they'd received so far in England and had made him tetchy. 'Sorry, Akiko . . .' he muttered, 'I'm a little tense at the moment.'

The delicate line of her jaw relaxed and her gaze returned his way. 'I didn't mean to upset you, Jack. But we're here to meet your sister, not the end of a sword! And it seems pointless fighting over something so small.'

'Well, certain samurai lords would chop off your head if you didn't bow low enough!' Jack shot back. He thought of the old blind tea merchant who'd suffered such a fate on the command of *daimyo* Kamakura – the man who'd become Shogun of Japan and expelled all Christians and foreigners from his domain.

'They are the exception,' defended Akiko. 'Most *daimyo* are fair and just.'

'*If* you are Japanese,' said Jack bluntly as they were brought to a halt beside an old oak tree in the middle of a meadow. 'Anyway, the same applies here. We've simply been unfortunate to meet such idiots as this man!'

Sir Toby was removing his fur-collared cloak with the affected grace of a royal courtier. Offloading the garment to his round-bellied and fawning friend, he examined the grassy duelling area, appeared satisfied, then began stretching his legs and flexing his arms. His other companion, the lank-haired drunkard, propped himself up against the tree, his eyes half-closed with intoxication. The growing number of spectators now formed a loose circle round them, hemming Jack and his friends in.

Yori, who'd been fearfully quiet all the way to Moorfields, now whispered to Jack, 'Do you *really* have to do this?'

'It looks like it,' he replied, as Sir Toby made a show of parrying and lunging, much to the delight of the crowd.

'But what if you apologize?'

Jack frowned. 'What do I have to apologize for? He's the one who should be apologizing to *us*!'

'I know, but for the sake of avoiding yet *another* fight today, perhaps we can swallow our pride, say sorry and return to the inn in one piece.' Yori looked up at him, eyes round and hopeful.

Jack sighed. Yori was right. He was about to risk everything over a perceived slight. He should just apologize and pray that would be the end of it, that his opponent's posturing was no more than an act of bravado. 'Yes, by all means try,' he said.

Summoning up his courage, Yori approached Sir Toby and bowed low. 'I understand, sir, the importance of honour and respect. I can assure you that my friend Jack did not wish to offend your good nature or imply that you're a liar. This is clearly a misunderstanding. So, rather than fight a duel, please accept our sincere apology.'

Sir Toby looked haughtily down his narrow nose at the submissive little monk. 'Some men are satisfied with words, some content with penance,' he replied, 'and others need to be answered with weapons. I, sir, am of this last opinion.'

With that, Sir Toby drew his rapier with a flourish. The weapon was long, slim and pointed as a needle. The ornate handguard was composed of a complex swirl of silver loops and prongs, and the pommel was large and round, a counterweight to the long blade as well as an effective striking ball. Sir Toby flicked the sword several times, its sharp tip whipping through the air with a high-pitched *swish*. Yori retreated rapidly.

'Well, it was worth asking,' consoled Akiko, as wagers started to be made among the crowd on the outcome of the impending fight.

Jack wasn't put off. Having gained experience of duelling in Japan, he was confident in his own fighting abilities. He was keenly aware that any combat posed the risk of injury, or even death, but he'd been trained in *kenjutsu* by the greatest swordsman in Japan, Masamoto Takeshi. From him, he'd learnt and mastered the Two Heavens, an almost invincible technique using both the *katana* and *wakizashi*. Furthermore, the samurai sword had by far the most lethal and honed blade in the whole world, and looking at the flimsy rapier in Sir Toby's hand, Jack almost pitied the man's chances.

'Is this your second?' Sir Toby asked him, pointing the tip of his rapier towards Yori. 'Not much of an opponent for Sir Francis here, but I suppose he'll do.'

'*Me?*' squeaked Yori, aghast. He glanced at the drunk yet towering gentleman leaning against the tree. 'I'm no fighter. I'm a monk. I've taken a vow of peace.'

Sir Toby shrugged away his protest. 'But we fight according to the French custom. The seconds on each side duel too.'

Yori backed away, his gaze darting round the crowd like a mouse seeking a bolt-hole.

'I'll be Jack's second,' said Akiko, stepping up.

Sir Francis's drooping eyes suddenly popped open. '*Zounds!* The girl really thinks she is a warrior!'

'You realize this is a man's fight,' said Sir Toby condescendingly.

The corner of Akiko's mouth curled into a faint smile. 'Then I'll be gentle with him.'

Laughter burst from the gathered onlookers and the excitement intensified at the prospect of such an unusual match. More eager bets were placed.

'So be it,' declared Sir Toby. 'Edmund, lend her your rapier.'

His portly friend reluctantly presented his sword. Akiko

41

weighed it in her hand, adapting her grip to the unfamiliar weapon. 'It's light!' she remarked.

'Of course it is,' said Sir Edmund. 'Italian steel. The finest.'

'Won't save you, though,' said Sir Francis, peeling himself away from the tree.

Jack and Akiko stood side by side, facing their opponents. The crowd fell silent in anticipation.

'*En garde!*' cried Sir Toby, dropping into a long low stance and holding out his rapier.

'I assure you that you don't want to do this,' said Jack, maintaining a calm composure as he and Akiko prepared for battle. 'Put away your swords now and we can forget all about our quarrel.'

'I believe they're scared,' slurred Sir Francis, his rapier tip wavering.

'I'm scared for *you*,' said Jack. 'Your last chance: sheathe your weapons.'

Sir Toby snorted his disdain. 'This is a matter of honour. I *must* draw blood to be satisfied.'

With that, he lunged at Jack. At the same time Sir Francis went for Akiko.

The speed at which Sir Toby moved was astounding. Caught off guard, Jack barely saw the rapier's sharpened tip as it thrust towards his heart. Only a deft, instinctive shift of his body saved him from being skewered. Meanwhile, Akiko was driven back by a series of sharp jabs from Sir Francis.

Recovering quickly, Jack drew his *katana* in one fluid movement and sliced down. The curved blade cut across Sir Toby, threatening to sever the man's sword arm clean off.

But Sir Toby was quick to pull back and the *katana* sliced through thin air, a fraction from the end of his nose.

'Your sword work is too slow,' sneered Sir Toby as if he'd only been testing Jack's reactions with his first attack.

Then the stiffened ruff round his neck parted, fell away and dropped into the dirt.

'Not that slow,' replied Jack with a cunning grin.

Sir Toby's face blanched at this indignity as sniggering spread through the crowd. The laughter caused Sir Francis to pause in his assault on Akiko, who'd been fiercely defending herself.

Sir Edmund waddled over in a panic and examined Sir Toby. 'No blood,' he declared with evident relief and Sir Francis resumed his attack on Akiko.

Although uninjured, Sir Toby was incensed. 'You ruined my ruff! You'll pay for that!'

He came at Jack like a thing possessed, his rapier stabbing for Jack's eyes. Jack deflected the first thrust, dodged the second, but the third caught him across the cheek. Pain flared in a sharp line.

'First blood!' cried an onlooker in delight.

'Sir Toby's won,' Sir Edmund announced with an official air.

Money began to exchange hands as bets were claimed and attention now turned to the ongoing duel between Sir Francis and Akiko. Despite her awkwardness with the rapier, she was putting up a valiant fight, deflecting his attacks and countering with a few well-placed jabs of her own. Sir Francis was forced to up his game when the tip of Akiko's rapier pierced his doublet and almost drew blood.

Sir Toby fought on too – regardless of taking first blood. Rapier and *katana* clashed as Jack warded off the multiple jabs. He was pricked in the arm, then the hand, but still Sir Toby advanced on him.

'It's first blood, Sir Toby,' called out his friend. 'Victory is yours.'

'My honour is yet to be satisfied,' he snapped, lunging again and again.

Each strike was like a bee sting to Jack. Despite his own sword skills, Jack found himself unable to match Sir Toby for speed and reach. More and more puncture wounds dotted his limbs and body. As he desperately fended off the flurry of attacks, Akiko continued to battle Sir Francis. Drunk as the man was, he proved to be a capable swordsman and Akiko was struggling to hold her own with an unfamiliar weapon and against such a vastly different sword style. But she seemed to be faring far better than Jack, who was fast becoming a bleeding pincushion.

Realizing he'd dangerously underestimated his opponent, Jack drew his *wakizashi* and took up a Two Heavens stance.

'You'll need more than two swords to beat me!' Sir Toby scoffed and thrust for Jack's chest.

Jack blocked the attack with his *wakizashi*, then brought his *katana* down hard on to the rapier. The steel of his blade being stronger than the rapier's, the clash of swords broke the tip clean off Sir Toby's weapon.

That should reduce his reach, thought Jack with a grin.

Sir Toby stared at his docked rapier in disbelief. Then flew into a rage. He stabbed, thrust and lunged repeatedly. But armed now with two swords and no longer at a disadvantage in terms of range, Jack had less trouble deflecting and countering the onslaught. A sudden yelp of pain caused him to turn. Akiko was backed up against the oak tree, her shoulder run through with Sir Francis's rapier, its slender blade pinning her to the trunk.

Distracted by her plight, Jack was caught off guard by a vicious slash from Sir Toby. The broken blade whipped across the back of his left hand, leaving a welt and forcing him to drop his *wakizashi*. Retreating awkwardly, Jack stumbled over a tree root and landed on his back. With a gleeful grin, Sir Toby saw his opportunity and prepared to plunge his broken rapier into Jack's exposed chest . . .

'CONSTABLES!' came a cry from the crowd.

A unit of armed men barged on to the scene and Sir Toby was denied his killing strike.

'Arrest these men!' ordered the chief constable as the spectators quickly dispersed. Then, somewhat taken aback at Akiko's involvement, he added, 'And the girl.'

The constables swiftly intervened, seizing the duellists and confiscating their weapons. Jack was forced to relinquish both his *katana* and *wakizashi*. Even Yori was made to give up his *shakujō* staff.

'Unhand me!' roared Sir Toby as he was being bound. 'Don't you know who I am?'

The chief constable, an officious man with a thrusting jaw and deep-set eyes, looked him up and down before replying, 'No.'

Sir Toby's face flushed with outrage. 'I am *Sir* Toby Nashe, second cousin of Sir William Harrington, who is friend to His Majesty the King.'

While the connection seemed pretty tenuous to Jack, it had the desired effect on the chief constable and Sir Toby and his friends were immediately released. But Jack, Akiko and Yori remained in custody.

'My apologies, Sir Toby,' said the chief constable, his tone polite but without any real effort at deference. 'Now will you explain what is going on here?'

'These *foreigners* tried to rob me,' Sir Toby declared, his two faithful companions nodding in vigorous agreement.

'That's a lie!' cried Jack.

'And besmirch my reputation,' added Sir Toby haughtily, holding his nose high.

'Please, honourable constable,' said Yori, managing a half bow despite being pinned by the arms. 'These three men insulted us, then challenged my friend Jack to a duel. We are innocent of these accusations.'

The chief constable eyed Yori's religious robes, then glanced at Akiko's wounded shoulder, the blood blooming on her silk kimono. For a moment it seemed he might be willing to believe them. Then his stubbled jaw hardened. '*You're* the ones who caused that disturbance at Cheapside market – I heard that three travellers in strange clothes had escaped capture.' Puffing out his barrel chest, he announced, 'I arrest you in the name of the King for brawling, robbery and disturbing the peace.'

Jack opened his mouth to protest, but was cut off by the constable's order: 'Take them away!'

6

GAOL

'At least this saves us the cost of lodgings!' said Yori, trying to sound cheerful as he crouched on his haunches in the grim confines of his little cell: no more than a cage of rusting iron bars and greasy granite walls with a filthy floor for a bed.

Akiko eyed the soiled bucket in the corner of her cell with disgust. 'I don't think much of the bath!'

Jack was slumped on the cold stone floor of his cell, his head hanging between his knees. While he appreciated his friends' attempts at humour, his heart was too heavy. They hadn't even been in England a day and they were prisoners in the city gaol, awaiting trial for crimes they hadn't committed. They could be incarcerated in this hell-hole for days, weeks . . . even months before they were brought before a court. Would he *ever* see his sister?

'I'm so sorry for dragging you all the way to England,' he mumbled. 'I shouldn't have asked you to come.'

'Forever bound to one another,' reminded Akiko with a weak smile.

Yori jangled the heavy iron shackles round his wrists. 'You can say that again!'

Like Yori, Jack was also shackled to a wall, but Akiko, being a girl, had been spared such undignified treatment. 'You must think England is a living hell,' he said.

'It's . . . not exactly what I'd pictured,' Akiko admitted kindly. 'But I'm with *you*, and that's what matters.'

Jack looked across to her prison cell. Weak sunlight squeezed through the bars of the tiny window above, casting a pale glow across her delicate features. He loved Akiko for her unwavering loyalty to him, but, despite that, she couldn't hide in her eyes the dismay and disbelief at what they'd experienced since arriving in London. And who could blame her! Jack, too, was astounded at the sheer savagery and uncivilized nature of his fellow countrymen, as well as repulsed by the primitive living standards compared to those in Japan. No wonder the Japanese considered Westerners to be barbarians. After seven years away from home, Jack no longer recognized his country. He was a stranger in his own land.

'How's your shoulder?' he asked, feeling guilty not only for dragging Akiko to this sorry country but for embroiling her in a duel.

She peeled away the silk of her kimono, the blood now dry, and peeked at her wound. 'It should be fine,' she said through gritted teeth, 'although it's a little painful. How about you?'

'All good,' lied Jack. In fact, he hurt all over; the numerous puncture wounds from Sir Toby's rapier still smarted as if he'd been rolled through a steel thorn bush. To add to his bleak mood, he couldn't forget that he'd been defeated in the duel. Never would he have believed that the samurai sword could be bettered, yet Sir Toby's rapier had proved an exceptionally nimble and effective weapon. His opponent had scored multiple strikes before Jack had managed to find any sort of weakness in his swordplay. If the rapier hadn't broken, Jack was convinced that Sir Toby would have run him through.

'*Nam-myoho-renge-kyo-nam-myoho-renge-kyo* . . .' Yori had begun chanting to himself, his shackles clinking in rhythm. Jack knew his friend was meditating, trying to distance himself from their dire circumstances.

'Perhaps we can escape somehow?' said Akiko, standing up and examining the bars to her cell.

A crazed cackle from a cell at the far end greeted her suggestion. '*Escape?* You'd need wings to escape this pit of despair!' said a dishevelled pile of rags.

Until then, Jack had thought they were the only ones in the prison block. But now a dirty, toothless face appeared between the gaps in the cell bars. The shrivelled creature licked its cracked lips and stretched its skeletal fingers out towards them.

'Abandon all hope!' it croaked. 'For we are all damned. The devil rules over this infernal prison.'

'Why aren't you shackled?' asked Jack, glad of the bars between them and this lunatic inmate.

'Been 'ere so long awaiting trial that the chains no longer hold me,' he replied with another skittish laugh. 'They just slide off me bones,' he said, showing Jack his stick-thin wrists.

Jack's low spirits plummeted even further. They would die of starvation before they were ever set free!

'Me name's Arthur, by the way,' the prisoner went on,

49

then frowned, 'or at least I think it was . . . Most people call me Mad Bob.' He offered a toothless grin. 'Pleased to make your acquaintance!'

Jack nodded a cautious greeting, then turned to Akiko. 'We have to get ou–' Jack almost leapt out of his skin. She was standing right outside his cell door.

'I already have,' she said with an impish grin.

He stared in astonishment. 'B-but how?'

'The bars are bent at the top, from the weight of the roof,' she replied, pointing to a wider opening high up in the ironwork. 'I was able to squeeze through.'

Though he was aware of Akiko's ninja skills, Jack was still taken aback at her extreme agility. He would have thought only a squirrel could have scaled the bars and slipped between such a narrow gap.

'The bird *does* have wings!' gasped their fellow prisoner.

'I'll go and find the keys,' Akiko whispered, heading towards a darkened stairwell, 'for the doors and your shackles.'

'Don't worry about me,' said Yori, who'd finished chanting. He held up his hands, free of their shackles.

Mad Bob's skull-like eyes widened into black holes of awe and fear. 'It's witchcraft!'

'No, the shackles were simply corroded,' Yori explained matter-of-factly. 'A little chanting – soft *kiai-jutsu*, as Sensei Yamada calls it – and with the right resonance, the brittle metal weakens and cracks.'

Jack looked at his own shackles. They were new. No chanting would break them.

'I'll be back with our weapons and hopefully your purse too,' said Akiko, before disappearing up the flight of stairs.

'We won't be seeing 'er again,' muttered Mad Bob peevishly.

Jack shot him an irritated look. 'She'll be back – you don't know Akiko.'

There was a snort of manic high-pitched laughter. 'Once a bird takes flight, it won't return to its cage.'

Trying to ignore him, Jack stood and pulled at his own shackles. While he had every faith in Akiko, there was a good chance she would not find the keys to his irons. So rather than sitting around and doing nothing, he yanked on the chains again. But the bolts held firm.

'Go on!' encouraged Mad Bob. 'Haul away, me hearty. I'd like to see ye trying to drag a whole prison wall with ye!'

Putting a foot against the brickwork and gritting his teeth, Jack wrenched hard. He jerked and tugged until his strength gave out and he collapsed on the floor, breathless, his heart pounding.

'I think it moved at least half an inch,' said Mad Bob earnestly.

Jack glared at him, then began trying to pull his hands out through the iron cuffs. But the shackles were far too tight and his efforts only resulted in scraping skin and bloodying his wrists.

'Oh, that looks like it hurts,' sympathized the inmate. 'But give it another few months and they'll slip right through –'

'Shut up, Bob!' snapped Jack, his patience worn thin. Just then, he heard a trickle of water and turned round. Yori stood in the corner of his cell, urinating.

'There's a bucket for that, don't you know!' said Mad Bob indignantly, as if such conduct was inappropriate in their already squalid surroundings.

Yet even Jack was surprised. Such ill manners were totally out of keeping with his Japanese friend's behaviour. 'What *are* you doing?' he demanded.

'Back-up plan,' Yori replied, now getting on his hands and knees and scraping away at the wall with the edge of one of his metal cuffs. 'The brickwork is eroded from frost and damp. My piss should help dissolve the crumbling mortar, and with a bit of extra encouragement –' he gouged out a lump of mortar, then worked away at the wall – 'there!'

Yori pulled out a brick. A back alley – and freedom – was visible through the narrow hole.

'Good work, Yori!' said Jack as another brick came loose, then another.

Mad Bob began tutting in disapproval. 'Julius won't be happy with that!' he remarked.

As Yori widened the hole, they heard the jangle of keys and footsteps descending the stairwell. Jack exchanged a hopeful look with Yori. When Akiko returned with the keys, they'd all be free.

'Don't know what you two are smiling about,' said Mad Bob. 'That ain't your friend coming back. That's Julius!'

And, as their fellow inmate began to cackle crazily, Jack realized he was right. The footsteps were too heavy to be Akiko's.

'*Go!*' Jack hissed to Yori. 'Get out while you can.'

Yori's eyes widened in horror. 'But what about *you*?'

'I'll be fine,' said Jack as lamplight spilled from the stairwell into the prison block. 'Now go!'

Yori dived through the hole a second before a large bearded man with a belly the size of a walrus lumbered in.

Holding up his oil lamp, the gaoler studied the two empty prison cells, then furrowed his thick brow in confusion. 'Weren't there three of you before?'

Jack said nothing, Mad Bob gave a toothless grin and shrugged.

'No matter,' said the gaoler, unhooking the keys from his belt and opening Jack's cell door. 'The court'll punish ye all the same.'

'Only if they find me guilty,' said Jack.

'*Guilty?*' cackled Mad Bob, as Jack was dragged away up the stairs by the gaoler. 'You're already guilty just by being in 'ere!'

7

JUDGE AND JURY

'Who comes next?' demanded the judge. A stern-faced man with sallow sunken cheeks, grey back-swept hair and a beard trimmed to a point, he could have been the devil in old age. He wore a fur-lined gown, a silk shirt laced at the neck and a heavy jewelled gold chain of office.

The court scribe studied his documents under the candlelight. 'The English seaman and two foreigners from the Japans.' He glanced across at the group of prisoners occupying the four rows at the back of the courtroom and called, 'Jack Fletcher, Akiko Dāte and Yori Sanada, come to the bar!'

Rising from his seat, Jack approached the judge, who sat behind a large and daunting mahogany bench. On either side of him, like vultures waiting for the kill, perched his deputies, tight-lipped and narrow-eyed.

'Where are your companions?' asked the judge tersely.

'They didn't like their welcome here in England so they left,' Jack replied, dearly hoping that Yori and Akiko were indeed long gone. A murmur of amusement rippled through the spectators gathered in the gallery overlooking the proceedings.

'Careful, young man!' warned the judge. 'I'll hold you in contempt of court with such surly replies. In their absence, you will stand for their crimes too. You're very fortunate we're holding session today, otherwise you'd be waiting a full season before being tried.'

But Jack, arrested and imprisoned on false charges, didn't feel very fortunate. He should have been with his sister by now, enjoying a warm meal in their father's cottage, celebrating his return in front of the fire, his two best friends at his side, while regaling her with tales of his adventures in Japan. Instead he was standing alone in a cold courtroom having to defend himself against a false charge.

One of the judge's deputies leant forward and rested his bony elbows on the bench. Peering from his perch with disdain, he enquired, 'What *are* you wearing?'

Jack glanced down and shrugged. 'A *hakama*.'

'I thought you were an Englishman, yet you dress like a foreigner!' he scoffed, sharing a derisive look with his associates.

'I've been in the Japans for the past seven years,' explained Jack.

'Well, they certainly haven't taught you manners there,' sneered the other deputy, glaring at him from beneath a pair of bushy black eyebrows. 'Or how to respect your elders.'

Jack held his tongue. The Japanese were *ruled* by etiquette and politeness. But it would be foolish and futile to argue that with these officious men.

The judge cleared his throat and began reading from the parchment he'd been handed by the court scribe. 'The charges brought against you are: disturbing the peace, wilful destruction of property, brawling in a public place, and violent robbery.' He eyed Jack with distaste. 'How do you plead?'

'Not guilty.'

Excited chatter burst forth from the gallery.

'Order in court!' called the scribe, and the crowd settled down again.

'Who brings these charges against the accused?' enquired the judge.

'Sir Toby Nashe,' said Sir Toby, striding forward with a self-important air. 'Second cousin of Sir William Harrington, who is fr–'

'Yes, yes,' said the judge, waving away the chronicle of family connections. 'Just give us your account of events, Sir Toby.'

Drawing in a dramatic breath, then addressing not only the bench but the gallery too, Sir Toby told his story. And what a story it was! He missed out entirely the insults he'd thrown at Jack and his friends, skipped the part where he'd challenged Jack to a duel, and even denied there'd been a formal fight for honour. According to Sir Toby, Jack, Yori and Akiko had tricked Sir Toby and his two companions into showing them round London, before setting upon them in Moorfields with the intention of robbing them with violence; only Sir Toby's virtuoso sword skills had saved him, apparently, from certain death at the hands of these foreign scum.

With every new embellishment to the truth, Jack's fury grew until he could take no more. 'What a load of lies! He's –'

'Silence!' barked the judge. 'You'll have your chance, prisoner, to speak in due course. Call the first witness!'

Sir Edmund waddled up to the bar. He repeated Sir Toby's

fabrication word for word. Next came Sir Francis, who also – predictably – corroborated the fairy tale.

'This is a farce!' protested Jack.

The judge narrowed his gimlet eyes. 'You question the court's authority?'

'No,' Jack replied stiffly. 'I question the validity of the witnesses. They're his *friends*!'

Pursing his thin grey lips, the judge gazed round the courtroom. 'Do we have an independent witness to these events?'

'Aye!' A rough-looking man in a battered feathered hat stood up and made himself known. Sir Toby looked alarmed and his face drained of blood. He was evidently fearful that his lies were about to be exposed in court. But it was Jack who had more reason to be afraid.

'And who might you be?' asked the judge.

'Porter,' replied the man, doffing his hat and offering a charming grin.

Jack groaned and hung his head. He was about to be set up good and proper.

'Approach the bar, Porter.'

The vagabond swaggered up to the judges, shooting Jack a roguish wink as he passed. The court scribe held out a heavy leather-bound bible and Porter, resting his grubby hand on it, vowed to tell nothing but the truth. But Jack spotted that the vagabond had crossed his fingers behind his back as he was making his vow, so knew Porter would have no qualms about breaking his oath.

'Pray tell us what you witnessed,' ordered the judge.

'Well, I wasn't exactly there, your honour, being

somewhat engaged in other matters,' Porter admitted with a playfully guilty expression. 'But I recognize this ruffler –' he pointed at Jack. 'I was minding me own business at market, Cheapside, when he and his foreign friends jumped me. He had this *massive* curved sword and all I had with me was my little dagger. It was lucky the constables came when they did, or I'd have been –'

'Thank you for your account, Porter,' interrupted the judge. 'We will, of course, bear in mind your willingness to cooperate here when it comes to your own trial. Now retake your seat.'

'My pleasure,' grinned Porter, bowing and scraping all the way back to his place.

The judge now turned to Jack. 'What do you have to say in your defence, prisoner?'

Jack had been rendered almost speechless by the catalogue of lies levelled at him. 'That isn't at all what happened! Porter and his gang tried to rob *us*. That man there, Sir Toby, offended my friends, tried to forcibly take my swords from me, then *he* threw down the gauntlet for a duel, not m–'

'Are you a knight?' interrupted the first deputy. He examined the parchment before him. 'I see no "Sir" before your name.'

Jack hesitated. 'Er, no . . . not exactly . . . not in England at least, but I –'

'Well, then –' the deputy crossed his arms smugly – 'Sir Toby was in the right to demand your swords.'

Sir Toby puffed out his chest at this validation.

'He has no right to take what *isn't* his,' Jack countered. 'The man's no better than that thief Porter there –'

'We'll have no slander in this court,' the judge cut in sharply. 'I think we've heard enough from you, Jack Fletcher. Unless you wish to call any witnesses in your defence?'

Through gritted teeth, Jack replied, 'I don't have any.'

'So it's your word against theirs,' observed the deputy with the bushy eyebrows. 'The word of a vagrant seaman against that of these three fine, upstanding knighted gentlemen.'

'This *isn't* a fair trial!' Jack protested again.

The judge glared at Jack. 'I believe it is *we*, as the judges appointed by His Majesty the King, who shall determine what is fair and just in this court.'

Jack opened his mouth to reply, then closed it, realizing anything he said now would only aggravate the situation. He stood in frustrated silence as the three men behind the bench conferred. It took but a few moments for them to reach a decision.

Ominously, the judge slipped on a black cap and gloves before addressing Jack. 'After careful consideration, and in light of the serious nature of your crimes and those of your two absent companions, this court finds you *guilty* of all charges. The law is that you shall return to prison and from there be taken to a place of execution, where you shall be hanged by the neck till your body is dead. May the Lord have mercy upon your soul.'

8

THE GALLOWS

The horse-drawn cart bumped and rumbled through the city, making its slow procession from the prison to the marketplace at Smithfield. Having been confined for the past three days to a stifling cell, the sunlight and comparatively fresh air were a relief to Jack. But he knew his enjoyment would be short-lived. Beside him in the cart were eight men and women, all unfortunate prisoners like him, sentenced to be hanged that morning. Two of them sat rocking in silent shock, while another two cried out for mercy and forgiveness; one man was blubbing to his wife as she trailed beside the cart, a screaming babe in her arms; two were stoic to their fate; and the last one was grinning.

'What are you so pleased about?' demanded Jack.

Porter's grin widened. 'I get to see *you* hang.'

Jack shot him an incredulous look. 'But you're going to hang too! The judges can't have taken your willing *co-operation* into account after all.'

'Oh, they did,' Porter replied grimly. 'This is lenient in their eyes. For my list of crimes, I should've been hung, drawn *and* quartered!'

Beyond the act of treason, Jack didn't dare think what this vagabond might have done to warrant such a brutal punishment as that. 'Well,' he said, 'I suppose, justice is a double-edged sword.'

'You call *that* justice,' said Porter, nodding ahead.

Jack looked up and a deathly shudder ran through him. His muscles going suddenly weak, he had to grasp on to the cart's sides just to stay on his feet. The cart had entered Smithfield. Standing tall and unremorseful in the centre of the market was the gallows. Nine nooses hung from a triangular wooden frame, supported atop three sturdy posts. A crowd had already congregated and a great cheer rose up when they saw the cart approach. Jack's stomach twisted into a leaden knot. His heart thudded hard and his throat tightened at the terrifying thought of swinging by his neck. Then, as if to add further insult to his misery, he was hit on the cheek by a rotten apple. One of his fellow prisoners laughed hysterically – until a lump of dung splatted him in the face. Then more rotten vegetables and fruit pelted the cart and its shackled occupants. Curses and jeers assailed them and Jack had to duck as stones flew past.

But Porter lapped up the attention. He rose and stood at the front of the cart, waving his hat as if he were the king in a royal procession. A clutch of women cooed and simpered at the swaggering vagabond. They blew him kisses and he threw his feathered hat to them. The women jumped and squabbled over it as if it was a bridal bouquet thrown at a wedding.

'How women love a condemned man!' said Porter with a wistful sigh.

The cart worked its way through the swelling crowd and eventually lurched to a halt between the three pillars. Above them, the nine loops of rope hung down expectantly.

The driver dismounted and held the horses' reins firm as the hangman, a beefy fellow with heavy jowls and dark bags under his sagging eyes, clambered aboard. He commanded the prisoners to all stand. One, a scrawny woman with a glazed pale expression, could barely raise herself off the cart bed and had to be manhandled upright. The hangman unshackled her and secured her wrists behind her back, before slipping the noose over her head. With workmanlike efficiency, he bound and noosed the other prisoners, coming to Jack and Porter last.

He slipped the rope round Porter's neck and gave it an extra tug. 'Tight enough?' he smirked.

'How should I know? I've never done this before,' quipped Porter, much to the amusement of the crowd – and the hangman's annoyance. Whatever his opinion of the vagabond, Jack couldn't deny the man's bravado in the face of death. Many a samurai would be proud to demonstrate such resilience of spirit. Jack only wished he could be so bold and defiant, but fear choked him in its icy grip.

Scowling, the hangman finally turned his attention to Jack. He bound his hands then fitted the noose, the rough hemp cord digging into Jack's Adam's apple. 'Tight enough?' he said with a leer. 'Well, it soon will be!'

This time the crowd were laughing along with the hangman.

With the rope heavy round his neck, Jack began to tremble. His breathing became fast and ragged with panic.

He gazed in anguish at the baying crowd. The throng stretched north, south, east and west, filling the marketplace all the way up to the Church of St Bartholomew. There wasn't a single friendly face to be seen. Even if his sister was somehow out there in the crowd, he probably wouldn't recognize her after so many years.

By now, an almost festive atmosphere had taken hold, as hawkers wandered amid the onlookers, selling apples and nuts and bottles of beer. Entire families had gathered for the event, and the local inn had ordered extra supplies: a whole wagonload of wine casks stood ready outside its door. An execution clearly provided more ghoulish entertainment than any play at the Globe!

Then Jack spotted a face he *did* recognize. A pompous, moustachioed, copper-haired head on a plate. It appeared Sir Toby had bought himself a brand-new ruff for the occasion. He sat astride his horse, drinking and laughing with his friends, Sir Francis and Sir Edmund, and when he saw Jack looking his way, Sir Toby raised his bottle in a toast, downed the contents, then smiled with malicious glee.

Jack seethed. He'd fought so hard to get home, escaped death on so many occasions, vanquished ninja and samurai foes alike; he'd sailed halfway round the known globe, only to be hanged by the neck by his fellow countrymen. *By an idiot in a ruff!*

The absurdity of his situation – the injustice of it all – was not lost on Jack. He just prayed that Yori and Akiko had managed to find Captain Spilbergen and had taken up his offer to return to the Japans. He wanted them to get as far away as possible from this cesspit of a country.

What has become of England? thought Jack bitterly. *Why was I ever so desperate to return home . . . ?*

Jess, of course. But now he would never see his sister. She wouldn't even know he'd returned to find her; she'd believe forever that her remaining family had perished at sea. Whereas the truth was that her brother was about to be hanged no more than a few miles from her doorstep. In all of the past seven years, Jack had never been so close to his sister, yet had never felt so far away.

'Cheer up!' squawked a familiar voice. 'Every cloud has its silver linin'!'

Jack glanced down. The crazed inmate from the prison cells was beside the cart, gurning up at him.

'You're *free*?' queried Jack in surprise.

'*Ta-da!*' And Mad Bob did a little dance on the spot, then winced in pain. 'They forgot what I was in for. The court let me off with twenty lashes.' He turned round and lifted his filthy shirt. Now it was Jack who winced, as the rake-thin man revealed a criss-cross of nasty welts across his bony back. 'I suppose it could've been worse,' Mad Bob went on. 'I could be hangin' like you!' He tugged at an imaginary rope, made a face and stuck out a lolling tongue.

Jack responded with a thin, humourless smile. 'Thanks, that's *really* comforting.' Then his gaze returned to the crowd.

'You lookin' for your friends?' hissed Mad Bob. 'I told you, once a bird takes flight, it won't return to its cage.'

'I don't blame them,' sighed Jack. 'I hope they've flown far away from this wretched country.'

'In my experience, birds often nest high up,' he mumbled, clearly not listening to Jack.

Mad as a March hare, thought Jack, as the man began picking his nose like he was digging for gold.

'Your friend's waving to you,' said Porter, jutting his chin in Sir Toby's direction.

Jack glanced over and saw the vile man holding up another beer.

'Take your time to die, Jack Fletcher,' Sir Toby called out over the crowd. 'I'm in no rush. I've a full bottle to enjoy here.'

The bell in the church tower struck the hour and the crowd fell silent in anticipation. The court official proclaimed each of the prisoners' crimes, then the hangman gave the order and the driver drew his horses away. One by one, the prisoners dropped off the back of the cart and swung from the gallows as the crowd shouted and cheered at the spectacle.

'See you in hell, Jack!' rasped Porter, as the cart went from under the vagabond's feet.

A moment later, Jack lost his footing too. His body dropped like a stone and the rope pulled taut round his neck.

SHOOTING THE BRIDGE

The gallows creaked under the weight of the nine swinging bodies. Taunts and insults thrown by the crowd drowned out the few anguished cries of friends and loved ones of the convicted, while death slowly and mercilessly choked the life out of the prisoners.

Jack gasped and gulped for air, the noose tight round his throat. With every passing second, the pressure built in his head. His arms went rigid and his legs began to jerk uncontrollably.

'Dance, Fletcher, dance!' called out Sir Toby, laughing heartily with his companions at Jack's death jig.

Porter now swung limp and lifeless beside him, but Jack's suffering was far from over. As the twitch in his legs gradually weakened, his heart pounded harder and harder and his lungs strained for the faintest morsel of air . . .

Stark visions flashed before Jack's eyes. His sister as a little girl making daisy chains for him in the summer sun . . . His mother embracing him with soft warm arms after he'd fallen and scraped his knee . . . His father standing proudly on the ship's deck showing him how to use a sextant and compass . . .

The green baleful eye of the ninja Dokugan Ryu looming out of the darkness . . . The bright gleam of the legendary Shizu blade as his guardian Masamoto gifted him his own samurai swords . . . His friend Yamato plunging to his death from the balcony of Osaka Castle . . . Yori folding a paper crane . . . Akiko bowing, her back to the setting sun . . .

As Jack felt the last of his life ebb away, Mad Bob crouched before him at the edge of the crowd like a demon waiting to drag him to hell. Through the ringing in his ears, Jack heard the lunatic cry, 'Here comes that birdie!' followed by a fluttering *swish* overhead. Then he was falling . . . falling . . .

He hit the ground hard with a thump. The noose round his neck loosened. Coughing and spluttering, Jack sucked in a painful stab of air. He blinked back to life and saw the rope lying in the dirt, the end of it now cut and frayed. Above him, quivering in the nearest wooden post of the gallows, was a hawk-feathered arrow.

As Jack's befuddled mind registered this, a small cloaked figure darted forward and helped him to his feet. Pulling a knife from the folds of his cloak, he cut away at Jack's wrist bonds.

'SEIZE 'EM!' bellowed the hangman, a thunderous expression on his ruddy face.

But the crowd were either too shocked or too entertained by the daring escape to react.

'Fly away, birdies, fly away!' Mad Bob chirped as the hangman charged towards them.

The cloaked figure bundled Jack towards the front of the cart, where the driver stood beside his horses, open-mouthed and dumbstruck. Then an ear-splitting '*YAH!*' was heard and the driver flopped to the ground like a sack of grain. Taking up the discarded reins, Jack's rescuer jumped into the driver's seat, his hood falling away.

'Come on!' cried Yori, offering his hand to Jack. Still weak and disorientated from his strangulation, Jack barely had the strength to clamber aboard. The hangman was almost upon him when someone leapt from the crowd. It was Mad Bob, blathering, 'Judgement Day is upon us all! The world is –'

'Out of my way!' the hangman roared, stumbling over the scrawny lunatic and sprawling headlong in the dirt.

Jack fell into the passenger seat. Yori flicked the reins and urged the horses on. As the cart pulled away, Jack glanced back at Mad Bob, who shot him a wink before vanishing into the writhing mass of onlookers.

'STOP THEM! Someone, STOP them!' yelled Sir Toby. The pompous sot was now so drunk and unsteady on his horse that he almost tumbled off as he tried to give chase. But gathering their wits, the crowd now closed ranks and attempted to block their escape.

Hands reached up to pull them from the cart. Other men tried to clamber aboard. Then all of a sudden a hay barrow burst into flames as a burning arrow, tipped with tar, buried itself in the tinder-dry heap. People screamed; panic quickly spread. Another arrow sliced through the rope securing the wine casks beside the inn. The wooden barrels tumbled from the wagon and rampaged through the crowd, scattering them like skittles.

Yori drove the horses on through the chaos. Clutching the

seat, Jack kicked away at anyone who still attempted to board the cart. But most people weren't fast enough or kept their distance, for fear of being trampled by the horses' hooves or crushed under the cart's wheels. As they approached the edge of the market, Jack noticed a unit of constables racing to cut them off.

'*Faster!*' he rasped.

But Yori did the exact opposite and slowed down beside the church.

'What are you stopping for?' cried Jack.

'To pick up a passenger!' replied Yori. There was a light *thump* and the cart rocked, and Jack spun round to see Akiko crouched cat-like in the cart bed, her bamboo bow and quiver of arrows across her back. He glanced up at the church tower. 'Did you just *jump*?'

'No time to take the stairs,' she replied. 'Yori, let's not hang around any longer. Jack's done enough of that today!'

'Ha, very funny,' said Jack, but he was overjoyed to be reunited with his friends. 'And unless you want to hang too, we've got to get out of here. Fast!'

Sir Toby and his two companions had finally managed to coordinate themselves and were now in hot pursuit. The constables were also on their tail, running down the street after them. Yori swung the cart into Cock Lane, the sharp turn almost tipping them over, then bore left on to Snow Hill. Pedestrians ran for cover as the cart picked up speed, the wooden wheels clattering over the cobbles.

'Your *daishō*,' said Akiko, presenting Jack with his swords. 'Looks like we might be needing them.'

Jack slid them into his *obi*, their weight familiar and

comforting on his hip, and with them he felt his strength return. 'Never thought I'd see these again,' he said, looking at Akiko – 'or *you*, for that matter. Thanks for rescuing me. But how did you know I was to be hanged?'

'Mad Bob told us,' explained Akiko, clinging on to the cart's sides as it bounced over a rut in the road. 'We'd been trying to find a way to break you out when we bumped into him leaving the gaol.'

'If it wasn't for him, we'd never have found Smithfield market,' said Yori. 'We only just got to you in time.'

'I guess he wasn't as mad as his name!' said Jack with a laugh.

'Oh, he's mad all right,' cried Yori, gripping the reins tight as the horses galloped towards Newgate. 'He wanted Akiko to dress up as a bird!'

As they approached the towering brickwork of Newgate, a bleary-eyed man emerged from the gatehouse and saw the cart hurtling towards him.

'GUARD! CLOSE THE GATE!' roared Sir Toby, tearing down Snow Hill with Sir Edmund and Sir Francis. The constables on foot had already given up the chase.

The guard rushed to release the portcullis and the old iron gate rattled down to block off the entrance back into the city. Yori yanked on the reins and steered the horses into Old Bailey Street. But they were going too fast. The cart tipped, then a wheel hit a pothole and flew off. They were thrown from their seats just before the cart smashed into the city wall. The terrified horses bolted away, dragging the splintered remains of the cart behind them.

Dazed, bleeding and bruised, Jack got unsteadily to his feet. 'Everyone all right?' he asked.

Akiko and Yori nodded. Practised in the art of *ukemi*, they'd each broken their fall and rolled smoothly across the pavement.

'*We have you now!*' shouted Sir Toby as he and his companions thundered down the road towards them.

Stumbling on, Jack led Akiko and Yori into a busy narrow side street. It would be less easy for Sir Toby to catch up with them and run them down. Weaving between the startled Londoners, Jack and his friends raced on into Fleet Ditch, past Ludgate and towards the banks of the River Thames. But that was where they ran out of road.

'What now?' asked Yori desperately.

Jack pointed to a rowing boat at the quayside. 'Quick, the skiff!'

Leaping into the boat, Jack untied its mooring rope. A ferryman shouted at them, waving his fist angrily, but Akiko took an oar and pushed away from the quayside and then began to row hard. A moment later, Toby, Edmund and Francis pulled up at the riverside.

'You cowardly swine! A pox upon ye!' bellowed Sir Toby. 'I'll have your guts for garters, Fletcher! Upon my life, I will run you through with my sword until you bleed like a stuck pig!' He continued to fume and curse, his face growing redder and redder with each insult, but he didn't jump into a boat and follow them.

'Why's he giving up?' asked Yori.

'Perhaps he's scared of water!' smirked Jack, just glad the chase was over.

The ferryman, apoplectic with rage too, gestured furiously downriver, yelling, 'The tide's going out, you blithering idiots!'

Akiko frowned at Jack as she continued to paddle. 'Why should that matter?'

Turning towards London Bridge, Jack's face drained of blood. 'That's why,' he replied weakly, staring in horror at the fierce rapids surging underneath the bridge's arches.

The skiff began to pick up incredible speed. Akiko rowed furiously for the bank, but to no effect. The current had the little boat in its grip and was carrying it and its three passengers towards the huge stone starlings of London Bridge. On the riverbank, Sir Toby had switched from hurling insults to delighting in the deadly predicament Jack and his friends now found themselves in. 'We'll fish you out on the other side! Every little piece of you . . .'

But his voice was soon lost to the roar of the approaching rapids. The waters grew choppier and the skiff rocked and lurched over the waves.

'What are we going to do?' cried Yori, his knuckles white as he clung on for dear life to the skiff's gunwale.

Jack sat down beside Akiko and took over an oar. 'We need to try and shoot the bridge!'

Akiko flicked him a look of alarm. 'What do you mean?'

'Aim for an arch and keep to the middle!' he replied, rowing hard to straighten up their line. 'Yori, you'll have to guide us.'

Yori nodded nervously. 'Akiko, row harder your side . . . Now you, Jack . . . Now together . . .'

The boat bobbed like a cork on the waves as the tide sucked the river through London Bridge. Faster and faster they went, the current drawing them on. Churches, houses and wharfs whisked by; a blur of people on the banks as they watched in astonishment the lone skiff tackling the wild waters. Jack's muscles strained as he fought to keep the bow on course. He knew that if they hit a stone starling, the boat would be smashed to smithereens . . . along with its three passengers.

As they drew closer and closer to the bridge, Yori continued to call out directions, his voice rising in pitch and urgency. 'More your side, Akiko, *MORE*!'

However, despite her frantic efforts, Akiko's shoulder was still hampered by the rapier wound and she struggled to correct their line.

'We're not going to make it!' yelled Yori. 'We're not g—'

In a flurry of spray they shot through an arch, the huge starling scraping along the side of the skiff and smashing Akiko's oar from her grasp.

'*Hold on!*' shouted Jack, throwing his weight the opposite way, as the boat began to tip and take on water. Battered by the violent swell, it veered sharply and crashed sidelong into a rushing wall of water, which drenched the three of them to the skin. Then the bridge spat them out on the other side . . .

And that's when the rapids *really* began. The Thames became a churning, frothing mass of mud-coloured waves. As the boat plunged into the raging torrent, the bow buried itself in the swell, the skiff broke apart and Jack, Akiko and Yori were tossed overboard.

The frigid shock of submersion knocked the air from Jack's lungs and he swallowed a bellyful of foul water. A moment later, he came up, spluttering and retching. He caught a brief glimpse of Yori and Akiko floundering in the foaming waters, before he was dragged back under again.

The rapids turned him over and over, barrelling him until he touched the bottom, where the cloying silt of the riverbed embraced him . . .

From the banks near London Bridge, all that could be seen by the curious onlookers was the wreckage of a small skiff drifting seaward, its three passengers having been lost to the murky waters of the Thames.

10

PLAGUE HOUSE

The seagulls squawked overhead as three sodden and half-drowned figures crawled from the river on to the marshy bank. They collapsed amid the reeds, gasping and exhausted, and lay in the warm early-autumn sun, slowly drying out.

Yori shook off a clump of water weeds from his *shakujō* staff and sighed. 'I suppose the one good thing is that Sir Toby and the others will believe us to be drowned.'

'We almost *were!*' Akiko exclaimed.

'Well, at least you've had your bath now,' wheezed Jack as he combed a hand through his straggly mess of straw-blond hair.

'It wasn't as warm or as clean as I'd hoped, though!' Akiko sat up and examined her mud-stained kimono in dismay. She untied a bedraggled leather pouch fastened to her *obi*. 'Your purse, by the way,' she said, tossing Jack his bag of coins from the prison before inspecting her bow and quiver carefully for damage.

'Thanks,' said Jack. He secured the purse to his belt, then began checking his own weapons. He thought how lucky he was to have left the *rutter* in his pack at the Mermaid Inn as he'd surely have lost it in the turmoil of their escape. He knew at some point they'd have to recover their belongings from the landlady – if she hadn't sold them, or the authorities confiscated them yet – but that would have to wait until after the reunion with his sister.

'Where are we?' Akiko asked as she looked around at the marshy wasteland.

Jack climbed to the top of the embankment and surveyed a patchwork of boggy fields dotted with flocks of scrawny sheep. 'We're on the Isle of Dogs, by my guess –' he offered his friends an encouraging smile – 'not far from Limehouse and my home.'

'Praise be for small blessings,' said Yori, scrambling up the muddy bank with the help of his staff.

They tramped across the fields, pockets of sheep bustling out of their way and giving them wary looks from a distance.

'Even the sheep think we're scarecrows!' muttered Akiko as she plucked yet another piece of reed from her hair. 'So much for appearing at our best to meet your sister.'

'Jess won't care,' assured Jack. 'She'll just be glad to see us.' Then his brow knotted in curiosity. 'I wonder what she'll look like – after seven years, I guess she won't be my *little* sister any more!' He turned to his friends. 'Do you think she'll even recognize me?'

'No one can forget *your* face!' replied Akiko, arching an eyebrow. For a moment Jack didn't know whether this was a compliment or an insult. But the curl of her lips gave away the gentle tease and Jack smiled, glad to see her sense of humour returning after their dunking in the River Thames.

'What's Jess like?' asked Yori.

Jack gazed up at the clouds passing across the sky. 'Kind,

caring, cheeky . . . and *very* competitive. But she was seven when I last saw her. I only hope Mrs Winters is still alive and caring for her.' That had been his great worry when he was stranded in Japan. Their mother had died from pneumonia when he was ten, and his father had employed their neighbour, Mrs Winters, to act as Jess's guardian and bring her up. But Mrs Winters had already been old when he and his father first set sail. She would be positively ancient by now, and the money their father had given her to look after Jess must surely have run out. Spurred on by these thoughts and his impatience to see his sister again, Jack quickened his pace.

Leaving the fields behind, they found a rutted road heading back towards London. Several small shacks built from timber and driftwood sprang up on either side. As Limehouse drew closer, these shacks gave way to a mix of wattle-and-daub cottages and tumbledown hovels. The dwellings grew in number, until they were shouldering one another for space, as if the city was spilling out in a slow yet steady flood.

'All this used to be fields,' said Jack, gazing around in astonishment.

When they were properly in Limehouse, Jack found himself a little lost. The roads and side streets were cluttered with new buildings, workshops and inns. 'I think it's down here . . . no, er . . . we turn left . . .'

Akiko and Yori trailed behind, silent and cautious.

'Where is everyone?' asked Yori.

Only then did Jack notice how empty it seemed. A number of dogs roamed the streets and a rat scuttled along a deserted alleyway. The sharp smell of bonfires tinged the air and the smoke from them left a permanent haze. The few people they did pass eyed the bedraggled trio with distrust and kept their distance, closing their doors as they approached. A sense of unease crept into Jack's bones.

Suddenly he recognized where he was and broke into a run.

'WAIT!' Akiko called after him.

But Jack didn't stop. He raced down a lane and turned a corner. 'Here it is!' he cried.

Akiko and Yori hurried to join him as he shouted, 'Jess! I'm home! JESS!'

Jack felt a surge of joy and relief to be finally home. After all these years he would be reunited with his sister again. They would be a family once more!

His father's thatched white-washed cottage with its garden plot of herbs and apple trees was just as he remembered it. *Except* . . . the windows were boarded up, the front door too – a large red cross was daubed on it, with the words: *Lord have mercy upon us.*

Jack's gut tightened, his joy instantly dissolving to ash. Sprinting up the overgrown garden path, he tore at the wooden planks blocking the doorway, screaming, 'No! No! NO!'

Akiko pulled him away from the door. 'Jack, don't – look! Is that wise?' she questioned, eyeing the ominous red cross.

Too shocked to think straight, Jack shook her off and yanked at the last plank. The iron nails protested but eventually gave way, the wood splintering in his grasp. Tossing the plank aside, he grabbed the latch and threw open the door. A waft of stale air assailed him as if he'd broken the seal to some ancient and cursed tomb. Nonetheless, he stepped inside the cottage.

The front parlour was shrouded in shadows, dark and dismal. The boards across the window were like bars to a prison cell. Blackened stubs of candles protruded from their holders and dust had settled on his father's armchair by the fire. Jack stood transfixed in the middle of the room, barely able to breathe. No longer was his home the warm and welcoming place of his childhood. It had become a crypt.

Akiko and Yori followed him tentatively inside.

'I really don't think we should be in here . . .' said Yori, glancing around nervously, a visible shudder running through his slight frame.

Akiko nodded in agreement. 'There's a good reason why the house is b—'

Jack held up his hand, silencing her. '*Jess?*' he called softly. 'Are you there?'

His voice sounded dead and dull in the heavy silence. He crossed the room, past the fireplace, its hearth cold and empty, and over to a door. Heading along a narrow passage, he made his way to the kitchen at the rear. The faint, sickly-sweet smell of decay lingered in the air there too. On the kitchen table, there appeared to be the remains of a meal, half-prepared and abandoned. Pewter plates, iron pans and knives were all there, but the food had rotted away. In one dark corner of the room lay a litter of bones, too small to be human. A dog or a cat? But they hadn't kept any pets.

'There's no one here, Jack,' said Akiko. She held the sleeve of her kimono to her mouth, breathing shallowly. 'I'm sorry, but let's go now.'

'No,' Jack replied firmly, 'not until I've searched this whole house for her.'

He knew he might not like what he found, but he had to know his sister's fate. He first looked in the pantry. Here the stench was strongest, the stores having turned rancid and rotten at least a month or more back. Gagging, Jack stuffed a fist into his mouth. It was all he could do not to vomit. A quick inspection, though, told him that Jess wasn't there.

Turning on his heels, he headed up the creaking staircase to the floor above and entered the main bedroom. Even here the dormer window was boarded up, condemning the room to a permanent dusk. Hidden in the gloom was a four-poster bed, hung with heavy drapes. Jack approached it and slowly drew back the drapes. The mattress was sunken and the blankets pulled aside, the sheets looked stained and musty: the bed had clearly not been slept in for some time.

'Any luck?' asked Yori, peering round the door frame, as Jack hesitantly lifted the lid to a large oak chest that stood against the far wall. It just contained spare bedding and some old clothes.

Jack shook his head and crossed the landing to his old room . . . Jess's room. In here was the wooden-framed bed he'd shared with his sister when they were little children. The blankets were in disarray, but the layer of dust on the floorboards suggested no one had entered the room for a while. It was as if Jess and Mrs Winters had vanished and left the house to rot.

Jack looked around for *any* evidence that she'd ever been there. On the windowsill he spied five small, smooth white bones. The knucklebones he and Jess used to play with! He picked them up, weighing them in his hand. Were these all that was left of their time together?

As he stashed the bones in his purse, he heard a scratching, like fingernails on wood. He glanced over at Akiko and Yori.

'It's coming from under the bed,' Akiko whispered.

His pulse racing, Jack crept over. 'Jess?' he asked gently.

Lifting the dusty covers, he peered into the inky blackness beneath. Two gleaming eyes stared back at him. Startled, the large black rat leapt out from its hiding place. Jack tumbled backwards in shock as the rodent scurried across the floorboards, between Yori's legs and down the stairs.

'Did you see the size of *that*?' squealed Yori, his eyes wide in horror. 'It was so big I thought it was a dog!'

Recovering his breath, Jack slowly got back to his feet. 'I think I've seen enough,' he said.

They returned to the kitchen, where Jack paused by the hearth. He could still recall its cosy warmth and the comforting smells of his mother's cooking. He remembered how the family used to gather round the fire in the depths of winter, his father regaling them with stories of his sea voyages, his mother smiling and stirring the pot, baby Jess cradled in her arms. He remembered burning himself once on the iron grate, how his mother had tended to him with herbs and a poultice. He recalled the day he'd said goodbye to Jess, his sister crying in Mrs Winters' arms as he and his father packed for their long voyage to the Japans. That was the last time he'd seen his sister.

'Are you coming?' asked Akiko, her tone gentle, her expression kind.

Jack nodded. At the same time a shadow passed across the boarded-up window. Darting over, he peered through a gap into the back garden and caught a glimpse of a black-garbed figure. Jack's breath caught in his throat. His first thought was . . . *Ninjas*. But that was ridiculous. He was about as far away from the *shinobi* warriors as he could get.

But *someone* was outside.

Putting a finger to his lips, he exchanged a look of warning with Akiko and Yori. They crept into the parlour and were almost at the front door when a tall figure in a black waxed cloak blocked their escape. His face was a nightmarish white-beaked mask, his eyes hidden behind thick circles of glass. Upon his head he wore a wide-brimmed black hat and in his gloved hands he carried a slim wooden cane.

'*What are you doing?*' The voice was harsh, nasal and muffled by the pointed beak.

'I . . . I . . . was looking for my sister,' Jack stammered. He found himself frozen to the spot as his childhood fears of the sinister plague doctors came rushing back.

'This is a plague house,' said the doctor. 'You should not be in here.'

'This is his father's cottage,' explained Akiko, her face pale, as she too was unsettled by the grim figure.

'Still, you shouldn't be here,' the doctor growled.

'You're right,' Yori replied, smiling cordially and making for the door. 'Our mistake.'

But the plague doctor beat him back with his cane. '*You* could be infected now. You can't leave.'

'But we haven't touched anything,' said Akiko earnestly. 'We've barely been here.'

The plague doctor appeared unmoved by her pleas. '*All* the occupants of this house perished. They're dead and buried in a plague pit. And now, because of your foolish risk-taking, you might be joining them too.'

Jack felt his knees go weak. Not for fear of himself but for his sister. He'd known from the first sighting of the red cross on the door that the plague had visited his home. But he'd held on to the slender hope that Jess was still alive, imprisoned inside. He'd heard stories of people being left untouched by the plague even when others in the household were struck down.

'*All?*' he asked tremulously.

The plague doctor responded with a single solitary nod.

'When did it happen?' pressed Jack.

'Some two months back, so the house is not yet cleansed.'

'Let us out!' demanded Akiko, her voice tight and panicky. 'There's no one here. We're *not* infected.'

'Not yet, maybe, but –'

The plague doctor suddenly broke into a coughing fit. He clasped the door frame to stop himself collapsing, and Jack, Akiko and Yori seized their chance to push past. Escaping the oppressive and poisonous air of the cottage, they dashed into the bright sunshine of the front garden, where life at once seemed to return to them. The plague doctor was now on his knees, still hacking. Akiko stopped and turned back.

'Are you all right?' she asked, offering her hand to help him up.

'No,' he replied hoarsely, waving her hand away, 'but there's little you can do for me, apart from pray.' He gazed at them from behind his glass-eyed bird mask. 'I should have you arrested, but what hope do any of us have against this scourge? God preserve us all!'

He rose unsteadily to his feet and sloped off down the road like a sickly crow.

11

ROSE

Jack stared morosely into his tankard of small beer, wishing it was something stronger. His head hung heavy. His shoulders were slumped, his face slack. He felt drained of all joy and hope. The gloomy recess he occupied in the little riverside tavern only added to the impression of a soul plunged into the darkest despair. After leaving his derelict and rat-infested home, Jack had led his friends into the Bunch of Grapes Inn, a disreputable establishment frequented by drunks, low-lifes and shady characters. However, even in his distress, Jack had recognized the need to keep off the streets and out of sight of the authorities, at least until matters quietened down.

Akiko and Yori sat at the table with him, their tankards untouched. They observed their grieving friend in anguished silence, ignoring the curious and hostile glares of the tavern's other patrons.

'She's dead,' Jack murmured, more to his drink than to his friends. 'Dead and buried.'

He turned the tankard in his hands, as if it was a crystal ball in which he could see an alternative future.

'All these years I've fought to get back home,' he went on.

'The obstacles I have overcome, the trials I have suffered, the enemies I have defeated, all with one aim in mind: to be reunited with Jess.' He swallowed hard. 'My sister was the *one* thing that kept me going, the single hope I'd held on to.' In frustration, Jack tightened his grip on his tankard. 'If only I'd got to England a few months ago *I could have saved her.*'

Akiko reached out and gently touched the back of his hand. 'Then you might have died from the plague too,' she said softly.

Jack glanced up, his eyes red and rimmed with tears. 'At least I would've been there for her. She wouldn't have died alone, terrified and tormented. And now I've risked *your* lives too, by dragging you into that death house!'

'We were careful not to touch anything and we covered our mouths,' said Yori. 'Besides, there was no one there to infect us.'

'Apart from the plague-ridden doctor himself! *Oh, damn this infernal country!*' Jack slammed his fist on the table so fiercely that he upset his tankard, and liquid slopped across the table. Several patrons shot him steely glares and muttered irritably under their breath. Jack ignored them and took a long swig of his remaining drink. 'I've come all this way, and for what? I've lost the *rutter* back at the Mermaid, my home and now my sister! I can't even mark her grave. The last of my family is gone, tossed into some unknown plague pit. I've no one left now.'

'You have us,' said Akiko.

Jack looked into her face, the earnest expression opening up a well of emotion inside him. 'I know, it's just —' burying his head in his hands, he broke down into sobs – 'I feel . . . like I'm . . . drowning in grief.'

'Grief is like an ocean,' consoled Yori, putting his arm round Jack's heaving shoulders. 'Your sadness will come in waves, ebbing and flowing. At times, the water will be calm. At others, rough and overwhelming. All you can do is learn to swim through it.'

Jack let himself be held as his tears ran freely. Akiko and Yori sat beside him in silent mourning, letting his grief flow. Jack thought his tears would never stop, but eventually his sobbing subsided.

'Perhaps we should retrieve our belongings and return to the *Hosiander*?' said Akiko gently.

Jack stared at her in disbelief. 'You want to go home *already*?'

She gave a non-committal shrug. 'Well . . . what do you suggest?'

Jack wiped away the tears with the back of his sleeve, then drained his tankard. 'Another drink! You want one?'

Akiko and Yori both shook their heads. Pushing back his chair, Jack looked around for the innkeeper and his eye was drawn to a hoary old seaman with a salt-and-pepper beard and skin as wrinkled and weathered as tree bark. He sat propped in one corner, buttressed by a handful of other old mariners cradling tankards of ale. They all huddled close, listening rapt to the seaman.

'I hear there's a galleon beached near Hole Haven,' he was saying in a hushed and husky tone. 'Rumours of a king's ransom in cargo! But no one will go near it.'

'Why ever not?' asked one of the others.

The man's close-set eyes narrowed. "Cause it's a . . . *ghost ship!*'

There was a collective gasp and Jack smirked as the old sea-dog continued to wind up his audience with his story. 'Whole crew murdered and stuffed into the hold. Eyes blank and staring like dead fish. They say the ship's cursed.'

'Who says it's cursed?' questioned a bearded fellow smoking a pipe.

'The watchman who first spied the ship,' the seaman replied, taking a slow and measured sip of his drink. 'He climbed aboard with a customs officer and a constable. But *he* was the only one to survive. Except he's gone mad. Says shadows killed 'em!'

Jack frowned at this description and unwittingly found himself leaning in to listen.

'*Shadows?*' said a red-cheeked drunk with a snort. 'The fella must be mad!'

'Must he?' questioned the seaman, fixing the drunk with a gimlet eye. 'Been reports all along the Thames Estuary of killer shadows, mysterious murders and dark deeds.'

Jack wondered if the old sea-dog could be talking about the missing Dutch ship, the *Salamander*. There'd been rumours her crew had seen moving shadows during their voyage, but her captain had dismissed such tales as superstitious nonsense. A shiver ran down Jack's spine at the thought.

"Ello, handsome, why the glum face?"

Jack flinched and spun round. A flame-haired serving girl stood near him. Entranced at the sight of her emerald-green eyes and ruby-red lips, Jack suddenly couldn't think of anything to say.

'Best close that mouth before some captain docks a ship in it!' she said, arching a slim eyebrow.

Suddenly aware he was gaping at her like a goldfish, Jack sat straighter and cleared his throat. 'Sorry . . . just thirsty, that's all.'

The girl sidled closer and bent down, placing her elbow on the table and resting her chin upon her palm. She locked eyes with him and smiled. 'So what can I get you?'

Just then, Akiko pounced on the serving girl and pinned her down on the table.

'Akiko! What do you think you're doing?' cried Jack in astonishment.

'Let me go!' snarled the girl as she writhed in Akiko's grip. But Akiko forced the girl to open her hand. Three silver coins tumbled out.

'She was stealing from you, Jack!' explained Akiko, keeping the thief pinned with an armlock.

Glancing down at the open purse on his hip, Jack cursed. *How could I have been so easily tricked by her?* The girl was a pickpocket, a highly skilled cutpurse.

'Jack?' The girl stopped struggling. She frowned and studied him more closely. 'Jack, as in . . . *Jack Fletcher*?'

He responded with a cautious nod. 'What's it to you?'

A smile burst across her lips. 'It's Rose. Rose Turner!'

Jack shrugged. 'Do I know you?'

'Do you *know* me?' she replied, incredulous. A twinkle entered her emerald eyes. 'Jack, we had our first kiss together. Moorgate – you chased me. Don't say you've forgotten?'

Like a key unlocking a door, the memory flooded back and Jack gasped, 'I was ten!'

Rose's grin widened. 'And I still remember it like it was yesterday.'

Jack shook his head in amazement. 'Let her go, Akiko. Rose is a friend.'

Akiko, her cheeks flushed, released the girl. Rose straightened her dress, shot Akiko a scathing look, then turned back to Jack. She handed him his coins. 'My apologies, Jack. I'd never steal from a friend. Now let me get you drinks on the house.'

A few moments later, Rose plonked three brimming tankards of small beer on the table. Then she pulled up a stool and sat next to Jack.

'So, who's the girl, then?' she asked, nodding but not looking in Akiko's direction.

'I'm Akiko Dāte,' replied Akiko with a tight-lipped smile. Bowing politely, she kept her gaze locked on Rose.

'And this is Yori Sanada,' said Jack.

'It's a pleasure to meet you, Yori,' said Rose, gracing him with a beaming smile.

His cheeks reddening, Yori bowed and smiled mutely back. Apparently lost for words, he didn't seem to know where to put his eyes, so looked up to the ceiling as if praying.

Rose glanced at Jack. 'Doesn't say much, does he?'

Realizing his friend was somewhat overawed by Rose, Jack replied, 'He's taken a vow of silence.'

'*Really?*' said Rose, intrigued. Then seeing that Jack was kidding, she began to laugh. 'Don't worry, Yori, I tend to have that effect on a lot of boys.' She returned her gaze to Jack. 'So where have you been hiding these past years?'

Jack took a swig of his drink. 'The Japans.'

Rose looked him up and down. 'I suppose that explains the dress.'

'It's a *hakama*,' sighed Jack, too tired to explain any further.

'You were always the great explorer,' said Rose with a smirk. 'You made your fortune yet?'

'No, not yet.'

Her eyes went to his hip. 'Judging by the heavy purse you carry, you must have had some success. I hear the Far East is a land of silver and gold!'

'That depends on what you are seeking,' Jack replied. 'It's an easy place to lose your head.'

'Or a finger, by the looks of it!' she said, nodding at his left hand gripping the tankard awkwardly.

Jack glanced at the stub of his little finger, the nail and first joint missing. '*Yubitsume*,' he replied bitterly.

'I'm sorry?' said Rose.

'My *taijutsu* master, Sensei Kyuzo, sliced it off as punishment for an alleged crime.'

Rose winced. 'I suppose it's better than losing your head. Is he responsible for the scar on your cheek too?'

Jack's hand went absently to the thin white line marking his left cheek. 'No, that's courtesy of Kazuki, the bane of my life in Japan.' He scowled, recalling all the bullying he'd suffered at the hands of his school rival. Kazuki had mercilessly taunted and tortured Jack from the very first day at the *Niten Ichi Ryū*, victimizing him for being a foreigner, a *gaijin*. They'd fought on numerous occasions – even duelled one another during the Battle of Osaka Castle, despite being on the same side! His rival had pursued him across Japan for over a year on the orders of the Shogun who wanted him dead . . . and to satisfy his own bloodlust.

'Is that why you're back?' asked Rose.

Jack shook his head. 'Kazuki's in prison now. He's no longer a problem. I came back to find my sister –' he put his tankard down, the heavy weight of grief returning – 'only to discover she's died . . . from the plague.'

Rose blinked and stared hard at him. 'Jess? She ain't dead, as far as I know.'

'*What?*' exclaimed Jack, jumping up.

'No, she left the area *before* the plague hit,' replied Rose. 'Your father's cottage was seized by some well-to-do gentleman – bad debts or something. He rented it out to three families. They're the ones that died.'

Jack fell back into his seat, stunned, his sorrow at the fate of the three families eclipsed by his relief at hearing his sister had survived. 'Where did Jess go, then?'

Rose shrugged. 'No idea. One day here, next day gone. But I bet you a silver coin that that old biddy, Mrs Winters, knows.'

'She didn't die of the plague either?' asked Jack breathlessly.

Rose shook her head. 'But she may as well have! After Jess left, I saw her around Limehouse a few times, quite a desperate look on her old face. I heard she helped care for those three families in your cottage when they caught the plague. Nasty job, but well paid.'

Jack leant eagerly across the table. 'Where's Mrs Winters now?'

'Now *that* I do know,' Rose replied, taking his half-empty tankard and draining the contents in one gulp. 'Bedlam!'

12

BEDLAM

They heard the screams and howls long before they reached the entrance to the notorious asylum. A former priory, Bedlam was a cluster of decrepit brick buildings situated just beyond the city walls in Bishopsgate.

'It looks more like a prison than a hospital,' Yori remarked, craning his neck upwards to see the small barred windows high in the wall.

'And so it should be,' said Rose. 'You wouldn't want any of the nutters inside it roaming London's streets. I pity poor Mrs Winters. If she wasn't crazy before, she will be by now.'

Jack stopped in his tracks. 'Are you telling me Mrs Winters is *mad*?'

Rose twirled a forefinger against her head. 'As a cuckoo!'

He frowned in dismay. 'I thought when you said she was in Bedlam that you meant she was helping to care for the patients. Not that she was one of them!'

'Sorry,' said Rose with a shrug. 'Thought that was obvious.'

Jack's shoulders slumped. *How would he get any sense out of a madwoman?*

'Perhaps her time in hospital may have helped her?' Akiko suggested hopefully.

Rose gave a dismissive snort. 'More likely made her worse! I hear they treat 'em worse than animals.'

Akiko's lips thinned in barely concealed annoyance at Rose's off-hand reply. The two of them had hardly exchanged a word since they'd first met, but Jack put that down to a clash of cultures. Rose couldn't be any more different from Akiko. Bold, brash and uninhibited, she was a typical London city girl; whereas Akiko behaved in the more reserved, calm and thoughtful way of the Japanese.

As they approached the asylum's front gate, a squat man with a balding head stepped out. Resembling a toad more closely than a gatekeeper, he had a large red boil on his neck and a bulging left eye that gave him a permanent squint. He studied the four of them with curiosity, evidently unsure what to make of this disparate band of a monk, a warrior girl, a serving wench and a boy in foreign dress. 'Are we visiting . . . or *staying*?' he chuckled.

'We're here to see Mrs Winters,' replied Jack.

The gatekeeper sniffed. 'You family?'

'No,' said Jack. 'Friends.'

The gatekeeper licked his dry lips. 'Then it's tuppence each for entrance.'

'Entrance?' queried Yori, leaning on his staff. 'Isn't this a hospital?'

The man nodded, limp strands of hair falling aside. He combed them back with his fingers. 'Aye, it is, but if you wanna have a laugh at the patients, you gotta pay.'

'We're not here to *laugh*,' said Jack indignantly.

With a dismissive snort the gatekeeper thrust out a greasy hand. 'That's what they all say. Now cough up.'

Reluctantly Jack paid the money. The gatekeeper gave them a black-toothed grin and waved them through.

Jack and the others entered the courtyard. They weren't the only visitors. A group of well-to-do young gentlemen stood round a bare-chested man, who was repeatedly knocking his head against a post.

'He beats a good rhythm!' scoffed one gentleman, clapping his hands. 'One could dance to this.' And he began a jig in time to the man's hammering. The others laughed and joined in taunting the poor patient. Jack didn't know who seemed crazier: the man bashing his head or the morbid spectators dancing round him.

Akiko and Yori looked on in shock but made no comment as they filed past the sorry scene into the main building.

The asylum was one long dark corridor with a series of small shadowy cells leading off on either side. Some of the doors were wide open; others were barred with iron gates. Two ladies in fashionable frocks, fluttering silk fans in front of their faces to keep away the stench of the blocked sewers, were peering into the nearest cell. A skinny hollow-cheeked man in rags stood behind the bars. He glared down his beaked nose at the paying guests and pompously declared, 'Bow before me, loyal subjects, for I am the King of England!'

The two women tittered behind their fans as the man strode regally round his tiny cell, oblivious to their ridicule. Jack eased past the women and headed further along the corridor. But any hope that Mrs Winters would still be of sound enough mind to tell him where he could find Jess diminished with every step.

The next cell contained a young woman chained to the walls. As they passed by the barred doorway, the woman leapt and spat at them like a wildcat. In the cell opposite, a shirtless man with festering sores all over his back was curled up and shivering on a bed of straw, while another patient was barking like a dog.

'Do people *pay* to see this?' said Yori, appalled.

Rose nodded. 'Not a bad day out. Once you see these sorry fellas, you realize your own life ain't so grim!'

'This is a hell on earth!' Akiko remarked, as the constant cries, screechings and rattling of chains threatened to drown out all sanity.

They eventually found Mrs Winters in a dingy cell at the far end of the corridor. The old woman, as sallow and scrawny as chicken's legs, wore a soiled nightgown and had a dull, defeated look in her grey eyes. She knelt in the corner of the room, her hands clasped together, rocking and weeping and muttering to herself.

Jack exchanged a doubtful glance with the others before addressing the old woman. 'Mrs Winters?'

She continued to rock back and forth. Either she hadn't heard him or she was beyond making sense of what he'd said. Jack entered the cell and crouched down beside her. She stank of stale sweat and urine. 'Mrs Winters? It's Jack . . . Jack Fletcher.'

The old woman broke off from her muttering and glanced up. Despite looking in his direction, she didn't seem to see him at all. 'Beware the red wolf at your door! Beware of false prophets, who come to you in sheep's clothing, but inwardly they are ravening wolves!'

She returned to her muttering, wringing her hands as if in desperate prayer. 'You shall know them by their fruits. Do men gather grapes of thorns, or figs of thistles? Even so, every . . .'

'Mrs Winters!' persisted Jack. 'Where's Jess?'

His sister's name seemed to stir something deep in the old woman's mind, for she stopped dead. '*Jess*? Dearest Jess? Is that you?'

'No, I'm her brother, Jack,' he replied, feeling a glimmer of hope at having got through to the old woman. 'Do you know where Jess is?'

Mrs Winters' eyes grew wide as full moons, her wrinkled skin turning pale as her whole body began to tremble. 'Beware the red wolf at your door! Beware of false prophets, who come to you in sheep's clothing, but inwardly they are ravening wolves! Beware the red wolf . . . the wolf in sheep's clothing . . . You shall know them by their fruits. Do men gather grapes of thorns, or figs of thistles? Even so . . .'

She repeated her incantation over and over. In spite of further attempts to communicate, Jack could get no sense from the old woman. She was lost to her ravings.

'Told you she's crazy!' said Rose, leaning against the cell door. 'And who'd blame her? Being locked up for months in a plague house as people slowly died and decomposed all around you. It's enough to send anyone mad!'

'What does she mean by "the wolf in sheep's clothing"?' asked Akiko.

'That's from a sermon in the Bible,' said Rose. 'The Gospel of Matthew.'

Jack turned to Rose. 'How do you know?'

'I *do* go to church,' said Rose, adopting an offended air before a mischievous grin broke through, 'despite my sins!'

Jack asked Mrs Winters again about his sister, but only got more babbling of scripture. 'You're right, Rose,' he sighed. 'This is a waste of time. She's just quoting from the Bible. Even if she does know where Jess is, she's in no state to tell me. Let's go.'

As Jack stood to leave, Mrs Winters grabbed his arm, her grip surprisingly strong. 'Beware the red wolf!' she hissed as she shoved a small hard object into his hand.

Jack slowly unfurled his fingers to reveal a silver locket. He prised it open. Inside was a tiny watercolour portrait of a young woman with hair like spun gold and eyes as blue as a midsummer sky. Jack instantly recognized her. *'Jess!'* he gasped.

He took hold of Mrs Winters by the shoulders and shook her. *'Where is she?* TELL ME, WHERE IS JESS?'

But Mrs Winters had once again reverted to weeping and rocking. He shook her harder, but she only wept more and babbled her sermon.

'Jack . . .' said Akiko, gently pulling him away. 'That's enough. You're going to hurt her.'

Jack let the old woman go. He realized she was little more than an empty shell, her mind having long departed. In a daze himself, Jack allowed Akiko and his friends to guide him out of the asylum. He felt almost as deranged as some of Bedlam's patients. Having got so very close to discovering Jess's whereabouts, yet unable to unlock Mrs Winters' madness, he wanted to bang his own head against a post.

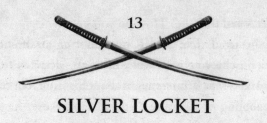

13

SILVER LOCKET

The next morning Jack lay on the sagging bed in a grimy room at the Bunch of Grapes, turning the silver locket over in his hand. He examined the intricate flower engraved on the front, then peered at the smooth polished surface of the back. He opened the locket and ran his finger over the soft blue cloth lining of the lid. Holding the locket up to the light, he studied the portrait of his little sister, who was no longer the little girl he'd last seen. Over the course of seven years she had changed so much. He remembered Jess as a slight girl with a button nose, wide eyes and a mischievous grin. Now she looked so grown up, so elegant, so beautiful.

'Do you really think the locket can lead us to Jess?' asked Yori, who sat in the corner of the room, his legs crossed in a lotus position.

Jack weighed the locket in his hand. 'It's the only thing we have to go on.' He propped himself up on the bed. 'Judging by how old Jess looks, the portrait was painted recently, within the last year. And I'm pretty certain my mother, God rest her soul, didn't own anything this fancy. Which means this locket must be a gift.'

'From whom?'

Jack shrugged. 'I've no idea. But whoever it is, he has to be rich. The locket's solid silver! And the portrait is expertly done. Only a master painter could've produced such fine work.'

'May I have a look?' asked Yori, holding out his hand.

Jack passed him the locket. Yori admired the engraving, then closely examined the miniature portrait inside.

'What's this?' he asked, pointing to two tiny marks along the bottom edge.

Leaning over Yori's shoulder, Jack squinted at the painting. 'I think it says . . . N . . . H . . .'

Yori frowned. 'The artist's initials?'

The bedroom door opened and Akiko entered. Her straight black hair was glistening, still wet from her bath. 'I've never bathed in such brown water!' she complained. 'How do you English ever get clean?'

'We don't,' replied Jack in all seriousness. 'I'm afraid this tavern isn't known for its high standards. The water was likely taken from the Thames – and who knows what's dumped in there!'

Akiko grimaced. 'Well . . . at least it was warm this time.'

'That's what worries me!' said Jack, triggering another shudder of revulsion from Akiko.

She perched herself on the edge of the bed and began vigorously drying her hair with a cloth. Then she noticed the locket in Yori's hand and smiled at Jack. 'Your sister's very pretty,' she observed. When he didn't smile back, she added, 'Jack, I know you're disappointed not to have found Jess yet, but there's every chance she's still alive – and you've got a picture of her now. Perhaps we can show the locket to some of the Limehouse locals and see if they recognize her? They might know where she is.'

'It's certainly worth a try,' said Jack, although privately he thought the task ahead of them insurmountable. London was a big place, some two hundred thousand citizens, and he realized they probably had a greater chance of finding a needle in a haystack than finding Jess. 'If *only* Mrs Winters hadn't gone mad!' he mumbled to himself.

Yori looked at Jack, his brow furrowed. 'Mrs Winters didn't strike me as mad, though . . . more *scared*.'

Jack frowned. 'Scared? Of what?'

Yori shrugged. 'I don't know. But she was going on about a red wolf. Maybe she has nightmares of the plague? Or perhaps it's just living in that hellhole Bedlam. Whatever the reason, she was definitely scared of something.'

'Or someone,' said Akiko darkly.

Jack exchanged a worried look with his friends. 'Do you think Jess is in trouble?'

'I pray not,' said Yori, his hands coming together, 'but it might explain her abrupt depart–'

All of a sudden the door burst open again and Rose bustled into the bedroom. She dumped two packs on to the bed with a triumphant flourish.

'You're in luck!' she announced. 'That old battleaxe at the Mermaid Inn still had your belongings.'

Jack and the others stared in astonishment at their missing packs. He'd honestly expected the authorities to have confiscated them after their arrest.

'Well, don't all thank me at once,' said Rose, planting

her hands indignantly on her hips. 'It took some doing, I can tell you. I had to sweet-talk that runt of a serving boy before I found out where his landlady had hidden them. She was planning to sell the contents at tomorrow's market.'

'Thanks,' said Jack quickly, searching his pack. His hand soon touched the familiar oilskin binding of his father's logbook and he breathed a deep sigh of relief. At least the *rutter* was back in his possession.

'Cost me a half-crown to bribe him, though . . .' and Rose held out her hand and beckoned with her fingers.

Jack pulled out a gold coin from his purse and tossed it to Rose. She caught it nimbly in mid-air.

But Akiko narrowed her eyes at Rose. 'That much? I thought you didn't steal from your friends.'

'I don't . . . though I might steal Jack's heart again,' Rose added, throwing a playful wink in his direction.

Akiko's jaw tightened. She snatched her pack off the bed and headed for the door. 'I'll be in my room. Let me know when you're ready to go, Jack.'

As Akiko shut the door firmly behind her, Jack wondered why she seemed annoyed. They'd got their belongings back after all. So what, if Rose made a little profit on the side? She'd brought him back the *rutter* and, to him, that was worth a half-crown.

Yori got to his feet and handed Jack his locket. 'Er . . . I'll get ready too,' he said awkwardly. 'Akiko will probably need my help re-bandaging her shoulder.'

As soon as Yori had left, Rose turned to Jack. 'Is Akiko always so irritable?'

Jack shook his head. 'She must be tired. Things haven't gone exactly according to plan since we arrived in England.'

'So what's the plan now?' asked Rose.

'We search Limehouse to start with.' Jack began laying out his new clothes on the bed. 'Akiko suggested showing the locket to some of the locals to see if anyone recognizes Jess and knows where she's gone. If we have no luck with that, I suppose we'll try the workhouses next.'

'Not much of a plan,' remarked Rose.

'Well, what else can we do? Jess has disappeared without a trace.' Jack held up the locket, letting it twirl on its chain. 'This is a mystery too. I mean, who would give my sister such an expensive gift?'

Rose raised an eyebrow. 'A suitor?'

'She's still a girl!' cried Jack, feeling instinctively protective of his little sister.

'But will soon be a woman,' replied Rose knowingly, 'and a sought-after one at that, judging by her portrait . . . *and* her brother's good looks.'

Jack laughed away the compliment. 'You haven't changed, Rose!'

'But you have.' A coy smile spread across her lips. 'For the better.'

Flustered by her playful manner, Jack busied himself with selecting a shirt. 'Look . . . I'm going to get changed. I'll meet you downstairs with the others.'

'If you want,' said Rose, nonchalantly making her way to the door. 'But do you really think you'll find Jess just by asking people you happen to meet in the street?'

Jack looked up. 'Have you got a better idea?'

Rose nodded. 'For sure! We visit the jewellers off Cheapside and show them the locket. One of them's bound to recognize whose work that portrait is. Then we can find the artist and ask him who paid for the portrait to be painted – and *that* person might know where your sister is!'

14

THE MINIATURIST

'This looks to be the place,' said Jack, having been directed by a goldsmith on Cheapside to a miniaturist portrait shop along Gutter Lane. The four of them stood outside a crooked little building tucked between a milliner's and a bookseller's. In the leaded window were a selection of small, blank, oval pieces of vellum and card, and some sample lockets.

They entered the shop's cramped confines. As their eyes grew accustomed to the gloom, they noticed a young man bent over a desk, painting by candlelight. He appeared to be copying a miniature portrait, stroke by stroke, and didn't stir from his work.

After a while, Jack coughed into his hand.

The young man looked up, startled. He had pale skin, curly black hair and a wispy moustache. 'My apologies,' he said. 'Nathan Holme at your service. How can I help you?'

'*Nathan Holme!*' whispered Yori, nudging Jack excitedly. '*The same initials as the portrait!*'

Jack hurriedly got out the locket and showed it to the miniaturist. 'Tell me, is this your work?'

The artist took the locket, cradled it gently in his palm

and inspected the portrait under the glow of the candle. His watery eyes widened in surprise, then a sad smile passed across his lips. 'I'm afraid not . . . that's the work of my father, *Nicholas* Holme.'

'Can we speak to your father?' asked Rose eagerly.

Handing back the locket, the young man mournfully shook his head. 'My father passed away last month . . . the bloody flux . . .' With a heavy sigh, he turned back to the two miniature portraits on his desk. 'I'm trying to match his style, but I never could master his technique. It's so elusive . . . his lightness of touch . . . the freshness he gave to his subject's countenance . . . the way he captured their features so gracefully . . .'

'I'm truly sorry for your loss,' said Jack earnestly as he attempted to regain the young man's attention. 'I know what it means to lose a father. But I'm hoping not to lose a sister as well.'

Nathan paused mid-stroke.

'She's missing,' Jack went on, 'and this locket is the only lead we have to her. Do you know who commissioned your father to paint this portrait?'

Nathan put down his brush and pulled out a leather-bound book from the desk drawer. Opening it, he ran a finger slowly down the lines of scrawled black ink. Jack waited impatiently, trying to decipher the handwriting upside down and garner a name. Nathan flicked to the next page, found only a few entries, tutted irritably, then snapped the book shut.

'I'm afraid I've no idea,' he said with an apologetic shrug. 'It appears to be yet *another* piece Bodley failed to account for, otherwise it would have been marked down in the ledger.' He shook his head in a world-weary manner. 'Typical of my father! He was terrible with money. He was always too wrapped up in his art to chase his debtors or handle his accounts himself. He left all that to Bodley, more fool him!'

Putting the ledger back in its drawer, Nathan resumed his painstaking copying of the portrait. But Jack wasn't willing to give up on the locket so easily. He planted his hands on the desk and leant forward, forcing Nathan to stop his work. 'Who's Bodley?' he asked.

A dark cloud descended over the artist. 'My father's *former* apprentice, Rowland Bodley.'

'Might Bodley know who commissioned this portrait of my sister?' pressed Jack.

Nathan blew away his wisps of moustache. 'Possibly. I dismissed him under suspicion of embezzlement. There was no real proof, though, but I'm sure he was taking commissions and payments off the books. Now that my father's gone, I've no way of knowing what pieces were crafted or sold.'

Jack straightened, eager to follow this new lead. 'So where can I find this Rowland Bodley?'

Nathan glanced at the afternoon sun slanting through his window. 'At this time of day, he usually frequents the Globe Theatre. You'll recognize the pompous idiot by his hat. He always wears an ostrich feather in the brim, dyed red.' At that, Nathan rolled his eyes. 'He's a bit flamboyant that way.'

'Well, what are we waiting for?' said Rose, clapping her hands together. 'Let's go to see a play!'

★

Some two thousand people had descended on the Globe Theatre for the afternoon performance of Ben Jonson's *The Alchemist*. Working men, shop owners, gentlemen in their finery, housewives and their servants and children, from London and abroad, all rubbed shoulders as they queued outside the timber-framed, three-storey playhouse on the southern bank of the Thames.

'See! Told you, Jack,' said Rose with a smug grin. 'Talking to the artist was a far better idea than wasting our time asking people at random in the street!'

A pained expression passed across Akiko's face.

'Are you all right?' asked Jack.

'My top is pinching me, that's all,' replied Akiko with a strained smile. 'How does anyone *breathe* in these clothes?'

Earlier that morning, Jack had managed to persuade Akiko to swap her kimono for English clothes in order that their appearance didn't attract so much attention. While the authorities might think they were all drowned, they still needed to keep a low profile. Courtesy of a shopping trip made by Rose, Akiko was now dressed in a figure-hugging bodice, billowing petticoat and wooden-soled shoes. Yori had kept to his simple saffron robes, and still carried his *shakujō*, but he had left the distinctive straw-bowl monk's hat behind at the inn. In the theatre setting, barely anyone gave them a second glance.

Rose called over her shoulder at Akiko, 'Sorry, did I tie your bodice a little tight? It's the fashion here.'

Akiko tried to adjust the lacings. 'But how am I even supposed to fight in this?' she complained. 'My legs are lost under two layers of petticoats!'

'You'll soon get used to the fashion,' Jack assured her. He thought back to the first time he'd worn a kimono and how disconcertingly draughty that had been for him! Now he was clothed like an Englishman again: cambric shirt, velvet doublet and damask breeches, along with his new pair of black leather boots. At first it felt odd to be dressed in such a manner after so many years in the attire of a samurai. But it was strangely familiar too, like slipping on a pair of old shoes. 'Anyhow,' he added, 'now we're presumed drowned, I hope we won't be getting into any more fights.'

Akiko cast him a doubtful look; whether that was to do with her dress or the likelihood of another fight, Jack couldn't tell. But he was determined to avoid any further confrontations. Now they had a solid lead to follow, his only priority was finding his sister and he wanted nothing to get in their way.

'Keep an eye out for a red ostrich feather,' said Jack, his eyes sweeping the sea of elaborate hats and headdresses. Everyone seemed out to impress. There were hats made of silk, velvet, fur and taffeta, and hatbands of almost every colour, from green to blue, and from purple to gold. Some were jewelled, others embroidered; some wide-brimmed, many high-crowned. Most were adorned with eye-catching plumes, plucked from the tails of pheasants, herons, guinea fowl or some other wild bird. But there didn't appear to be a single ostrich feather in sight.

They shuffled along until they reached the theatre's main entrance. Squeezing through the doors, they entered a magnificent open-air amphitheatre with three tiers of galleries round the outer wall overlooking a large rush-covered yard. A rectangular stage jutted out into this central pit area, and on either side of the stage, two marble columns supported a ceiling painted with wispy clouds and a sea-blue sky. An ornate balcony overhung the stage at the back and a thatched roof sheltered those rich enough to afford seats in the galleries.

Jack and his friends stood in the central pit along with all the other groundlings who'd paid their penny to watch the play. Looking around, Jack searched the galleries for the elusive Mr Bodley. There were several lords and their retinue of servants, many well-to-do gentlemen and ladies, but no red-feathered artist's apprentices.

'Can anyone see him?' asked Jack, beginning to think that the miniaturist had sent them on a wild goose chase.

Rose shook her head. 'Not yet, but I don't think everyone's in.'

A buzz of conversation, laughter and merrymaking consumed the spectators as they waited for the play to begin. A young woman bearing a large wicker basket threaded her way through the crowd, selling apples, nuts and bottles of beer. As she passed by, Rose subtly lightened her load of a bag of nuts.

'Did you just *steal* that?' asked Akiko, horrified.

'I can't deny my nature,' said Rose, popping a nut into her mouth and grinning. She offered Akiko the bag. 'Want one?'

'No, thank you,' she replied, then turned away to resume the search.

'I'll have one,' said Jack, only catching the last part of the conversation. He chomped on the nut as his eyes continued to scan the galleries and pit, but, with the audience constantly shifting around, it was impossible to keep track of anyone.

'I'm afraid I can't see much,' said Yori, whose ringed staff was the only visible presence of him amid the throng.

'Don't worry, Yori. You keep a careful watch on Jack's purse,' Rose replied, gently patting his shoulder. 'In a crowd like this, one needs to be wary of pickpockets.'

'It takes one to know one, I suppose,' said Akiko under her breath.

Rose glared at her. 'What was that?'

Akiko smiled politely. 'I was just saying, that's good to know –' Her eyes suddenly focused and she pointed towards the front of the stage. 'There he is!'

Spinning round, Jack followed the line of her finger to a tall man with a thin face, pinched mouth and a large white ruff round his scrawny neck. A bright red ostrich feather stuck out proudly from the front of his black velvet hat. He had a dandyish air about him and held a lace handkerchief to his nose. Ignoring the mutterings and complaints of his fellow groundlings, Jack barged his way to the front row, his friends trailing in his wake.

'Mr Bodley?' he asked hopefully.

'Yes,' replied the man in a high shrill voice. 'And who might be enquiring?'

'Jack Fletcher. I believe you're an apprentice of Nicholas Holme.'

'Was,' replied Rowland Bodley, peering down his long nose at Jack, 'but I'm now an artist in my own right.'

'Why, of course,' said Jack, sensing the man's obvious pride. 'That's the very reason I wish to seek your opinion on this . . .'

His ego flattered, Rowland condescended to look at the

locket in Jack's hand. His eyes widened in both recognition and what appeared to be . . . *alarm*. 'Who sent you?' he demanded.

'No one sent us, but Nathan Holme told us where you might be,' replied Jack.

Rowland glanced down at the swords on Jack's hip, then smiled nervously at him. 'Oh, look!' he cried. 'The play's about to start.' As soon as Jack turned his head, Rowland bolted and disappeared into the crowd.

15

CONFESSION

'Where did he go?' shouted Jack, looking round the theatre pit in fury.

Rose pointed to the tip of a red feather weaving its way through the crush of spectators. 'He's heading for the main door!'

'I'll stop him,' said Akiko. Nimbly mounting the stage in spite of her two petticoats, she sprinted to the edge and leapt for the nearest gallery. There was a gasp of amazement from the audience as she flew through the air and caught hold of the upper gallery's balustrade. Then she dropped down on to the lower gallery's rail and, with the agility of an acrobat, ran round its circumference to the theatre's entrance.

Fighting his way against the tide of incoming theatre-goers, Rowland spotted Akiko and, realizing that she'd get there first, turned on his heel and headed in the opposite direction. Jack could see the red feather bobbing along as the artist zigzagged across the pit like a pheasant fleeing the huntsman.

Jack pushed through the crowd, shouldering people aside in an effort to cut the man off. Not looking where he was going, he bounced off a prodigious beer belly.

'Oi! Watch it!' growled its heavily bearded owner as ale slopped from his bottle.

'Sorry,' said Jack, trying to circumnavigate the massive man. But Rowland had already diverted back towards the stage. He had a clear run to the area behind the stage and its exit on to the street. Their quarry was about to escape! Then he heard the jangle of gold rings on a *shakujō* staff as Yori admirably tried to locate the fleeing artist and block his path. Whether by luck or good judgement, Yori converged with Rowland at the foot of the stage.

'Out of my way!' cried Rowland, coming face to face with the diminutive monk. But Yori stood firm, his *shakujō* staff planted in the packed earth. Rowland tried to push him aside, but Yori proved immovable as stone, his whole being grounded with the power of *ki*.

Jack hurried over to trap the artist as Akiko leapt off the lower gallery and closed in from the opposite direction. Hemmed in on all sides, Rowland clambered on to the stage and made for the back curtain. However, as he dashed across the open stage, Rose threw her bag of nuts at him. Scattering everywhere, the nuts rolled under his feet and sent him crashing to the floor. The spectators roared with laughter at the pratfall.

Jack jumped on to the stage and advanced on the flailing artist. Judging by his instinct to flee, the man clearly knew about the locket and who had commissioned the miniature, and he was obviously scared . . . like Mrs Winters. *But why?*

Jack's gut tightened. He now feared even more for his sister's safety.

Scrambling to his feet, Rowland seized a rapier from the

back wall – a theatrical prop yet real and sharp enough to cut. 'Stay back!' he warned Jack, brandishing the weapon.

Considering how wildly the sword's tip wavered, Jack realized the artist was no swordsman. Still, following his recent duelling experience, Jack no longer underestimated the deadliness of a rapier's reach and speed. He drew his *katana* in readiness, triggering an awed intake of breath from the audience.

'I said, stay back!'

Rowland lunged forward, thrusting the rapier at Jack's chest.

Jack deftly moved aside, at the same time striking down with his *katana*. Their swords clashed. Rowland retreated, then thrust again. Having no wish to kill the man, Jack deflected the attack with the edge of his blade before slamming the flat of his sword across Rowland's wrist. He howled in pain and dropped his rapier. As the weapon clattered on to the stage, Jack surged forward with his *katana* out straight. Its tip touched Rowland's bare throat above his ruff and forced him back against one of the stage columns.

Fishing the locket from his pocket, Jack held it before the artist's eyes. 'Tell me what you know about this!' he demanded.

'I've never seen it before in my life,' declared Rowland.

'*Really?*' said Jack, twisting the blade of the *katana* ever so slightly and making the artist wince. 'Then why did you run?'

Rowland glared defiantly back at him. But there was a glint of fear too. 'You won't get another word from me!'

Jack applied the lightest of pressures to his *katana*. Its

razor-sharp point pierced the artist's skin like a peach, drawing a bead of blood. Rowland yelped in shock and pain.

'Stop! Stop!' he begged, holding up his trembling hands. 'I confess, I confess . . . it was *me* who killed Master Holme.'

A collective gasp of astonishment ran round the audience.

Rowland broke down into sobs. 'I-I-I poisoned him . . . with arsenic . . . after he discovered I was stealing his money and commissions . . . but I only did it because he wouldn't acknowledge my skill as an artist!' Rowland looked up, furious indignation in his eyes. 'Half those portraits were *my* doing!'

Jack stared at the quivering man, astounded at this unexpected confession. 'That isn't what I wanted to know . . . I was asking who commissioned this locket?'

Rowland stopped sobbing and blinked. 'Why, I-I-I don't know.'

'Surely you were there when this portrait was painted?'

Rowland peered at the picture and nodded vaguely. 'Yes . . . I do remember the girl coming in for her portrait. Fine cheekbones . . . angelic hair . . . and eyes as deep blue as the ocean –'

'Was she with anyone?' pressed Jack, his hopes rising.

'I believe there was an old woman,' said Rowland, furrowing his brow, 'her chaperone, but I don't recall anyone else.'

'That must have been Mrs Winters,' said Jack. Still holding the *katana* to Rowland's throat, he asked, 'Don't you have *any* idea who paid for the locket? The girl in the portrait is my sister – and she's missing!'

Seeing his blood drip from the blade, Rowland began

babbling, 'My master was secretive – didn't want me stealing his most valued clients – so I rarely met them. Whoever it was, he must have been a gentleman of some wealth to afford such a fine piece!' Then Rowland scowled. 'Although . . . I'm as sure as I can be that he *didn't* ever pay. I'd remember a commission worth eight sovereigns! So, truly, I never met the man. Any knowledge of who ordered the locket went with Holme to his grave!'

Upon hearing this disheartening news, Jack let his sword drop. The trail offered by the locket was now as dead as the man who painted it!

'Don't despair, Jack,' said Akiko, joining him on stage. 'We'll find Jess another way.'

'But how?' replied Jack. 'The locket's a dead end.'

'If a box has no hinges, it may still contain gold,' called Yori sagely from the pit. 'Don't give up so easily. Remember, Sensei Yamada's *koan* of the Daruma Doll: seven times down, eight times up.'

Jack smiled sadly. *How could I forget?* he thought. That philosophy had kept him going throughout his time in Japan. But with only a picture to go on, what chance did they have of finding his sister in a city the size of London? How could they even be sure she was still in the city and *still* alive?

Out of the corner of his eye he noticed Rowland edging away. With a snap of his arm, the steel tip of his *katana* was back at the artist's throat. 'You must remember *something* useful,' he insisted.

Rowland froze where he stood, the *katana* poised over his main artery. 'I-I-I do recall the girl and the old woman talking about going to Stratford-upon-Avon . . . how she wasn't happy about it . . . but had no choice . . .'

'*Stratford?* Are you sure?' questioned Jack.

Rowland nodded and swallowed nervously. 'Now, be a good lad, and let me go.' He offered a grovelling smile. 'I rightfully should charge you for that unpaid locket . . . but in light of our, er, discussions here I'm willing to write off the debt . . .'

Jack lowered his sword once more. Taking that as his cue, Rowland bolted and fled through the backstage curtains. After a moment's hush, the whole of the audience burst into thunderous applause and shouts of '*BRAVO! BRAVO!*'

Jack gazed in disbelief round the theatre, at the whooping and cheering crowd.

They all thought it was the first act of the play!

'*Stratford?*' Jack pondered as they trailed out of the theatre. 'What would she be doing in Stratford-upon-Avon?'

Rose shrugged. 'Only one way to find out.'

'Is it far?' asked Akiko.

'It'll take us about a week to walk there,' replied Rose, 'less if we had horses –'

'*Fletcher!* Is that you?' boomed a voice.

Jack turned to see a portly gentleman with a pointed white beard hurrying out of the theatre after them. He wore a thick padded-velvet doublet and a gold chain round his neck, and a rapier hung loosely at his hip.

'Sorry, do I know you?' asked Jack.

'John, I know it's been a long time,' replied the man good-naturedly, waddling over, 'but surely you haven't forgotten *me?*'

Jack smiled politely as the man approached. 'I think you're confusing me with my father, John Fletcher, the pilot. I'm *Jack* Fletcher.'

The gentleman peered closer at Jack's face. '*Zounds!* Why, I can see that now. My eyesight ain't what it used to be, but you're the spitting image of your father!' He shook Jack firmly by the hand. 'I'm Sir Henry Wilkes, a good friend of John's. When did you get back? Is John here too?' He looked around eagerly.

Jack bowed his head, the weight of grief upon him once more. 'I'm sorry to say, my father was killed by Japanese *wako* pirates. By a ninja, in fact.'

Sir Henry stepped back. 'Good heavens, no! It cannot be true. He was such a fine seaman, the best pilot I ever knew. And what on earth is a "ninja", anyway?'

'An assassin,' explained Jack. 'The worst kind.'

Sir Henry clasped Jack by the shoulders. 'I'm truly sorry to learn this, dear boy. This is tragic news indeed. If there's anything I can do for you, *anything* at all, you have only to let me know.'

'That's very kind of you,' Jack replied.

'You may not be aware,' the gentleman went on, 'but I'm one of the directors of the East India Company. I *personally* invested in your father's voyage to the Japans.' His gleaming gaze now swung towards Akiko and Yori. 'And, by the looks of it, you've brought back some friends with you, as well as a quantity of treasures, I hope!'

Sir Henry kissed Akiko's hand in greeting and inclined his head to Yori. In return, they bowed to him. Then Sir Henry wheeled back to Jack, his plump face flushed with excitement. 'I daresay the ship is unloading as we speak!'

Jack went to reply, but Sir Henry cut him off as the sound of applause came from inside the theatre. 'No, don't tell me now. The play's about to start. Come to my house on the Strand tomorrow evening at six. I'm holding a small party. I want to hear all about your adventures and what riches you've returned with.'

Jack once more opened his mouth, this time to politely decline. Although he was heartened to meet an old friend of his father's, the party would only delay their departure for Stratford-upon-Avon.

But Sir Henry was already rushing away. 'No excuses! You're all invited.'

16

AN UNEXPECTED GUEST

'Remind me again why this is a good idea,' whispered Jack the following evening, as a well-heeled footman led them from the marble-floored entrance hall of Sir Henry Wilkes' London residence, along a passageway and towards the banqueting chamber. Besides being anxious to find his sister, Jack was concerned that they might draw unnecessary attention to themselves among high society. Someone could alert the authorities and they'd find themselves back in prison. Moreover, Jack had no great desire to inform Sir Henry of the failure of the trading expedition, especially as the man had invested his own money in the venture.

'It's a good idea because a man of Sir Henry's standing could help us find your sister,' explained Rose, who'd put on her best and only other dress for the occasion. Jack was in his finery too, as was Akiko, who'd insisted upon wearing a kimono to impress their host. Yori had been content to remain in his monastic robes. And, despite the risk of them being recognized, Jack couldn't deny that Akiko looked resplendent in her glimmering silk gown of red and gold dragons.

As they approached the banqueting hall, they could hear

chamber music and lively chatter. With due ceremony the footman swung open the double doors and swept them into a grand room with a high ornate ceiling, a dark polished-wood floor and a magnificent white-plaster fireplace. Tapestries depicting hunting scenes hung from the walls, luxurious Persian carpets were laid out on the dining tables, and expensive silverware gleamed in the glow shed by a dozen candelabras.

'This is a *small* party?' gasped Akiko, gazing around in awe at the throng of elegant guests mingling in the hall. Upon a raised platform there played a quartet of musicians, and some of the guests were already dancing.

'So this is how the other half lives,' said Rose, taking Jack's arm.

As she led him through the room, Jack noticed Akiko lagging behind. 'Are you coming?' he whispered.

Akiko responded with a stiff smile and nodded. Yori bobbed alongside her, struck dumb by the sheer extravagance of the event. Servants carrying huge silver platters offered them a bounty of sweetmeats, preserved fruits and floral-shaped marzipan confections.

'Talk about a banquet!' said Rose, popping a rose-shaped marzipan into her mouth. 'I could get used to this!'

Curious and admiring gazes – especially from the ladies at Akiko's attire – followed them as they wandered through the party. Jack looked around for their host, then noticed Rose taking a more-than-casual interest in the silverware on the dining tables.

'Rose . . . we're guests here,' he said pointedly, pulling her away.

'I was only *looking*,' she replied, a curl to her lips as she returned the ornate silver spoon to its place setting.

'Jack!' boomed the now-familiar voice of Sir Henry. Their pot-bellied host was waving them over to join him and two other gentlemen. 'So glad you could make it. I was just telling these gentlemen of your fortunate return. Sir Isaac,' he said, turning to a wizened old man with white hair, 'and Sir Thomas –' he now turned to a handsome young man sporting a trimmed goatee beard – 'this is Jack Fletcher, and these are his guests from the Japans.'

Bows were exchanged and introductions made. Rose offered her hand to the dashing Sir Thomas. 'I'm Rose,' she said, surprising Jack by affecting an upper-class accent, 'London-born and -bred.'

Sir Thomas touched his lips to the back of her hand. 'A true English rose, if ever I saw one!' he replied with a grin.

'That's a pair of fine-looking swords on your hip, young man,' observed Sir Isaac to Jack. 'Are you knighted?'

Jack stiffened, his hand instinctively going to his *katana* for fear of another confrontation. 'In Japan I was honoured with the rank of *hatamoto*,' he explained, 'the *equivalent* of being knighted.'

'Don't worry, I'm not questioning your right to bear arms,' replied the old man. 'I'm more interested in seeing your swords. May I?'

At his request, Jack partly withdrew his *katana* to reveal its sharpened steel blade, the cloud-like swirls of its *hamon* shimmering in the candlelight. Leaning in, Sir Isaac inspected the weapon and nodded appreciatively.

'That is truly exceptional craftsmanship,' he declared,

before turning to Akiko's kimono with the measuring eye of a tailor. 'And that's a magnificent silk dress too. Are these typical of your country's workmanship, madam?'

Akiko bowed her head. 'My people like to perfect our artistry.'

The old man grinned and fixed his rheumy eyes on Jack, an avaricious glint to his gaze. 'So, Japan *is* the promised land of silk and steel! Are there riches of silver and gold to be had too?'

'It's certainly a place of untold treasures,' Jack replied. 'But –'

Sir Henry patted Jack hard on the back, almost knocking the wind from him. 'Excellent news! Didn't I tell you, Sir Isaac? The Land of the Rising Sun is a goldfield just waiting to be mined.'

'And what of the trading routes?' Sir Isaac continued keenly. 'I heard rumour of a young pilot navigating the fabled North-East Passage. Would that be *you*, by any chance?'

Jack nodded humbly. 'Yes, although –'

'Extraordinary!' exclaimed Sir Isaac, clapping his hands in delight. 'No pilot has ever successfully navigated that route. Our company will have a monopoly on it. We can corner the market!' He looked at Sir Henry. 'You have my backing for another expedition, sir. Why, with the voyage cut by a year, the company's profits would be doubled, perhaps *trebled*!'

'I will make the arrangements forthwith, Sir Isaac,' said a beaming Sir Henry as he put his arm round Jack. 'Will you excuse us for a moment, gentlemen and ladies?'

Sir Henry drew Jack aside, leaving Sir Isaac to question

Akiko and Yori further about Japan; Sir Thomas was still engaged in conversation with Rose.

'Pray, tell: where's the *Alexandria* docked? What of the other ships in our trading fleet?' asked Sir Henry, his voice low. 'I haven't been able to track them down at the quay.'

Jack gazed awkwardly at his feet. 'I'm afraid a typhoon sent the fleet to the bottom of the ocean, Sir Henry. Only the *Alexandria* survived, thanks to the piloting skills of my late father. We made landfall in Toba, several hundred leagues north of Nagasaki. But, as I told you, we were then attacked by pirates and the whole crew were slaughtered. The journey is treacherous!'

Sir Henry's face grew as gloomy as the storm itself. 'Not a *single* ship returned? Our whole investment – sunk? But you've been gone some seven years!'

'I only survived by the grace of God and the kindness of a local samurai warrior, Masamoto Takeshi,' Jack explained. He then told Sir Henry how Masamoto had taken him in, adopted him and trained him in the Way of the Warrior. How, following a civil war, he'd journeyed across Japan to Nagasaki, where he'd had the good fortune to meet with the captain of the *Hosiander*, the Dutch trading vessel that had eventually brought him home.

As Jack related his tale, Sir Henry's demeanour brightened. 'So, you are well acquainted with the Japans and the Japanese? You speak their language, know their customs?'

Jack nodded. 'Yes, but I returned to Eng–'

'Then *return to the Japans* you must! With a new fleet. As soon as possible. You still have your father's *rutter*, don't you? May I . . .?'

Jack hesitated. The *rutter* was with him in his shoulder bag. He hadn't dared leave it at the Bunch of Grapes. However, as honourable as Sir Henry Wilkes seemed, Jack didn't yet know the man well enough to trust him with such a valuable heirloom. 'I'm sorry, Sir Henry, but I *can't* return to Japan.'

Sir Henry blanched. 'Why ever not?'

'I need to find my sister. She's missing.' Jack pulled out the silver locket and showed him her picture. Sir Henry squinted at the portrait. 'I believe she might be in Stratford-upon-Avon,' said Jack.

Sir Henry frowned. 'I thought you lived in Limehouse, so why on earth would you think she's in Stratford?'

'I'm baffled myself,' replied Jack, 'but the artist Rowland Bodley said he overheard her talking about going there.'

'Did he, now? Hmm, it's unusual for a young woman to travel so far alone.' But, after a moment's consideration, Sir Henry patted Jack amiably on the shoulder. 'Of course, Jack, family must come first. Visit my stables before you go and take whatever horses you require for your journey.'

'*Really?*' gasped Jack, stunned by Sir Henry's offer. Rose had been right about enlisting Sir Henry's help. Having horses at their disposal would cut days off their journey to Stratford.

Sir Henry nodded. 'Yes, really. We can talk more about your return to the Japans when you get back to London. But do be careful on the roads. Trust *no one* – these are dangerous times.'

'Of course, Sir Henry. I thank you for your generosity –'

Jack felt a tug on his sleeve and looked round to find Yori at his side, a strained expression on his face.

Pulling Jack closer, Yori whispered in his ear, 'We have to leave. Right now!'

'Why?' breathed Jack.

Yori nodded towards the door. A guest with a tight crop of copper-red hair and a preened moustache was entering the room. 'Sir Toby Nashe is here!'

17

SHADOW

'Are you leaving so soon?' said Sir Isaac, a disappointed pout on his lips as Jack extricated Akiko from his company.

'I'm afraid we've a long journey tomorrow,' Jack explained. 'Thank you, Sir Henry; it has been a splendid party. Goodbye, Sir Isaac –' and with that he began ushering Akiko and Yori away. 'Come on, Rose!'

'Sorry, it looks like we're going,' said Rose to a forlorn-looking Sir Thomas. As she was dragged towards a side door, she hissed at Jack, *'What's the hurry?* I was just starting to enjoy myself!'

'See that man over there?' Jack replied, his eyes directing Rose's attention to the main entrance. 'He's Sir Toby Nashe, the idiot who challenged me to a duel, then had me arrested and sentenced to hang!'

'Oh dear,' said Rose, barely suppressing a smirk, 'you *are* in a pickle!'

Keeping their heads low and weaving between the other guests, they crossed the room as swiftly as possible. Then Yori stopped short and gasped, 'Sir Francis is here too!'

The lanky, long-haired fencer was sampling the sweetmeats

from a tray offered by a servant. Doubling back, Jack and his friends headed towards the rear set of doors . . . only to run straight into Sir Toby himself! By a stroke of good fortune, however, their nemesis had his back to them and was exchanging greetings with a grave-faced man in a black fur robe. Before Sir Toby could turn round, Jack and the others darted behind a group of ladies, the wide hooped skirts of their dresses providing partial cover for the four fugitives.

'Did you hear about the fiasco at the Globe yesterday?' said one of the ladies, too wrapped up in their conversation to notice anyone hovering in their shadow.

'Yes . . .' said another, 'I heard it was a rogue theatre company . . .'

'I heard someone confessed to a murder . . .' chipped in an older lady, 'and the Justice of the Peace is investigating . . .'

'And what about that ghost ship along the Thames . . . do you *believe* the tales of killer shadows?'

Jack's ears pricked up. *Killer shadows* . . . that was the second time he'd heard the phrase. The women tittered nervously as they discussed the series of grisly garrottings. To Jack, the manner of death sounded disturbingly like a ninja technique. But such a notion was absurd. He was in England, not Japan. He was simply reading too much into the rumours. Besides, he had more pressing concerns to deal with at that moment.

Sir Toby and his companion were coming their way. Edging round the chattering group of women, Jack and his friends managed to keep out of sight. Still, he overheard the man in the black fur ask Sir Toby, 'How's that young filly of yours? Tamed her yet?'

'No, she's as disobedient as ever,' Sir Toby replied, a sour look on his face. 'She almost escaped the other day!'

His companion tutted disapprovingly. 'You need to keep her on a short rein. At least, that's how I handle my wife!' They laughed cruelly at the expense of a timid, mousey-looking woman trailing a few feet behind.

'You're right,' said Sir Toby, a sneer on his lips. 'She deserves a good whipping!'

Jack watched, silent yet fuming, as the two men walked up to Sir Francis. The more Jack learnt about Sir Toby, the less he liked him. But he knew that now was not the time to settle old scores. Quietly slipping away, he and his friends headed for the rear doors. They had almost made their escape when a portly man clutching three brimming glasses of wine stepped into their path.

'*YOU!*' gasped Sir Edmund, his pudgy eyes widening in disbelief.

Rose, quick off the mark, stepped in front of Sir Edmund, blocking his momentary glimpse of Jack and the others.

'Is one of those for me?' she asked, taking a glass, then promptly spilling it over his velvet doublet. 'Oh dear, I'm so sorry!'

She grabbed a napkin from a table and began mopping him down vigorously. As Sir Edmund flailed and flustered under the onslaught, Jack, Akiko and Yori dashed out of the banqueting hall.

Rose joined them a few seconds later. 'I couldn't delay him any longer,' she explained. 'He's getting Sir Toby and Sir Francis!'

As they sprinted down the corridor and round a corner,

they heard the doors behind them crash open and heavy footsteps coming after them.

'In here!' said Jack, opening a door to their left and diving through. They found themselves in a wood-panelled library room with an upholstered armchair beside a fireplace and two walls lined with books. Akiko closed the door behind them, barely a second before Sir Toby and his two companions rounded the corner.

'Are you sure you saw them?' demanded Sir Toby, his gruff voice echoing along the hallway.

'I'm certain . . .' replied Sir Edmund, 'well, sort of . . .'

'But we watched them . . . drown!' hiccuped Sir Francis, the drunken slur already apparent in his voice. 'Methinks, Sir Edmund, you've had too much wine this evening!'

'I've not yet had my fifth glass!' protested Sir Edmund.

As their voices drew closer, Jack looked around desperately for another exit. However, aside from a closed leaded window, the library had no other way out except the doorway they'd come in by. He and his friends could only wait in anxious silence, listening to their enemies' approach. As the creak of floorboards grew louder and ever nearer, Jack's eyes were drawn to the book-lined walls. He crept over to the nearest bookcase.

What are you doing? whispered Akiko.

Quickly and quietly, Jack pulled out the *rutter* from his shoulder bag. 'Hiding this!' he whispered.

'Just another tree in the forest,' Yori murmured under his breath, as Jack parted two leather-bound tomes to create space on the shelf. The *rutter*'s oilskin cover was similar enough to the bindings of Sir Henry's books and would blend in easily.

What better place to hide a book than in a library? thought Jack. He didn't want to risk losing his father's precious logbook to the authorities if he was caught again. As he slid the *rutter* into the gap he'd made, the hairs on the back of his neck bristled and he was seized by the unsettling sensation of being watched. He spun round. But there was no one there. His friends, still clustered by the door, were no longer even looking his way.

Yet Jack couldn't shake off the uneasy feeling. His gaze swept the library . . . the empty fireplace . . . the vacant chair . . . the row upon row of books . . . until it finally settled on the window overlooking the street. The sun had long since set and the thoroughfare had become a murky underworld lit by the faintest of moonlight. Jack peered out into the night and what he saw made his heart stop and his blood run cold.

A shadow stood in the darkness. Black against black. Unmoving. A silhouette of a man, sinister and spectral.

Jack couldn't speak . . . couldn't scream . . . could barely even breathe. Against all reason, he saw Dokugan Ryu – Dragon Eye – the ninja who'd killed his father, who'd hunted him mercilessly, who'd dragged Yamato to his death.

Yet that was impossible. The assassin was dead. So too was his *kagemusha*, his successor and doppelgänger. Then Jack recalled the final words of Dragon Eye's shadow warrior: '*I'll haunt you to your grave*, gaijin.'

A shudder ran down Jack's spine. For what he saw was more terrifying than any ghost.

Jack flinched as the door to the library rattled and Akiko and the others threw their full weight against it.

'Muss be locked,' slurred Sir Francis on the other side.

'I've had enough of this drunken nonsense!' growled Sir Toby. 'Back to the party.'

The footsteps receded down the corridor and, when all was silent, Akiko peeked out. 'They're gone,' she whispered.

When Jack turned back to the window, the shadow was gone too.

18

PROPHECY

The sun had barely risen above the horizon when Jack and his friends left the city through Newgate and headed west along the old Roman road. Sir Henry's stable boy, yawning and rubbing his eyes, had provided them with horses, saddles and some basic provisions. Even at this unearthly hour in the morning, the highway was bustling with traffic: messengers in their riding gear, farmers driving their cattle into market, travellers in their carriages bound for Oxford. But the further they left the capital behind, the more the traffic thinned out until they were seemingly the only ones on the road.

Jack rode in silence, his thoughts consumed by the demonic shadow of the previous night. He knew that it could only have been his imagination – the shadow had been a trick of the light or else a nightwatchman merely going about his business. That seemed the most likely explanation for the black-robed figure he'd seen. Still, he couldn't get the horrifying image out of his head . . .

'You're quiet,' remarked Akiko, trotting up alongside him. 'What's troubling you?'

Jack nodded vaguely, unsure whether to share his concerns

or not. He *knew* Dokugan Ryu and his successor were dead. Moreover, this was home – this was England, a world away from Japan and its ninjas. So the idea that he'd seen Dragon Eye was simply ludicrous. Not wanting to worry Akiko unnecessarily, or have her think he was going mad, he said, 'I was just thinking about Jess, wondering why she'd be in Stratford-upon-Avon, of all places.'

'From what Bodley said, it sounds like she didn't have much choice,' said Akiko.

'But was Jess running away, or being taken away?' Jack questioned. 'There's a big difference.'

'Well, we know Mrs Winters is scared of something . . . or someone,' said Yori, bouncing atop his mare like a bobbin on a spindle. 'Perhaps Jess is too.'

'I guess the only way to find out is to find her,' said Rose, and she geed up her horse.

As they crested the brow of a hill, Jack took one final glance back at the hazy city in the distance. He was glad to be leaving London behind with all its perils and problems. But he feared what lay ahead for them too. Would he find his sister? Or would he discover her dead and buried? What would he do then? He'd spent so many years with one goal in mind – being reunited with Jess – that he hadn't really thought beyond that. And after their rude and violent welcome to England, would Akiko and Yori really want to stay with him in this country? His future – and their future – was as open as the road that lay ahead of them.

Fields spread out on either side of the highway, carpeting the countryside in a patchwork of golden barley and rich brown earth. Woodland came and went. So did babbling brooks and streams. Hamlets of a dozen or so houses sprang up every so often, congregated round an old stone church or a creaking watermill. As Jack and his friends passed through the settlements, the farmers and their families watched their progress with wary curiosity, many perturbed by the sight of the Japanese monk and Japanese girl on horseback. Jack was reminded of the strange and often hostile looks *he*'d got when he travelled through Japan. But if the farmers' stares made Akiko and Yori uncomfortable, they were doing a good job of hiding it.

After riding most of the day, they entered a village and stopped at a water trough to give their horses a chance to rest and drink. With the barley harvest being brought in, the village was all but deserted, everyone, including the children, working in the fields. However, as Jack dismounted, he noticed a grizzled old farmer on a stool outside a small thatched cottage. He was chewing on a long piece of straw and eyed the four travellers with guarded suspicion.

'Good day to you,' greeted Jack. 'What village is this?'

'Oakfield,' grunted the farmer.

'Do you mind our horses drinking?'

The man offered a shrug of his bony shoulders. 'Bit late to ask, considerin' they already are.'

Yori stepped forward and bowed. 'Thank you for your kindness. It's an honour to visit your village.'

The farmer snorted. 'An *honour*?' He gave Jack a sidelong look. 'Can your friend see with those eyes? This place be just a patch of mud!'

'Yori and Akiko are from the Japans,' Jack explained, as

Akiko bowed respectfully too. 'It's their first time in England.'

The farmer gnawed thoughtfully on the straw's stem. 'Don't they 'ave mud in their country?'

Jack laughed. 'Yes, lots. But this is *English* mud. Nothing finer!'

The farmer's frosty demeanour slowly gave way to a toothless grin. 'Aye, it's good mud!' He offered his hand to Jack. 'My name's Jon Tiller. There's some hay for the horses round back if you want.'

'Thank you,' said Jack. Rose walked off behind the cottage and soon came back with an armful of hay.

'Where you folks travelling?' asked Jon, his eyes never leaving Akiko or Yori.

'Stratford-upon-Avon,' Jack replied.

The farmer spat out a chewed wad of straw. 'Long way to go. You 'ave business there?'

Jack shook his head. 'Looking for my sister. She's gone missing.'

His brow furrowing like a ploughed field, Jon sighed. 'Lots of folk gone missing, what with the plague an' all.'

They both fell into a gloomy silence. Jack tried not to imagine that gruesome fate befalling his sister, but, after seeing his father's cottage all boarded up, it was hard to suppress his dread. Perhaps the plague was the reason Jess had been forced to move? But . . . *why Stratford?* As far as he knew, they didn't have any family connections to the town . . . although it was possible Mrs Winters did.

The horses having finished their hay, Jack unhooked the reins and remounted. Their break had been short, and he still felt saddle-sore after their long ride out of London. 'How far to the nearest decent coaching inn?' he asked.

The farmer rubbed his stubbled chin. 'Hmm, I'd say some fifteen or so miles. Travellers do say the Fox and Pheasant ain't bad, tho' I never been there myself. But if you don't tarry, you'll get there 'fore sunset. Bear right as you leave the village, then carry on along the road till you come to the corner of a wood, then take the left-hand fork.'

'Any thieves in the wood?' asked Rose.

'Nah,' said Jon, selecting a fresh piece of straw from the ground and popping it in his mouth. 'There's a witch, you see. Scares 'em off, she does!' The old farmer chuckled. 'Keep away from the woods and you'll be fine.'

'This must be the fork,' said Jack. They had come to a junction marked by a set of old stocks on which someone had heaped a pile of leaves and old rags.

Yori glanced nervously towards the dark wood. 'Do you really think there is a witch in there?'

'England has its fair share of them,' Rose replied. 'I wouldn't go wandering off, if I were you.'

'Don't worry, Yori,' said Jack, seeing his friend go pale. 'The farmer was just trying to frighten us, that's all.'

But no sooner had he spoken than the pile of rags twitched, causing his horse to rear up in fright. Mouldy leaves tumbled aside to expose a grey-haired, wrinkled old crone in the stocks. The creature looked more dead than alive: her face was lined and rough as a piece of bark, her eyes little more than slits, her hands curled and blackened like crow's feet, and her skinny legs protruded through the holes of the stocks like the limbs of a dead tree. Then the crinkled corpse of a woman gave a dry cough.

'She's still alive!' Akiko gasped, scrambling down from her horse.

'Careful!' warned Rose. 'She could be the witch.'

'She's just an old woman,' said Akiko. 'What harm can she do?'

Rose gave her a sober look. 'A witch can do a lot of harm, from what I hear.'

'We don't *know* she's the witch,' said Jack, dismounting.

Remaining in her saddle, Rose shook her head doubtfully. 'Who else would be put in stocks out here?'

'Well, we can't leave her like this,' insisted Akiko. 'She'll die.'

Witch or not, Jack agreed with Akiko. He dismounted and opened the satchel on his saddle. Sir Henry's stable boy had given him a leather water bottle and he took it out. Pulling the stopper, he pressed the spout to the old woman's parched lips. Her tongue sought out the water like a wriggling worm. She swallowed, then coughed and spluttered.

'Kindness can kill,' she rasped.

Ignoring the warning, Jack offered her more. This time she drank, glugging greedily. Once she had slaked her thirst, she rose stiffly to a sitting position. Through limp strands of her dirty hair her eyes fixed on Jack.

'*You!*' she croaked. 'You seek one missing!'

Jack almost dropped the water bottle in shock. 'H-h-how do you know?'

A grim twist of a smile threaded its way across her cracked lips. 'One sees much on this road . . . especially when one has little choice.' She looked down despairingly at her legs in the stocks.

Jack pulled out the locket from under his shirt and showed her the portrait. 'Have you seen this girl?' he asked urgently.

'Ooh, pretty little thing . . . Jane, isn't it . . . no, Judith . . . no, Jess . . . yes, Jess!'

Jack's hands began to tremble with hope. 'Where is she? Where's Jess?'

The old woman raised a finger, crooked as a knotted twig. She held it up before Jack's eyes. 'When a wise man points at the moon –' Jack followed her fingertip in an arc through the air – 'the fool looks at the finger!'

She let out a cackling laugh.

Jack frowned in dismay, while Rose sighed heavily.

'She's just playing games with you,' she said impatiently. 'Come on – let's go.'

'Then how did she know my sister's name?' challenged Jack.

'She guessed it,' Rose replied, and she pointed at the locket. 'The letter J is inscribed within the flower engraving on the front.'

Jack looked and saw it now for himself. Annoyed at being duped by a simple parlour trick, Jack shoved the stopper back in the water bottle.

'Oh, Jack, don't be so petulant!' chided the old woman.

'What!' exclaimed Jack in shock. 'You know *my* name as well?'

'However far the stream flows, it never forgets its source!' the old crone answered cryptically.

Jack crouched down closer to her. 'So tell me, what else do you know? Has my sister passed this way?'

The old woman gave a gap-toothed grin. 'I know not everyone who travels these roads, but I do know the world has taken much from you. So ponder this on your journey: when you feel furthest away, you're closer than you think.'

'Don't get drawn in by her trickery!' Rose cautioned. 'Let's leave before this witch curses us all!'

The old woman scowled at Rose. 'A bird may be known by its flight, so why don't *you* just fly away!'

'At least I ain't bound to the ground like you,' Rose shot back.

Gazing mournfully at her pinned legs, the old woman sighed. 'Aye, it's a cruel fate when they clip the wings of an old bird.'

Akiko knelt down and inspected the padlock and iron clamp holding the top piece of wood in place. 'It'll be impossible to get this off,' she said.

Looking to Yori, Jack asked, 'Can your chants break them?'

Yori shook his head. 'Even *kiai-jutsu* has its limits.'

'Ah! Foreign magic,' muttered the old woman, licking her dry lips. 'But not everyone who wears a cowl is a monk.'

'And not every wise woman is a witch,' replied Yori with a nervous smile.

Jack examined the stocks themselves. While the padlock was solid and secure, the stocks were old and worn, the wood weathered and riddled with woodworm. 'I might be able to free you,' he offered.

'It would take a strong man to break these bonds,' replied the witch.

'I don't need strength,' replied Jack, 'just technique.'

Recalling his *tameshiwari* training, Jack knew it was possible to break through three blocks of wood in a single punch. He'd only ever managed two blocks, but the stocks looked to be about the same thickness. Breathing deeply and harnessing his inner energy, Jack channelled the *ki* into his fist. Then, with a mighty shout of '*KIAI!*', he punched the brittle wood . . .

CRACK!

But the wood wasn't as brittle as it looked. The stocks splintered but refused to snap, his knuckles crumpling instead. Grimacing in pain, Jack clutched his hand.

How Sensei Kyuzo would be laughing in his grave at such a failure! he thought grimly.

'Good try, dear,' soothed the old woman as Jack nursed his throbbing fist. 'Seems you broke your hand rather than the stocks. Here, let me have a look at your injury.' Then, with startling ease, she slipped her ankles out of the stocks and creakily got to her feet.

They all stared dumbfounded at the crone.

'You . . . you could get out? *Any time?*' gasped Yori.

'Oh yes,' replied the old woman, smirking. 'Stocks can't hold a witch.'

'I warned you the hag was playing tricks on us!' cried Rose.

The witch laughed. 'Don't worry, I won't curse any of you. Not even you, Rose.'

Flinching at the use of her name, Rose fearfully backed her horse away.

'But I did want to test you,' the witch went on. 'Most travellers ignore me, or they taunt or abuse me. Few show compassion . . . although there was a girl, blonde-haired . . . eyes like the sea . . .' She smiled at Jack, a hideous, crooked, black-toothed smile.

A flicker of hope ignited in Jack's heart. 'Are you talking about *Jess*?'

The witch's grin suddenly vanished and she stared wide-eyed down the road, as if a storm was fast approaching. 'Make haste! For the sun soon sets, and your shadows grow longer. And you don't want *your* shadow catching up with you . . . do you, Jack?'

The old woman fixed him with such a piercing look that Jack wondered if she somehow knew of the dark figure he'd seen outside Sir Henry's house in London. The flicker of hope he'd felt a moment ago now turned to cold fear.

'For your kindness to an old woman, I offer you this prophecy.' She held up her gnarled hand, raising her fingers, one at a time, with each line she uttered:

> *'One will live . . .*
> *Two will love . . .*
> *Three will cry . . .*
> *Four will die!'*

Jack exchanged a look of alarm with his friends, their party of four suddenly feeling cursed despite the witch's promise not to. Then, cackling to herself, the old woman limped off into the woods, her words hanging in the air like a spell.

19

THE COURTESY-MAN

Dusk was descending by the time Jack and his friends reached the Fox and Pheasant Inn. The ostler met them at the gates and led their horses through a wide archway into the cobbled yard. While the horses were unsaddled and taken through to the stables at the rear, a young lad gathered their bags and bade them follow him into the main hall. A roaring fire was burning in the stone hearth and the smell of woodsmoke mingled with the mouth-watering aroma of roasted pheasant coming from the kitchen. At a long table sat a group of travellers, drinking and feasting, as a lank-haired musician played a lively jig on his fiddle. In the corner nearest the fire, a well-dressed gentleman and lady were afforded more privacy in their own booth, a pair of manservants attending to their every need. Jack, Akiko and Yori took an empty table close to the fire, while Rose went to negotiate with the innkeeper over their rooms and board.

'It seems like a respectable establishment,' said Jack, glancing round at the candlelit bar, cushioned benches and painted-cloth hangings on the walls.

'Do you think they'll have a bath?' asked Akiko hopefully.

'Probably . . .' replied Jack, 'but whether they have enough hot water is another matter.'

Akiko frowned in disappointment. 'This country is so strange. Even the most basic tea house in Japan would be able to provide its guests with a *proper* bath.'

Jack scratched at the dirt on his neck from the long journey. He too missed the daily ritual of bathing, but was loath to admit it. 'We English are a hardy lot,' he said by way of an excuse. 'Tell me,' he said, changing the subject, 'do you believe what the old woman said?'

The witch's words still played on Jack's mind: her prophecy was deeply troubling. After his encounter with the Riddling Monk in Japan, and the crazed man's predictions that came true, he gave more credence to the forecasts of oracles and soothsayers.

Yori rested his staff against the table, its bronze rings jingling softly. 'Divination is an unproven art,' he said. 'There's always more beyond the horizon than one can see.'

Jack swallowed hard. 'But she said the four of us will *die*!'

Yori nodded. 'She did. But prophecies aren't always direct predictions of future events. Often, they're symbolic of *possible* outcomes.'

'I hope you're right, Yori,' said Akiko, her expression as equally worried as Jack's. 'Because she was very convincing.'

'And I'm convinced that that witch has met my sister on the road,' said Jack. 'How else could she have –'

'Good evening!'

They all looked up as a young man in a plush velvet jerkin, with silver buttons and shoulder wings, sat himself down at their table. 'You look like you've come far,' he said cheerily to Akiko and Yori.

Jack stiffened, instinctively on guard. 'And what's it to you?'

The young man raised an eyebrow. 'Don't take umbrage, my good man. I'm only being friendly to our foreign visitors here.' He offered his hand. 'Sorry, rude of me not to introduce myself. The name's Harold Westcott. And you are?'

Jack relaxed a little. From his dress and manner, their uninvited guest appeared to be a gentleman. Jack shook hands with him, and introduced himself and his friends.

'The Japans, eh?' remarked Harold, regarding Yori and Akiko with open curiosity. 'Can't say I've ever heard of the place. But it must be a fine country to produce such fine people as you.' His gaze rested on Akiko.

Akiko inclined her head, smiling politely, and Jack felt a stab of envy at their guest's easy charm and charisma. Both Akiko and Yori attracted a lot of attention in England, and Jack felt protective of them as his guests in his homeland.

'If I may say so,' Harold went on, 'that's an exquisite hairpin you're wearing, miss. Solid gold?'

Akiko nodded, her hand going to the slender *kanzashi* pin that held her long dark hair in a bun. One end was crafted into the shape of a *sakura* flower. But Akiko's *kanzashi* was as beautiful as it was deadly – its tip sharpened to a fine point for use as a secret lethal weapon. *Not that our new friend need know that*, thought Jack, reminding himself that Akiko was more than capable of protecting herself.

'And you look to be a learned young man,' remarked Harold, turning to Yori. 'What's that staff you're carrying?'

'It's a *shakujō*,' Yori explained enthusiastically. 'We use it in prayer, as an accompaniment to our chanting.'

Harold examined its spiked bronze tip and six metal rings. 'Looks more like a spear than a musical instrument!'

Yori responded with an enigmatic smile. The man was closer to the truth than he realized. Not mentioning the staff's purpose as a self-defence weapon, Yori replied, 'I am a Buddhist. We believe in not harming any creature. The jingling of the rings warns insects and other animals of our approach so that we don't step on them accidentally.'

'Admirable,' said Harold. 'But why *six* rings?'

'They represent the Six Perfections.'

Harold listened attentively as Yori told him of the Six Perfections of Generosity, Virtue, Patience, Diligence, Contemplation and Wisdom. Harold glanced at Jack. 'And there I was thinking England was the font of all knowledge!' He let out a good-natured laugh. 'So what's your story, Jack? How come you've been to the Japans?'

'You're certainly full of questions,' said Jack, becoming mindful of Sir Henry's warning not to trust anyone on the road.

Harold gave a nonchalant shrug. 'Well, he who asks a question is a fool for a minute; he who does not remains a fool forever. Isn't that right, Yori?'

Yori nodded approvingly at such wise words. Harold took a sip from his pewter wine goblet, then, sensing Jack's reluctance to open up, jutted his chin in the direction of the richly dressed couple in their own private booth. 'There appear to be a lot of fine people on the road this evening. That's Lord Robert Percival and his wife, Lady Catherine, don't you know.'

Jack glanced over at the silver-haired man and his elegant

wife, who was younger than her husband. 'I've never heard of them,' he said.

Harold's mouth fell open in shock at this admission. 'Lord Robert Percival's a member of the Privy Council – a very important man, an adviser to the King himself!'

Jack studied the elderly man again. Attired in red velvet robes and seated ramrod straight in his booth, Lord Percival certainly carried an air of authority as he talked with his wife; the two manservants hovering close by at his beck and call.

Harold leant in and whispered, 'Lady Catherine is . . . *French*.' He took another swig from his wine goblet and sat back. 'I presume you've ridden up from London today? I bet you're glad to be out of the city, what with those plague doctors wreaking havoc!'

Jack looked up suddenly at Harold. 'What are you talking about? What plague doctors?'

Putting aside his goblet, Harold lowered his voice once more, his expression turning grave. 'You ain't heard? It's as if the four horsemen of the Apocalypse have descended. They appear only at night – dark as shadows – leaving death in their wake.'

Jack felt a chill run through him. Plague doctors conjured up nightmarish images in his head, but it was Harold's mention of shadows that really troubled him.

'Yet it's not the plague that kills,' Harold went on. 'It's the doctors themselves. I heard some poor soul was found with his right eye pierced straight through with a red ostrich feather after they visited him!'

Jack's mouth went dry as a bone. The victim could only be one person – Rowland Bodley.

'They say he's not the first, and he won't be the last!' Harold went on, not noticing the uneasy looks being exchanged between Jack, Yori and Akiko. 'Rumour has it there's a whole trail of bodies, from Limehouse to Ludgate. These are dark and dangerous times, my friends!'

Picking up his wine goblet, he took a long draught and finished it off. 'Anyways, where are you folks headed?'

'Stratford,' Jack replied distractedly, his thoughts consumed by Harold's story. *Was the apparition outside the window last night a plague doctor? Or was it something even more sinister . . . something connected to the rumours of killer shadows?*

'Well, if you're going that way, take the high road out of town,' advised Harold. 'The low road's flooded and has become almost impassable.'

'Thank you for the warning,' said Akiko, smiling warmly at him.

'You're welcome, miss.' Setting down his empty goblet, Harold's eye was caught by the glint of silver round Jack's neck. 'That's a fine locket. Is it your sweetheart inside?' he asked, glancing at Akiko.

'No, it's my little sister,' replied Jack, opening up the locket and showing Harold Jess's portrait. 'She's missing. Have you seen her by any chance? I believe she may have travelled this way.'

'Let me have a closer look.' Harold peered at the miniature, then regretfully shook his head. 'Sorry, no, but I'll keep an eye out for the lass.'

'I'm sure you will!' said Rose, inserting herself between Jack and their guest. 'Now be gone and try your luck with those coneys over there.'

Harold scowled at Rose, who unflinchingly stared back. Then he stood and bowed stiffly to Jack, Akiko and Yori. 'A pleasure meeting you. May you continue safe on your journey.'

As he traipsed off to the other table of travellers, Akiko stared in astonishment at Rose. 'Why were you so rude? He was just being friendly.'

'Too friendly,' replied Rose. 'Seems like a courtesy-man to me.'

'What's a courtesy-man?' asked Yori.

'A courtesy-man is a con man, a thief. You see those fine clothes he's wearing?' said Rose. 'Likely they ain't his. Probably stolen off the last traveller who fell for his charm.'

Akiko looked aghast. 'I don't believe it. He seemed so nice. Surely not *every* Englishman's a thief?'

'Of course not,' Rose replied, the corner of her mouth curling into a sly grin as she produced a small leather purse. 'Women can be too. But we're better at it!' She nodded in Harold's direction. 'Dinner's on him tonight.'

'Well, *we*'re not thieves!' said Akiko, snatching the purse from Rose. She chased after Harold, calling, 'You dropped this.'

Harold blinked in surprise. 'Why, thank you, Akiko,' he said, reattaching the purse to his belt. 'It's rare to come across such honest folk these days. I do hope I can return the favour one day.'

After a supper of roast pheasant and sweet turnip, Jack and his friends turned in for the night. The long ride from London had tired them all out. As they ascended the stairs to the gallery overlooking the moonlit yard, Yori asked, 'Do you think the man killed by those plague doctors *was* Rowland Bodley?'

'There can't be too many other Londoners who wear red ostrich feathers in their hats,' said Jack grimly.

'The feather could just be a coincidence,' suggested Akiko.

Jack glanced at her. 'Too much of a coincidence, for my liking.'

'I reckon Nathan Holme did it,' said Rose, leaning against the balcony rail. 'To avenge his father.'

'Nathan didn't seem like a murderer to me,' said Yori.

'Grief can push a man to the brink,' argued Rose. 'If he didn't do it, then he hired someone to do it for him.'

'But why hire plague doctors?' questioned Akiko, unconvinced.

Rose shrugged. 'The men he hired likely *dressed* as plague doctors so they could move freely round the city and not rouse any suspicion.'

That's certainly what a ninja would do, thought Jack, the notion flashing through his mind like a *shuriken* star.

'What's the matter?' asked Akiko, noticing the troubled look on Jack's face.

'Nothing,' he replied, dismissing his concerns with a shake of his head. He realized that he should be focusing on finding his sister rather than worrying about rumours of shadows. 'Whatever it was, Bodley's not our problem any more.'

'Or anyone else's, for that matter!' said Rose with a gallow's laugh. 'Right, I'm off to bed. See you in the morning.' And, as she passed Jack on her way to her room, she kissed him goodnight on the cheek.

Yori headed to his and Jack's chamber, yawning, and Jack followed. But Akiko lingered in the darkness. '*Jack*,' she called softly.

'What is it?' he asked, turning back to her.

Akiko stood stiffly, her usual warmth towards him absent. 'How *well* do you know Rose?'

Jack could still feel the press of Rose's lips on his cheek. 'We're childhood friends, that's all,' he reassured her.

'That was over seven years ago,' said Akiko. 'A person can change in that time. I don't think you can trust her.'

Jack frowned. 'Why ever not?'

'She's a *thief*,' replied Akiko, as if the answer was obvious. 'And I think she's taking advantage of you.'

'How can you say that?' argued Jack. 'Rose is helping us find my sister.'

'Not without payment,' said Akiko. 'I saw her pocket one of the coins you gave her for board and lodging. She's *stealing* your money.'

Jack frowned. 'Rose negotiated a good price for the rooms. She gave me back more change than I expected, so I'd be surprised if she'd taken any for herself. Besides, she may be a thief, but she's got a good heart.'

Akiko stared unexpectedly hard at Jack. 'Why are you defending her?'

'And why are you attacking her?' replied Jack. 'This isn't like you. Can't you be more friendly?'

'Well, she's certainly being friendly with *you*.'

Jack sighed. 'Akiko, there's no need to be jealous, I –'

'Jealous? Of *her*?' Akiko shot him an affronted look and crossed her arms. 'Jack, you do what you want. This is your country. I'm only a guest. If you prefer a rose to a *sakura* blossom, that's your choice. I'm just trying to protect you, that's all. Goodnight.'

With that, she turned on her heel and strode off towards her chamber, leaving Jack alone on the gallery. He gazed up in bewilderment at the stars, wondering what he'd said to upset her. He imagined she was just tired from the journey.

But as he stood in the darkness, listening to the whinny of the horses in the stables, Jack thought again about what Akiko had said. Was she right about not trusting Rose? It was true that his only acquaintance with Rose before last week consisted of a childhood kiss under Moorgate. But it was Rose who had led them to Mrs Winters, and suggested seeking out the miniaturist, and was now guiding them through a country he was no longer familiar with.

Rose was a godsend . . . wasn't she?

20

TARGET PRACTICE

The next morning, by the time they'd polished off a breakfast of buttered bread and sage, the ostler had their horses saddled and ready to ride. Jack tipped the man, then set off out of town with his friends. Along the highway a mist hung over the fields, the dew glistening in the early-morning sunlight. Rose led the way, followed by Jack and Yori, with Akiko trailing a little behind. Besides a polite 'Good morning', Akiko had not said much.

'I think she's homesick,' Yori whispered to Jack, noticing him look back several times to check on her.

'You think so?' said Jack. He hadn't mentioned the previous night's quarrel to his friend, but maybe that explained why Akiko was being so distant with him.

Yori nodded and offered him a weary smile. 'I'm starting to appreciate how you must have felt, arriving in Japan. Everything is so different, so alien . . . the food, the beds, the people . . . it takes time to grow accustomed to it . . .' He gazed longingly at the rolling meadows with the mist beginning to lift from them.

'Do you want to go home too?' asked Jack, unable to keep the disappointment out of his voice.

'We haven't found your sister yet!' Yori replied heartily.

Jack noticed that his friend hadn't directly answered his question, and he thought this was telling in itself. Jack realized Yori *was* homesick, but doing his best to hide his true feelings from him.

'Besides,' Yori continued, putting on a smile, 'the real voyage of discovery consists not in seeking new lands but in seeing with new eyes. I think Akiko just needs to look at things in a different way.'

Sighing, Jack nodded his understanding. After the welcome they'd received, he couldn't blame his friends for wanting to return home. There were many times in Japan when, feeling homesick, *he*'d snapped at his friends and taken his frustration out on them. No wonder Akiko had been irritable with him; it was more surprising that it had taken so long for those feelings to surface. The fact that both his friends insisted on helping him search for his sister, rather than returning home to Japan, proved their loyalty to him. Their unwavering devotion made Jack feel simultaneously fortunate and guilty . . . yet hopeful too. With such friends at his side, he couldn't fail in his quest.

As the mist dispersed with the warmth of the coming day, they arrived at a wooded valley. Here the road split, one route going high, the other low.

'Harold said the low road is flooded,' reminded Akiko.

'Did he, now?' said Rose, tugging her reins to the left and heading along the low road.

'But –'

'How naive can you be, Akiko?' she remarked over her shoulder. 'Harold, or whatever his real name is, was most likely lying. He'll have set up an ambush with his friends on the high road.'

'Not everyone thinks like you!' said Akiko, bristling.

'Well, it's a good thing *I* do, then, otherwise you wouldn't even have got this far. I don't know what qualifies you to be a samurai, but it ain't common sense, that's for sure!' she said, laughing.

'We learn *bushido*!' snapped Akiko. 'The Way of the Warrior. Perhaps you'd benefit from learning its seven virtues – in particular, the virtue of respect.'

Rose brought her horse to a sharp halt and glared at Akiko. 'You don't know me, so you've no right to judge me!'

The two girls held each other's fierce stares. Yori's eyes grew wide with alarm at the escalating argument. Seeing Akiko's muscles tense like a cat primed to pounce, Jack quickly rode between the warring parties.

'We're on the same side!' he reminded them. 'I heard Harold's advice too, Akiko, but there's a chance Rose is right.' He tried to placate Akiko with a conciliatory smile. 'Let us do the opposite of what Harold said, just in case. If the road is flooded, we can always turn back.'

'Fine,' relented Akiko, giving him an inscrutable look, before spurring on her horse.

They rode on in silence, Akiko remaining aloof as they followed the course of the river. Jack realized he'd upset Akiko by defending Rose again, but there was little he could do about that now. It was better to be safe than sorry in this case.

Making their way beneath overhanging branches, and through muddy patches, they discovered some stretches so waterlogged that the road was almost marshland. And for a while it appeared that Akiko might be vindicated: the road had clearly been flooded at some point. With careful riding, however, the route eventually proved passable.

'See?' said Rose smugly as the road began to slope gently upwards, the ground drying out the higher they got. 'We can get thr–'

A woman's scream pierced the air, causing several birds to take flight from the tree canopy. They reined in their horses and glanced at each other in alarm.

'It came from the woods,' said Jack, his eyes scanning the treeline.

'It could be a trap,' Rose warned, as another scream rang out.

'Trap or not, someone needs our help,' said Akiko.

Jack was in two minds. He didn't want to delay their search for Jess. Then again, he couldn't ignore someone clearly in need. The code of *bushido* compelled him to help. There had been occasions during his escape through Japan when strangers had stepped up for him and saved his life, so it was only right that he did the same in return, especially in his own homeland.

'Akiko's right,' he said. 'It's our duty as samurai to help.'

With a flick of his reins, he rode for the woods. Yori and Akiko did the same.

'But I'm *not* samurai!' Rose called after them.

Leaving their horses tied to a tree, Jack and the others crept through the forest. As the sound of voices grew louder, they hunkered down behind a clump of ferns and peered into a small clearing. They saw a gang of a dozen or so ruffians. Some of them were binding an elderly man and a younger woman, dressed only in their undergarments, to the trunk of an oak tree, while others rifled through their saddlebags. Two manservants lay bleeding on the ground at their master's feet, having been badly beaten.

'Isn't that Lord and Lady Percival, the couple who were dining in the private booth last night?' asked Yori under his breath.

Jack nodded. A pair of robbers had stripped them of their finery and were now parading around in the clothes, pretending to be the lord and lady of the manor, much to the amusement of their fellow robbers. A tall, bearded man with a thick knotted staff stood at the centre of the clearing, presiding over the mayhem. He bore a long scar that curled from the corner of his right eye down to his jawline. Next to him stood a young woman with a tangle of hawthorn hair and a spray of girlish freckles that was at odds with the cruel sneer on her lips.

'That tall one, with the scar, he's what we call an upright-man,' whispered Rose. 'He's the leader of this gang. You don't want to mess with him, or his doxy.'

'What's a doxy?' asked Yori.

'His girlfriend, only a lot more vicious!'

'We might have to – mess with him, I mean,' Jack said, as he noticed the flintlock gun on the upright-man's hip.

Rose stared at Jack. 'This isn't our problem. Why get involved?'

'Because if *we* don't, no one else will.'

'But there must be ten or more of them!' protested Rose.

'We've battled worse odds,' said Akiko, nocking an arrow in preparation. 'You stay here if you're scared.'

Rose bristled. 'I *ain't* scared. Just realistic! I mean, why risk our lives for two nobles we don't even know?'

'Next to creating a life, the greatest thing a man or woman can do is save one,' explained Yori, his hands clutching the shaft of his *shakujō* so tightly that his knuckles were white.

In the clearing, the upright-man approached his bound victims. 'Today's your lucky day, sirrah.'

'*Lucky?*' growled Lord Percival, struggling against his bonds. 'How can you call this *lucky*?'

'Well, I ain't in a killing mood this morning,' the thief replied with a grunt of a laugh. 'However, Hazel 'ere does need some target practice with my pistol.' He drew the flintlock gun from his belt and handed the weapon to his doxy. Then he pulled an apple from his pocket, and took a large bite out of it before placing the fruit upon Lady Catherine's head.

'Don't move,' advised the upright-man. He strode over to where his doxy now waited a dozen metres from the tree. 'I'm sure you've heard the story of William Tell? Well, if Hazel manages to shoot the apple from your wife's head . . . I'll let her go free.'

'*Est-ce vrai?*' asked Lady Catherine, glancing in hope at her husband.

The gang leader nodded. 'Except Hazel ain't a very good shot.'

'No, I don't see so well, do I, Guy?' his doxy said. She adopted a wide-legged stance, raised the pistol, closed one eye and took an unsteady aim.

'No . . . no . . . wait!' begged Lord Percival, as his wife trembled so much that the apple threatened to tumble to the ground.

Hazel pulled the trigger. The flintlock ignited the powder and a loud *crack* rang out. Lady Catherine yelped as the bullet struck the tree, bark exploding in a shower of splinters just above the apple – and her head.

'Not bad,' encouraged Guy, grinning at his girl. 'Have another go.'

Hazel began the process of refilling the pistol barrel with powder and shot. Lady Catherine, her face pale as a lily, started sobbing, while her husband pleaded for her life.

'If we don't rescue them,' said Jack, 'that girl's going to blow that poor woman's head off sooner or later.'

'Rather her than one of us!' replied Rose. 'You're here to find your sister, not be a hero.'

An ominous click signalled that the gun was ready to fire.

'A little lower,' advised the upright-man, standing behind his doxy and adjusting her arm.

Hazel closed her eye and took aim for a second time. The gun went off, the bullet blasting another chunk out of the tree . . . and this time clipping Lady Catherine's ear. The woman screamed as blood splattered down her white smock.

'So, so close,' said the upright-man, relishing the look of horror and panic on Lord Percival's face. 'One last go, my sweet.'

Jack hurriedly whispered his plan to Akiko and Yori, then nodded a silent command, and they spread out round the clearing. While Hazel reloaded for a third and final shot, Guy delighted in further taunting his captives.

'Ear, ear! Cheer up!' he laughed. 'Hazel's definitely getting better. I reckon the next bullet will be *dead* on target –'

Jack stepped out into the clearing. The robbers all stopped their rifling of the saddlebags and turned to face the intruder. Lord and Lady Percival stared at him, their eyes pleading for rescue.

'You're surrounded!' Jack declared, with as much confidence and authority in his voice as he could muster. 'Put down your weapons and surrender.'

'And who might you be?' demanded the upright-man, unfazed.

'Jack Fletcher,' he replied, ensuring the gang leader could see the swords on his hip. 'Now do as I say and no one need get hurt.'

Guy stroked his beard and measured Jack up. Then his grey eyes scanned the forest. 'I admire your gall, young man. But I call your bluff. I don't believe there's anyone –'

An arrow whistled through the air and pierced the apple on the woman's head, pinning the fruit to the tree.

The robbers looked nervously around, suddenly fearful of the hidden enemy. A clump of bushes shook to their right giving the impression of several men approaching. Some of the gang immediately dropped their weapons, a couple even bolted for the woods. Jack tried to suppress a grin – their plan was working!

'Impressive bowman you have,' acknowledged the upright-man, still unperturbed. He took a step towards Jack.

'The next arrow will go through your eye, if you don't release the two captives,' warned Jack, his hand on his sword. 'Let's avoid any more bloodshed, shall we?'

Scowling, Guy turned to his doxy as if to issue the command, then he spun back and whipped the end of his staff up so fast that he caught Jack under the chin.

'The only blood that will be shed today is *yours!*' he spat.

Jack saw stars and reeled backwards. An arrow shot past in instant retaliation, flying straight for the robber's right eye. But, forewarned of the attack, he blocked it with his weapon, the arrow tip embedding itself deep into the wood. He then jabbed Jack in the gut.

Jack doubled over and crumpled to the ground. This *wasn't* part of the plan.

'I guess I *am* in a killing mood after all,' snarled Guy, raising his staff high over his head to crack Jack's skull like an egg.

Yori broke from his hiding place in the bushes and leapt to Jack's defence. As the staff came hurtling down, Yori deflected the lethal strike with his *shakujō* – then countered with a thrust of the bronze spear tip, the rings jangling as he hit the upright-man in the solar plexus. Winded, Guy staggered away – but he soon recovered and flew into a furious rage. A David-and-Goliath battle ensued as Yori fought the onslaught, matching the thief blow for blow. The young monk couldn't match his enemy for strength, though, and was soon forced into a retreat.

Jack, tasting blood from a split lip, struggled to his feet. He *had* to help Yori. However, a young robber with a cudgel had other plans for him. Jack ducked as the club almost took his head off. Another swipe nearly bust his nose. A third came down like a hammer . . .

Akiko appeared in the clearing, an arrow drawn on her

bow. She let it loose, the arrow flying so fast and true that it went straight through the young robber's raised arm and pinned him to a nearby tree trunk.

'Now don't run off!' said Jack with a grin, leaving the poor lad hanging by his skewered limb.

But Jack wasn't out of danger yet. The two robbers dressed as the lord and lady confronted him with rapiers. Mindful of their weapons' lethal reach, Jack unsheathed his *katana* and *wakizashi* and began to fend off their thrusts. While the robbers quickly proved to be no swordsmen, two against one meant Jack couldn't afford to drop his guard for a single moment. He deftly dodged one thrust, deflected another and blocked a third. Then he slashed right with his *katana* and left with his *wakizashi*, creating space between his two opponents. Moving into position, he baited them to lunge. One tried to run him through the chest, the other through the back, but Jack nimbly skipped aside and the two men impaled themselves instead.

'What happened to the plan?' Akiko cried, as she side-kicked one muscle-bound ruffian into a gorse bush and elbowed another in the face.

'We're on to Plan B,' replied Jack, clashing swords with a bare-chested brute of a man.

Akiko drew an arrow from her quiver. 'What's Plan B?'

'Fight for our lives!' said Jack, blocking a vicious slash to his head, then retaliating with an upward cut and scoring a line of blood across his attacker's chest.

Meanwhile, Yori had been backed up against a tree. The upright-man hammering him with blows of his staff, Yori darted from side to side, like a shrew evading the talons of a hawk, his small stature playing to his advantage as each attack struck the tree trunk instead. With each missed blow, the gang leader's fury and frustration grew, but so did Yori's exhaustion.

Jack and Akiko had seen his plight and were fighting their way across the clearing, desperate to help their friend.

Suddenly Yori dived between the robber's legs, catching him with the bronze tip of his *shakujō*. The gang leader let out a pained groan. Then, hooking his ankle with the end of the *shakujō*, Yori swept him off his feet. The upright-man landed in the earth with a heavy *whump*, his head hitting a protruding root, and he was knocked senseless.

'Not so upright now, are you?' panted the victorious Yori.

On seeing their leader bested, the remaining members of his gang fled the clearing.

'Good work, Yori!' said Jack, sheathing his swords.

Yori grinned. 'The bigger they are, the harder they fall!'

But the upright-man wasn't out for the count. He slowly began to rise.

Akiko drew her bow once more, pressing an arrow to the back of his head. 'Don't move!'

'That's good advice!' said a voice behind them, just before they heard the distinctive *click* of a flintlock pistol being primed.

21

THUNDERSTORM

Jack and the others turned round, to find Hazel pointing the barrel of the pistol at them. Jack cursed himself. They'd forgotten all about the upright-man's doxy in the mayhem of battle. Holding Jack and his friends at gunpoint, Hazel sneered, 'Now it's your turn to drop your weapons and surr–'

A bone-jarring *thunk* stopped her mid-sentence and she slumped to the ground, the pistol clattering from her hand.

'I reckon you did need my help after all!' said Rose, emerging from the bushes, casually tossing a rock in her hand.

'Nice shot!' said Jack. He examined the growing lump on the back of the unconscious girl's head. 'Where did you learn to throw like that?'

'At the May Day fair,' replied Rose. 'Always hit the skittles off.'

'Will someone please untie us?' requested the well-mannered voice of Lord Percival.

Jack turned to the nobleman and his wife, who were still bound to the oak tree. With one slash of his *katana*, he cut through the knot and the ropes fell away. Lord Percival rushed to tend to Lady Percival's ear, finding a handkerchief to stem the bleeding. Then, rather formally, he addressed his rescuers. 'My wife and I are deeply indebted to you,' he said, inclining his silver-haired head.

'*Oui, vraiment . . . merci beaucoup,*' said Lady Catherine in a tremulous voice, still pale and shaken from the attack. Then she added, in accented English, 'We are truly grateful that you didn't pass on by . . . I think most travellers would save their own skins first, rather than risk themselves for strangers.'

Akiko gave Rose a reproachful look but said nothing.

'A person has two hands,' Yori explained. 'One for helping himself, the other for helping others.'

'Wise words, young monk,' said Lord Percival, regarding Yori's saffron robes and *shakujō* with curiosity. 'I don't know where you're from, but I thank God that you came our way.'

'Well, I don't thank no one!' growled the upright-man, making a wild grab for Yori's legs.

Akiko pressed the arrow tip harder into the back of the man's skull. 'Stay where you are!' she warned.

Lord Percival peered down his arched nose at the gang leader lying in the dirt. 'I believe this fellow here is the notorious highwayman Guy Rakesby.'

'What do you want us to do with him, my lord?' asked Jack.

'If it was my decision, I'd hang him on the spot!' The nobleman glanced up, as if searching for a suitable branch. 'But we must respect the law of the land. So tie him up, along with his gang here. I'll have the local Justice of the Peace send a band of constables to arrest them. Then they can be tried in court.' He glared at Guy. 'And after what you did to my wife, I can assure you the punishment will *not* be lenient.'

Holding each other by the arm, Lord Percival led his wife away to reclaim their clothes. Jack bound Guy and his dazed doxy to the oak tree, while Akiko gathered her arrows, carefully prising out the one in the young robber's arm before tying him up with his fellow gang members. Meanwhile, Yori tended to the lord's manservants, reviving them with water and incense.

'Which way are you going?' asked Lord Percival, dressed once more in his plush red velvet robes. He took the reins and mounted his horse.

'Stratford-upon-Avon,' replied Jack as he helped Lady Catherine into her saddle. 'I'm hoping to find my sister there.'

Lord Percival raised an eyebrow. 'She's missing?'

Jack nodded and related their story: returning to England and discovering his home was now a plague house; their fortunate encounter with Rose and learning that his sister might still be alive; their visit to Bedlam and Mrs Winters' wild ramblings about red wolves; the silver locket that led them to Rowland Bodley and to their belief that they might find Jess in Stratford.

'That is all quite strange,' remarked Lord Percival.

'Are there such wolves in England?' queried Lady Catherine, with a nervous glance round the woods.

Lord Percival shook his head. 'Not red ones, that's for sure.' He turned to Jack. 'When I'm back in London, at the royal court, I'll ask about it for you. Perhaps someone will know what some of it means. In the meantime, would you do me the honour of accompanying us along the road, at least as far as our journeys coincide. Your presence would greatly reassure my wife.'

'Of course,' said Jack, realizing that travelling in such noble company would ease their passage through the towns on their way. Collecting their own horses, they left Guy and his gang of thieves bound and gagged in the clearing – Guy hurling muffled insults at them as they departed.

Resuming their journey on the main highway, Lord Percival asked Jack about his adventures in Japan, while Lady Catherine conversed with Akiko, fascinated by her stories of golden temples and samurai warriors. But as they travelled along the road, the sky darkened and ominous thunderclouds loomed on the horizon.

'This is where we must part,' said Lord Percival, coming to a halt at a crossroads. 'Stratford is north from here.' He looked up at the menacing sky. 'You'd best make haste to Banbury first, though. It's the nearest town to here, and you'll likely reach it before the heavens open.'

'Thank you,' said Jack, 'and safe travels to you.'

'And to you too, Jack. I wish you every luck in finding your sister. And if I can be of any service, don't hesitate to call upon me.'

Bidding them farewell, Lord and Lady Percival, and their two manservants, headed west in the direction of Oxford. Jack and his friends took the road north, riding into the gusting wind. The thunderclouds raced to meet them, bringing an iron sheet of heavy grey rain rolling across the landscape to consume every hill and field in its path. Despite galloping their horses flat out, they couldn't beat the advancing storm and soon found themselves in a torrential downpour. The rain was so heavy they could barely see their way ahead, the highway fast turning into a quagmire.

'Over there!' cried Jack, spying the dark silhouette of a barn through the maelstrom of mud and rain.

Soaking and shivering, they dismounted their horses and entered the timber-framed building. The barn was musty and full of hay, but its thatched roof afforded them shelter from the storm. After wringing out their clothes, the bedraggled group each plumped up a mound of hay for themselves and settled down for the night.

Yori was out almost as soon as his head hit the hay, but Jack lay there, listening to the rain drumming on the thatch. They were just one day's ride from Stratford – little more than twenty miles lay between him and his sister, if she was there. Despite his exhaustion, Jack could barely sleep for thinking about their reunion.

Just then, he heard a rustle in the hay and felt a body nestle up close to him. He thought it must be Akiko, but it was Rose's voice that whispered in his ear, 'I'm cold.'

Jack took off his coat and laid it over her. But she moved closer and put her arm round him. He pulled away. 'Rose, no . . .'

'Don't you remember our first kiss?' she murmured.

'Of course,' replied Jack, 'but my heart belongs to another now.'

Rose drew him to her. 'Can't I steal it back?'

Jack gently shook his head. 'Akiko and I are forever bound to one another.'

'You're so loyal, Jack,' replied Rose, her tone both approving and disappointed. 'Perhaps too loyal. Do you *really* think she'll stay in England, for you?' Rejected, Rose disentangled herself and turned her back to him, taking his coat with her.

Jack stared up blankly into the darkness, as unsettled by his emotions as by the storm. He was sorry he'd upset Rose, but added to that she had pricked the doubt that was clouding his heart from the moment they had stepped on to English shores. There was always the question of whether Akiko would stay or not, although he'd harboured the hope that she would. But now, after everything that had happened, he couldn't see why she would want to stay in this cold, brutal and unforgiving country.

Jack glanced over to where Akiko lay. She wasn't there, and he saw her crouching by the barn door, peering into the rain-soaked night. He rose quietly and joined her. She didn't acknowledge him, just kept her gaze on the lightning in the distant clouds.

'I'm sorry about last night . . .' he began.

'And tonight?' she asked pointedly.

Jack let out a regretful sigh. She'd seen him and Rose together. 'It's not what you think. Rose was cold, so I gave her my coat.'

'Oh? She looked warm enough to me,' replied Akiko, her eyes glistening with tears.

Jack took Akiko's hand, her soft skin cold to the touch. 'I told her that you and I are forever bound to one another, that my heart belongs to you.'

Akiko turned to him, a hesitant smile upon her lips. He gently wiped away her tears.

'I realize England is not what you hoped for . . . or I hoped for . . . or even promised,' Jack went on. 'I know you're homesick. Once we find Jess, I can arrange passage on a ship back to Japan for you . . . if that's what you want.'

'And what will you do?' asked Akiko.

Jack thought for a moment. 'I honestly don't know. I've been so focused on being reunited with my sister that I haven't planned what would come afterwards. I believed that once I got home, things would just fall into place. But I'm not sure where I belong now. Perhaps I'm destined to be a pilot like my father.'

'Always travelling, then,' said Akiko with a resigned look.

'Well, that depends upon where you are,' replied Jack, gazing deep into her eyes.

Akiko tenderly placed a hand on his heart. 'I am here, always and forever.'

22

THE BAILIFF

Jack was woken by the stirring of the horses. He sat up, shaking the straw from his hair, and rubbed sleep from his eyes. A faint dawn light seeped through the slats in the barn walls, catching dust motes in the air. The storm had blown itself out during the night, leaving behind only the soft drip of rainwater trickling from the thatched roof. Akiko lay asleep next to him, her face serene; Yori was curled up almost in a ball on his pile of hay; and Rose – was nowhere to be seen.

He looked around for her and found his coat discarded in the hay. A flicker of sunlight alerted Jack to movement outside the barn.

'*Rose?*' he whispered, pushing his arms through the sleeves of his coat. There was a low murmur of voices and the soft squelch of feet in mud. He tensed, straining to listen. Suddenly the barn doors were flung open and a band of constables charged in. Before Jack could react – or Akiko and Yori even open their eyes – they were seized by rough hands and dragged to their feet.

'Strip them of their weapons and belongings,' ordered the

chief constable, his double chin stubbled like a fallow field, his hangdog eyes mean and wary.

'Wait! What's the meaning of this?' Jack protested, as his swords were taken and his hands bound. 'We haven't done anything wrong –'

'Shut up!' snarled the chief constable. 'You're under arrest.'

Jack stared at the man in disbelief. Yori, bowing his head low in humble respect, said, 'I believe you may be making a mistake, constable. We're not the ones you should be arresting!'

'*Really?*' questioned the chief constable. He made a show of looking round the barn. 'Then who *should* we be arresting? The field mice? I suppose, you're small enough to be one!'

The other constables laughed heartily as they secured Yori and Akiko, confiscating his *shakujō* along with her bow and quiver, and their packs.

'Lord Robert Percival sent for constables to arrest the highwayman Guy Rakesby and his gang ... not us,' explained Yori timidly.

'Guy Rakesby, you say?' The chief constable raised a bushy eyebrow and snorted. 'Well, good luck to those constables! Rather them than us, eh, boys? We're here to apprehend vagrants and horse thieves.'

'*Horse thieves?*' gasped Akiko as the constables unhooked the reins and led their mounts out of the barn. 'I can assure you, sir, we didn't steal these horses.'

'That's not what the owner says.' The constable gave her a disparaging look up and down. 'Besides, you're clearly vagrants and therefore not welcome in Banbury.'

Jack opened his mouth to object, then caught sight of

Akiko and Yori. Their fine clothing was caked in mud from riding through the previous night's storm and the dirt had fused with clumps of hay to make them look like dishevelled scarecrows. He looked down at his own clothes too, and saw how dirty they were. It's no wonder the constable mistook them all for vagrants. 'We only stayed here to take shelter from the storm,' said Jack. 'I can promise you –'

'Shut your trap!' snarled the chief constable, backhanding Jack across the jaw and making stars burst before his eyes. 'I've heard all the excuses in my time, so don't try my patience. There's a perfectly good inn just down the road for proper folk. It's obvious you ain't got the money for that – and that makes you vagrants in my book.'

'I have money,' Jack assured him, reaching for his purse . . . only to discover it missing. He looked desperately around at the barn floor and hay bales but couldn't spot any leather pouch. 'At least I did have . . .'

'Enough stalling!' barked the chief constable. With a jerk of his head he ordered his constables to lead them out on to the road. There, they were secured by a long rope to Jack's horse, the chief constable now sitting smugly astride it on his ample behind. 'Let's see what the bailiff makes of you three,' he said, urging his mount on and pulling the rope taut.

As they were frogmarched along the muddy highway, Yori whispered to Jack in Japanese, *'Where's Rose?'*

'I don't know,' Jack replied. He too spoke in Japanese so their captors wouldn't understand. *'Perhaps she saw the constables and ran.'*

'Or else she turned us in!' said Akiko under her breath.

Jack shook his head. *'Rose is a friend. She wouldn't do that.'*

'*Then where's your purse?*' asked Akiko.

'*It must have come loose while I was asleep . . .*'

Akiko gave him a look. '*Once a thief, always a thief!*'

'*Rose* wouldn't *steal my purse*,' insisted Jack. But doubt was creeping in again. Had Rose been so hurt by his rejection that she'd decided to cut loose, with his money? He remembered her wrapping her arm round his waist. Had that all been a ploy to take his purse? When they'd met her in the Bunch of Grapes Inn back in Limehouse, she'd flirted with him simply in order to pick his pocket. Jack didn't want to believe it, but it seemed possible that Rose *had* betrayed him.

'*I assume the rose did have her thorns*,' said Yori sadly.

'*I'm sorry, Jack*,' said Akiko, '*but I did try to warn –*'

'Quiet back there! Save your babbling for the bailiff!' growled the chief constable, tugging hard on the rope and making the three of them stumble in the mud.

The bailiff was a mournful-looking man with heavy jowls, bulging eyes, and a pouting lower lip that pushed through his beard like a slimy pale slug. His dress sense was equally sombre. He wore a brown fur-trimmed robe, a padded woollen doublet and a black velvet cap, his gold chain of office being his only concession to adornment. Seated behind a heavy oak table in the town's draughty market hall, the bailiff regarded the three vagrants before him with glassy disdain.

Jack returned his cold gaze with as much dignity as he could muster. Unfortunately, the forced march into Banbury had left him and his friends looking even worse for wear. Their hair was tangled and knotted with dirt and straw, their already dirty boots were plastered afresh with mud, and their garments were stained and ripped from the countless times they'd fallen along the way. Hungry for want of breakfast, bone-tired from dragging their feet through the muck, they appeared little more than homeless beggars.

A hostile muttering hemmed them in on all sides. Their sorry procession through Banbury's streets had drawn a crowd, curious to see the two foreigners in their midst, and now half the townsfolk seemed to be crammed into the market hall to get a better look.

'I hereby open this session of the Hundred Court,' declared the bailiff, his voice flat and monotonous. 'The accused stand charged with vagrancy and horse thievery.' He eyed Jack and his two companions. 'How do you plead?'

'Not guilty,' replied Jack firmly. 'There's clearly been a misunderstanding, sir. You see, we're –'

'Were you or were you not found in possession of Sir Henry Wilkes' horses?' cut in the bailiff.

'Yes,' said Jack. 'But –'

'Then you are horse thieves.'

Jack stared, open-mouthed, at the bailiff. 'I don't understand . . . Sir Henry gave us permission to use his horses.'

'Not according to this arrest warrant,' stated the bailiff, studying a piece of parchment lying upon the table. 'Four of his finest horses were taken yesterday. And his stable boy is dead.'

'*Dead?*' gasped Jack, recalling the young, tawny-haired lad who'd kindly packed their saddlebags with provisions. He exchanged a stunned look with Akiko and Yori.

'Are you able to shed some light on the matter?' enquired the bailiff.

Jack blinked in shock. 'What? You don't think we had anything to do with it, do you?'

The bailiff's dour expression hardened. 'According to this warrant, every finger of the boy's hands had been broken. He was tortured before he was killed.'

A cry of outrage erupted in the crowd and Jack felt a sickening twist in the pit of his stomach.

'That's awful! But we couldn't have done it,' he protested. 'We were on the road yesterday,' he added, having to raise his voice over the hisses and jeers. 'In fact, we stayed in the Fox and Pheasant Inn the previous night.'

The bailiff leant across the table and, like a poisonous toad, fixed Jack with his bulbous eyes. 'Yet you slept in a barn *last* night. Why should I believe that penniless vagrants like you had the means to stay at an inn the night before?'

'Ask the landlord,' said Akiko, stepping forward. 'He's sure to remember us.'

The bailiff glowered, as if the audacity of a woman to speak out of turn was a sin. 'The landlord's not here to ask,' he said sharply, spittle spraying out of his mouth. 'And I'm not minded to waste my time or his for foreigners and thieves.' He waved to the chief constable. 'Lock them up, constable, and send word to the Justice of the Peace that we have apprehended the horse thieves. He will arrange to have them transported back to London for trial.'

'NO!' cried Jack. He struggled in the chief constable's grip and was rewarded with a heavy blow of a cosh to his kidneys. He dropped to his knees, winded and bruised. As they were dragged away, Jack began to despair. They *couldn't* be sent back to London. He *had* to find his sister. If they went back to the capital, he and his friends would hang for their earlier false convictions. Oh, how Sir Toby would be delighted to see him swing from the gallows again!

Then Jack spotted a familiar face in the crowd: Harold Westcott.

'Harold!' he shouted, but the charming gentleman from the Fox and Pheasant didn't appear to hear him.

'HAROLD!' he shouted again, then pointing his bound hands in Harold's direction, Jack appealed to the bailiff. 'Please, sir – that man can vouch for us.'

All eyes turned to the young man in the plush velvet jerkin adorned with silver buttons and shoulder wings. Harold was pushed forward by the crowd and made to stand before the bailiff.

'Is this true?' demanded the bailiff. 'Do you know these people?'

Jack looked imploringly at Harold, willing him to confirm their story. But it appeared their friendly traveller was reluctant to get involved. 'Harold,' Jack pleaded, 'tell the bailiff we were with you the other night at the inn. You owe us this favour, remember?'

After what seemed like an age, Harold looked at Jack, smiled and nodded. 'Yes,' he announced, 'I know them.'

Jack felt a wave of relief. They had their alibi confirmed.

Then Harold's smile turned sour and he added, 'They're thieves, all right. They stole my purse *and* my precious locket.'

'*What?*' cried Jack in horror. Akiko and Yori stared in equal disbelief.

Harold, theatrical tears now in his eyes, pointed an accusing finger at Jack. 'He took it. He took my silver locket!'

The chief constable pulled Jack's shirt aside and ripped the locket from his neck.

'That's mine!' shouted Jack, reaching desperately for the only link he had to Jess. 'Harold's lying. *He's* the thief! He –'

Jack was cut short by a jarring punch to his jaw and knocked to the ground. As he lay on the packed earthen floor of the market hall, his head ringing, the bailiff questioned Harold. 'This is a fine piece, sir,' he began. 'Can you prove your ownership of it?'

'Yes,' Harold replied confidently. 'If you care to look inside, the locket has a portrait of my sweetheart inside. She has hair like golden wheat and eyes as blue as the midsummer sky.'

The bailiff inspected the miniature painting inside. 'I have no reason not to believe you,' he declared, handing Harold the locket. 'Here, keep her safe from now on.'

'Why, thank you,' said Harold, inclining his head respectfully and pocketing the locket. 'And what about my purse?'

The chief constable regretfully shook his head. 'No purse was found on him, I'm afraid, sir.'

Harold sighed heavily, as if the troubles of the world were upon his shoulders. 'That's a great shame. But at least I have my precious Judy back next to my heart.'

'*Judy!*' exclaimed Jack, incredulous at Harold's barefaced lies. 'Her name's Jess and she's my sister!'

As Harold walked away, swallowed up by the crowd, Jack fumed. Rose had been right: Harold was a courtesy-man – a con artist, a thief – just like Rose.

The bailiff returned his attention to Jack, sprawled in the middle of the hall. 'As much as it galls me to say so, it appears you have an alibi for yesterday. Which means you can't be held accountable for taking the horses or murdering the boy . . .'

Despite his fury, Jack felt a spark of hope. They would be freed! Then he would chase down that swindler Harold Westcott and get back his locket, if it was the last thing he did.

'However,' continued the bailiff, 'we've now learnt, from what that gentleman said, that you're a petty thief. Therefore, within my powers as bailiff for this town, I confiscate your belongings, and furthermore sentence you to be put in the pillory a day and a night before being whipped out of town.'

His fishy eyes then settled on Yori. 'Since you're a man of the cloth, I'll show leniency in your case. You shall not be whipped and only put in the stocks.'

His cold gaze fell last upon Akiko, who whispered under her breath to Jack. '*Kore de jūbundesu! Watashitachi wa koko kara denakereba narimasen, Jakku.*'

Jack understood. *Enough of this! We need to fight our way out of here, Jack.* But to the townsfolk in the crowd, Akiko's words had sounded strange and disturbing.

'She's speaking in tongues!' cried a dough-faced woman.

'She's trying to curse us,' screeched another, pointing a fat finger at Akiko. 'She's a WITCH!'

All of a sudden, the crowd's mood grew fearful and dangerous. A chant of '*Witch! Witch! Witch!*' went up. Akiko looked around in horror at the baying mob, their cries and catcalls vicious in their intensity.

'ORDER!' bellowed the bailiff, as the constables tried to hold back the mob intent on attacking the sorceress in their midst.

The townsfolk fell silent.

The bailiff stood, glared at Akiko, and pronounced, 'The devil woman shall face trial by water!'

23

DUCKING STOOL

Jack watched helplessly, his head and hands imprisoned in the pillory, as Akiko was tied to a wooden chair. His frustration was only matched by his fury at the small-minded and cruel townsfolk, who set about their punishment of Akiko with religious fervour.

Yori, his legs pinned by the stocks, was equally powerless to stop what was happening. Akiko did her best to resist her captors, but many hands made light work of strapping her to the ducking stool. Once her limbs were bound, the chair was fixed to a long oak beam set on a fulcrum post and lifted high into the air.

A great cry of 'Witch!' went up. The townsfolk, eager to witness Akiko's trial by water, crowded round the reed-fronded pond at the edge of the marketplace. They continued to hurl abuse as her chair was swung over the frigid and stagnant water.

'She's *NOT* a witch!' Jack shouted. 'She was only speaking Japanese!'

An old woman nearby rounded on him. 'Sounded like a witch's curse to me,' she snarled, then lobbed a rotten apple at

Jack. She was an infuriatingly good shot, and the apple hit him square on the forehead, the fruit exploding in his face, smothering him in its sticky sour mush.

Prior to Akiko's trial by water, the mob had slaked their thirst for violent punishment by pelting Jack and Yori with rotten fruit, mud and horse muck. The two friends had suffered several hours of humiliation, abuse and torture at the hands of the citizens, while the ducking stool was constructed beside the pond's edge. By the end of the day they were filthy, stinking and bruised. But their experience had been nothing compared to what awaited Akiko.

'Leave her alone!' Jack begged, blinking away the slimy remains of the apple. 'I tell you, she's not a witch!'

'That's for *me* to decide,' said the bailiff, marching self-importantly across the marketplace, his gaoler's keys jangling on his hip. The crowd parted to let him through to the pond, where two burly men still held Akiko aloft. The bailiff gazed up at his prisoner, his thumbs tucked firmly into the belt that secured his ample belly.

'You have been accused of witchcraft,' he pronounced. 'Do you confess to being a witch?'

'No, of course not!' Akiko replied defiantly. 'That wou–'

At the nod of the bailiff's head, the ducking stool was tipped into the pond. Akiko plunged beneath the surface, her words lost in a bubbling slosh of foul water. The crowd let out a jubilant roar. Jack and Yori watched horrified, as their friend disappeared entirely, only a swirl of froth marking her entry into the water. After several excruciatingly long seconds, the bailiff waved for the ducking stool to be raised.

Akiko emerged, gasping and spluttering, covered head to foot in pondweed, sludge and reeds.

The bailiff repeated his question. 'Do you confess to being a witch?'

'N-n-no,' Akiko spluttered, spitting out a clump of waterweed. 'Why would I con–'

The bailiff signalled the two men again, and Akiko was once more dunked into the pond. The townsfolk all leaned in, trying to make out Akiko's flailing figure under the murky waters.

'What's the point of this trial?' demanded Yori, his voice trembling.

The bailiff turned towards him, a sneer on his slimy lips. 'To prove whether she's a witch or not.'

Yori frowned in bewilderment. 'But *how*? You're simply torturing her.'

'If she doesn't drown, then we know she's a witch,' replied the bailiff as if Yori was stupid. 'Of course, she could simply confess and avoid all this needless suffering.'

Yori stared at the rippling surface of the pond in mounting distress. 'But what if she *does* drown?'

'Then at least we know she isn't a witch.'

'But then it's too late!' cried Yori.

The bailiff shrugged indifferently. 'Better to be safe than sorry, I say.'

After a couple of minutes, he waved to the men to raise the ducking stool. Akiko came up, bedraggled and shivering. She was evidently weaker this time. Gagging, she spewed up the revolting pond water into her lap.

'Do you confess now?' asked the bailiff.

Akiko shook her head, her long hair hanging in dark wet tendrils across her pale face. Once again, the ducking stool plunged into the pond. Once again, the crowd cheered.

Jack raged and kicked against the pillory, trying to loosen the wooden post that held him fast. But the frame was solid and its foundation too deep. He could only watch in terror as the water in the pond settled and the bubbles gradually fizzled out.

'She's drowning!' he yelled in desperation. 'Let her up! I beg you, let her up!'

The bailiff, however, ignored his pleas. The crowd grew anxiously quiet as the seconds passed, then minutes. No movement could be discerned in the pond's depths. Finally the bailiff gave the command to raise the stool. A limp and lifeless form came up. Weeds clung to Akiko's hair like green braids. Sludge spattered her gown in sorry streaks. And white reeds garlanded her head, as if she already lay in her grave.

'NO!' screamed Jack in agony. 'NO!'

Yori mournfully bowed his head, screwed his eyes tight shut and sobbed out a prayer for Akiko.

With solemn slowness, they pivoted the chair back over dry land and deposited Akiko's body on the bank. Her bindings still held her upright, but her head lolled unnaturally to one side. Her skin had a bluish tinge and there were no signs of her breathing. The bailiff briefly inspected her, then declared, 'The girl is no witch.'

'Of course she isn't!' cried Jack, tears streaming down his cheeks. 'She was my friend! My dearest friend!'

Thunder rolled in the distance and dark clouds smothered

the setting sun. As heavy drops of rain began to fall from the darkening sky, the crowd silently dispersed.

The bailiff walked over and rested his hand on Jack's shoulder, for a moment appearing to console him. Then he said, 'Tomorrow you shall be whipped.'

As the jangle of the bailiff's keys faded up the street, Jack wept. His tears mixed with the rain until his whole world seemed to swim in despair. Akiko's silhouetted form was slumped in the ducking stool, her body abandoned by the townsfolk, who were more eager to take shelter from the storm than to lay her to rest.

Yori was curled up in an awkward ball, his feet still pinned by the stocks. His chest rose and fell with soft sobs of sorrow. 'Akiko is . . . *dead*,' he moaned. 'How can a light so bright . . . ever be put out?'

Jack, too grief-stricken to reply, clenched his fists and trembled with fury. His one true love had been drowned by the ignorance and unfounded fear of his fellow countrymen. What a fool he had been to invite Akiko and Yori to England! What reception had he imagined they would receive? As a stranger in Japan, he himself had been the subject of discrimination, ridicule, torture – even threats of burning and beheading. Why on earth had he imagined it would be any different for Akiko and Yori in England? While it had been the bailiff who'd sentenced Akiko to trial by water, ultimately *he* was to blame for her death: he had brought her here, he had put her in danger.

Jack let out an anguished cry; the pain of the pillory was nothing compared to the pain in his heart.

But no one heard him above the downpour – not even the gatekeeper, huddled in his hut beside the town gate, a little down the road from the marketplace.

The marketplace grew darker still as the storm took hold. Sheet lightning and the cannonball rumble of thunder warred angrily in the clouds overhead. Rain drummed on the roofs of houses and pummelled the earth-packed streets, until puddles turned to streams that grew into torrents. The deluge became so great that it was as if the heavens themselves wept for Akiko's loss.

Jack hung his head, the pillory holding his body at an unnatural and excruciating angle. When, after a time, his neck had become stiff and sore, he forced himself to look up and stretch out his aching back. The rain having eased slightly, he spied through the evening gloom four figures riding up the road towards the town gate. Their pace was slow yet measured, like a funeral procession, their bearing sinister and menacing, a clear warning to anyone to keep out of their way.

Nevertheless, the gatekeeper emerged from his shelter to challenge the late-night visitors. Jack watched as he held aloft a fiery torch and, in the glow of its guttering flame, rivulets of rain gleamed on the riders' waxed black cloaks, and – briefly – a ghostly vision of four white, beaked masks appeared. The gatekeeper stood stock-still, apparently frozen with fear. Then he dropped the torch and turned to run, but, following a flash of steel, he slumped face-first in the mud, beside the torch's dying flame.

Jack blinked away the rain in his eyes, uncertain of what he'd just seen. The movement had been almost too fast to catch in the darkness.

'Did you see that?' he whispered to Yori.

'What?' said Yori, uncurling himself and peering into the gloom.

'I thought I caught a glimpse of a sword,' Jack explained breathlessly. 'A *samurai* sword.'

Yori stared into the rain, trying to make out the four horsemen riding up the street towards them. 'I don't see any samurai sword,' he replied timorously, 'but I *do* see four plague doctors!'

A sudden flash of lightning scorched the sky, revealing in all their morbid horror the riders' birdlike masks and black hats and cloaks. Jack recalled the courtesy-man's warning of plague doctors terrorizing London and felt again the paralysing fear from his childhood. Harold had been right to describe them as the horsemen of the Apocalypse: their unearthly appearance struck terror into his heart.

The four figures pulled their horses up at the edge of the marketplace. They looked cautiously around until their cold, dead gaze fell upon Jack and Yori imprisoned in the pillory and stocks. Dismounting, they began to approach.

That was when Jack's survival instinct overcame his crippling grief. He started pulling on his arms and straining with all his might against the pillory. 'We've got to get out of here, Yori . . . *now*!' he hissed.

Yori, for his part, had begun tugging at his ankles, in vain. 'But how?'

'Use *kiai-jutsu* on the lock!' cried Jack. 'Like you did in prison.'

'But those chains were rusted!' Yori exclaimed in panic.

Seeing their prey pinned and powerless, the four figures

took their time crossing the marketplace, one in front, the other three behind. Their long cloaks hid their feet so that they appeared to glide across the puddle-strewn square like wraiths.

Jack struggled more and more wildly, desperation threatening to overwhelm his reason. Then he stopped dead and a chill ran through his bones. The leader was drawing a long, curved blade, the *hamon* along its steel glinting like the lightning in the storm.

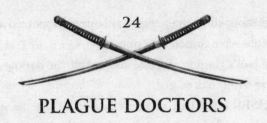

24

PLAGUE DOCTORS

Immobilized by the pillory, Jack was helpless. In one easy swipe of the sword, the plague doctor could sever his head from his torso, along with both his hands for good measure. Jack had no idea who was behind the white-beaked, glass-eyed mask – and had no desire at this perilous point to find out. But the presence of a second *katana* in England both puzzled and disturbed him. *How have these plague doctors acquired a samurai sword?*

As the four ominous figures drew nearer, Jack noticed Yori gulping in several deep breaths, preparing to repel them with his *kiai-jutsu*. Jack knew, however, that each and every *kiai* strike took a great deal of effort to generate, and Yori would not have enough energy to deal with all four attackers. Jack, meanwhile, had nothing but his legs to defend himself with, and his movements were severely restricted. All he could do was clumsily shovel a mound of mud at his feet in readiness.

Then a loud clanging broke through the monotonous *thrum* of rain. The town bell was ringing frantically, sounding an alarm that would wake even the dead. The four plague doctors stopped in their tracks as lanterns appeared and the townsfolk were roused to action.

The bell's ringing stopped and out of the darkness ran a familiar flame-haired girl.

'ROSE!' cried Jack in shock and relief. As she sprinted across the marketplace, Jack heard a jangle of keys. Spotting the would-be rescuer, the plague doctors advanced on Jack and Yori once more. But Rose reached them first.

'Sorry,' she panted. 'Had to wait for the bailiff to fall asleep 'fore I could steal 'em!'

Her hands shook as she tried a key in the pillory's padlock.

'Where did you go? Are you all right?' asked Jack, overjoyed to discover his childhood friend hadn't betrayed him after all.

'Save the questions for later!' Rose replied as the first key failed and she tried a second – but that one wouldn't fit either.

The plague doctors' leader bore down on them, sword raised high above his masked head. Both Jack and Rose were directly in line of the blade's lethal path. Jack kicked out with his boot, flicking a clump of mud into the plague doctor's face. It splattered across his glass eyes, blinding him and halting his attack.

As the plague doctor furiously wiped away the muck, Rose tried the fifth and final key. The padlock clicked open at last and Rose flung back the top bar that imprisoned Jack.

'Free Yori!' ordered Jack, as he let loose a side kick that sent the sword-wielding plague doctor tumbling backwards into the mud.

Rose rushed over to Yori. But one of the other plague doctors had drawn a knife from the folds of his cloak and was intent on slitting Yori's throat. Unable to run or evade the slash of the blade, Yori roared, '*KIAI!*'

The force of the shout stunned the plague doctor. The knife fell from his grasp and he dropped to his knees in a puddle, clasping his chest in pain.

Hurriedly, Rose inserted a key into the stocks' padlock and got lucky first time. Yori shook the blood back into his little legs and leapt to his feet.

Jack ran over to his friends just as the two remaining plague doctors began closing in on them. One wielded a chain with pointed weights at each end; the other brandished a straight-edged sword with a distinctive square handguard. They were quickly joined by the other two, both now recovered but more wary of their foe.

Jack raised his fists in defence.

'We don't stand a chance!' hissed Rose, glancing nervously from Jack's bare hands to the array of deadly weapons confronting them. 'We're outnumbered – and out-weaponed!'

Yori started hyperventilating, in panic and in preparation for another *kiai* strike.

'The bailiff has our weapons,' Jack growled, as the plague doctors slowly began to encircle them.

'Then follow me!' said Rose, backing away. 'I know where he lives.'

'We can't leave Akiko,' insisted Jack, holding his ground. He felt an insistent tug on his arm.

'What cannot be saved can be remembered,' Yori said solemnly, retreating with Rose.

Jack shot one last longing look in Akiko's direction – her slumped body a shadow in the rain – then took off after Yori and Rose, barely a second before the lead plague doctor lunged with his sword.

As the three of them fled the market square, their attackers gave chase. By now, the town was on full alert: the chief constable was barking orders and rallying his men, people were spilling on to the streets, alarmed by all the commotion. When they saw Jack, Yori and Rose sprinting across the square, their immediate thought was that they were escaped prisoners. Then the four plague doctors materialized out of the darkness and pandemonium broke out.

'PLAGUE!' yelled a man in horror.

Several people screamed and mothers gathered up their children and bundled them back inside, bolting their doors behind them. Townsfolk ran in all directions, desperate to avoid contact with anyone else. The chief constable tried to maintain order, but he was fighting a losing battle.

Chaos reigned – to Jack and his friends' advantage. Losing themselves in the melee, they shook off the plague doctors, slipped past the constables and disappeared down a side street. Rose led them to a large brick house overlooking the Cherwell river.

With no time to waste, Jack hammered on the heavy oak door, yelling, 'Open up!'

No one answered. Jack threw his shoulder against the door; the frame split and the door swung open. Inside in the hallway, they found the bailiff packing a trunk, evidently in a hurry to leave. When he saw Jack and Yori, his goldfish eyes almost bulged out of their sockets.

'*You!*' he cried, pointing an accusing fat finger at Yori.

'You and your devil witch brought the plague upon us!' And he cursed them bitterly.

'We did no such thing,' said Yori fiercely, in a rare show of temper. 'You *killed* Akiko!'

The bailiff snorted. 'Good riddance, I say, to that plague-infested –'

'Give us back our weapons, you slimy toad,' Jack demanded.

The bailiff puffed out his barrel chest. 'No one speaks to me that way! I'm the bailiff of this town. You will –'

He suddenly clasped his fleshy throat and began to spit up blood. Through his fingers Jack glimpsed the gleam of a silver metal star. Jack spun round to see the black waxed cloak of a plague doctor filling the doorway. Before they became the next victim of a *shuriken*, Jack shoved his friends into the nearest room and slammed the door shut behind them.

'We need to find our weapons,' he said, as Yori and Rose helped him drag a heavy wooden bench across the doorway. They scoured the front room for their belongings, then dashed through another door into the dining chamber, but their frantic search turned up nothing. Behind them they heard the splintering of wood and the scrape of furniture as the plague doctor barged his way into the front room. Cutting through the kitchen, they crossed into the parlour, then took a servant's passageway leading to a wood-panelled music room. There they found a lute and a harpsichord – but no swords, no bow, not even Yori's *shakujō*.

'We'll have to try upstairs,' said Jack, hearing the clatter of pans as the plague doctor entered the kitchen.

They raced back into the main hallway, where the bailiff now lay dead, his blood oozing across the floorboards. Then, just as they were mounting the staircase, Yori caught sight of Jack's *katana* on a desk in the front study. Jumping over the bailiff's body, Jack made a dash for his sword . . . but was too late.

The plague doctor had doubled back and was now blocking their way.

25

KANZASHI

As Jack, Yori and Rose stood motionless in the hallway, the plague doctor gave a shrill birdlike whistle, then drew a gleaming straight-edged sword from the sheath on his back. Up close, Jack recognized the weapon for what it was – a razor-sharp *ninjatō*.

'Who are you?' Jack demanded. 'What do you want with us?'

But the bird-masked plague doctor gave no reply. His very silence was more unnerving than the blade he wielded.

Jack glanced past his assailant. His *katana* was so tantalizingly close, if only he could get past his attacker . . . But, no, there was little room for manoeuvre or mistake in the hallway, just enough space to swing a sword, so that any false move would result in Jack being run through or having his head cleaved clean from his shoulders.

'Why doesn't he attack?' whispered Yori, sheltering behind Jack.

'Perhaps he's waiting for the others?' said Rose.

Jack spoke again. This time in Japanese. *'Anatahadare?'*

This seemed to get a reaction. But not the one Jack hoped

for. The plague doctor suddenly raised the *ninjatō* to strike. Having nowhere to hide and nothing to defend himself with, Jack prepared to dodge the sword – then realized that, if he moved, Yori would be directly in its path. There was no way on earth Jack could sacrifice his friend like that. As the *ninjatō* sliced down, Jack caught the glint of a gold candlestick stuffed into the trunk the bailiff had been packing. Snatching it up, he tried to deflect the blade . . .

At the very last second, the plague doctor let out a sudden gasp of pain. His whole body went rigid; he dropped the *ninjatō* and toppled face first to the floorboards. Jack stared in stunned bewilderment. Protruding from his back – exactly in the paralysing *ryumon ki* point – was a golden hairpin, its end shaped in a *sakura* flower.

Jack had never thought he'd see that *kanzashi* ever again. Or the person it belonged to. But, like an angel sent from the heavens, Akiko stepped out of the darkness and into the light.

'Akiko!' cried Yori, his eyes widening into full moons. 'You're *alive*!'

'Not for much longer if we don't get out of here,' she replied, smiling at Jack's dumbfounded expression.

'B-but I saw you drown –' began Jack, his heart almost exploding with joy as he rushed over and hugged her.

'You did,' Akiko replied, returning his embrace, then pulling away. 'But there is no time to explain now. The other plague doctors heard that whistle too and are right behind me!'

Recovering their weapons – Yori finding his *shakujō* propped against the wall and Akiko her *yumi* and *ya* next to a bookcase – along with their packs, they dashed out into the rain-drenched street. A line of flaming torches marked where the constables stood at the top of the road, a wary distance from the three remaining plague doctors. In their black waxed garb, the plague doctors fanned menacingly out and slowly advanced towards Jack and the others.

'So, do we stand and fight?' Akiko asked, nocking an arrow on to her bow.

Jack clasped the hilt of his *katana*, deliberating whether to draw it or not. 'If we defeat the doctors, we still have the constables to deal with. This could turn into a bloodbath.'

Yori swallowed nervously and held out his *shakujō* like a talisman against the three approaching wraiths. 'He who fights and runs away may turn and fight another day.' He glanced up at Jack. 'That's what Sensei Yamada would say anyway.'

'Well, I don't have a weapon,' said Rose matter-of-factly, 'and I ain't that keen on catching the plague either. So I agree with Yori – let's scarper!'

Turning on their heels, Jack and his friends fled down the street towards the river. The plague doctors swooped after them, moving swiftly over the mud and puddles that pockmarked the road. The constables followed cautiously, a good twenty paces behind.

Before they saw the river, they heard it, a great roaring torrent fed by the storm. Debris, branches and even thick logs were borne upon its wild white waters. As Jack and his friends drew closer, an arched wooden footbridge materialized out of the gloom. Putting on a spurt of speed,

Yori and Akiko reached it first. But Rose, crying out, stumbled along the way and Jack had to catch her. Taking her hand, he helped her onwards, but she still struggled to run.

'What's the matter?' he asked, noticing her face was screwed up in pain.

'My leg!' she cried, wincing.

Jack looked down and saw a *shuriken* embedded in the back of her calf. He quickly prised it free, blood blossoming on her smock. With Rose's arm over Jack's shoulder, they hobbled on – the plague doctors rapidly gaining on them. Jack stopped at the bridge where Akiko and Yori waited anxiously.

'You go on with Rose,' he urged his friends. 'I'll hold them back.'

'You can't do it alone!' said Akiko, as Yori handed Rose his staff as a crutch and took Jack's pack.

'No time to argue,' Jack insisted above the roar of the river. 'Just *GO!*'

As his friends disappeared across the bridge, Jack unsheathed his *katana* and turned to face the advancing plague doctors. They halted several paces from him and drew their weapons too.

'Come on, then,' Jack baited, his *katana* at the ready. 'Let's see whether you really know how to use that sword!'

The plague doctor with the *katana* strode forward and took up a left-handed *waki-gamae* stance.

Jack had his answer.

His adversary knew *exactly* what he was doing: body open but side-on, feet planted wide, blade hidden behind the torso, only the pommel of the sword visible. In such a stance, Jack couldn't see the length of his opponent's sword and therefore wasn't able to safely judge the range of its attack. Furthermore, with the sword concealed, he couldn't see the orientation of the blade, so had no clue as to his opponent's intended first cut.

Seizing upon Jack's momentary hesitation, the plague doctor struck. His blade arcing through the rain like a lightning bolt, the sheer speed of the attack took Jack off guard. He barely managed to slip aside and deflect the cut with the edge of his own blade, before being driven back on to the bridge with a second slice upwards. Jack jerked his head away, but not quickly enough. He felt the sting of steel as the tip of the *katana* just caught his chin. The cut wasn't deep but it bled freely.

Fired up by the indignity of first blood against him, Jack retaliated with his own series of slices and slashes. But the plague doctor proved to be a formidable opponent. Every cut was met with steel; every thrust evaded with catlike agility; every slice ducked, dodged or deflected. Jack fought with fury, calling on all his skill as a samurai. Still the plague doctor matched him, strike for strike, cut for cut.

Suddenly the whole bridge shuddered. Debris in the water below had struck it, and Jack lost his footing on the slippery planking, falling backwards. The plague doctor wasted no time in taking advantage of Jack's misfortune. Standing over him, he held his *katana* to the heavens, ready to drive the steel straight through Jack's undefended chest.

But then, like a battering ram, a tree trunk carried by the surging river smashed into the bridge, taking out the central supporting posts and splitting the structure in two. The plague doctor leapt back on to the bank, to avoid tumbling into the raging waters below. Jack, stranded on what was left of the far end of the bridge, desperately reached out, clinging on to a plank for dear life. He dangled over the churning river, one hand gripping the collapsing structure, the other still holding on to his sword.

He would have to make a choice: either drop into the flood waters . . . or let go of his precious *katana*.

From the bank, the plague doctor watched, wordless and wicked, relishing Jack's predicament. But in the end Jack didn't have to make that choice. A hand reached down and took his arm.

'I told you you couldn't do it alone,' said Akiko, pulling him to safety. Together they raced for the bank as the remains of the broken bridge were swept away, victims of the swollen river.

On the opposite bank, the three plague doctors stood in a line, their frustration apparent in their very stillness.

'They'll need to find another bridge now,' panted Jack with relief.

Akiko glanced up and down the river. 'And where would that be?'

Jack shrugged and sheathed his *katana*. 'Who knows! Let's not wait around to find out.'

26

THE SLEEP OF THE DEAD

Jack and Akiko caught up with Rose and Yori taking shelter beneath the branches of a large beech tree, the rain rolling off the leaves in heavy drops. Yori was tending to Rose's wound, applying a herbal ointment and binding her calf with a strip of cloth torn from his robes. Jack crouched beside them, his brow etched with concern.

'How bad is it? Do you think you'll be able to carry on?' he asked.

Rose winced as Yori tied off the makeshift bandage. 'I'll be able to walk, but don't ask me to dance,' she said, giving him a pained smile.

'Luckily for Rose the *shuriken* wasn't poisoned,' said Yori as he packed away his pouch of medicines. 'The herbs should stop any infection.'

'Thank heavens for small blessings,' said Jack, taking out the gleaming ninja star from his pocket and weighing it in his palm. Seeing such weapons in England greatly troubled him. It confirmed his fear that the rumours of killer shadows weren't rumours at all.

'Small blessings or not, it hurts a lot,' Rose complained, as

Yori helped her get to her feet. She glanced over at Akiko. 'I hope that plague doctor you stuck with your hairpin is in as much pain as I am!'

Akiko smiled and nodded. 'Probably a lot more. Unless the other plague doctors know *kyusho-jitsu* and the correct pressure points to release him, he won't be going anywhere!'

Rose nodded approvingly. 'You're certainly full of surprises, Akiko.'

'So are you,' Akiko replied, raising an eyebrow. 'I didn't expect to see you again.'

Rose glared at her. 'Is it so hard to believe that *I* came back, when *you* came back from the dead?'

Akiko shook her head. 'I just thought –'

'Thought *what*?' snapped Rose. 'That I'd abandoned you? Betrayed you? Run off at the slightest sign of danger?'

'Well . . .' began Akiko, 'you *did* disappear at the same time the constables arrived!'

A prickly silence fell between them, broken only by the soft patter of raindrops on the leaves.

'We were worried about you, Rose,' said Jack, trying to ease the tension.

Rose gave him a look as if she only half believed him. Then she explained, 'I was woken by the horses; something had unsettled them. When I spotted the constables outside the barn, I hid in the hay.'

'Why didn't you warn us?' questioned Akiko.

'There was no time, and it wouldn't have been any use if I'd been arrested too,' Rose replied. 'So I stayed hidden, then followed you into town. I couldn't do much, not with so many constables around.' She glanced apologetically at

202

Jack and Yori. 'I had to watch as you two were put in the stocks and pillory, stand by while they pelted you with rotten fruit and whatever else! I stayed hidden even as they drowned you, Akiko. Believe me, I *wanted* to save you. But it wasn't until nightfall that I could be of any help. Stealing the keys off the bailiff was the only plan I had – the *only* skill I really have.'

Jack smiled sheepishly at Rose, feeling guilty for ever thinking she'd betrayed them. 'Well, thank heavens you did, otherwise those plague doctors would've cut us into eight pieces. We owe you our lives.'

'Not mine,' stated Akiko.

Jack and Yori braced themselves for another quarrel, but when Akiko spoke her tone was unexpectedly contrite. 'I didn't think I'd ever say this . . . but clearly being a thief has its merits, at times.' She bowed deeply to Rose. 'Please accept my apologies for doubting you. I thought you'd stolen Jack's purse and run away.'

Rose laughed at the remorseful Akiko.

'*What?*' said Akiko, both confused and offended by Rose's reaction.

Rose stifled her giggles. 'You Japanese are so formal! A simple "sorry" would've sufficed. But you're right about one thing . . . I did steal Jack's purse.' She produced a leather pouch from the folds of her dress.

Akiko's mouth fell open, as did Jack's.

'But I only stole it,' continued Rose, holding up a finger against Akiko's protests, 'to stop the bailiff and his constables taking it. They'd have pocketed the money for themselves and denied all knowledge of it. *They're* the real thieves!'

She tossed the purse to Jack, who deftly caught it, yet he still looked less than pleased. 'Oh, don't be angry with me, Jack,' pleaded Rose. 'I only did it for the best.'

'It's not that,' Jack replied, as he tied the purse to his belt. 'I'm still furious that Harold Westcott took my sister's locket!'

'Sometimes we have to lose something precious in order to gain something priceless,' consoled Yori. 'Perhaps the locket has already fulfilled its purpose. It's shown you what your sister looks like now, and has guided us to Stratford. Soon you could be setting eyes on her for real!'

Jack brightened at the thought. 'You're right, Yori, as always. There are far worse things to lose in life.' He looked tenderly at Akiko. 'Like you. I thought I'd lost you forever.'

Akiko bowed her head, her ebony hair hiding the flush to her cheeks. 'You could never lose me, Jack. *Forever bound to one another*, remember?'

She lifted her chin and Jack gazed into her eyes. Having almost lost her, he realized just how precious Akiko was to him. In that moment, he was captivated by her and wanted to kiss her . . .

'Shouldn't we get moving?' said Rose abruptly.

Yori stood to one side, apparently intent on studying the stars, even though none shone through the clouds. 'The rain's easing,' he observed.

'Yes, of course,' mumbled Jack, regaining his composure. Akiko shot Rose a reproachful look.

They resumed their journey along the highway, the night hanging like a cloak over the countryside. Jack remained close to Akiko. He still couldn't believe that she was alive and walking beside him. 'You've yet to explain how you survived the trial by water,' he prompted her. 'We all thought you'd drowned.'

The rings of Yori's *shakujō* jingled softly in the rain-soaked silence as they walked along, waiting in anticipation for Akiko to reply. Akiko cleared her throat. 'You'll recall, Jack, when we first met that I used to dive for pearls? So I'm practised at holding my breath . . .'

'Surely not for *that* long?' challenged Jack.

Akiko shook her head. 'The second time under, I had to use a pond reed as a breathing tube – a simple yet effective ninja trick. But I quickly realized the bailiff intended to continue until I either confessed or drowned. So I *had* to die.'

'You certainly fooled the bailiff!' said Rose.

'Along with Yori and me!' exclaimed Jack. 'Your skin was *blue*.'

Akiko gave him a rueful smile. 'I'm sorry if I worried you, but I had no other choice. It had to be convincing. During my *ninjutsu* training at the Temple of the Peaceful Dragon, the grandmaster taught me *Shisha no Nemuri*.'

Yori gasped in shock. Jack frowned. Rose stared at them both, bewildered by their reactions. 'Er, would anyone care to translate for me please?'

'The Sleep of the Dead,' Yori explained breathlessly, his eyes wide with awe. 'It's a secret meditative state that suspends breathing and almost stops the heart beating. It's like human hibernation, but it's highly dangerous. Many people have never awoken from it.'

'That's why it took me so long to recover,' explained Akiko.

Jack nodded and smiled, everything now making sense. 'I should've guessed! I didn't think about your *ninjutsu* training.' Then his expression turned grave as he pulled out the *shuriken* again. 'Talking of ninja, those plague doctors *aren't* plague doctors. The costumes are merely a disguise. They move like ninja, fight like ninja – even use ninja weapons.'

'But what would ninja be doing in England?' asked Yori, his eyes now darting around as if every shadow along the highway might leap out at them.

'That's the very question I've been asking myself,' said Jack, flipping the *shuriken* over in his hand, 'ever since I heard rumours of killer shadows.'

'Isn't it obvious?' said Rose. 'They're after *you*.'

'But why?' said Jack.

Rose shrugged. 'You'll have to ask them, won't you.'

'Judging by their actions so far, they're not here to talk,' said Akiko.

Jack grimaced. 'Perhaps we should've faced them down rather than run like cowards.'

'A gazelle runs from the lion, not through fear but for love of life,' said Yori sagely.

'Yori's right,' said Akiko. 'We're not here to fight; we're here to find your sister.'

'But who would send ninja on an assassination mission halfway round the world?' asked Jack.

'Dokugan Ryu?' suggested Yori, swallowing hard at the mere thought of Dragon Eye.

'Impossible. He's dead,' said Jack bluntly. Although, after the nightmarish vision in London, he wasn't so sure. The ninja's spirit clearly continued to haunt him.

'But his clan isn't,' reminded Akiko. 'His successor might consider that Dragon Eye's death still needs to be avenged, just like the *kagemusha* before him.'

'Or maybe it was Shogun Kamakura?' said Yori. 'I wouldn't be surprised if that man's dying wish was to have you killed at any cost!'

Jack nodded thoughtfully, recalling the late samurai lord's determination to wipe out all foreigners from Japan, in particular the '*gaijin* samurai', whom he considered an abomination. 'That might at least explain why the plague doctor was carrying a *katana*,' he said.

Yori frowned. 'Did you get a close look at the blade?'

'Too close!' replied Jack. 'But to be honest, I wasn't studying its craftsmanship at the time.'

'That's a pity,' said Yori. 'If its design contained a *kamon*, we might be able to identify the owner from their family crest.'

Akiko shook her head. 'Not necessarily. Ninjas sometimes take the weapons of their victims. They believe the spirit of those they have vanquished in battle transfers to the weapon and adds to its power. So that *katana* could be wielded by anyone.'

'Well, whoever they are, and whatever they want, let's not find out in the middle of nowhere, in the middle of the night!' said Rose, glancing behind at the dark and forbidding road. 'If those ninjas have tracked you all the way from Japan, then a river – even in flood – isn't going to stop them.'

'I agree with Rose,' said Jack, quickening his pace. 'We need to stay one step ahead of them.'

27

HARVEST FESTIVAL

As dawn broke the next day, Jack and his friends were struggling to put one foot in front of the other. They'd been walking all through the night, the fear of the plague doctors driving them on, and had covered some twenty miles, despite no longer having Sir Henry's horses at their disposal. Tired, cold and hungry, they urged their weary bodies along the deserted highway. The chill morning mist that hung over the meadows slowly turned golden with the rising sun and the birds struck up their dawn chorus. As the world awoke, the peal of a church bell rang softly in the distance. Jack glanced up from the muddy road. A wooden spire could be seen piercing the glowing coals of the horizon.

'That must be Stratford!' he exclaimed, feeling a renewed vigour enter his stride.

The others, encouraged by his burst of enthusiasm, hurried after him.

The road soon met with the main highway and they joined a steady procession of people heading from the countryside into the town, farmers driving their cattle, herdsmen their sheep, itinerant labourers, assorted tradesmen, and villagers bearing baskets, with their children in tow.

'Is it market day?' Rose asked an apple-cheeked boy who was leading a rather large and reluctant pig by a ring through its nose.

'No, it's harvest festival,' he replied, casting a wary eye over the four dishevelled travellers before giving his swine a tug and moving on ahead.

Rose grinned at Jack. 'It's your lucky day, Jack! If your sister's in Stratford, she's bound to be out and about for the festival.'

Impatient to get into town, Jack threaded his way through the stream of farmers and villagers, all the time keeping his eye out for a glimpse of a girl with barley-blonde hair. Akiko, Yori and Rose followed close behind as the flow of people thickened into a bottleneck at a long bridge spanning the great river.

Crossing over the fourteen stone arches, Jack and his friends finally arrived in Stratford-upon-Avon. The main thoroughfare, Bridge Street, was already bustling with tradesmen and women arriving early for the festival. Stalls had been set up on both sides, as well as crammed down the centre. They passed needle-makers and hosiers, wool merchants and weavers, glovers and tailors; there were butchers, bakers and fishmongers, barbers and ironmongers. A band of wandering minstrels played and people were laughing and dancing to the music in a circle round them. Games of chance were being won and lost on street corners, and the mouth-watering aroma of freshly baked bread and roasted meats laced the air. On two sides of the busy marketplace, and forming a grand backdrop to it, were rows of timber-and-brick houses, three storeys high, with glazed windows with lead lattices. Stratford was in all ways a prosperous and popular town.

'Let's spread out,' instructed Jack, eager to find his sister. 'We'll have a better chance of spotting Jess.'

'What about breakfast?' Rose asked, hungrily eyeing a stall selling figs, apples and freshly picked blackberries. 'I'm starving!'

'That'll have to wait,' replied Jack, even though his own stomach cried out for food.

So, fanning out, they headed into the thick of the market. Jack impatiently pushed his way through the throng, his eyes sweeping the multitude of faces for a glimpse of blonde hair, a flash of blue eyes – in fact, any young girl who might remotely be his sister. Akiko and Yori drew many curious stares as they passed through the marketplace, their progress marked by Yori's strange, jingling *shakujō*, but no one attempted to stop or question them.

At the top of the street, they regrouped. 'Any luck?' asked Jack.

'Sadly, no,' replied Akiko with a regretful look.

Jack gave a heavy sigh. 'It's like trying to find a needle in a haystack!'

'At least we've found the haystack,' said Yori encouragingly. 'It's only a matter of time before we find the needle.'

After a second sweep through the market, they found themselves back at the bridge.

'Has anyone seen her?' asked Jack, his tone barely concealing his desperation. His three friends solemnly shook their heads. 'She *has* to be somewhere. Look again!' he urged.

Resuming their search, they went more slowly this time, stopping at each stall. Jack felt his frustration building as the number of people seemed more and more overwhelming. Jess could be but a few metres from him yet he might not spot her.

'Is that her?' called Rose suddenly, pointing to a blonde bob in the crowd.

Jack looked keenly. He couldn't see her face; too many shoppers in the way. He stood on tiptoe, peering over their heads, and caught a glimpse of golden hair. 'JESS!' he cried out, his heart lifting.

Several people turned towards the shout, including the blonde bob . . .

But she proved to be a thin-faced girl with a pinched nose and mud-brown eyes. Definitely not his sister.

His hopes dropped. Then he heard the familiar chime of Yori's staff as he rushed towards him.

'Jack! Jack!' yelled Yori. 'I just saw Jess!'

'Where is she?' he cried, a sudden surge of euphoria raising his spirits again.

'I spotted her near the flower stall,' Yori replied, pulling him along. 'She's wearing a blue shawl . . .'

Yori guided Jack over to the flower-seller, collecting Akiko and Rose along the way. A number of women and young women clustered round the fragrant nosegays and posies on display, but none of them wore a blue shawl or even had a wisp of blonde hair.

Jack looked frantically around, but the shifting sea of

shoppers made it difficult to follow anyone beyond a few stalls away. Unable to locate his sister, he blurted out, '*Oh, why didn't you just go up to her, Yori?*'

'I-I-I'm sorry,' stuttered Yori, bowing his head. 'I did try, but I was blocked by the crowd. So I thought it better to find you instead.'

'You did the right thing, Yori,' said Akiko, with a reproachful look at Jack for his outburst. 'She can't be too far away. Come on!'

With a rushed apology, Jack headed down the centre of Bridge Street. Akiko and Yori took the left side, Rose the right. Jack felt terrible for snapping at Yori, but his exasperation at being so close to finding his sister yet so –

A flash of blue cloth caught his eye. Halfway down the street, beside a fruit stall, a young woman with curls of blonde hair was inspecting a basket of red apples.

There she is!

Jack could scarcely breathe. His heart pounding, he hesitantly approached from behind. 'Jess?' he asked softly.

The young woman turned round and smiled. Her locks of blonde hair, like spun gold, framed her pretty face, and her pale blue eyes gazed back at him with kindness and enquiry. 'Sorry, do I know you?' she said.

Jack stared at her, unable to believe what he saw before him. The girl did indeed look like his sister. But it *wasn't* Jess.

Compared to the portrait in the locket, her eyes were a shade too light. Her nose a fraction too wide. Her lips a touch too thin. But her gaze was what settled the matter. On a deep, instinctive level, Jack didn't feel any sibling connection with this young woman. They were total strangers. Their souls were unrelated.

With a sorrowful shake of his head, he backed away. 'I'm afraid not, madam. My apologies . . .'

Disappointment hit him hard. The rapid see-sawing of his emotions plunged him sharply into despair. Letting the crowd swallow him up, Jack felt more alone than he had since that first year in Japan. He was an island in an ocean of strangers, not one of whom was Jess. He'd sailed so far – both in miles and in life – in the hope of being reunited with her. Yet the port he'd plotted his ship for seemed cruelly elusive. He realized now that he might never find her, that Jess was probably lost to him – and possibly forever.

Slumped on a bench outside the bustling Greyhound Inn, Jack numbly watched the flow of people passing by on the High Street. So many faces. So many strangers. None of them Jess. After a fourth fruitless sweep through the market, they'd abandoned their search and sought out a tavern for a late but much-needed breakfast.

'Are you certain that girl wasn't Jess?' asked Yori. 'I mean, she looked exactly like the portrait. Seven years is a long time, and people change. Is there a chance you could be mistaken?'

Jack glumly shook his head. 'No, I *know* my sister. A whole lifetime and a whole ocean couldn't break the bond between us. In here,' he said, pointing to his chest, 'I'll always recognize Jess – and when I spoke to that girl my heart felt nothing.'

'Don't despair, Jack,' said Akiko, as Rose ducked inside

the inn to order food and enquire about lodgings. 'We've come this far, we'll finish the journey. We *will* find your sister.'

Jack sighed and looked at her. 'But what if she's not here? What if we're on a wild goose chase after all? Bodley could have made up that story just to save his own skin!'

Akiko gently closed her hand over his, in an effort to reassure him. 'I believe Bodley was telling the truth. His eyes weren't lying. So we'll stay in Stratford as long as it takes to find Jess.'

Despite Akiko's determined optimism, Jack wearily shook his head. 'I'm beginning to think we never will, though.'

'You *can't* think like that!' chided Yori. 'Remember what the witch said: *when you feel furthest away, you're closer than you think.*'

Akiko nodded. 'Yori's right. If you feel like giving up, just remember why you held on for so long in the first place.'

His friends' wise words gave Jack pause for thought. The idea of reuniting with his sister had been the seed of his survival in Japan. It had sustained him during his training at the *Niten Ichi Ryū*. It had been his shield during the Battle of Osaka Castle. It had carried him across Japan, all the way from Kyoto to Nagasaki and back home to England. To give up on his sister now would be to give up the very thing he'd always fought so hard for.

Jack sat up straighter. 'You're right. As Sensei Yamada said, there's no failure except in no longer trying.' And once again he began scanning the crowd with renewed determination.

'I've got us lodgings for the night,' announced Rose, emerging from the inn with four tankards.

'That's good news,' said Akiko, moving along the bench to make room for Rose. 'I'm so tired I could sleep on a board!'

Rose laughed. 'You might have to. There were only straw beds above the stable loft. We're lucky to even get those – Stratford's heaving because of the harvest festival.'

'*Straw!* It sounds like luxury to me!' said Yori, taking a polite sip of his drink.

A servant came out with four plates heaped with buttered bread and dark meat in gravy. He plonked them on the table, stared wide-eyed at Akiko and Yori, then cautiously backed away. Akiko studied her plate dubiously. 'May I ask what we're eating?'

'Goose,' replied Rose, tearing off a chunk of bread and dipping it in her gravy. 'They say, "He who eats goose on Michaelmas Day shan't money lack or debts pay." It brings good luck.'

'And we'll need all the luck we can get,' said Jack, hungrily devouring his meal while keeping a constant eye on the crowd.

With the arrival of their food a scrawny man had appeared near them, little more than skin and bones. 'Spare some bread?' croaked the beggar, his cracked lips salivating at the sight of such succulent meat.

'Go away!' said Rose, irritably waving him off.

But Yori handed the beggar his whole plate. The man's eyes almost popped out of his skull. With a muttered thanks, he ran off before the generous offer could be withdrawn.

'Why did you give away *all* your food?' said Rose, aghast.

'He's more in need of it than me,' Yori replied, as several

other beggars, spotting a soft touch, came over and made their appeals.

'It won't make a jot of difference,' said Rose, shooing away the vagrants, 'and *you'll* just go hungry instead.'

Yori placed his hands in his lap and turned to Rose. 'Do you know the tale of the ten thousand fish?'

Biting into her buttered bread, Rose shook her head.

'One morning,' began Yori, 'after a tsunami had washed ten thousand fish up on to the shore, a monk went down to the beach. He saw the fish flapping on the sand, slowly dying. One by one he started to pick them up and throw them back into the sea. A samurai sitting nearby spotted the monk and laughed at him. "Foolish monk!" he cried. "What difference can one man make against the fate of nature?" In reply, the monk picked up a gasping fish and tossed it back into the ocean. "I made a difference to that one!" he answered.'

'A nice story,' said Rose, through a mouthful of goose, 'but I prefer not to go hungry myself.'

Yori responded with a contented smile. 'And I prefer to be a monk rather than see other people go hungry.'

'Well, I won't see a friend go hungry either!' said Jack, handing Yori a hunk of his own bread and a slice of meat.

Then, as he was picking the bones of a goose wing clean, Jack glimpsed out of the corner of his eye a girl with golden hair. '*Jess?*' he gasped.

Dropping the bone on to his plate, Jack leapt up and plunged into the crowd after her.

'Wait!' cried Akiko, as Jack dashed off down the street.

But Jack would wait for no one. He'd seen his sister. Of that he was sure.

He raced along, pushing people aside, fighting his way through the crowd. She was heading into the market. He shouldered past a farmer, knocking the man's ale out of his hand. Yelling an apology over his shoulder, Jack tripped over a group of men playing dice on the street corner and fell to his knees – and in that moment he lost sight of Jess. Scrambling back to his feet, he looked desperately around. *Where is she? Where's she gone?*

Bridge Street was teeming with tradesmen and farmers, with villagers, entertainers and travellers. His eyes darted from one face to the next in his feverish search. Then he spotted her heading down Wood Street.

'JESS!' he shouted. 'JESS!'

The girl turned towards the sound of her name, seeking out the caller. Yes! Her angelic face matched the locket's portrait down to the finest brushstroke. It *was* her!

Jack waved, trying to get her attention across the crowd. 'JESS! JESS!' But he suddenly saw her being pulled roughly away by an older gentleman with a tight crop of copper-red hair and a curling preened moustache – and a ludicrously large ruff.

For a second, Jack froze in shock, his voice becoming stuck in his throat. He recognized that man.

It was Sir Toby Nashe.

28

BEAR-BAITING

Jack fought his way through the heaving market. He could hardly believe what he'd seen. Sir Toby, of all men, was behind his sister's disappearance! That scoundrel had taken Jess. Rage rose in Jack and he raced after them. At the crossroads with Rother Street, he saw Sir Toby pushing Jess into a horse-drawn coach, then climbing in after her. The driver flicked his reins and the coach took off.

'JESS!' cried Jack, running to catch them up.

Her head appeared at the window and across the distance their eyes met. A brief moment of puzzlement registered on her face, then a flicker of startled recognition. But, as the coach pulled away, a huge man stepped into Jack's path, blocking her out of sight. A large hand was planted in Jack's chest, stopping him dead in his tracks.

'Well I never!' said a sly grating voice. 'I've been looking all over for *you*.'

Wheezing from the run and the blow to his chest, Jack stared up into the scarred, sneering face of Guy Rakesby. The bearded highwayman towered over him, almost as tall as his heavy knotted staff.

'Out of my way!' yelled Jack, frantically trying to get past him and give chase to the fast-disappearing coach.

But the sharp point of a dagger in his back halted his escape.

'Not leaving us so quickly, are we?' taunted Hazel, the hawthorn-haired doxy, giving the knife a twist.

Jack winced, feeling the blade bite, as several other members of Rakesby's gang materialized from the crowd and encircled him.

'Wasn't nice of you to leave us tied to a tree like that,' snarled Rakesby, 'not nice at all.'

'I thought Lord Percival was to send constables to arrest you,' replied Jack fiercely. To his dismay, he saw the coach turn a corner and it was gone.

The upright-man snorted a laugh. 'He did, but they didn't send enough men to handle the likes of *me*.' He leant in, his stale breath wafting in Jack's face. 'So I've a bone to pick with you, young Jack Fletcher.'

With the man so close, Jack drew his *katana* – fast and hard – to hit him in the gut with its pommel. But Rakesby seized Jack's wrist first and forced the sword back into its *saya*.

'Now, now – that's no way to treat an old friend,' he said through gritted teeth, his iron-like grip crushing Jack's wrist.

With practised light fingers, Hazel relieved Jack of his *daishō*. Then she gave another prod of her dagger, just to remind him of his predicament.

'Talking of friends,' said the highwayman, his gaze raking the crowd, 'where are yours?'

'They're around,' Jack replied boldly. 'So you'd better let me go if you don't want to be felled like a tree again!'

Rakesby spat on the ground. 'That pint-sized monk got lucky! Next time I'll crush him under my foot. Now, where are they?'

Jack defiantly held his tongue. But he, too, wondered where his friends had got to. Were they still waiting back at the inn? Or had they followed him in his mad dash after Jess? Wherever they were, he desperately needed their help right now.

'No matter,' said Rakesby, when Jack didn't reply. 'We'll find 'em soon enough.'

He nodded to his gang, and Jack found himself roughly seized by the arms and ferried through the market, his feet barely touching the ground. He struggled to free himself. To have seen his sister, only to have her snatched away and himself apprehended by Rakesby and his motley crew – it was beyond torture. He kicked and spat, a wildcat in their unyielding grip.

'Help!' he shouted. 'I'm being kidnap–'

Rakesby whipped his staff around and caught Jack across the jaw, the heavy blow stunning him into silence. As Jack reeled drunkenly, his captors holding him up, Rakesby apologized to the onlookers for Jack's delirious behaviour, blaming it on too much wine. The townsfolk, some equally merry, laughed and paid him no more attention. The gang moved swiftly on.

Jack tried in vain to spot his friends in the crowd. He let out a desperate cry – '*Tasukete! Abunai!*' – calling for help in Japanese, in the faint hope that they might hear him above the hubbub.

'Go ahead, Jack! Wail all you like,' said Rakesby, grinning. 'When the piglet squeals, the mother comes running!'

Jack ceased shouting, realizing that he was doing exactly what the highwayman wanted. He was being used as bait to draw the others. At the end of the street, his captors frogmarched him west towards the cattle market and on to the outskirts of town where a wooden arena had been constructed. Spectators sat on tiered benches, shouting, clapping and cheering. From down in the pit itself there arose a violent cacophony of barks, yelps, growls and roars.

'Do you like blood sports, Jack?' asked Rakesby, as he and his gang pushed to the front, ensuring Jack had a good view. Towards one side of the arena a post had been driven into the ground to which a huge bear had been chained. The creature, bloodied and fierce, gave a gut-wrenching roar as she tore with her claws at four muscled dogs attacking her. The dogs, their jaws dripping with saliva, snapped and bit into the flesh of the chained bear, even as they were clawed and bitten themselves.

'I so admire mastiffs,' Rakesby went on, not waiting for Jack to answer. 'Despite being mauled by the bear, they never give in. That's true fighting spirit.'

'Although it's not really a fair fight, when the bear's chained and her teeth blunted,' Jack observed bitterly. Trapped by Rakesby's gang, he felt as chained as the poor bear.

'Never underestimate the bear!' warned Rakesby, wagging a finger. 'For they are formidable warriors. How can you not admire their sheer power? See how this one crushes that dog at the neck!'

The mastiff in question gave a pained yelp, then fell limp.

The bear tossed it away just as another leapt on her back. She twisted and tumbled in a wild effort to dislodge the beast. Jack looked away, sickened at the spectacle. All round the arena spectators were feverishly placing bets on the outcome of the fight. He could never understand how some people could take pleasure in seeing one poor beast tear and kill another for the sake of mere entertainment.

'Why have you brought me here?' demanded Jack, as the bear finished off a bulldog.

'We've come to make a bet,' the upright-man replied with a fiendish grin.

'New dogs!' yelled the pit owner, a fat man with heavy jowls and a sweat-stained shirt, rolled up at the sleeves.

Rakesby raised a hand. 'I've a fresh dog for the pit.'

The owner glanced over, questioning with his rheumy eyes. 'Let's see if it's worthy, then.'

Without warning, Jack was picked up and tossed into the arena. He landed hard in the dirt, jarring his shoulder on impact. The crowd gasped, then fell silent. Winded and hurting, Jack looked up. The two remaining dogs – another large mastiff and a muscular bulldog – halted their attacks on the bear and now glared at him, their jaws open, their fangs dripping with blood. The wounded bear pawed the ground, her great head turning towards the intruder in the pit.

'He's no dog!' exclaimed the pit owner.

Rakesby shrugged. 'What can I say? He's the runt of the litter!'

Ever so slowly and carefully, Jack got to all fours. The two dogs stalked towards him, growling deep in their throats. In their frenzied bloodlust, they didn't see a young man before them. They saw a young bear to rend and tear to pieces. A primeval fear seized Jack. The dogs sensed his weakness and closed in. At the last second, Jack made a dash for the arena wall. He threw himself up, clinging to the top of a wooden panel as the two dogs barked and snapped at his heels. However, as Jack tried to scramble to safety, Hazel met him with her dagger.

'Oh, Jack! Don't spoil the entertainment for everyone,' she said with a smirk, and she brought the knife's hilt down.

Pain flared through his fingers and he was forced to let go. As he fell back into the pit, the bulldog went for him – but Jack leapt aside. The dog hit the arena wall and was stunned – but now the mastiff was giving chase. Rakesby laughed, and the rest of the spectators joined in, as Jack sprinted for the opposite wall. Almost tripping over one of the dead dogs, Jack dodged round the frenzied bear. A huge paw, the size of a cannonball, lashed out at him and he was caught on the arm by the bear's claws.

'Watch out, Jack!' Rakesby taunted gleefully.

On reaching the far side of the pit, Jack glanced back and saw the mastiff launch itself at him. He barely managed to get his arms up before the dog was upon him. They fell to the ground and wrestled in the dirt, the beast's slobbering jaws snapping inches from his face.

As he continued trying to hold the mastiff off, Jack was vaguely aware that around him wagers were being laid on his survival. Given his dire situation, he didn't put the odds much in his favour.

29

BULLDOG

Jack had fought many enemies, but never a dog. The mastiff was relentless in its fury, its claws scrabbling at his chest as if digging for a bone. Blood soon soaked through Jack's tattered shirt. Yet he grimly kept the dog's slobbering head at bay. He had everything to fight for, not only his life but Jess's safety too. He *had* to survive to rescue her from Sir Toby's clutches.

The spectators looked on in morbid fascination. Above their shocked gasps and shouts of encouragement, Rakesby's voice boomed loud and clear. 'Keep fighting, Jack, I've put sixpence on yer!'

But Jack was rapidly weakening under the mastiff's ferocious onslaught. None of his training had prepared him to fight a rabid wild beast. There were no punches to block or kicks to counter. No blades to deflect or weapons to disarm. The dog had no battle strategy – it simply wanted to rip, tear and bite.

Then Jack remembered Sensei Kyuzo's *katame waza* training. Surely his teacher's grappling techniques would be as effective on a dog as on a man? In a bid to gain the advantage, Jack rolled over until he was on top of the mastiff. Then, pinning a forearm across the dog's throat, he began to choke the animal. It spluttered and writhed beneath him. But, in rolling, Jack had made the fatal error of entering the bear's domain. Straining on her chain, the enraged beast took another swipe at Jack. Her sharp claws ripped through the cotton of Jack's shirt and scored four red lines into his back. Crying out in pain, he lost his grip on the dog and the mastiff's jaws clamped on to his forearm.

Caught between teeth and claws, Jack realized he was as good as dead.

The shouts of the crowd grew to fever pitch and Rakesby leant over the arena wall to gloat at Jack's demise. 'I told you, Jack: never underestimate the bear!'

His words cut through the pain and Jack knew what he had to do. Rather than rolling away from the bear, he rolled *towards* her, with the dog still gripping his arm. Using the mastiff as a shield, Jack let the bear attack, and her claws dug deep into the dog's back. The mastiff yelped, releasing Jack's arm, and was almost immediately torn from him. The bear killed it with a single bite to its throat.

Jack scrambled away to safety. Although many had bet against him, the crowd now cheered his miraculous escape. But the gladiatorial battle wasn't over yet. The remaining bulldog, recovered from its impact against the arena wall, stalked towards Jack. Injured and exhausted, Jack didn't know whether he had the strength left to fight it off. Weakly, he raised his fists into a fighting guard.

'This isn't a boxing match!' heckled Hazel, prompting a wave of laughter.

But Jack had nothing else with which to fend off the savage animal.

The beast bared its teeth and growled. Jack braced himself.

Then a dagger landed at his feet, a slim stiletto blade with a pair of ornate curved prongs above the hilt.

Jack snatched it up.

'Foul play!' yelled Rakesby, scanning the crowd for the dagger's owner.

Jack had no idea who his benefactor was – he couldn't spot Akiko, Yori or Rose among the spectators – but he was thankful nonetheless. He held out the blade, warding off the animal.

The bulldog sensed the danger and became wary, eyeing the silver point as if it was a bear's claw. The crowd began jeering and booing, some demanding that all bets be called off. But Jack realized that, even if he managed to defeat the dog, Rakesby and his gang wouldn't let him go. They intended he should die one way or another, which meant Jack needed to escape the pit *and* Rakesby's gang.

So, rather than killing the bulldog, Jack backed slowly away to the far side of the arena and the post that tethered the bear. The abused beast swung towards him, her eyes red with pain and fury. Jack tried to unhook the chain, but discovered it was padlocked to the post. Roaring, the bear reared up on her hind legs to take a swipe at him. Jack furiously tugged on the chain but to no avail. Then the bear spotted the bulldog prowling towards Jack and lashed out at its old enemy. As bear and dog fought, Jack thrust the tip of the dagger into the padlock and tried to jimmy it open. The bear knocked the bulldog aside with a brutal slash of claws, and the dog landed in a bloody heap and lay still. Then the bear turned back to Jack, intent on finishing off her last threat.

His hands slick with sweat and blood, Jack frantically jiggled the blade in the lock. At the very last moment, he heard a *click* and the padlock sprang open. The iron chain fell to the earth; the bear hesitated. She looked at her shackles . . . then at Jack . . . then gave a mighty roar. Jack feebly raised the dagger, a toothpick against the claws of a fully grown brown bear – but the bear swept past him and bounded over the arena wall. Despite her injuries, she clambered into the stalls with ease. Spectators scattered in panic, screaming for their lives. A woman's cloak was torn from her and a man was crushed under the heavy paws of the wild animal. Pandemonium reigned and, in the confusion, Jack scrambled up the wooden wall and out of the pit . . .

'Not so fast!' hissed Hazel. She thrust her knife at Jack's heart.

Jack blocked the blade with the curved prongs of the stiletto dagger, then, twisting the hilt, disarmed her. He followed up with a side kick that sent Hazel tumbling into the pit – taking Jack's stolen *katana* and *wakizashi* with her. She landed next to the wounded bulldog. Unfortunately for her, the dog wasn't quite dead and in its death throes the animal latched on to her with its slobbering jaws.

Jack went to jump into the pit after her, but two of Rakesby's gang came rushing at him with rapiers. Armed only with the dagger, Jack managed to fend off the first jab but was caught on the arm by the second attack. Smarting from his wound, he retreated through the fleeing crowd, the bear still on the rampage. But now more gang members materialized to block his escape. Surrounded by rapiers, cudgels and knives, Jack had nowhere left to run.

Rakesby appeared with his knotted staff. 'Enough of this blood sport!' he spat. 'Kill the runt!'

Jack pivoted on the spot, trying desperately to ward off any attacks. But he was outnumbered seven to one.

Then a slim gentleman with an upturned moustache stepped into the circle. He was dressed in a fine purple doublet and hose trimmed with lace. A black velvet cape hung stylishly off one shoulder and a wide-brimmed feathered hat adorned his head. With a flourish, he unsheathed his rapier – a long sliver of elegant steel.

'And who are you?' demanded Rakesby, furiously.

'I, sir, am Signor Horatio Palavicino,' announced the swordsman, with a grand air and distinctly foreign accent.

Rakesby sneered. 'A fop from Italy? Get lost! This ain't your fight.'

'It is now,' replied Signor Horatio, sinking into a low guard, his rapier out straight, his left arm held high for balance.

Rakesby shrugged. 'So be it. Kill 'em both, lads.'

His gang rushed in. Jack readied himself to fight to his last breath, but he barely got a thrust in. Signor Horatio lunged, deflected and disarmed all six attackers in a matter of seconds. His sword work was almost too fast to see, the rapier blade whipping through the air like a hornet, stinging its victims and wounding them into immediate submission.

Rakesby gazed round at his men. Then he turned his outrage on the newcomer. 'You may be quick with a rapier,' he snarled, 'but I daresay you ain't as quick as a bullet!'

Pulling his flintlock pistol from his belt, the highwayman took aim at Signor Horatio. The swordsman held his ground, noble and proud even in the face of certain death. There was nothing Jack could do to save his saviour –

A guttural roar issued from the arena. Rakesby spun back round to face the approaching bear, re-aimed and fired his pistol. The bear flinched and howled in pain, but kept coming. And Rakesby fled for his life.

'Ah, how Shakespeare would have approved!' Signor Horatio laughed, as the highwayman hightailed it into the woods, with the enraged bear close behind. *'Exit, pursued by a bear!'*

SWORD MASTER

Jack stood surveying the aftermath of their escape, his and the bear's. The tiered benches round the arena were abandoned and in disarray, having been knocked over during the audience's hysterical flight. Some spectators were still present, wandering around in a daze or tending to the shocked and injured. A few more unprincipled individuals were scouring the ground for dropped coins and lost possessions. But most had retreated into the relative safety of the town. Surrounding Jack in a ring lay the groaning and writhing bodies of Rakesby's gang, each nursing a painful and potentially fatal wound.

The threat over, Signor Horatio resheathed his rapier. 'May I have my dagger back, *per favore, signor?*' he asked, holding out a gloved hand.

'By all means,' said Jack, returning the fine stiletto blade. 'Thank you for saving me. I owe you my life.'

'*Pah!* It was nothing!' replied the swordsman, flicking a speck of dust off his velveted shoulder.

'Your sword work cannot be described as *nothing!*' exclaimed Jack, astounded at the man's blasé attitude. 'Your skill with a blade is extraordinary!'

His saviour puffed up like a peacock at the compliment.

Jack studied the man's dark and handsome face. 'I don't believe we've met before. I'm Jack Fletcher. May I ask you why you came to my aid?'

Signor Horatio pursed his lower lip and shrugged nonchalantly. 'I was impressed by your fighting spirit.' He raised a slender finger and pointed at Jack. 'Also, your balanced posture suggests you're a trained swordsman too. I am right, no?'

Jack nodded and Signor Horatio beamed at his educated guess. 'What school did you train at, and who was your master?' he asked.

'The *Niten Ichi Ryū*,' Jack replied. 'Under Masamoto Takeshi.'

Signor Horatio frowned. 'I've not heard of that sword school.'

'It's in the Japans,' explained Jack.

'Ah! That must be why,' said Signor Horatio, nodding to himself. 'Well, you've no doubt heard of mine,' he said, then paused dramatically before announcing: '*Signor Horatio's School of Fencing!*'

From the way the swordsman spoke, it was obvious he was supremely proud of his institution. Jack hated to disappoint his saviour, but replied honestly, 'I'm afraid not, Signor Horatio . . . I've been out of the country a while.'

For a moment the swordsman appeared somewhat deflated. Then he smiled again. 'No matter. One day *everyone* will have heard of *Signor Horatio's School of Fencing!*'

Of that Jack had no doubt, not only because the man kept announcing the school's name so loudly and emphatically, but also because of the spectacular skill he had shown earlier with his rapier. Aside from Masamoto Takeshi himself, Jack had never witnessed such a consummate display of swordsmanship.

'I hope one day I can repay the courage and kindness you have shown me,' said Jack with a grateful bow, 'but I must go now.'

'You should rest, *signor*,' Signor Horatio advised, as Jack limped over to the arena. 'Those cuts are deep and need tending.'

'I'll be fine,' said Jack, wincing. His only thought was to find his friends and rescue Jess, and he began carefully climbing down into the baiting pit to recover his swords.

By now, the bulldog had died from its injuries, but the same couldn't be said for its last victim. Hazel lay moaning and weeping beside the animal, her arm still clamped in its jaws. Jack took his *daishō* back from her, and her knife for good measure, but he couldn't bring himself to leave her like that. Prising the dog's jaws apart, he freed her arm, then tore a strip of cloth from her ragged sleeve and bound her wounds to stem the bleeding.

'You have a good heart,' observed Signor Horatio with approval. 'Not many men would show such mercy to their enemies.'

'She's not my enemy,' replied Jack, his mind fixed on his real foe: Sir Toby. As he tied off the makeshift bandage, he heard the familiar jingling of a prayer staff. Then Yori appeared in the arena, followed by Akiko and Rose.

'We heard about the bear-baiting . . .' panted Rose, 'and someone being thrown into the pit . . . and knew it could only be *you!*'

Yori's eyes widened at the carnage of matted fur, spilled guts and bloody carcasses strewn across the arena. 'You survived *this*?' he gasped.

'Barely,' replied Jack, handing Rose the knife. 'Here,' he said, 'you have this, Rose. It could come in useful.' Then, with Akiko's help, he clambered out of the pit.

Akiko stared, aghast, at Jack's tattered and bloody shirt. 'Are you badly hurt?' she asked.

Jack grimaced in pain. 'My chest feels like it's been raked with a hoe and my back whipped with a cat-o'-nine-tails, but I'm alive, thanks to this gentleman.'

Rose cast an admiring eye over the fancifully dressed stranger. 'And who might you be?' she asked curiously.

'Signor Horatio Palavicino, at your service, *signorina*!' replied the swordsman, bowing low with a flourish of his feathered hat. He took Rose's hand and kissed it lightly. '*Ah, un angelo mandato dal cielo!*'

Rose's cheeks flushed. 'I've no idea what he said, but it sounded divine!'

Yori inspected Jack's wounds. 'Jack, we should go back to the inn so I can tend to these.'

'They can wait,' said Jack firmly. 'I've found Jess!'

'*Really?*' exclaimed Akiko, her face lighting up. 'Where is she?'

'That I don't know!' Jack replied in fierce frustration. 'She was taken away in a coach – by Sir Toby Nashe!'

Akiko, Yori and Rose all stared at him in dumbfounded disbelief.

'What would Sir Toby be doing with your sister?' asked Yori.

Jack's expression turned thunderous. 'I fear he's the one who's been courting her.'

Rose gasped. 'So that "young filly" we heard him talking about at the party must have been your sister!'

'No wonder Mrs Winters was so scared,' said Akiko. 'Sir Toby must have threatened her.'

'If he's laid one finger on my sister,' said Jack vehemently, gripping the hilt of his *katana*, 'I swear on my life that I will run Sir Toby Nashe through with my sword!'

'Wait, did you say . . . Sir Toby *Nashe*?' enquired Signor Horatio.

Jack nodded. 'Why, do you know him?'

A sharp look of distaste flashed across Signor Horatio's face. 'Let's just say I have crossed swords with him!'

'Me too,' said Jack with equal bitterness. 'The pompous idiot challenged me to a duel, and despite all my years of samurai training he danced rings round me.'

'No wonder,' said Signor Horatio, glancing at the *daishō* on Jack's hip. 'With those swords you've little chance against a rapier.'

Jack stiffened. 'A *katana* is the ultimate sword,' he argued, feeling defensive in face of the insult to his prized weapons. 'No steel is sharper!'

Signor Horatio shrugged. 'Maybe in the Japans it is the ultimate sword, but here the rapier rules – as you discovered to your cost. That *katana* of yours would appear deadly when it comes to slashing and cutting, but it's no match for the rapier's speed and reach.'

Jack opened his mouth to argue further, then closed it. He had to accept the hard truth: he'd been resoundingly beaten in the duel and had yet to get over the shock. Setting aside his samurai pride, he muttered, 'Well, if only I'd known that before I fought that knighted imbecile.'

Signor Horatio studied Jack closely, then seemed to come to a decision. 'We share a common enemy, Jack Fletcher. When Sir Toby wounds one of my students, he wounds me too!'

Jack frowned. 'But I'm not a student of yours.'

'You are now!' declared Signor Horatio, clapping a hand on Jack's shoulder. 'And as your sword master, it's my duty to ensure you're never at that low-life's mercy again. So the next time you encounter him, to take back your sister, you'll have the skills to defeat him in open combat. For I shall instruct you in the fine art of fencing!'

31

HORATIO'S SCHOOL
OF FENCING

'*Buongiorno!* I hope you're well rested, for your training now begins at Signor Horatio's School of Fencing!' announced Signor Horatio the next day, as Jack and his friends joined him in a cloistered courtyard of a large timber-framed building off the High Street. Galleries overlooked the paved area on three sides, and a path led behind the house through to a well-tended garden of herbs and vegetables.

'This is where we train,' Signor Horatio explained, sweeping his hand round the courtyard. A row of rapiers, their tips capped with leather, lined one of the walls. A suit of battle-worn armour was mounted on a stand and, in one corner, a dummy stuffed with straw and barley hung from a beam like a convict from the gallows. 'And in here,' continued the sword master, opening a wooden door and showing them a dimly lit room with a long table, 'is where we dine. And up there —' he pointed to the galleries — 'is where you can sleep.'

Jack exchanged a hopeful look with his friends. After their betrayal by Harold, the courtesy-man, it was refreshing and reassuring to meet someone genuinely on their side.

Signor Horatio had invited them to stay at his premises until they located Jess and Sir Toby. Despite being desperate to start the search, Jack had accepted the offer. He realized that if he was to have any chance of overcoming Sir Toby, he needed the sword master's rapier skills.

Signor Horatio planted his hands on his hips. 'So, what do you think?'

Jack nodded enthusiastically. While it couldn't compare to the *Niten Ichi Ryū* with its awe-inspiring *Butokuden*, its exquisitely decorated Hall of Butterflies, and its incense-infused Buddha Hall, Signor Horatio's school boasted all the necessary facilities required to live and train under one roof. 'It's impressive,' said Jack.

'You've a fine collection of weapons,' added Akiko, showing an interest in a long sword and heavy chain mace that were mounted next to the armour.

Signor Horatio beamed. 'A student must learn to defend himself against a wide range of attacks. You can't expect everyone to fight with a rapier!'

'I see you're an accomplished gardener too,' remarked Yori, looking down the path at the flourishing plot to the rear. 'May I explore? There might be some herbs that can help heal Jack's wounds.'

'But of course,' replied Signor Horatio. *'La mia casa è la tua casa!'*

As Yori scampered off, Rose glanced round the deserted courtyard. 'Where are all your students?' she asked.

Signor Horatio's beaming smile faltered. 'Ah, well, you see . . . I've only been open for a few weeks . . . and it seems people are more interested in drinking beer and gambling than in learning the noble art of fencing.' He took a deep breath and thrust out his chest. 'But I am confident that my reputation will bring in students from far and wide.'

'I'm sure it will,' said Rose kindly. 'But given England is at peace, I'm not surprised at the lack of interest.'

Signor Horatio snorted. 'Peace is but a fragile gift, and with this country no longer helmed by your dear departed Queen Elizabeth, it will surely run into a storm sooner or later.' He nodded in the direction of Yori, who was picking leaves from a primrose bush. 'As I tell my students, it is better to be a warrior in a garden than a gardener in a war.'

'You sound like my old Zen master, Sensei Yamada,' said Jack, smiling at the memory of his wise mentor.

'Why didn't you set up your school in London?' Akiko asked. 'Everyone there seems very eager to duel.'

A dark cloud passed across Signor Horatio's face. 'I did, *signorina*. And my school was full, my skills were respected, my reputation was untarnished.'

'What happened?' asked Jack.

Signor Horatio stared at the straw dummy in the corner, as if weighing up an old enemy. 'I was challenged to a duel by none other than Sir Toby Nashe! He considered that, as a foreigner in England, I'd got above my status. He insulted me and my students. So I had no choice but to accept the challenge, for the honour of my school.' Signor Horatio's eyes narrowed. 'To give him his due, he was an accomplished swordsman – talented yet arrogant. Still, I bested him. He was furious at losing, couldn't accept that I'd beaten him fair and square. So he took a pistol from one of his fawning followers and shot me . . . in the back!'

Rose gasped, putting a hand to her heart.

'That sounds like Sir Toby to me,' said Jack. 'No sense of *bushido* at all.'

Signor Horatio scowled. 'He has no grace, no valour, no honour. Such men aren't worthy of the title *Sir*. And, although I survived, I discovered he'd blackened my name – he claimed that it was I who'd lost and that *I'd* tried to shoot *him*! My school was forcibly closed by the Defence Guild and I was hounded out of the city.' He looked Jack square in the eye. 'That's another reason I want to train you, Jack. I have a score of my own to settle with Sir Toby.'

After a light breakfast of buttered bread, sage and fresh blackberries picked from the garden, Jack and his friends returned to the courtyard for the first lesson of the day. Yori and Rose elected to watch from the sidelines, but Akiko was keen to learn this Western style of sword-fighting, especially in view of her painful encounter with Sir Francis. She took up a position next to Jack as Signor Horatio emerged from his lodgings, now attired in black breeches, a fine white shirt and a tight leather jerkin, his slender rapier slung on his hip. Upon seeing Akiko, he stopped and blinked in surprise. He offered her an awkward smile, before saying, 'I must confess, I've never instructed a *woman* before.'

Akiko held his gaze. 'Well, I've never been taught by an *Italian* before, but I'm willing to take that risk.'

Signor Horatio stared at her a moment, then laughed. '*Touché, signorina.* You shame me with your wit and virtue.' He inclined his head. 'I apologize for my small-mindedness. You are a most welcome student.' He glanced in Yori and

Rose's direction. 'In fact, *everyone* is invited to train at Signor Horatio's School of Fencing.'

Bowing his gratitude, Yori excused himself. 'I thank you, Signor Horatio, but I need to blend some more herbs for Jack's wounds.'

Thanks to Yori's medicinal skills, Jack was recovering fast from his ordeal in the bear-baiting pit. After just one night the scratches across his chest and the claw marks on his back were already beginning to heal, and Yori had assured him that within a week he'd be fighting fit again – although a week seemed a long time in the search for his sister.

'How about you, Rose?' asked Signor Horatio, inviting her to take a sword from the rack.

Rose shook her head, her red hair blazing like the morning sun. 'No,' she replied. 'I'm just watching *you*.'

Signor Horatio raised an eyebrow at her, and Rose smiled coyly. 'Besides,' she added, 'my leg still needs to heal.'

With a gentle inclination of the head, Signor Horatio strode over to the sword rack and selected a pair of leather-capped rapiers. He presented them to his two students. 'You'll find that the rapier handles very differently to a *katana*. Feel how the weight is concentrated in the hilt. This allows the blade's tip to make rapid, agile and long-reaching attacks.'

'It's almost weightless,' Jack remarked, balancing the sword in his hand.

'And so it should be. The rapier,' Signor Horatio explained, unsheathing his own sword, 'should be a natural extension of your arm. While I can appreciate your *katana*'s superiority as a cutting blade, in a fencing duel the shortest distance between two opponents isn't the curved line of a cut – it's the straight line of a thrust.' And in one fluid movement he lunged at the straw dummy hanging in the corner of the courtyard. Covering the distance in a single bound, the rapier's tip plunged into the heart of its target. The straw dummy bled several grains of barley as Signor Horatio swiftly withdrew the slender blade and returned to his position in the centre of the yard.

'As you can see,' he said, 'the rapier combined with a lunge has a range well beyond the effective reach of a *katana*. That's why, Jack, you found yourself at such a disadvantage duelling Sir Toby. Before you could even begin to attack, he would have been able to land a potentially lethal strike.'

Jack grimaced, recalling the peppering of small wounds Sir Toby had inflicted on his body, face and hands.

'But once you're past the tip of a rapier, the blade is relatively harmless,' argued Akiko. 'All you need to do is evade the first attack, then move in.'

Signor Horatio gave an arch grin. 'Ah, *signorina*! That's why we carry a parrying dagger in our other hand,' he said, patting the slim stiletto blade on his hip. 'We can parry or bind the opponent's blade, disarm them or deliver a strike – but we're getting ahead of ourselves. You may be experienced in sword work but one step at a time. Let's begin with the basic warding posture and a straight lunge.'

Signor Horatio took up a duelling stance: his left leg to the rear, his right foot pointing forward; his sword arm out in front, his left hand close to his chest. 'Notice how I lean back and hold my head as far away from my opponent as possible,' he explained. 'Most sword masters' stances are more centred, but with *my* stance the vital organs of head and heart are kept at a safer distance from my opponent's rapier. Moreover, when I make a lunge, my range is very deceptive – and far greater than anticipated.'

Jack and Akiko imitated his stance. Signor Horatio examined them both, making small adjustments as he went. 'Hold your left hand higher . . . it's a secondary guard for your body and head . . . Point the front foot forward, your back one at right angles for maximum stability and power . . . good . . . Now I want you to lunge like *this* . . .'

Signor Horatio took a step with his front foot, leaning sharply into the attack and extending his sword arm out straight, while flinging his left arm back. He looked like an arrow in flight. The sword master repeated the move several times until he was certain his students had understood the technique. 'Now lunge!'

Jack and Akiko leapt forward, their rapiers thrusting at imaginary enemies. To Jack, who was used to a more upright and guarded posture in *kenjutsu*, the sheer boldness and apparent overreach of the lunge felt distinctly unsettling.

'Don't extend your knee past your toes, *signor*,' advised Signor Horatio. 'It results in a slower recovery. And you, *signorina*, throw your left hand back for balance . . . Both of you, hold the sword hand a little higher – the hilt needs to protect your face . . .'

And so it went on. The rest of the morning was taken up with warding and lunging, until Signor Horatio was wholly convinced that both his students had mastered the two techniques. He then moved them on to the straw dummy, ensuring their thrusts were true and straight and would penetrate their target each and every time. When their teacher finally called a break, the muscles in Jack's legs and arms were aching and a blister had formed on his thumb where he'd been gripping the hilt. But he felt a deep satisfaction at having learnt the basics of a new sword style, as well as a renewed confidence that, under Signor Horatio's tutelage, he would be more of a match for Sir Toby.

As they returned their rapiers to the rack, he smiled at Akiko. 'It's like being back at the *Niten Ichi Ryū*!' he said.

Akiko nodded and smiled too. Yet in her eyes there was also a longing. An undeniable yearning for her homeland.

32

PARRY AND RIPOSTE

'Come on, Jack – we can't sit here all afternoon,' said Akiko, getting to her feet. 'We need to train.'

'But this is where I spotted Jess,' he replied, not taking his eyes off the people passing by. He was perched on an empty beer barrel at the corner of the High Street, a position that afforded him clear views of all Stratford's main thoroughfares and the marketplace. Signor Horatio had made enquiries with a number of town officials about Sir Toby and Jess, but so far they'd come to nothing. No one appeared to know the gentleman or to have seen a blonde girl fitting his sister's description. Jack realized that his task would be a whole lot easier if he still had the locket to show people her portrait. So with no clue as to where the coach might have been heading, beyond due west, Jack felt his best option was to stand watch and hope Jess or Sir Toby made a return visit to town.

'Signor Horatio will be waiting for us,' urged Akiko. 'It would be disrespectful to turn up late.'

Jack didn't move. He was torn between the need to find his sister and the need to learn to handle the rapier. Jess was being held against her will – of that Jack was sure – which meant he needed every skill he could get in order to free her. And yet . . . what if he missed seeing his sister in town?

Rose, who leant against the wall eating an apple, gazed round at the quiet streets. 'It might be better to wait for market day,' she suggested, 'or else Sunday, when most of the parish will be here for church. Otherwise, you could be wasting your time.'

'This is *not* a waste of time!' insisted Jack, his tone sharper than he'd intended.

Rose held up a hand in her defence. 'Sorry! Just saying, though, you've a greater chance when there are people *actually* around.'

'I'll keep watch,' Yori offered. 'I can stay here and meditate.'

Jack turned to his friend, who sat on the ground, his *shakujō* across his lap. 'But how will you spot her with your eyes closed?' he asked.

'I can meditate just as well with my eyes open,' Yori replied. 'In fact, your sister would be a good focus for my meditation. Meanwhile, the focus of *your* training would be good for *you*,' he suggested gently. 'It's important to keep a sharp sword . . . but not necessarily a sharp tongue.'

Jack glanced sheepishly at Rose. 'I'm sorry I snapped at you . . . I'm worried about my sister with that arrogant . . .'

'No need to apologize, Jack. I'd be out of my mind if it was my sister!' Finishing her apple, Rose tossed the core away. 'Now,' she said, 'Signor Horatio's asked me to get in some provisions for tonight's dinner. I'll see you later.' With that, she strolled away towards a baker's shop.

Leaving Yori to keep watch, Jack and Akiko headed up

the High Street to the fencing school. As they passed a cluster of people gathered outside the Greyhound Inn, they heard a familiar voice telling a familiar tale.

'. . . It's as if the four horsemen of the Apocalypse have descended . . . It's not the plague that kills; it's the doctors themselves . . .'

Jack stopped dead in his tracks. He'd been so focused on finding Jess that he'd almost forgotten about the four ninjas on his trail. A shudder ran through him. He knew it was only a matter of time before the assassins caught up with them.

'So how did you escape, then?' a wide-eyed woman was asking him in concern.

'To tell you the truth, madam, I barely made it out alive,' the storyteller replied pitifully. 'I lost everything . . .' he added, with a sorrowful shake of his head. 'I had to abandon all my belongings . . . and am left with only the gentleman's clothes that I wear . . .'

Jack, followed by Akiko, pushed through the knot of listeners to find the storyteller being comforted by the woman.

'Harold!' said Jack with a broad smile, as if greeting an old friend. 'I trust you didn't lose *everything*.'

Harold Westcott glanced up sharply and his face blanched. 'I-I-I didn't expect to see you here,' he stuttered.

'I bet you didn't,' said Jack.

Before Harold could make a bolt for it, Jack unsheathed the rapier on his hip and thrust the tip against the courtesy-man's throat. Pinned against a wall, Harold swallowed hard in panic. The crowd of onlookers all took a hasty step back.

'Where's my silver locket?' demanded Jack.

Feeling only the blunt leather cap against his skin, Harold regained his courage. 'Oh, it's a *practice* rapier!' he sneered. Then, laughing off Jack's threat, he pushed the blade aside and rose to leave. But in a lightning-quick flick of his wrist, Jack slashed the blade's edge across Harold's face, leaving a thin line of blood along his cheek. Harold gasped.

'Sit down!' ordered Jack. 'Now, unless you want a matching scar on your other cheek, give me back my locket.'

Offering no further resistance, Harold hurriedly removed the chain from round his neck and shakily passed the locket to Jack. 'I hope you don't bear me any ill-will,' Harold pleaded with an ingratiating smile. 'I looked after it well.'

Looping the chain over his own head, Jack considered the grovelling thief before him. Then he flicked the leather cap off the rapier's tip and thrust the blade at Harold's gut.

'NO!' shouted Akiko in alarm. The courtesy-man screamed and the gathered onlookers gasped in horror.

Slowly, Jack withdrew the blade. There was no blood. But the rapier's tip had pierced a red leather purse that he now extracted from the folds of Harold's jacket. 'No doubt as well as you looked after this lady's purse!' said Jack, as Harold, pale-faced and panicking, checked himself for serious injuries.

'Oi! That's mine!' cried the wide-eyed woman in outrage.

Tossing the purse back to its rightful owner, Jack then sheathed his rapier and strolled away from the scene. He'd got what he wanted.

Akiko hurried to catch him up. 'For a moment, I thought you were going to kill him,' she said.

Jack shook his head. 'No, I'll leave justice to take its

natural course.' And behind them there came a sharp cry followed by a plea for mercy as an angry mob dealt with the thief.

'Offence is defence,' Signor Horatio declared, as Jack and Akiko again took up their positions in the courtyard. 'Any direct attack by an opponent must be defended and countered in one fluid action – parry and riposte.'

He beckoned Jack forward. 'Lunge at me, *signor*!'

Jack thrust for the sword master's heart. Before the blade could make contact with its target, his rapier was deflected and Jack felt the hard prod of a leather tip against his own heart, his sword master's parry and riposte quicker than the blink of an eye.

Signor Horatio grinned, enjoying the look of astonishment on both Jack and Akiko's faces. 'I'll slow the action down to teach you.'

This time Jack was able to see how the sword master rode the rapier with his own blade, redirecting the attack even as he counter-thrusted. It reminded Jack of Masamoto's Flint-and-Spark strike.

'Be sure to use the forte of the blade against the debole of your opponent's,' explained Signor Horatio, first indicating the stronger half of the rapier near the hilt, then the thinner weaker section towards the tip. 'This gives you the leverage you need in your parry. And, by keeping contact, you maintain control of your opponent's blade. Now you try, *signor*.'

Jack waited for Signor Horatio's thrust. As the attack came, slow and steady, he met the debole with the forte.

Signor Horatio's sword was deflected off-target while his own struck home in the middle of the sword master's chest.

'Bravo! A perfect parry and riposte,' congratulated Signor Horatio. Jack smiled at the praise. 'Now to do it at speed!'

Slow had been easy. Fast was an entirely different matter. It took Jack several attempts even just to catch the blade, let alone deflect it. By comparison to his *katana*'s broader blade, the rapier's slender strip of steel was almost impossible to see coming. As their rapiers tangled, Jack missed his target yet again. Cursing in frustration, he lowered his sword.

'Don't despair, Jack,' encouraged Signor Horatio. 'Like any martial art, fencing takes practice. Rarely does anyone master it first time.' He turned to Akiko. 'Now, *signorina*, let's see how you do.'

Signor Horatio thrust his rapier at her. With a deft touch, Akiko deflected the attack and landed a strike dead centre upon his heart. Signor Horatio's eyes widened. '*Magnifico!* Perhaps one *can* master it first time. Why have I not taught women before? Your skill is astounding, *signorina!*'

Akiko bowed humbly. 'I've had the benefit of watching Jack first.'

'*Pah!* You're a natural!' said Signor Horatio, as she repeated the feat. Jack merely smiled, accustomed to Akiko's talent at picking up new techniques.

After several more rounds of practice, Signor Horatio announced, 'It's time you two had a duel. *En garde!*'

Jack and Akiko stood in the centre of the courtyard, both in warding stances, their rapiers outstretched, their eyes locked. Despite being no match for her innate skill with a rapier, Jack couldn't help but feel elated at their imminent duel. Once again he was reminded of the *Niten Ichi Ryū* and of all the times he'd trained with Akiko and his other friends, like Saburo, Emi and his late Japanese brother-in-arms Yamato. While the samurai school had been tough, challenging and at times unbearable, it had also been a place of friendship, love and loyalty. He knew Akiko missed Japan – but he was slowly coming to realize that he did as well.

'*Allez!*' called Signor Horatio, commencing the duel.

Jack tensed as Akiko stood poised like a scorpion ready to strike. Assessing each other as if old enemies, they sought the familiar telltale signs that one of them was about to attack. Jack shifted his foot. Akiko flinched. She twitched the tip of her rapier. He reacted with a flick of his blade. Then, just as he lunged, Rose entered the courtyard.

'Good news!' she announced, putting down a heavy basket of bread and other provisions.

Distracted, Jack's face immediately turned to look at her. At the same time his attack was parried and a lightning-fast riposte struck him in the chest. '*Touché!*' cried Signor Horatio. 'Akiko wins!'

But Jack didn't care who had won or lost. He only cared about what Rose had to say.

'Sorry, Jack, nothing to do with your sister,' said Rose, answering his querying look. 'But they have found Rakesby . . . or at least what's left of him!'

33

POMMELLING

'*Can you see how Jack invites an attack?*' whispered Signor Horatio to Rose, as they leant over the balcony watching the duel play out in the courtyard below. 'He's intentionally left his high outside flank open to encourage Akiko to strike there.'

'Then why isn't she attacking?' asked Rose under her breath.

A sly smile crept across Signor Horatio's lips. 'She's too clever to fall for that old trick.'

In the courtyard, Jack and Akiko warily circled each other, rapier and parrying dagger in hand. The two students had a right to be cautious. Over the course of the week, their sword master had introduced them to feints, parries, presses and binds. He'd shown them how to glide down an opponent's blade. How to void an attack. Perform circular thrusts. And strike with accuracy at the hands, face, throat, eyes and even the teeth. Their previous experience with the samurai sword had meant they both picked up the rapier techniques swiftly, and they progressed faster than the average student. But it was their unique training in the

Two Heavens that had enabled them to master the dual combination of rapier and dagger so quickly.

Akiko stamped her front foot loudly on the flagstones. Jack tensed for an attack. But none came.

'Nice attempt at an *appel* by Akiko to startle and distract Jack,' whispered Signor Horatio approvingly.

But Jack was used to *kiai* shouts in his *taijutsu* training and didn't overreact. Instead he made a feint to Akiko's hip. She parried his sword and immediately responded with a riposte. Jack countered with a beat parry, knocking Akiko's blade aside and leaving her open to a thrust to the heart. He lunged forward. Akiko leapt back, recovering with a deflection, followed by a glide along his blade. His rapier forced off line, Jack missed his target as she retaliated with a jab to his face. The leather tip almost caught his eye, but Jack ducked at the last second, whipping his sword under hers and fending off the assault.

'What a conversation of blades!' exclaimed Signor Horatio, his eyes wide as he followed the action. 'Did you see that *prise de fer*? How she took Jack's blade with a bind and forced it on to a different line?'

Rose nodded as if she knew what the sword master was talking about.

Panting from his exertions, Jack retreated across the courtyard. After numerous bouts, he and Akiko were now familiar with each other's personal fencing style. While she had beaten him in every duel so far, he was learning her tells and becoming wise to her tricks. He was no longer fooled by her every feint, or beaten by every riposte she made. Sometimes he could gauge just by the angle of her lead foot the attack she intended, at others by the way she held her head. Occasionally, though, he had no clue at all –

And there it was! The twitch near the hilt. He knew she was about to lunge, but this time he'd get in first. Jack thrust with his rapier a moment before she did. Their blades passed each other, flying like silver arrows for their targets. Yet Jack felt the leather tip of Akiko's rapier press against *his* throat first . . . his own sword still an inch short of Akiko's slender neck.

'*Touché!* Akiko wins . . . *again*,' Signor Horatio declared, as Rose applauded the outcome.

His rapier still held out straight, Jack studied his sword arm against Akiko's and frowned. 'How do you *always* manage to hit me first when your arm is shorter than mine?' He narrowed his eyes in suspicion. 'Are you using a longer sword?'

Akiko shook her head. 'Of course not.'

'Then how do you do it?' asked Jack, exasperated.

'Pommelling,' she replied.

Jack looked to Signor Horatio; he'd clearly missed something during their lessons. 'What's *pommelling*?'

The sword master leant over the balcony and grinned. 'While you've been keeping a lookout for your sister, I've had the honour of tutoring Akiko in some more advanced techniques.' He pointed to her sword hand. 'By gripping the hilt at the pommel, one can extend the reach of a rapier by a good few inches. That can make *all* the difference in a duel. But it is a trade-off. One loses some control over the blade work, so you need a strong grip and a skilled hand to pommel effectively.'

'So Akiko *cheated*?' questioned Jack with good humour.

'No, *signor*, she won fair and square,' Signor Horatio replied, 'and, as you well know, that's all that counts in a real duel –'

Suddenly the doors into the courtyard burst open and Yori came running in, ushering a young lad ahead of him. 'Jack! Jack!' he cried. 'This boy says he's seen your sister!'

Jack rushed over, his heart in his mouth. 'You have? Where?'

The lad, dressed in a leather apron and smock, his hair a tangle of wiry black curls, struggled to get his breath back. (Yori had clearly dragged the witness at high speed across town.) 'Aye . . .' he panted, 'I seen her . . . or a girl that looks like that one in that there locket o' yours.'

'But *where* did you see her?' pressed Jack.

'In the garden,' replied the boy, wiping the sweat from his brow. 'I was 'elping me father deliver a cartload of wine and beer they'd ordered. I think they must be 'aving a party or summut –'

'But what garden? WHERE?' demanded Jack in exasperation.

'Lupus Hall.'

34

LUPUS HALL

The coach rattled along the potholed highway, its iron-rimmed wheels making the bones of its occupants shudder. Jack sat rocking between Akiko and Yori; Signor Horatio and Rose perched on the seat opposite. They passed rolling fields, with the earth stubbled and brown after the harvest, and Jack stared impatiently at them out of the window. The coach they'd hired couldn't go fast enough for him. He gripped the hilt of his *katana* in one hand; his other nervously thumbed the pommel of the rapier Signor Horatio had lent him. Jack hoped that he wouldn't have to use them, that he could recover his sister without a fight, but he knew from experience that Sir Toby was rash and quick to take up arms. So he was ready to duel for his sister's life if it came to it.

'We're here!' the driver called out gruffly.

The coach passed beneath a large stone gateway and into the grounds of a country estate. The rutted road turned to gravel and, as they approached the main house, lush lawns took over from the pastured fields. Marble statues of Roman emperors formed an imperial procession up to a stone bridge, beyond which stood the imposing manor house of red brick, tiled roofs and tall corkscrew chimneys. Four storeys high in places and protected by a wide square moat, the house was more akin to a castle than a country residence.

Crossing the bridge, the coach clattered through a gatehouse into a large cobbled courtyard, where the driver drew the horses to a halt. Jack and his friends clambered out, stiff from the ride and cautious at their unannounced arrival. Signor Horatio paid the driver as Jack's eyes swept round the yard, deserted apart from another coach which looked to be the one that had borne his sister away. He gazed up at all the glazed windows encircling the inner yard, astounded by the huge quantity of glass in one building. Suddenly his breath caught in his throat. High up on the top floor, through the smallest window, a pale girl's face peered down at him –

'*Fletcher?* Is that you?' boomed a voice.

Jack spun round to see a portly figure with a pointed white beard emerge from the main house.

'Sir Henry Wilkes!' gasped Jack. 'What are *you* doing here?'

'I might ask you the same, Jack! This is my family home,' Sir Henry replied. Jack snatched another glance at the upper window but the face had gone. 'Too much talk of plague doctors in London,' Sir Henry went on. 'So I thought I'd escape to the country – but it seems the doctors are everywhere!'

'*Everywhere?*' gulped Yori, a visible tremble making the bells of his *shakujō* ring.

'Yes, I fear so. Aylesbury, Buckingham, Banbury . . . they've all been visited. The last sighting of them was in the village of Kineton.' Sir Henry shook his head in dismay. 'I pray that the plague doesn't spread any further north. Kineton is little more than ten miles from here!'

Jack exchanged a troubled look with Akiko and Yori. The four ninjas must have picked up their trail. *Are they* that *close to Stratford?* thought Jack. The need to find Jess had just become even more pressing.

Sir Henry suddenly noticed their sword master and squinted. 'Why, Signor Horatio Palavicino!' he exclaimed. 'I thought you'd returned to your homeland, sir.'

Doffing his feathered hat, Signor Horatio bowed. '*Che piacere vederti*, Sir Henry. No, I've been in Stratford establishing a new fencing school. In fact, you're talking to some of my best students.'

Sir Henry raised an eyebrow at Jack, then laughed. 'You really are a jack of all trades! Well, come in – let me offer you some refreshment. This is fortunate timing indeed! I'm holding a masque tonight – you know, a masked ball – and you'll be among some most distinguished company.'

'Will Sir Toby Nashe be here?' asked Jack.

'Why, yes, of course. He's a good acquaintance of mine,' replied Sir Henry. 'Do you know him?'

'We've met . . .' Jack admitted. 'I believe he might know where my sister Jess is.'

Sir Henry frowned. 'Your sister? You haven't found her yet?'

'I spotted her a few days ago with Sir Toby in Stratford,' Jack replied. 'And a brewer's boy swears he saw her here at Lupus Hall when he was delivering beer the other day . . . and *I* believe I just saw her in *that* window.' He pointed to the upper floor.

Sir Henry's face went pale. 'Oh . . . then you've seen it too!' he said, peering up anxiously at the blank window.

'*It?*' questioned Jack, suddenly confused.

'The ghost girl,' Sir Henry replied gravely. 'To be honest, no one goes up there. The attic is empty. The servants say this manor house is haunted – and I'm inclined to believe it too. But I suppose that's what comes from acquiring a house on the cheap from a fleeing Catholic.' Sir Henry forced a laugh, then stifled his amusement when he saw the indignant look on Signor Horatio's face. 'I'm sorry. I forget that you're of that religion. But, well, we *are* in England, don't you know.'

'*Certo, signor,*' said Signor Horatio with a tight smile.

'Are you telling me it was a ghost I saw?' said Jack.

Sir Henry nodded. 'Come inside and I'll explain,' he said, ushering Jack and the others through to a vaulted entrance hall. 'This manor house was originally designed and built by Humphrey Pakington, but Nicholas Owen had a hand in its construction too. That devious Jesuit had a knack for concealing priest holes within the design.'

'What's a priest hole?' asked Yori.

Sir Henry stopped at the foot of a main staircase: a square spiral set of wooden steps, each flight leading to one of the four floors of the house. Ascending the staircase a little, he lifted the wood on the fifth step to reveal a hidden cavity beneath. 'It's where traitors such as Humphrey Pakington hid Catholic priests from the authorities,' he explained darkly. 'You see, Pakington was a Catholic who refused to give up his religion and become a Protestant. When Queen Elizabeth passed a law banning Catholic priests, he had his friend Owen build secret hiding places for them in his house. This manor has as many holes as a Dutch cheese! I doubt I've managed to find them all.' He lowered the wooden step back into place. 'The story goes that a servant girl hid in one of these priest holes; she became trapped and was never found again, and her restless spirit haunts the house still.' Sir Henry raised an ominous eyebrow at Jack. 'That's who you may have seen in the attic. But enough of the ghost stories! Sir Toby will be here this evening. You can ask him yourself about your sister, but I daresay he'll be perplexed by what you tell him. As far as I'm aware, he hasn't been in Stratford this past week – he's still travelling up from London.'

Jack frowned. He was *certain* that it had been Sir Toby with his sister. *Could I have been mistaken?* he thought.

'In the meantime,' continued Sir Henry, 'I've something that may be of interest to you and your warrior friends.' He waved them through to the next room: a Gallery of Arms. Lining the wood-panelled walls were racks of iron-tipped pikes, a dozen longbows each with a sheaf of arrows, twenty or so arquebuses and flintlock pistols, several broadswords and a variety of rapiers. Shining sets of armour were mounted beside a collection of crested steel helmets. And above this impressive array of weapons hung a coat of arms – a white stag and a red wolf rampant either side of a black-and-white shield.

'There's enough for an entire army here!' said Signor Horatio, his eyes widening.

'Probably not an army,' Sir Henry conceded, 'but certainly enough to fulfil my duty of supplying the local militia.' He patted an arquebus rifle. 'All the weapons are loaded and sharpened so they're ready at a moment's notice.'

Jack examined one of the broadswords. He weighed it in his hand. It felt like a sledgehammer compared with the finesse of a rapier and the elegance of his *katana*. Akiko seemed even more taken by the display. She immediately went over to the longbows, comparing their D-shaped curves to the serpentine shape of her *yumi*.

'By all means, try one out,' offered Sir Henry.

Akiko selected a bow and strained as she attempted to pull back its string. 'The draw strength must be at least double that of my *yumi*!' she exclaimed.

'They can shoot up to *four hundred* yards,' Sir Henry said proudly.

Akiko's mouth fell open. 'That's twice the range of a Japanese bow!' she said, impressed.

Yori appeared more taken with a huge portrait on the opposite wall. It was of their host, in a steel breastplate, striking a heroic pose.

'A fine work, don't you think?' boasted Sir Henry, crossing his arms and assuming a stance very similar to the one in his portrait.

Yori leaned in, studying it closely. 'Mmm, wonderful brushwork,' he murmured.

'You get a better perspective from here,' advised their host.

Yori stepped back a little and nodded his head in respectful appreciation.

'I think the *further* away, the better,' mumbled Signor Horatio under his breath. Rose overheard his jibe at Sir Henry and smothered a giggle.

Missing the remark himself, Sir Henry escorted them

through to the main hall, a high-ceilinged, wood-panelled chamber with lattice casement windows overlooking the lawns and formal knot garden. A group of musicians were setting up at the far end, while actors were rehearsing their parts and scenery was being erected upon a makeshift stage. Servants bustled to and fro, putting up decorations, stacking the central fireplace with fresh wood, and preparing a long table for what promised to be a sumptuous banquet.

'This is the Great Hall where the festivities and feasting will take place this evening,' Sir Henry explained. 'Now if you'll excuse me, I have much to do. Please be back here at six o'clock sharp. Until then, make yourselves at home. I'll arrange with the servants to prepare rooms for you on the second floor and leave costumes on the beds. Do please dress up this evening – it is a masque, after all!'

Their host strode out of the hall, barking orders to his servants as he went. The five of them stood for a moment amid the chaos and manic preparations. Then Rose said, 'Do you believe Sir Henry's story about the ghost?'

'Well, *he* seemed convinced,' said Signor Horatio.

'In Japan we call ghosts *yūrei*,' explained Yori. 'Such spirits are thought to be the souls of people robbed of life and denied a peaceful afterlife. So his story would fit in with our beliefs.'

'But I swear it was *Jess's* face I saw in that window,' said Jack. 'Not some ghost.'

'Then why don't we take a look?' suggested Akiko. 'After all, Sir Henry did say to make ourselves at home.'

'We should be cautious,' Yori warned, as Jack and Akiko approached the small wooden door that led to the attic room.

The narrow corridor was gloomy and threaded with spider's webs, suggesting no one had come this way for quite some time. It had taken a good deal of exploration just to find the right room. The manor house was a warren of corridors, staircases and chambers. Jack had had to return to the courtyard twice to gauge which window he'd seen Jess's face in and work out from that which part of the building to search next. Rose and Signor Horatio had elected to stay at the foot of the main staircase as lookouts, in case they needed to make a quick exit.

Jack's hand hesitated on the latch. 'You're right,' he said, drawing his rapier. 'Sir Toby could be here too.'

'It's not Sir Toby I'm worried about,' Yori replied, a slight tremor in his voice. 'It's the ghost. *Yūrei* often haunt this world to exact revenge, and will not rest until they have done so.'

'There's nothing to fear,' said Akiko kindly. 'We're not in Japan.'

Yori's eyes grew wide in the gloom. 'Ghosts are ghosts wherever they are! *Yūrei* can never be destroyed. Desire is the key to such malevolent spirits – they want something. This is what drives them, gives them purpose. They may just want to pass on a message to a loved one . . . or tear their victims apart in revenge for their own murder! But whatever they want, it's best not to seek such ghosts out.'

Ghosts or not, Jack had to know one way or another whether his sister was there. He tried the latch. It was stiff but gave way under a little effort. The door creaked slowly open to reveal a surprisingly small and drab room. The floorboards were bare, an old writing table stood by the window and there was a disused fireplace in the far corner. The timber-beamed walls were crumbling where the damp had eaten into the brickwork and the musty smell of mildew hung in the chill air.

'Jess . . .?' asked Jack tentatively, almost fearfully.

There was no reply.

Jack stepped inside, the floorboards groaning underfoot. For a moment he thought he could hear whispering, but, when he listened hard, all was quiet. Akiko joined him in the room.

Yori peeked in, keeping to the threshold. 'Do you see anyone or . . . *anything*?'

Jack shook his head in dismay and sheathed his sword. 'The room's empty.' His heart felt equally empty. His expectation at finding Jess shrank to disappointment.

Akiko ran a finger through the sheen of dust on the table. 'It looks like it's been empty for a while.'

Growing bolder, Yori entered the gloomy attic room. He gazed nervously around at the dank walls, keeping away from the darkest corners. Jack peered out of the small lattice window into the courtyard below. The guests were starting to arrive for the masked ball, which meant Sir Toby would be arriving too.

A floorboard suddenly creaked, making Yori jump. 'If Jess isn't here, then . . . perhaps that servant girl's ghost . . . Can we go, *now*?'

Jack nodded and they headed for the door.

35

THE MASQUE

Flaming torches illuminated the night, fiery beacons lining the paths and guiding the procession of costumed guests towards the masque. Greek gods, Egyptian pharaohs, Turkish sultans, medieval knights, fairy kings and queens . . . a fantastical treasury of characters and opulent costumes wended their way over the bridge and into the manor house. On arrival in the Great Hall, they were greeted by servants dressed as mythical creatures and served with goblets of wine and plates of sweetmeats. Above the hubbub of noise and chatter, the musicians played sprightly tunes to which the guests were encouraged to dance and make merry. At the same time, the actors, in biblical dress, played out scenes from the tale of King Solomon and the Queen of Sheba for everyone's amusement.

'I've never seen anything quite like it,' said Akiko breathlessly, as they entered through an archway of glittering blossoms.

'Nor have I!' replied Rose, gazing in awe at the sheer extravagance. 'This is a world away from the life I've known.'

But Jack barely noticed the lavish decorations or gargantuan buffet. His eyes were trained on the multitude of guests, seeking out Sir Toby's pompous moustachioed face. With everyone wearing masks, however, it was proving an impossible task.

'Jack? Is that you?' called a hearty voice. A rotund Egyptian king in a golden face mask came barrelling up to them. Sir Henry lifted the mask and winked. 'Look, it's me! I must say, I like your choice of costume – very jolly.'

Not wishing to give Sir Toby Nashe any warning of their presence, Jack and his friends had decided to get into the spirit of the ball and wear the fancy-dress costumes their host had provided. Jack wore the red-and-black chequered suit of Harlequin, its full-face black mask reminding Jack of the hood of a ninja's *shinobi shōzoku*.

Akiko was wearing a long, shimmering, red silk kimono, complete with Jack's *katana* on her hip, and a fearsome battle mask adapted from a knight's costume to look more like a traditional Japanese *mempō*. Sir Henry stepped back to take her in. 'May I ask who you have come as?' he enquired.

'Tomoe Gozen,' replied Akiko, 'the greatest female samurai to have ever lived.'

Sir Henry raised an eyebrow. 'Well, it seems female warriors are the theme,' he went on, now admiring Rose's costume: a pleated green gown with silver armoured breastplate and a half-visor helmet. 'If your armour, shield, spear and red hair are anything to go by, I'm guessing you're Boudicca, the Queen of the Celts.'

Rose curtseyed. 'Full marks, Sir Henry.'

Beside her stood Signor Horatio, who'd chosen to come as a Roman emperor, resplendent in a white toga, a crown of golden laurel leaves on his head, and a decorative mask covering one side of his face. Unable to bear being parted from his cherished rapier, he still carried the weapon on his hip, its sheath slipped into the belt of his toga.

Meanwhile, Yori had opted for a simple costume made out of a bedsheet. He'd painted his face white and had somehow managed to find an old wig. He'd blackened it with soot and teased out the hairs, and now wore it in a long, dishevelled mess over his face instead of a mask. When Sir Henry enquired as to who he represented, Yori dangled his hands limply from his wrists and glided across the floor, moaning and groaning, 'I'm a *yūrei*!'

Sir Henry looked bemused, and Akiko explained for him. 'Your story of the servant girl inspired him to dress up as a Japanese ghost!'

'Well, he frightens the wits out of me!' replied their host, laughing. When a servant came up offering drinks to the group, Sir Henry pulled Jack to one side and whispered, 'By chance, have you had any more thoughts about returning to the Japans? I've just been conversing with Sir Isaac and he's decidedly keen to press on with the trading expedition, as am I.'

Jack was taken by surprise by his host's question, particularly at that moment. 'Not really . . .' he admitted. 'I've yet to find my sister.'

'Of course, how insensitive of me,' blustered Sir Henry, putting an arm round Jack's shoulders. 'I realize her welfare must be your first priority. However, whether you find her or not, you must have considered your future, no?'

'My future depends on being reunited with Jess,' explained Jack. 'And I have no plans to leave so soon after my arrival.'

Sir Henry withdrew his arm. 'I understand,' he said. 'You must do what you think is best.'

Grabbing a goblet of wine from a passing servant, Sir Henry downed the entire contents in one gulp. He suddenly seemed lost in deep thought and the conversation appeared to be over.

'Do you know if Sir Toby's here?' asked Jack.

'I'm sure he's here somewhere,' Sir Henry replied distract-edly, sweeping his gaze over his guests. 'But I'm afraid I've no idea what he's come as. But I'll keep an eye out for him, you may be certain of that.' Then, pulling his golden mask back on, he plunged into the thick of the festivities.

Jack watched Sir Henry go, wondering why he was behaving somewhat strangely. He put it down to the stress of hosting such a lavish masked ball. Jack rejoined his friends near the banqueting table. 'Has anyone spotted Sir Toby yet?' he asked.

Signor Horatio shook his head. 'No sign of the scoundrel, I'm afraid.'

Jack peered down the length of the hall. Masked dancers weaved in and out, performing an elaborate pavane, but none offered up a clue as to their real identity. Jack felt his frustration growing. Sir Toby had to be *somewhere* amid the guests – and, dare he hope, maybe even his sister was there too!

'Perhaps we should spread out?' suggested Akiko. But, before they could move, the musicians fell silent and the actors gathered on the stage for the play. The Queen of Sheba, resplendent in her jewelled gown, presented gifts to King Solomon as the players enacted their fabled romance before the hushed audience.

Rose whispered, 'This ball must have cost Sir Henry a fortune!'

'A fortune he doesn't have, as far as I'm aware,' muttered Signor Horatio.

Jack frowned. 'What do you mean?'

Signor Horatio leant in and lowered his voice further. 'It's perhaps improper of me to talk ill of our host . . . but before I was forced to leave London, I heard that Sir Henry, having made some unwise investments over the years, had lost *all* his money.'

Akiko turned to the sword master. 'So why is he putting on a masked ball if he has no money?'

'For show, I presume,' replied Signor Horatio. 'He's calculated that, by appearing to afford a lavish lifestyle such as this, he will convince his creditors that he's a man of power and influence and good social standing and that, more importantly, he can repay his debts.'

'Ah, but all that glitters is not gold,' said Yori, wiping his finger through the fairy dust sprinkled on an extravagant floral arrangement.

'Too true,' replied Signor Horatio. 'You can be as bankrupt as a beggar, but if you look rich and act rich, any fool will lend you money.'

'Well, we had best enjoy his hospitality while we can,' said Rose, selecting a crystallized date from the banqueting table and popping it into her mouth.

Jack now began to understand why Sir Henry was so desperate to send another expedition to the Japans. A lucrative trading mission would earn back his lost wealth and, with Sir Isaac willing to bankroll the voyage, Jack was his ticket to the Far East and the prospect of untold riches.

The play ended to wild applause and the music struck up again, heralding the start of the dances. The constant movement of the guests now made it doubly difficult to keep track of everyone. After several turns, a man dressed as Zeus, in a toga with a thunderbolt headdress and porcelain-white mask, approached Akiko.

'May I have the pleasure of this dance?' asked the suitor, holding out a hand.

Akiko hesitated and glanced uncertainly in Jack's direction, knowing they weren't there to dance.

'It's bad manners to refuse an invitation,' said Rose. 'Isn't that right, Signor Horatio?' she added, offering her own hand to the sword master.

'*Certo, signorina!*' Signor Horatio smiled as he escorted Rose on to the dance floor.

With a polite bow of her head, Akiko accepted Zeus's invitation and followed him into the centre of the room, where the other guests had begun a processional galliard dance. Jack watched Zeus expertly whirl Akiko round and lead her smoothly through the set moves. Then her partner began to show off with hops, twists, sidesteps and high kicks, prompting a round of applause from the audience as well as Akiko. Jack felt a pang of jealousy at the man's dazzling display and its evident effect on Akiko. He turned to the banqueting table as a means of distraction, choosing from a plate of exotic foods something he'd never tried before: a slice of potato. As he sampled the strange vegetable, Jack looked from guest to guest, trying to work out which masked person was Sir Toby. Beside him stood a squat Turkish sultan and a tall medieval knight gorging on the sumptuous delights. Neither looked to be Sir Toby.

Jack wandered through the hall, casting his eyes over fairies and sprites, kings and queens, gods and goddesses. Then he spotted the pale ghostly form of Yori by the fireplace. His friend was stood upon a chair and studying Sir Henry's coat of arms hanging over the mantelpiece. Jack sighed with exasperation. Why weren't his friends focusing on the task at hand? *They're either dancing or gazing at paintings!* he thought. As he headed in Yori's direction, the music ended and Akiko returned with Zeus.

'You're a magnificent dancer,' complimented Akiko, slightly out of breath.

Zeus inclined his head and replied smoothly, 'It always helps to have a magnificent partner.'

Jack felt like he might be sick – and it wasn't because of the potato. Then Yori appeared beside him and whispered, 'Jack, we need to talk. I've –'

'Ladies and gentlemen!' Sir Henry proclaimed loudly as he stood upon the stage in his Egyptian costume, swaying slightly. 'The time has come to reveal who we *really* are!'

With a flourish, their host removed his golden mask to thunderous applause. Then the rest of the guests followed suit, casting aside their disguises. There was much laughter and many shrieks of surprise. Ignoring Yori's insistent tug on his sleeve, Jack removed his black Harlequin mask to have a better look for Sir Toby . . . at the same time as Zeus took off his porcelain-white face . . .

Their eyes locked upon one another.

'*YOU!*' cried Zeus, his jaw dropping in outraged disbelief. 'But I thought you'd drowned!'

36

FIRST BLOOD

Jack was standing toe to toe with Sir Toby Nashe – the belligerent dueller who'd almost run him through in Moorfields . . . the liar who'd got him arrested and almost hanged in London . . . the mystery suitor who'd taken his sister! Jack felt his fury rise up inside him like a furnace fire.

But Sir Toby appeared equally outraged. His preened moustache quivering and his face as thunderous as Zeus himself, Sir Toby grabbed Jack by the lapels of his chequered Harlequin suit. 'You won't escape this time, you slippery fish!' he spat. 'Sir Edmund! Sir Francis! Come, quickly!'

At once, the sultan and the knight beside the banqueting table dropped their wine goblets and surrounded Jack, cutting off any way of retreat. But Jack, for his part, was also swiftly backed up by reinforcements: Akiko, Yori, Rose and Signor Horatio all rushed to his aid. With a sharp upward thrust of his forearms, Jack broke Sir Toby's grip on his costume and pushed the self-righteous bully away. Sir Toby stumbled and fell on to his backside, much to the amusement of the other guests.

'How dare you!' he cried, his face flushing as red as his

hair in mortified fury. 'I'll have you thrown into the Tower of London for that! Put in irons and hung by your hands! Stretched on the rack until your arms pop out of their sockets! Tossed into the pit!'

The guests sniggered at his outrageous threats. But Jack wasn't laughing.

'It's *you* who'll be put in the Tower,' said Jack. 'Now, tell me, where's my sister?'

'Your sister?' sneered Sir Toby, a dark gleam entering his eyes. 'I've no idea what you're talking about.'

'Of course you do. You've abducted her!'

'That's slander!' snarled Sir Toby, scrambling to his feet with the help of his stooge Sir Edmund. 'I'll not have my reputation besmirched like this. Seize the rascal!'

Sir Francis was the first to advance on Jack, but Signor Horatio blocked his path and a tussle broke out between them. No one else stepped forward to apprehend Jack, so Sir Toby took it upon himself. As Jack prepared to fend off his foe, Akiko and Rose squared up to Sir Edmund. The portly sultan, nostrils flaring and belly wobbling, blurted, 'I don't fight *women*.'

'That's mighty noble of you,' said Rose, before bopping him on the nose with her shield.

As Sir Edmund howled in pain and Sir Toby grappled with Jack, Yori became trapped in the middle of the fray, not knowing which way to turn. Sir Henry bustled over, pushing through the throng of guests, who were all clamouring to watch the altercation. 'Stop this at once! This is a ball, not a bearpit!' he yelled, putting a swift end to the fight.

With a look of outraged indignation, Sir Toby spluttered, 'Did you invite this ruffian and his foreign scum?'

'They were last-minute guests,' explained Sir Henry. 'What offence has Jack caused you, Sir Toby?'

'This upstart is a wanted criminal!' Sir Toby proclaimed, stabbing an accusatory finger at Jack. 'He escaped the hangman's noose little more than two weeks ago, after being convicted of trying to rob me and my fellow gentlemen at sword-point. He's just pushed me over – and, to cap it all, he's accused me of kidnapping his sister!'

'Have you, Sir Toby? Have you kidnapped Jack's sister?' enquired Sir Henry.

Sir Toby stared at his host in perplexed astonishment. 'Of course not! It's an outrageous claim.'

'I *saw* you with Jess in Stratford!' said Jack fiercely. 'And I *never* tried to rob you. You are a barefaced liar, Sir Toby!'

Gasps of horror burst from the gathered guests and once more Sir Toby's face turned as red as his hair with rage. 'Once again you have given me the lie, sirrah!' he snapped. 'I won't have my name so publicly besmirched!'

All of a sudden Sir Toby pulled a dagger from the folds of his toga and lunged at Jack.

'Not so fast!' said Signor Horatio, drawing his rapier with such speed that its tip was at Sir Toby's throat before the man had barely taken half a step.

'Signor Horatio Palavicino!' sneered Sir Toby. 'Why am I not surprised to find *you* among such lowly company?'

The sword master pressed the rapier tip harder beneath Sir Toby's jaw, threatening to draw blood. 'Still the sore loser, aren't you?' he said.

Sir Toby narrowed his eyes. 'I didn't lose. *You* cheated!'

'*You* shot me!'

A tense stand-off occurred as the two parties venomously eyed one another.

'Gentlemen, gentlemen, perhaps we can settle this *disagreement* with a gentlemanly duel?' Sir Henry suggested, lightly resting his hand upon the rapier's blade and encouraging Signor Horatio to lower it. 'That way we can avoid *too much* bloodshed at my ball.'

At the merest suggestion of an arranged fight, a chant of 'DUEL! DUEL! DUEL!' went up from the eager guests.

'I have no interest in challenging Signor Horatio again,' declared Sir Toby, lifting his nose snootily into the air.

'Scared of losing again, are you?' Signor Horatio taunted.

'No, of course not. My beef is with Jack Fletcher,' Sir Toby replied haughtily, 'and Jack Fletcher alone.'

Sir Henry raised an eyebrow and cast a troubled glance in Jack's direction. 'And how about you, Jack?'

'I want the truth,' replied Jack. 'If Sir Toby won't willingly tell me, then I'll duel him for the truth.'

'So be it,' said Sir Henry with a sigh, 'a duel to first blood.'

'But he gave me the lie, so it should be to the *death*!' Sir Toby protested dramatically.

'My house, my rules,' said Sir Henry firmly. Jack realized that his host wasn't restricting the fight purely out of the goodness of his heart; Sir Henry had a personal interest in keeping Jack alive for the hoped-for trading mission. Besides, Jack had no desire either in killing Sir Toby. He only needed to force him into revealing Jess's whereabouts.

Jack found himself being borne into the Gallery of Arms by the enthusiastic crowd. It seemed the whole ball wanted to watch, and Rose even had to keep some of the guests at bay with her shield as Jack readied himself for the fight. Yori took the Harlequin mask from him and Akiko presented his *katana*.

'No *foreign* weapons!' said Sir Toby contemptuously, as he selected the sharpest rapier from the rack on the wall. 'This is a proper *English* duel.'

'Use my rapier instead,' said Signor Horatio, offering up his blade of finest Italian steel.

'Pah!' Sir Toby sneered. 'Your sword won't save him, Signor Horatio.'

Signor Horatio responded with an assured smile. 'I've not only given Jack my weapon, *signor*, but my training too!'

'Then you really are putting the poor lad at a disadvantage!' scoffed Sir Toby, as he made several practice swipes with his sword, its tip whistling through the air. The guests laughed heartily at his jibe, but Sir Toby's grim expression suggested he was more unsettled by Signor Horatio's words than he let on.

Ignoring his opponent's taunts, Jack weighed his sword master's rapier in his hand. It was as light as a feather and quick as lightning. The grip felt like the handshake of a good friend, the blade was long and slender, and the hilt was expertly crafted into a helix of steel to deflect and catch an enemy's blade. It was truly a magnificent weapon.

Akiko passed him a parrying dagger from the rack. 'Remember,' she whispered, 'offence is defence. Parry and riposte. Keep your guard up before your face. Don't overreach –'

'I'll be fine,' Jack reassured her. But he didn't feel fine. His heart thudded and his blood pumped loudly in his ears, his palms became slick with sweat and his breathing elevated. In this duel, he wasn't fighting for *his* life; he was fighting for his sister's.

37

THE TRUTH

'*En garde!*' cried Sir Toby, dropping into a warding stance. All the guests fell silent in tense anticipation as Jack took up position in the centre of the gallery. From painful experience, he knew Sir Toby was a formidable swordsman. He'd have to fight at the top of his game if he was to have any chance of defeating his opponent. On the sidelines, Yori shifted nervously from foot to foot, appearing even more anxious about the impending duel than Jack was.

Sir Toby stared scornfully at Jack, his whole stance exuding a sense of superiority. Jack returned the glare with a blank expression, trying not to give away any of his thoughts, feelings or fears. Whether with weapons or with fists, a fight was first fought in the mind; a battle of wills often determined the outcome. Jack was well versed in such mental combat, so he didn't let his opponent's fierce look faze him, despite the rush of adrenalin coursing through his body.

'*Allez!*' cried Sir Henry, commencing the duel.

The two swordsmen stood poised with dagger and rapier in hand, neither willing to make the first move. The crowd watched with bated breath as the two slowly circled one another. This time, Sir Toby was evidently more cautious than in their previous duel. So Jack stamped his front foot, performing an *appel* and making a feint with his sword.

But Sir Toby wasn't taken in by the tactic. He stood his ground and didn't even bother parrying the fake attack. 'Is that all you've taught your mouse, Signor Horatio? To squeak?'

Another round of laughter rippled through the crowd. In that moment of disturbance, Sir Toby lunged, his rapier tip lancing for Jack's left eye. Thanks only to the rearward stance Jack had been taught was he saved a blinding – the tip stopped a fraction short of his eyeball. Parrying the blade away with his dagger, Jack responded with a rushed riposte. Sir Toby easily deflected the strike and advanced with another jab to the face. Beating the rapier off, Jack bluffed an attack to the head before lunging for the body. Sir Toby leapt aside and blocked the blade with his own dagger. Then he began to force Jack down the hall with a surge of lunges and thrusts.

'I'll teach you to give me the lie!' snarled Sir Toby.

'You're the one that's lying!' replied Jack, frantically fending off the attacks. 'I *know* you have my sister!'

The guests began applauding Sir Toby's virtuoso display of swordsmanship. And, despite a growing frustration at failing to land a hit, Sir Toby started to show off. He danced round Jack, executing flamboyant blocks and dramatic lunges, playing to his audience.

'You're dressed as a fool and you fight like a fool!' taunted Sir Toby, his rapier probing Jack's guard for weaknesses.

Jack was forced to retreat under the barrage of blows.

'Don't dance to his rhythm!' Signor Horatio called out. 'Steal his sword and attack in every defence!'

Heeding his sword master's advice, Jack managed to perform a *prise de fer* – taking control of Sir Toby's blade and shifting it into another line. This broke his opponent's rhythm, allowing Jack to retaliate with a stab to the throat. Sir Toby blocked it and immediately countered. But now, for every deflection made, Jack had a follow-up attack. The week of intense training under Signor Horatio had paid dividends and Jack found he was able to match Sir Toby strike for strike, thrust for thrust. The clink of steel rang out through the gallery as the two duellers fought furiously.

The crowd now applauded Jack's comeback and soon shouts of encouragement to Sir Toby were met by calls of *'Jack! Jack! Jack!'*, his friends' voices loudest among his supporters.

No longer overwhelmed by the speed or reach of his enemy's attacks, Jack regained some ground. Still Sir Toby showed off, hopping and skipping round Jack's rapier like a springtime hare. But Jack didn't discourage this boastful behaviour; he was biding his time for the moment his opponent made a fatal mistake.

'You couldn't stick a pin in a pincushion!' Sir Toby laughed, avoiding Jack's strike to the hip and countering with a circular thrust. And *there* was the mistake. Sir Toby had inadvertently opened up his guard with the circular attack.

Jack made a lunge at Sir Toby's exposed heart . . . but immediately found his rapier pressed off line and Sir Toby's own blade heading for the target of *his* heart. Jack resisted the press, jumping aside, but the blade tore through his costume. A gasp went up from the crowd, followed by a hesitant shout of 'First blood!'

However, when Sir Toby retracted the blade, there was no blood. The sword had pierced only cloth, not flesh. Before Sir Toby could attempt a second thrust, Jack rapidly retreated again.

'Don't be fooled by his flashy sword work, *signor*!' called Signor Horatio from the sidelines. 'He's showing off on purpose to draw you in.'

'I realize that now!' gasped Jack before resuming his attack.

But, whatever he tried, Sir Toby had a counter. Thrust met parry. Lunge met block. Feints were ignored and binds resisted. He even performed a second *prise de fer* to no avail. It seemed that Sir Toby had got bored with playing with Jack and was now fighting to finish the duel.

Jack was at a loss as to what to do. He was flagging and on the verge of losing. He *couldn't* be defeated. He had to force Sir Toby to surrender, to give up what he knew about Jess. Suddenly, Jack remembered how Akiko had beaten him every time in training. With a quick adjustment to his grip, Jack pommelled his rapier. A moment later, he spotted a gap in Sir Toby's defence and stabbed for his opponent's face. The sudden extended reach took Sir Toby off guard . . .

In a miracle of reaction he turned his cheek at the very last second and the rapier tip missed him by a mere whisker.

Beating away Jack's rapier, Sir Toby snorted a laugh. 'Don't go thinking Signor Horatio's underhand tactics will outwit me. He may have got away with it *once*, but never twice!'

Sir Toby now went on the offensive, driving Jack down the gallery with a relentless flurry of jabs and thrusts.

Jack was out of ideas. Sir Toby was wise to all the tricks and techniques of fencing Jack knew. His opponent couldn't be fooled or faked, and Jack realized it was only a matter of time before he would be run through with Sir Toby's blade. How he wished he could wield his *katana* now! That would at least give him a different edge over his opponent. He could do Flint-and-Spark strike . . . Autumn Leaf . . . or even Mountain to Sea. Then Jack recalled how similar the parry and riposte technique was to Masamoto's Flint-and-Spark strike. *What if I use an unfamiliar Two Heavens technique with the rapier?* he thought. East meeting West. A fusion of style and weapon.

As Sir Toby thrust for his heart, Jack retaliated with an Autumn Leaf strike. Surging forward, he hit Sir Toby's rapier twice in quick succession with his blade. To Jack's delight, the sudden and deft double strike knocked the rapier from Sir Toby's grip and it clattered to the floor. Sir Toby stared aghast at the surprise disarming. With only a parrying dagger to defend himself, he was unable to match the speed of Jack's follow-up attack – a deceptive and unpredictable thrust upwards that finished with the tip of the rapier up his nose!

'I bet you've never seen *that* move before!' said Jack, lifting the blade slightly and forcing Sir Toby on to his toes. A snigger of amusement rippled through the gathered guests as Sir Toby danced at the end of the blade.

'Now tell me,' hissed Jack, *where's my sister?*'

Sir Toby glared defiantly back. 'I've told you – I don't know what you're talking about.'

'Perhaps this will jog your memory.' With a light flick of his wrist, Jack withdrew his rapier and sliced through the end of Sir Toby's nose. A thin stream of blood ran from his nostril.

'First blood!' Sir Henry declared, and the crowd burst into rapturous applause at Jack's skilful and unexpected victory.

Sir Toby dabbed the back of his hand to his nostril. 'It's only a nose bleed! Let us continue!'

But his protests were drowned out by the clamour and handclapping. Unwilling to concede defeat, Sir Toby grabbed another rapier from the rack and launched a furious assault on Jack, the blade whipping through the air like a whirling dervish. But knowing Sir Toby was a man without honour, Jack had been prepared for such a move – he'd remained on guard and was now quick to parry the attacks.

'Sir Toby, lay down your arms!' commanded Sir Henry.

Defiant and seething, he pressed on. Sir Toby thrust again and again, determined to skewer Jack through the heart. This time Jack responded with a different Two Heavens technique: Mountain to Sea. Attacking in a highly unexpected manner, Jack threw his parrying dagger at Sir Toby. The blade went spinning, end over end, and the hilt struck him dead centre in the forehead. Sir Toby staggered and fell to the floor, where Jack planted the needle-sharp tip of his rapier on his heart.

'I swear I will run you through,' threatened Jack, 'unless you tell me the truth!'

All the colour drained from Sir Toby's cheeks as he realized he was defeated. 'You want the *truth*?' he spat, his voice quavering. 'Then you shall have it. Your precious sister is dead!'

'Dead?' said Jack, the word sounding like a church bell's toll in his head. 'How can that be? I saw her but a week ago, alive, in Stratford.'

Sir Toby held Jack's questioning gaze. 'She fell from the carriage, trying to get out to see you, and was run over by the wheels.' Sir Toby gave a great sob, a tear ran down his cheek. 'Believe me, I tried to save her but she was beyond help.'

'*You lie!*' cried Jack, pressing down on the rapier until its tip pierced his opponent's chest.

'NO!' Sir Toby screamed as blood seeped from the wound. 'I swear that's the truth. On my life!'

'Lower your sword, Jack!' commanded Sir Henry. 'He has no reason to lie. You have him at your mercy.'

For a moment, Jack thought about driving the blade all the way home. *Surely a just punishment to avenge Jess?*

Then Yori was at his side, a small hand resting upon his to stay his sword. 'Killing him will not bring Jess back,' said his friend quietly. 'Think about the consequences, Jack. People who fight fire with fire usually end up with ashes!'

Jack was reminded of his old Zen master's words from his first year in Japan: *You must never forget your* bushido. *Rectitude, your ability to judge what is wrong and what is right, is the keystone to being samurai . . .*

He looked to Akiko, who gently shook her head. Jack felt all the fight drain out of him and he let his rapier drop. If Jess was dead, it was over. He had nothing more to fight for.

'Sir Edmund, Sir Francis – detain Sir Toby in his room until further notice,' ordered Sir Henry, as Jack stood numb and paralysed by grief in the centre of the room.

Sir Toby, his head hung low in shame, was escorted out of the gallery. He was almost at the door when, in a fit of fury, he snatched a loaded flintlock pistol from the rack on the wall. Cocking the weapon, he took aim at Jack.

'No one humiliates the Right Honourable Sir Toby Nashe and lives!' he cried in outrage, pulling the trigger.

'NO!' yelled Signor Horatio, shoving Jack to one side.

The pistol shot resounded like a thunderclap through the gallery. Jack flinched as he fell to the ground – but Signor Horatio's quick reaction had saved him. A startled and pained cry caused everyone to turn. For a second, Jack thought Signor Horatio had been struck, his courageous act having put him in the line of fire. But, when he looked, Signor Horatio was unharmed. Instead, it was Rose who slumped to the floor, blood pouring from the bullet hole in the breastplate of her costume.

38

PRIEST HOLE

The sounds of the masked ball resumed in the Great Hall, the music and chatter more muted than before. Up on the first floor of the house, Rose was laid out on a four-poster bed, a circle of concerned faces watching as her armoured breastplate was carefully removed. A blossom of blood stained the front of her green dress. Taking a knife, Signor Horatio cut away a patch of cloth and inspected the wound in Rose's belly.

'Can you save her?' asked Jack.

'I can see the lead shot,' the sword master replied gravely as he washed his hands in a bowl of hot water. 'Thankfully her costume's armour slowed the round. If I can get it out, she has a good chance.'

Rose groaned in pain, her face ashen and glistening with sweat. Akiko dabbed Rose's brow with a cool cloth, while Yori held her hand and hummed '*Vam*', the healing mantra for the stomach. Over the flickering flame of a candle, Signor Horatio heated the knife to sterilize it before letting the steel cool.

'This might sting a little, *signorina*,' he warned Rose, as he prepared to insert the knife into the wound.

Rose forced a smile. 'At least . . . I know you're skilled . . . with a blade,' she whispered.

Jack offered her a wooden spoon.

'No thanks . . . I'm not hungry.' She attempted a laugh, but ended up grimacing in agony.

'It's for you to bite on,' Jack explained. 'Here, take it.'

Holding the wound open, Signor Horatio dug the knife into her flesh. Rose clamped down on the spoon's shaft and, through clenched teeth, let out an anguished cry. Ever so slowly, Signor Horatio prised the lead shot from her belly. As the bullet came free, Rose gasped and passed out. Now the blood flowed freely, and Signor Horatio pressed his hand hard against the wound.

'Over to you and your herbal magic, Yori,' said the sword master, stepping aside.

From his pouch of medicines, Yori selected a dark paste that he'd previously prepared for Jack's injuries. Gently applying the healing salve, he began to bandage Rose and was almost finished when there was a knock on the door and Sir Henry looked in. 'How's the patient faring?' he enquired.

'Signor Horatio has succeeded in removing the bullet,' replied Jack, helping Yori tie off the bandage.

The sword master tenderly pushed aside a lock of red hair from Rose's face. 'By God's grace, she'll live.'

'That's good to hear,' said Sir Henry, the relief evident in his voice. 'I've spoken with Sir Toby and he's deeply remorseful. He's agreed not to inform the authorities of your whereabouts, if in turn you'll overlook the, er . . . *accident* with the pistol.'

'*Accident?* That was no accident!' roared Signor Horatio,

anger flashing in his eyes. 'The idiot tried to shoot Jack and ended up almost killing Rose!'

Sir Henry offered a conciliatory smile. 'I understand you're upset, sir. But it's best for everyone that we don't involve the authorities. While I may have *some* influence, I could not promise to stay the heavy hand of the law completely. And we don't want you arrested again now, do we, Jack?'

'But what about my sister?' demanded Jack, feeling hot tears sting his eyes at her loss.

With a regretful look, Sir Henry replied, 'A tragic accident. Sir Toby can barely bring himself to talk about it.'

'Then where's her body?' he persisted. 'Where was she buried?'

'I believe she lies in the parish graveyard,' said Sir Henry, making the sign of the cross in respect. 'I can take you there tomorrow. But, for now, I'd advise agreeing to Sir Toby's terms. It is far better to be a free man nursing your grief than an imprisoned man trapped with it.'

Jack cursed Sir Toby's cunning. He had Jack and his friends at his mercy with that false conviction. The vile man had not only shot Rose but was responsible for Jess's death too, yet he would get away scot-free. 'Just ensure Sir Toby keeps his word.'

'But of course,' Sir Henry replied. Then, as the others tended to Rose, Sir Henry drew Jack to one side. 'Forgive me for bringing this up again at such a delicate time, Jack. But, in light of your sister's sad passing, have you by chance had any further thoughts as to my proposal?'

Jack was stunned by the insensitivity of his host's

request. Why would Sir Henry raise the matter again this evening, and at such a sorrowful time? Jack knew the answer, of course. He was now aware how desperate the impoverished Sir Henry was to secure a trading mission.

For his own part, having found out that Jess was dead, Jack had little left to bind him to England – and England no longer seemed bound to him. This past couple of weeks his homeland had at times felt more foreign to him than Japan.

Then he was struck by another thought too: *How exactly am I going to survive in this country anyway?* The money in his purse would soon run out. He needed a livelihood . . . and a new purpose. The only means he knew of making a living was as a pilot aboard a trading ship. So returning to Japan was the obvious solution . . . and perhaps a way he could escape his grief. More to the point, with the four deadly ninjas on their trail, it would be prudent to leave England behind. He already knew that Akiko and Yori would be glad to return home. So, with all things considered, the decision had been pretty much made for him.

Jack gave a deep sigh. 'I accept your proposal,' he announced.

'Excellent!' Sir Henry grinned and clapped him on the back. 'You won't regret it, Jack. And all that sea air will do you the world of good, help you get over your loss. Now if you will excuse me, I must return to my other guests downstairs.' With that Sir Henry departed.

Akiko looked curiously at Jack. 'Why is he so cheerful?'

Jack stared out of the bedroom window at the moonlit sky, its silvery light casting a sheen across the lawns. Shining bright in the heavens was Polaris, the great North Star that was the celestial reference point for navigation. 'I've agreed to pilot his trading mission to the Japans,' he told her.

Akiko's eyes sparkled almost as bright as the North Star. 'That's wonderful! But . . .' The sparkle faded and a sadness entered her voice. 'You've fought so hard to get home, Jack. Are you sure you don't want to stay?'

He rested his head against the cool lattice panes. 'Now that Jess is forever lost to me, I have no reason to be here. I appreciate all you and Yori have done to help me find her. Your friendship and your loyalty have meant a great deal to me. But it's time I took you both home . . .'

Yori cleared his throat. 'Before we do that, can I show you something?'

Jack frowned. 'Of course. What is it?'

'It's best you see it for yourself and make your own mind up,' he replied cryptically.

Jack glanced over at Rose, who was slowly coming round. 'Yori, can't it wait?'

Yori shook his head adamantly.

'Don't worry,' said Signor Horatio, helping Rose to take a sip of water. 'I'll look after her.'

So, leaving their injured friend in the sword master's care, Jack and Akiko followed Yori down the stairs and back into the Gallery of Arms. The room was now deserted, the guests all in the Great Hall, only a patch of drying blood marking the spot where Rose fell.

'Look at this,' said Yori, beckoning Jack and Akiko over to Sir Henry's towering portrait over the fireplace.

Jack peered at the painting. 'It's very impressive, but what exactly are we supposed to be looking for?'

'Here!' said Yori, pointing to an inscription of two letters in the right-hand corner.

'N . . . H . . .' Jack read out aloud. He furrowed his brow. 'And?'

Yori let out a heavy sigh, as if the answer was obvious. 'Your locket! It's the same artist.'

Tugging the silver locket from round his neck, Jack compared the initials, trying to ignore the swell of sadness at seeing his sister's face once more. 'N. H. – Nicholas Holme. So what of it? He's probably painted countless portraits.'

'It's true that, on its own, it's just a coincidence,' agreed Yori. 'But I've checked other paintings in Lupus Hall, and Sir Henry appears to have commissioned a number from this particular artist. He clearly favours his style. Maybe he was even his patron for a while.'

'That doesn't mean Sir Henry has anything to do with the locket, though,' said Akiko.

'No, it doesn't,' conceded Yori. 'But there is a *possible* connection.' He turned away from the portrait and headed over to the racks of arquebuses. 'Earlier, at the ball, I overheard some guests talking about Sir Henry's claim to his coat of arms. There's a rumour he *bought* it and has no true family connection to a noble lineage.'

'That's not uncommon,' said Jack, unsure where his friend was taking them with this. 'Many successful merchants have bought themselves the right to bear a coat of arms.'

'Well, it would be odd in Japan,' observed Akiko, 'like a fisherman buying a *katana* to become a samurai!'

'No, that's not the issue,' said Yori. 'It's the coat of arms itself.' He pointed to the black-and-white wooden shield hanging above the rack of rifles. 'Don't you remember what Mrs Winters in Bedlam said? *Beware the red wolf at your door!*'

Jack studied the design on the shield – a white stag opposite a red wolf. A sense of unease began to creep into his heart.

'But the old woman was mad,' Akiko reminded him. 'Why take her ravings seriously?'

'She wasn't mad – she was afraid!' insisted Yori. 'Afraid of the red wolf.'

Jack looked sidelong at Yori. 'Are you suggesting that Sir Henry is the *red wolf*? Then perhaps you should be in Bedlam for thinking it! Sir Henry was a dear friend of my father's. He's *our* friend. He's been helping us look for Jess. He's offered me a job.'

'Exactly,' said Yori. 'He *needs* you to sail back to the Japans to regain his lost fortune. I fear he would pretend to be your long-lost uncle if he thought it would persuade you. But I think he's hiding something. A treasure far more precious than silver or gold.'

Yori led Jack and Akiko out into the moonlit courtyard. He pointed up at the window where Jack had thought he'd seen his sister's face. 'How many windows do you count on that floor?'

Jack looked. 'Five,' he replied.

'Now come with me –' With that, Yori scampered back inside, grabbing an oil lamp before heading up the central staircase.

Halfway up, they bumped into a servant coming down the other way, his face haggard and drawn in the sudden glow of the lamp. He carried an empty tray. 'No guests are allowed on the upper floor,' he muttered.

'We just need to look for a window,' said Yori, his reply perplexing the grim-faced servant as he pushed on past.

Jack and Akiko hurried after him, leaving the servant behind in the gloom. Reaching the top landing, Yori guided them round to the cobwebbed corridor. He stopped, the oil lamp spilling a wave of light across the floorboards to the attic room at the far end.

'Count the windows again,' he instructed Jack.

Starting at one end, Jack worked his way down the corridor and into the room. 'One . . . two . . . three . . . four . . .'

But there was no fifth window. He re-counted. 'Where's the other window?' he asked.

'My point exactly,' said Yori, crossing his arms in satisfaction. 'Which means . . .'

'There must be a priest hole!' said Akiko breathlessly. Jack felt a sudden surge of shock.

Placing the oil lamp upon the writing table, they immediately set about searching the attic room. They tapped on the walls, listening for hollows. They checked the floor for loose boards, tested the ceiling for a trapdoor. But they found nothing.

'Perhaps we counted wrong,' suggested Akiko, her tone despondent.

Yori shook his head. 'No, there are definitely five windows from the outside.'

Jack stood in the middle of the room and turned a full circle, his gaze exploring every nook and cranny. 'The priest hole has to be *somewhere*,' he said. Then he heard a faint scratching and he looked at the others. 'Do you hear that?'

Akiko and Yori nodded, straining their ears to locate the sound.

The scratching was getting louder. Then a small grey creature scurried out from the fireplace.

'It's just a mouse!' groaned Jack.

'Yes, but where did the mouse come from?' asked Yori, peering into the firebox.

Jack now noticed there were no cold cinders in the grate. In fact there wasn't anything at all. He went over and ran his finger down the brickwork of the firebox. 'It's been blackened to simulate smoke!'

Stepping on to the hearth and ducking beneath the mantel, he found a secret sliding bolt. He eased it open and pushed the wall at the back. It gave a little, then, with the help of another shove, it swung wide open. Jack looked back at Akiko and Yori in astonishment. 'A false fireplace!'

39

PRISONER

The priest hole was a mirror version of the attic room, except there was a small altar for daily prayer and a wood-framed bed in the far corner. Through the one sole window – the missing fifth lattice – a shaft of moonlight illuminated a half-eaten meal on the writing table. The rest of the room was in shadow. As Jack's eyes adjusted to the dark, he thought he spied a hunched figure on the bed. Then Yori and Akiko came into the chamber with the lamp and the darkness was chased away to reveal a young woman. She shielded her eyes from the lamp's bright glare. Yori dimmed the flame and the girl lowered her arm.

Jack stared at the vision before him. So familiar, yet so different. So much older, yet still so young. Traces of the girl he once knew present in the growing woman. Golden hair longer than he remembered. Blue eyes darker but still full of playful mischief. The slim jawline of their mother. The strong brow of their father. The lips and button nose of his sister.

She stared back, afraid yet curious of the three intruders in her room.

'Jess?' said Jack, so softly in case he shattered the illusion.

The girl slowly nodded, comprehension entering her sky-blue eyes. '*Jack?*'

Needing no further confirmation, Jack rushed over and enveloped his sister in his arms. He held her tight to his chest, determined *never* to let her go again. Only now was he truly home. The journey he'd begun seven years earlier was at last over. He'd found his sister, against all the odds, all the obstacles and all the enemies. They were family once again.

Jess hugged him with equal delight and desperation. 'I prayed . . . and prayed . . . and prayed for your safe return,' she sobbed. 'I had all but given up hope.'

'Your prayers have been answered,' replied Jack, kissing her forehead and glancing towards the small wooden cross above the altar. 'As have mine.'

'I thought I spotted you at the harvest festival,' she explained, 'but Sir Toby said it was my fevered imagination. Then I saw you in the courtyard and *knew* you'd returned. I tried to get out to find you, but my room was locked, as always.'

'Sir Toby told me you had died!' said Jack bitterly.

'He's a devil of a liar . . . and cruel,' Jess muttered. 'But now you're back I have nothing to fear.' Daring to loosen her embrace, she looked up at her brother. 'Where's Father?'

In that instant the elated smile on Jack's face turned to ashes. 'He didn't –' his voice caught in his throat – 'he didn't survive the voyage, Jess . . . We were attacked . . . he died protecting me . . .'

Jess buried her head in her brother's chest, tears of woe now mixing with her former tears of joy. Their reunion was bittersweet indeed! Having lived with the tragedy for the past five years, Jack now felt a fresh wave of grief overwhelm him and he cried with her. How he wished his father could have been there for this moment. He would have wrapped his great arms round them, pulling not only him and his sister in, but their dear departed mother too, the whole family together . . . But it was not to be – nor would it ever be. Still, he had to be thankful for small miracles: Jess was alive and safe in his arms.

Their sobs gradually subsided and the joy of their reunion returned. Smiling, Jess glanced over at the two other people in the room, who were respectfully and quietly keeping their distance.

'Aren't you going to introduce us?' she asked her brother.

'Of course!' replied Jack, opening his arms wide and beckoning his friends closer. 'This is Akiko, and this is Yori. Without their help, love and loyalty, I'd never have survived Japan . . . let alone found you. They are my strength, my wisdom and my best friends.'

Akiko and Yori bowed to Jess. 'We're deeply honoured to meet you at last,' said Yori.

Jess returned the bow. 'I cannot thank you enough for bringing my brother home safe. I am forever in your debt.'

Akiko smiled kindly. 'Be assured it is a debt that never needs to be repaid.'

'But there are other debts that *do* need to be repaid!' said a cruel voice from the fireplace.

Jack and his friends spun round to see Sir Toby enter through the priest hole, brandishing a pair of flintlock pistols. He wore the satisfied grin of a cat that had just cornered its prey. A moment later, the grim-faced servant they'd met on the stairs emerged into the room too, followed by . . . Sir Henry.

Jess retreated into Jack's arms, her body trembling like a little bird's.

'Ah! A family reunion – how touching,' said Sir Henry with a hollow smile.

'Sir Henry! Explain yourself!' demanded Jack, both angry and bemused at the apparent deceit of his benefactor. 'Are *you* responsible for holding my sister prisoner? Why didn't you tell me she was here?'

'Holding her *prisoner*?' said Sir Henry, making a show of being shocked. 'What talk is this of *prisoner*? Jess is my betrothed – my future wife as soon as she comes of age.'

'*What?*' exclaimed Jack, his jaw dropping in abhorrence. He looked to his sister for a denial, but she couldn't meet his eye.

'It's true, Jack,' she replied meekly. 'I had no choice, you see. He took possession of Father's cottage to settle a debt he said our family owed him. I'd have been thrown out on to the streets, like Mrs Winters, if I hadn't accepted his proposal. I had no money, the plague was rife – I'd have been dead within a month. You do see, don't you?'

Jack felt sick to the pit of his stomach. He wrenched the silver locket from his neck and held it out to Sir Henry. 'Was this *your* courtship gift to her?'

'Why, yes!' said Sir Henry, his eyes lighting up at the sight of it. 'And it cost me a pretty penny too –' His face suddenly soured. 'Not that your ungrateful sister appreciated it, though. She'd lost it within a week!'

Jess, emboldened by the presence of her brother, replied, 'No, sir – not "lost". I *gave* it to Mrs Winters.'

Sir Henry's cheeks flushed red with rage. 'Why on earth would you do *that*, girl?'

'So she could pawn it,' explained Jess, holding his fierce gaze, 'and keep herself from starving because of *you*!'

'As my future wife, you'll learn to respect me *and* my property!' bellowed Sir Henry. He raised the back of his hand to strike her but Jack stepped between them, shielding his sister.

'Mrs Winters was right,' said Jack, as Sir Henry grudgingly backed down. 'You are indeed a wolf in sheep's clothing!'

'Don't be like that, Jack,' said Sir Henry, his tone at once conciliatory. 'I always say, family must come first, and one day you and I will be brothers-in-law.'

'Over my dead body!' snarled Jack. He advanced on Sir Henry but was warded off by one of Sir Toby's pistols.

Jack now regretted leaving his rapier in his room for the masked ball. Yori was equally defenceless. Akiko was twitching to use the *katana* on her hip – but Sir Toby had his second pistol trained on her, his finger to the trigger. Fast as Akiko was with a sword, Jack doubted she'd beat a speeding bullet.

'Oh, don't talk of dead bodies. I hope it won't come to that, Jack,' said Sir Henry with a thin mean smile. 'And, anyway, you have a debt to pay first.'

'What debt? I owe you nothing!' said Jack.

Sir Henry snorted in disagreement. 'I made significant losses funding your father's trading expedition to the Japans. In fact, it's *his* fault I'm bankrupt now. The sale of his cottage barely covered a single interest payment. The debt is hereditary. So, as his son and the sole survivor of the shipwrecked *Alexandria*, *you* carry the burden of your father's debt.'

'My father wasn't to blame for your losses!' argued Jack. 'As an investor, you knew from the start the risks of such an expedition. Father was employed to pilot the fleet, not guarantee you returns on your investment.'

'He may have piloted the fleet on its way there, but he didn't pilot it *back*, did he?' countered Sir Henry. 'The way I see it, your father is directly responsible for the trading mission's failure. You yourself told me that he navigated the fleet to the wrong port!'

'Not true! We were blown off-course by the storm,' argued Jack. 'He died defending the ship from pirates!'

'Hmm, such a tragic loss . . . But there is no avoiding the fact,' Sir Henry went on, ignoring Jack's protests, 'that, as his sole surviving male heir, you inherit that debt. A debt you will repay a thousandfold by sailing back to the Japans and recouping my losses.'

'I won't go,' stated Jack boldly.

Sir Henry narrowed his eyes. 'Oh yes you will, because you see, Jack – Jess is your collateral. My guarantee that you'll return from Japan with a handsome payload. If you succeed with this trading mission, I'll *consider* ending my engagement to your sweet sister –' he gave Jess an oily smile – 'as much as that would break my heart.'

'You don't have a heart!' Jess shot back. 'Your only love is money.'

Sir Henry shrugged off the accusation. 'And your brother's love for you, my dear, is why he *will* return to Japan.'

Jack glared at Sir Henry. He knew he was being emotionally blackmailed, yet what could he do about it? 'But I'll be away for at least two years, if not more!'

'Don't worry, I'll take *very* good care of her,' replied Sir Henry.

Jack clenched his fists. Although he lacked a weapon, he just might be quick enough to get his hands round Sir Henry's throat before Sir Toby could get a shot in. Akiko, sensing he was preparing to attack, flexed her fingers in readiness to unsheathe her *katana*. Yori began drawing in a deep breath, filling his lungs for a *kiai* strike . . .

Then from the courtyard below came the sound of panicked screams. Footsteps clattered up the echoing staircase, then pounded along the corridor. A moment later a wide-eyed and gasping servant scrambled through the fireplace into the room.

'What is the meaning of this?' demanded Sir Henry, peering out of the window to see his guests dashing for their coaches and horses. 'What has happened down there?'

The servant, regaining his breath, gulped. 'Sir Henry – plague doctors!'

40

LAST STAND

'Let us out!' shouted Jack, hammering his fists on the bedroom door. At gunpoint, they had been forcibly marched back to Rose's bedroom, where all six of them – Jack and his sister, Akiko, Yori, Signor Horatio and Rose – were now being held captive. 'We need our weapons!'

From the other side of the door, Sir Edmund grunted a laugh. 'I'm sure you do. That's *exactly* why Sir Henry has you locked up, you dullard!'

Jack beat his fists upon the wood again. 'You don't know what you're dealing with!' he insisted. 'You *need* our help.'

More snorts of laughter, and this time Sir Francis replied. '*You're* the one in need of help, Jack. You'll be strung up by your neck, good and proper this time. Reckon they'll hang, draw *and* quarter you!'

Jack grabbed the door latch and rattled it – but it was futile. The lock was cast iron and the door solid oak. It wouldn't budge an inch. 'They're not plague doctors,' he cried. 'They're NINJAS!'

'What did he say?' mumbled Sir Francis to his friend.

'I think he said they're *whingers*!' replied Sir Edmund, before collapsing into a fit of laughter.

Jack kicked out at the door. 'Idiots!' he muttered.

'Aren't we safer in here?' said Jess, who was perched at the foot of Rose's bed. 'I mean, if we can't get out . . . then those ninjas can't get in either.'

Jack shook his head. 'We're like fish in a barrel in this room. Without our weapons, those ninjas will hunt us down and slaughter us.'

'I still have my rapier, *signor*,' reminded Signor Horatio. In Sir Henry's haste to deal with the plague doctors, he'd overlooked the sword master tending to Rose at her bedside. Rose was now propped up against the pillows. Her cheeks had regained some colour and her strength was gradually returning.

'One sword against four ninjas? Our chances aren't good,' said Akiko, shaking her head. 'We're dealing with trained assassins.'

'What about the window?' suggested Rose, wheezing slightly. 'Can't one of you climb out . . . and over to the next bedroom?'

'Maybe,' said Jack. He looked at Akiko, knowing that out of all of them she had the necessary skills.

'I'll try,' she said, securing her kimono.

Yori was already peering through the glass. 'There's something very strange going on . . .'

Jack and Akiko joined Yori at the casement window. Under the silver sheen of the moon, the four plague doctors stood in a line, their black gowns flapping in the chill breeze like crows' wings. Moonlight was reflected, ghostlike, in their glass eyes; their beaked masks appeared deathly white, terrifying to behold. Sir Henry's guests were fleeing down the gravel paths, keeping as far away as possible from these harbingers of pestilence. But it was the very disorder of their flight that threw into sharp contrast the plague doctors' unnatural stillness.

Akiko frowned. 'They're not moving . . .'

'But why not?' asked Yori, squinting to get a better look. 'Do you think they're waiting for everyone to leave before attacking us?'

Studying the layout of the ornamental garden below, Jack's eyes widened in grim comprehension. 'No!' he gasped. 'They're not moving because they're *statues*! The ninjas have covered them with their plague doctor clothes. It's a trick!'

Suddenly a shadow appeared at the window, only a pair of eyes gleaming in the dark. A small diamond of glass was knocked from its lead frame and a blowpipe pushed through.

'Watch out!' cried Yori, throwing himself at Jack. They both fell to the floor as a poisoned dart shot out of the pipe. Missing Jack by a fraction, the dart embedded itself in the nearest post of Rose's four-poster bed. Jess let out a startled cry and dived under the bed for cover.

Before the ninja could reload another dart, Akiko spun on her heel and back-kicked the casement window. Glass shattered and the frame flew open, sending the ninja plummeting earthwards. A second later, they heard a distant *splash* as the assassin fell into the moat. Akiko leant out of the broken lattice to see the dark figure swimming for the bank. 'He'll be back,' she warned. 'Have no doubt of that!'

'Hey, what's going on in there?' shouted Sir Francis, his voice muffled by the door.

'Nothing,' Signor Horatio replied casually. 'I've just dropped the water jug, that's all.'

'Thanks for saving me,' said Jack, as Yori helped him to his feet.

Yori smiled. 'It's becoming something of a habit here in England!'

'At least we have a way out now,' said Akiko, inspecting the brickwork for possible handholds.

However, before she could climb out of the window, they heard Sir Edmund's tremulous voice in the corridor. 'Wh-wh-who goes there? Relight the lamps! Show yourself!'

From the other side of the door, there was a pained gasp then a heavy *whump*, followed by a high-pitched whimpering. A key rattled in the lock and the latch began to lift. Jack, Akiko, Yori and Signor Horatio took up a defensive guard round the bed as the door swung open. Sir Edmund's portly figure filled the doorway. He wore a petrified, dead-eyed expression. The iron key fell from his hand with a clatter, then he toppled forward and landed face first on the floorboards, a *tantō* embedded in his back.

Behind the bleeding body of Sir Edmund lay his companion, Sir Francis, still dressed in his costume armour. Only his feet were visible through the doorway, the muscles spasming in a gruesome death twitch. The corridor was swallowed in darkness, the lamps snuffed out. From the gloom a shape detached itself and materialized into a shadow warrior. Dressed head to toe in black, the ninja slipped serpent-like into the room and retrieved his knife. Hissing, he then drew a razor-sharp *ninjatō* from the sheath upon his back.

'God help us!' breathed Jess, her eyes round with fear. ''Tis truly a demon!'

'Leave this one to me,' said Signor Horatio, unsheathing his rapier and advancing. 'You get your weapons.'

'Be careful,' warned Jack as their sword master prepared to engage. '*Never* underestimate a ninja.'

Signor Horatio threw Jack a cocky wink. 'And *never* underestimate *un Italiano*!'

With that, he launched himself at the assassin. A blaze of lightning-quick lunges took the ninja by surprise and drove him back through the doorway. Steel rang against steel, the duel echoing down the corridor.

As soon as the way was clear, Jack, Akiko and Yori dashed to their rooms, collected their weapons and regrouped in Rose's bedroom.

'What's the plan, then?' asked Yori, the rings of his *shakujō* jingling nervously in his grip.

Tying off his *obi*, Jack secured his *daishō* to his hip. 'We either keep running . . .' he said, sliding the *shuriken* he'd retrieved from their last encounter with the ninja into a fold of his belt – 'or face down these ninjas once and for all.'

'I vote we take a stand,' said Akiko, armed with her *yumi* and a sheath of arrows on her back.

Jack drew his *katana*. 'A *last* stand!'

He glanced at Yori, who looked less certain, but he nodded his agreement anyway. Jack picked up the iron key and handed it to his friend. 'Stay with Rose and my sister. Block that window and lock the door behind us.'

Yori tightened his grip on his *shakujō* and tried to stand tall. 'I'm not scared of ninjas,' he said determinedly.

Jack laid a hand upon Yori's shoulder. 'I know, my friend. That's why I trust you to protect my sister.'

Yori's chest swelled with pride. 'I won't let you down, Jack,' he promised, with a bow.

As Yori locked the door, Jack and Akiko hurried along the corridor towards the staircase. On reaching the landing, they heard the clash of swords coming from the floor below.

'Signor Horatio needs our help!' said Akiko, racing down.

But when they got there, it wasn't Signor Horatio after all. In the Gallery of Arms they found Sir Toby fearlessly fending off another ninja. This one wielded a *katana*.

'Whatever devil you are, you won't defeat the mighty Sir Toby!' he boasted, as he parried a slash to his head and countered with a thrust to the chest.

The ninja nimbly evaded the thrust and came back with a devastating slice across the body. Light-footed as a ballet dancer, Sir Toby leapt away, dodging the blade before retaliating with a peppering of jabs that forced the ninja on the retreat – his rapier's reach giving him a crucial advantage over the *katana*. As much as Jack despised the man, he once again had to admire Sir Toby's skill with a sword. It was rare to see a ninja on the back foot in a fight.

The assassin was stung on his left sword hand, then his right arm, then his shoulder. None were fatal, but each strike perturbed the ninja. He began to lose more ground, becoming wilder and more desperate in his defence.

'You can't best an English sword master!' laughed Sir Toby, becoming bolder in his lunges.

Then the ninja overblocked a thrust with his *katana*, leaving his chest open for an attack. Sir Toby instantly spotted the gap in his adversary's guard and lunged. As the thrust came for his heart, the ninja looked certain to be run through . . . but, at the last second, he twisted his body, corkscrewing out of the way of the rapier's needle-sharp tip. The blade passed beyond its intended mark – and beyond posing any immediate threat to the ninja. Surging forward, he delivered a rapid combination of hand strikes as fast as a rattlesnake, each targeting a specific pressure point.

Sir Toby, mid-lunge, was paralysed where he stood, his front leg forward, his sword arm outstretched, his rapier quivering.

'What . . . have . . . you . . . done . . . to . . . me?' he groaned.

Jack knew exactly what the ninja had done. *Dim Mak*. The Death Touch.

As Sir Toby trembled in his immobilized state, the ninja took his time. His composure was absolute now, his former apparent panic merely a ploy to coax overconfidence from his opponent. With calm Zen-like motion, the ninja raised his *katana* high into the air, then cut cleanly down in a swift arc.

'NO!' cried Jack as Sir Toby was decapitated, his red-haired head sliced clean off.

At Jack's cry of protest, the ninja glanced up and their eyes locked. In that moment, Jack could have sworn that behind the mask the ninja actually smiled. Then, raising a hand, the assassin beckoned Jack and Akiko into the gallery.

Jack looked at Akiko. 'I think we fight first, ask questions later?'

'Agreed,' said Akiko, stringing an arrow.

Weapons raised, they entered the gallery. Two against one, Jack thought they could swiftly dispatch this ninja. But he hadn't reckoned on walking into a trap. As they passed through the doorway, another ninja ambushed them from above. Dropping down from the wooden lintel, the assassin landed on Akiko's back like a black panther.

'You left *this* behind!' hissed the ninja in Japanese.

A gleam of gold flashed through the air. Akiko shrieked in pain as the sharpened hairpin was driven into her shoulder blade. Her whole body arched and she dropped to her knees. Jack elbowed her attacker hard in the face, knocking the ninja off Akiko's back. In so doing, he dislodged the ninja's mask, revealing . . . a female face. A *kunoichi*. While this didn't shock Jack, he still hesitated in his follow-up attack, giving the *kunoichi* a chance to retreat to a safe distance.

Squirming in agony, Akiko desperately reached for the *kanzashi* protruding from her shoulder. The hairpin, thanks to her quiver, had missed the paralysing *ryumon ki* point by a fraction, yet it still sent shockwaves of pain through her body. Jack went to help her, but was kicked aside by the other ninja and he slid across the polished floorboards. Winded heavily by the brutal attack, Jack lay sprawled on the floor, and it was a few seconds before he could get back to his feet. The ninja strode towards Jack, *katana* raised. A succession of lethal slices from the sword forced Jack to retreat along the gallery, separating him further and further from Akiko.

Meanwhile, the *kunoichi* had by now taken a broadsword from the weapons rack and was bearing down on Akiko to finish her off. With the *kanzashi* lodged in her back, Akiko could only feebly raise her *yumi* in defence. The bamboo bow shattered under the force of the *kunoichi*'s strike but was still enough to deflect the blade's heavy blow. Scrambling away, Akiko snatched a rapier off the wall and retreated down the hallway. The *kunoichi* went after her, slow and certain as a hunter stalking a wounded prey.

'Akiko!' cried Jack, desperate to follow and save her. But the ninja with the *katana* blocked his path, leaving Jack no option but to battle his way through. Taking up a fighting guard, he demanded, 'Who are you? Why are you trying to kill us?'

The ninja didn't reply. But his sword did.

The blade struck out like a bolt of lightning, thrusting for Jack's heart. Jack spun to one side, evading the blade. Then he sliced with his own *katana* across the ninja's neck. The ninja leant back, bending like a reed in the wind, the steel edge of Jack's sword passing within a hair's breadth of his mask. Whirling round, the ninja then cut for Jack's legs. Jack jumped high into the air before bringing his own sword down as if to cleave the ninja in two. His attacker dived aside, rolled out of harm's way and effortlessly sprang back to his feet.

'Who sent you?' growled Jack, his frustration at the ninja's agility increasing with his concern for Akiko. The fight in the hallway had gone ominously quiet.

The ninja's continued silence was equally disturbing – just as he probably intended. The only conversation was the conversation of blades as they fought through the length of the gallery and into the Great Hall. The masked ball had been abandoned. The musicians were gone, the stage was empty, the great banquet left to spoil and go to waste. All the guests, the servants – everyone, in fact – had run away, no one willing to risk any possible exposure to the plague.

With the Great Hall deserted, the only sounds came from the roaring of the fire in the hearth and the battling of the samurai and the ninja. Their *katanas* engaged in a deadly dance; steel against steel singing out. Jack soon found himself pushed to the limit of his skills. The ninja seemed to have a counter to his every attack, an answer to his every riposte, almost as if he could read Jack's next move.

Jack realized he had to do something different, something *unexpected* – just as he had in his duel against Sir Toby. But before he could work out *what*, the ninja struck the back of Jack's blade twice in quick succession. The sudden double hit disarmed Jack of his *katana* and it clattered to the floor. An instant later the razor tip of the ninja's sword was pressed to his throat. Jack stood stock-still, feeling his racing pulse pump against the sharpened steel. An ounce more pressure and the blade would pierce his artery and he'd bleed to death like a stuck pig.

But Jack was more stunned at the ninja's sword technique than his own imminent demise . . . *Autumn Leaf strike*.

Somehow the ninja knew Masamoto's *Two Heavens*!

'Before you kill me, at least tell me who you are,' begged Jack, staring into the dark hooded eyes of his assassin.

Keeping the *kissaki* firmly to Jack's throat, the ninja turned the blade with his left sword hand. Firelight rippled along the steel's *hamon*, guiding Jack's gaze to the sword's bronze *tsuba*, where the rays of a sun *kamon* could be seen, glinting.

'*God forbid . . .*' gasped Jack, recognizing the samurai family crest as the ninja pulled off his hood.

41

VENGEANCE

Imperious. Arrogant. Superior. The scornful expression was as recognizable as the ninja's face. High cheekbones. Shaved domed head. Dark hooded eyes shot through with pure malevolence. There was no denying who the assassin was. Still, Jack couldn't believe he'd become a ninja. '*Kazuki!*'

His former school rival responded with a malicious grin. '*Gaijin!*'

'*B-but how?*' spluttered Jack in Japanese, slipping back easily into his enemy's native language. 'You're supposed to be in prison.'

Kazuki gave a spiteful laugh. '*No one* imprisons the Oda clan. Not even the great Masamoto-sama. I was released the very next day by a loyal subject of my father's.'

'That doesn't explain how you got to *England*, though,' said Jack, still keenly aware of the blade at his throat.

Kazuki smirked. 'As ever, you underestimate the resourcefulness and determination of a samurai.'

'You're no longer a *samurai*!' retorted Jack, instantly regretting his rashness as the *kissaki* dug into his flesh, threatening to sever his artery.

'I *don't* need reminding!' snarled Kazuki, his eyes flashing with fury. '*You're* to blame for my fall from grace. After Masamoto-sama stripped me of my samurai status, I had no option but to turn to the Way of the Ninja. I had to debase myself to survive . . . but I eventually came to appreciate the cunning and skill of a *shinobi*. And I had a whole year aboard the *Salamander* to learn and master their arts.' He smiled thinly. 'In particular, *Dim Mak*.'

'The *Salamander*?' Jack's thoughts turned to the Dutch trading vessel that had failed to make port in London. The beached galleon at Hole Haven, with its dead crew and supposed 'killer shadows', had to be one and the same. During the fleet's long journey home from Japan there had been rumours of ghosts aboard that ship, of shadows on deck, of crew simply vanishing. But no one, of course, had suspected ninjas. *Kazuki had been a stowaway on the* Salamander *all that time!*

'But what ninja would ever teach you his arts?' questioned Jack.

'My time in prison may have been brief, but it was fruitful,' Kazuki replied. 'In the cell with me were three ninjas of the Fūma clan. These Wind Demons, it turned out, also had a vendetta against you . . . the *gaijin* samurai.'

Jack's heart sank. The Fūma clan were ninja pirates. During his arduous trek to Nagasaki, he'd encountered the Wind Demons crossing the Seto Sea. Their clan had been all but wiped out in a battle with Sea Samurai, their secret lair destroyed and their Pirate Queen killed. Jack had been accused of cursing the Wind Demons and being responsible for their downfall. No wonder Kazuki had found such willing assassins to teach him their dark arts and accompany him on the treacherous voyage to England.

Kazuki grinned when he saw Jack's defeated expression. 'As you clearly appreciate, the Fūma were eager to help me in my task – a task bestowed upon me by the mighty Shogun Kamakura. And even though my lord is dead, his dying wish lives on.' Kazuki's grip tightened round the hilt of the *katana* and Jack braced himself for the fatal blow. 'I've colluded with ninjas . . .' Kazuki went on, his tone bitter, resentful, 'crossed half the world . . . scoured this filthy country . . . all with one purpose in mind: to kill you and restore my honour!'

Even in the face of certain death, Jack couldn't believe the lengths his enemy had gone to. He'd been wrong to think that Kazuki's spirit had been broken in Nagasaki. Like a shattered sword, Kazuki's fury had merely been reforged and strengthened in a fire of hatred and revenge. Kazuki had demonstrated that he was willing to go to the ends of the earth to satisfy his bloodlust.

'I only need your head to prove it,' said Kazuki, swinging back the *katana* to decapitate Jack with one final savage slice.

Jack's life flashed before his eyes, his thoughts consumed by memories of his sister and the cruel twist of fate that had cut short their long-awaited reunion.

Assured of victory at last, Kazuki couldn't resist one final jibe. Pausing at the top of his swing, he snarled, 'Vengeance is mine, *gaijin*!'

And in that moment of arrogant self-indulgence Jack pulled the *shuriken* from the fold of his *obi* and flicked it at Kazuki's face. Kazuki howled in pain as the throwing star struck him in the eye. Jack grabbed his *katana* from the floor, at the same time unsheathing his *wakizashi*, and took up a Two Heavens stance.

'Curse you, *gaijin*!' snarled Kazuki, pulling out the *shuriken*. Half-blinded, he glared at Jack from his one good eye. Now more than ever, Jack's school rival resembled his arch-enemy Dokugan Ryu, not only in the blackness of his heart but in his appearance too.

'An eye for an eye,' said Jack, his two swords gleaming in the firelight. 'That was for murdering Sir Henry's stable boy.'

Kazuki wiped the blood from his cheek. 'I want you to know, *gaijin*, that once I've killed you, I'll not only behead your beloved Akiko, I'll cut your sister into eight pieces and feed her to the dogs!'

A surge of protective rage rose up in Jack. He roared a battle cry of *kiai* and launched himself at Kazuki. Blades whirling, he drove his enemy back with cut after cut. Despite his partial loss of vision and the obvious pain he was in, Kazuki managed to deflect and evade the onslaught. Retreating into the Gallery of Arms, he snatched a parrying dagger from the weapons rack with his claw of a right hand and took up his own Two Heavens stance.

'We *both* know Masamoto's sword style,' reminded Kazuki. 'And we both know I'm better at it!'

'Are you sure of that, Kazuki?' replied Jack. Attacking with a Flint-and-Spark strike, he ran his blade down the length of Kazuki's *katana*, the move so fast that sparks actually flew from the scrape of steel against steel. Kazuki's weapon pushed aside, Jack then thrust for his enemy's heart.

But Kazuki stopped the blade with the parrying dagger and retaliated with a Fire-and-Stone cut. The force of the hammer blow almost knocked Jack's *wakizashi* from his left hand, the whole sword shuddering in his grip. He came back with a Running Water strike, flowing forward with all the force of a wave. Yet Kazuki rode out the attack, twisting and turning like the wind.

For all his arrogance, Kazuki was right. He knew the Two Heavens. Knew what to expect. Knew how to counter it.

Jack was driven back into the Great Hall as Kazuki now went on the offensive. A Serpentine strike cut through Jack's guard and the *kissaki* of Kazuki's sword tore across his chest, slicing through the diamond-chequered cloth and leaving a razor-like wound. Jack cried out and staggered backwards, stumbling into the banqueting table. Plates of meat and bowls of fruit went crashing to the floor.

'I'm going to carve you up like that pheasant!' snarled Kazuki, pointing with his dagger at the roasted fowl still sitting upon its silver platter.

Jack glanced down at his wound. The cut wasn't deep, but it bled freely and it now hurt to move his left arm. There was no doubt he was losing the duel. And Kazuki knew it too. With a triumphant smirk, Kazuki raised his sword for another Serpentine strike. Hampered by his injury, Jack would be hard-pressed to fend off the lethal attack. Then a thought struck him: *If a Japanese Two Heavens technique works using a Western rapier, then why not try a Western technique using a Japanese sword . . .?*

Jack quickly pommelled his *wakizashi* as Kazuki bore down on him. With his *katana* held high to deflect the Serpentine strike, he thrust out with his short sword. The extended reach was enough to surprise his old enemy. The *kissaki* pierced

Kazuki's belly and the blade sank in. Kazuki faltered in his attack before dropping to his knees, his sword and dagger clattering to the ground.

'H-h-how . . .?' he gasped, his face a knot of pain and confusion as he tried to figure out how a *wakizashi* could have outreached a *katana*.

Jack stood over the wounded Kazuki. He kicked away his enemy's weapons before pulling out the *wakizashi*. Groaning in pain, Kazuki clasped his bleeding abdomen.

'That's something you'll never know,' replied Jack, sheathing his *wakizashi* before laying the edge of his *katana* against Kazuki's neck.

Kazuki glared up at him with his remaining eye. 'Do it!' he said, coughing up blood. 'Or don't you have the guts?'

Jack's sword wavered. To kill his enemy this way would give Kazuki the honourable death he desired as a samurai. Yet twice before Jack had let his rival live, and both times Jack had lived to regret it. This time, he knew Kazuki *had* to die. Not out of any desire for revenge. But for protection. Not only for himself and Akiko, but for his sister. He couldn't allow *anyone* to harm Jess.

'Call yourself a samurai?' spluttered Kazuki. 'You're a pathetic . . . worthless . . . *gaijin* –'

Jack whipped back his sword, determined to finish their feud once and for all. Then as he swung the blade, a shout of *KIAI* – cut short into a strangled yelp – echoed through the manor house, followed by a girl's terrified scream.

'*Jess!*' exclaimed Jack, stopping his sword mid-strike.

A bloodstained grin crept across Kazuki's face. 'That'll be Kuma . . . meeting your little sister.'

Caught between killing Kazuki and saving Jess, Jack made the only decision he could. Leaving the wounded Kazuki on his knees, Jack sprinted out of the Great Hall, back through the Gallery of Arms and up the staircase. Wet footprints dotted the steps and continued in a trail along the corridor to Rose's bedroom. The door had been smashed open and Jack could hear the sounds of a struggle coming from inside.

He dashed in and found Yori lying dazed on the floor, a *manriki* chain wrapped tightly round his neck. His *shakujō* lay beside him, snapped in half. Beside the four-poster bed the ninja Kuma had Jess, a garrotte pulled round her throat. Her fingers were clawing at the wire digging into her soft skin.

Jack rushed at Kuma, his *katana* raised. But Kuma turned and held Jess in front of him as a shield, and Jack no longer dared strike at the ninja for fear of mortally wounding his sister. Kuma tugged on the garrotte, making her cry out again in panic. Jack had a horrifying flashback to when his father had been garrotted by Dokugan Ryu and his clan aboard the *Alexandria* — and now the nightmare was happening all over again!

In desperation, Jack dropped his sword and held up his hands in surrender.

'*Kanojo o tebanasu!*' he cried, pleading in Japanese for Kuma to let her go. 'You want *me*, not her.'

'Your self-sacrifice is admirable,' hissed Kuma. 'But this is the price you must pay!'

42

MILITIA

'*Sumimasen* . . .' begged Jack, tears stinging his eyes as Jess's struggle grew weaker, 'she's but a young girl, and unarmed.'

The ninja kept the garrotte taut and Jess's hands fell away from the wire, her eyes closed and her body went limp.

'NO!' cried Jack, feeling like his whole world was being torn from him. A fury so monstrous and fierce was unleashed within him that he lost all sense and reason. His sole thought was to *destroy* his sister's killer . . . but as he launched himself in enraged revenge, the ninja stiffened. His grip on the garrotte loosened and he slumped to the floor, dragging Jess down with him. Behind him, Rose knelt upon the bed with the doxy Hazel's knife in her hand, the one Jack had given her at the arena.

'Takes a woman's touch to deal with these devils!' she declared, wincing from her gunshot wound as she eased herself off the bed. Then she spotted Jess's body lying lifeless beside the ninja. 'Jess! No! Was I too late?'

His blind fury abating, Jack bent down over Jess, held his hand close to her face, but couldn't feel the warmth of her breath. 'She's not breathing!' he cried. He hurriedly pulled the wire from her neck and felt for her pulse. 'No, wait,' he said, 'her heart is still beating ... weakly, but she's still clinging on to life!'

At a loss as to what to do next, Jack turned Jess over on to her side and rubbed her hard on the back, much like he'd done when she was a baby and needed winding. She suddenly gasped and drew in a sharp breath. Her eyes flew open, wild and panicking like a startled bird's. Then she saw Jack's face above her, felt his arms cradling her, and she relaxed into his safe embrace.

'Thank the heavens!' said Rose, leaning for support against the four-poster bed.

Jack held his sister tight, thankful too for her miraculous return.

Wearily, Jess sat up. '*Y-Yori*,' she rasped with great effort. '*Is he . . .?*'

Jack spun round. 'Yori!' he shouted, having momentarily forgotten his friend amid the shock of his sister's near-death.

Yori was laid out on the floor, the *manriki* chain still twisted round his neck. Hobbling over, Rose helped Jack to untangle it, and Yori drew in several wheezing breaths. He was fortunate the chain had not completely strangled him, but he had a large lump on the back of his head where one of the chain's end-weights had struck him.

'Are you all right?' asked Jack, offering his hand to his dazed friend to help him up.

But, instead of getting to his feet, Yori dropped to his knees, bowed his head to the floor and began sobbing, 'I'm sorry, Jack, sorry ... I failed ... I failed to protect your sister ... I promised to, but I didn't! I'm so –'

'You've nothing to apologize for, dear friend,' cut in Jack. 'Jess is alive!'

Yori, his eyes swimming with tears, still looked regretfully at Jack. 'B-b-but I couldn't stop the ninja . . . I failed in my duty . . .'

'You *didn't* fail,' said Jess in a hoarse whisper. 'When the ninja broke in, you fought like a warrior, not a monk. He had those horrific weapons –' she glanced in revulsion at the garrotte and *manriki* on the floor – 'and you only had your staff. Yori, you were so brave – so, so brave.'

Yori stopped bowing. 'Really?'

'Absolutely.' Jess smiled, going over to him and taking his hand. 'Your courage is what saved us.'

Yori looked uncertainly at Jack again, who nodded in agreement with his sister.

'Without your protection, Jess wouldn't be alive now,' said Jack earnestly. 'You fulfilled your duty in every way. You're a true samurai. You proved you were willing to lay down your life for my sister. I couldn't ask for more from a friend.'

Wiping away his tears, Yori replied, 'The greatest gift in life is friendship. That's why I treasure yours, Jack . . . and now your sister's.'

On an impulse, Jess hugged Yori. For a moment the monk looked startled at the unexpected affection, then he put his arms round her and returned the hug.

Rose coughed politely into her fist. 'And what about *my* part in all of this?' she asked. 'It was me who had the knife. I struck the fatal blow, don't forget.'

'How could we, Rose? You'd *never* let us forget!' said Jack with a laugh. 'Joking aside, though, I'll be forever in your debt too.'

Rose raised an eyebrow. 'I wouldn't be so quick to promise such things. I might ask you to repay it one day –'

She stopped as urgent footsteps pounded towards them along the corridor. Jack grabbed his *katana* and Rose raised the knife. Yori picked up the remains of his staff and stood protectively in front of Jess. A moment later, a Roman emperor in a bloodied toga burst into the room.

'Thank God you're all still safe!' gasped Signor Horatio, his rapier's blade slick with blood.

Casting aside her knife, Rose threw herself into his arms. 'My sweet Horatio, you're injured! Look, you're bleeding!'

'It's mostly my opponent's blood,' said Signor Horatio with a grim smile. He looked over her shoulder at Jack. 'You are right never to underestimate a ninja, *signor*. They've no honour in a duel!'

'They live by a different code,' replied Jack, knowing that not all ninjas acted like the ones they had faced that evening, 'but in a fight *anything* goes.'

'Never a truer word said!' agreed Signor Horatio. 'That ninja set fire to the kitchen during our fight. We need to leave, *now*, before the whole place burns down.' Wincing from a wound to his side, he began gathering up their belongings. Then he glanced round the room and frowned. 'Where's Akiko?'

Jack stopped at the threshold, his heart suddenly sinking like a stone. 'I lost sight of her while I was fighting Kazuki.'

'*Kazuki!*' exclaimed Yori, almost dropping the remains of his *shakujō*. 'He's *here*?'

Jack nodded. 'Kazuki was the ninja with the *katana*. I'll explain later. We have to find Akiko first. She's wounded and up against a *kunoichi*.'

With Yori protecting Jess, and Signor Horatio supporting Rose, Jack led the way along the darkened corridor. He kept his sword on guard as they approached the staircase. The acrid stench of smoke tinged the air and an eerie silence had fallen over the manor house. There were no sounds of a struggle, no clash of swords, just the distant crackle of the fire. Jack began to fear the worst for Akiko. As they descended the stairs, he could see into the Gallery of Arms. Sir Toby's headless body lay spread-eagled on the floor – but Kazuki was nowhere to be seen, a drying pool of blood the only evidence of the wound Jack had inflicted upon his rival. Jack's sword had run deep . . . *but not deep enough to be fatal?*

'I'll go first,' Jack whispered, cautiously heading down the final flight of steps into the hallway. The others waited on the middle landing for the all-clear. As his foot touched the fifth step from the bottom, the wood creaked loudly in the smoke-filled silence. Jack looked sharply around, praying he hadn't alerted anyone. But neither Kazuki nor the *kunoichi* appeared. He breathed a sigh of relief. Then a blade shot up through a narrow gap in the staircase, its steel tip spearing straight between his legs. Jack dived and rolled across the floor, the blade catching the cloth of his Harlequin suit and tearing a hole in his trousers . . . but thankfully nothing else.

Flipping back to his feet, Jack spun towards the staircase, *katana* at the ready. As the mystery blade disappeared, the step was flung open, and Jack charged at the figure emerging from the priest hole. He brought his sword slicing down to end the deadly ambush . . .

'NO!' cried Akiko, her face pale and fresh blood staining her kimono. Only at the very last second did Jack manage to halt his attack, his *katana* stopping a hair's breadth from her neck. Akiko let out an unsteady breath. 'That was close . . . *too* close.'

'You can say that again!' replied Jack, lowering his sword and inspecting his torn trousers.

'I thought you were . . . the –' Akiko suddenly collapsed into Jack's arms, her battle with the female ninja having taken its toll. She still had the golden *kanzashi* buried in her shoulder blade. With great care, Jack removed the debilitating hairpin and almost immediately Akiko revived a little.

'That *kunoichi*'s around somewhere . . .' she groaned. 'I had to hide . . . I couldn't fight . . . not with *that* in my back . . .'

'Don't worry,' said Jack, supporting her full weight. 'We're all getting out of here.'

He beckoned to the others and they hurried through the haze of smoke, down the hallway and out into the courtyard. The night was lit up by the flames of the burning manor house. The fire had taken hold in the east wing and was spreading rapidly through the whole building, windows shattering under the intense heat, and smoke billowing up in a dark cloud and smothering the stars in the sky. Sir Henry's coach was beside the gatehouse, the horses, agitated by the blaze, whinnying and straining in the traces.

'Come on!' said Jack, helping Akiko down the steps and towards the coach, the others following close behind.

As they opened the carriage door, though, a shadow leapt from the gatehouse on to the roof of the coach. The *kunoichi* held the broadsword high over her head, its steel glowing red in the wavering light of the flames. Before Jack or Akiko could react, she brought the great blade down. With one arm supporting Akiko, Jack was unable to raise his sword to deflect the fatal strike –

Then a gunshot rang out. The ninja was suddenly thrown backwards and, rather than finding Jack and Akiko, her broadsword embedded itself in the wooden bodywork of the coach. Tumbling to the ground, the *kunoichi* was dead before she even hit the gravel.

'Another rat exterminated!' bellowed Sir Henry, standing furious upon the entrance steps to the house. His beady eyes glared as fierce as the flames of Hell as Jack and his friends bundled themselves into his coach.

'More rats escaping!' yelled Sir Henry, frantically reloading his pistol. '*Militia! Militia! Seize them!*'

Men armed with Sir Henry's pikes and muskets started surging out of Lupus Hall. Jack and Signor Horatio hurriedly lifted Rose into the coach, before helping Jess and Akiko inside too. Signor Horatio dived in after them. Yori leapt into the driver's seat and took up the reins. Jack jumped up on to the coach's runner as Yori urged on the horses. They bolted through the gatehouse and down the gravel paths towards the stone bridge, only too eager to escape the blazing manor house.

'STOP THEM!' ordered Sir Henry, apoplectic with rage.

The militia took up formation and began firing muskets

at the fleeing coach. Bullets peppered its wooden frame and Jack clung close to the carriage as the others huddled in the footwell. Yori flicked the reins harder, urging the horses on again. Another volley of gunfire echoed through the grounds, bullets whizzed past, but fewer hit their target. Then they were through the estate's stone gateway and on the main road. Leaving the inferno of Lupus Hall behind, the coach and its fugitive passengers disappeared into the enveloping night.

43

THE LIBRARY

'*Twosies!*' exclaimed Jess, applauding Yori as he picked up a pair of knucklebones from the floor before catching a third in mid-air. 'Can you manage *threesies*?'

With a determined look, Yori re-cast the bones, the knuckles clattering across the floorboards of the little attic bedroom up in the Bunch of Grapes Inn. They'd chosen the establishment in Limehouse as a safe hide-out, since the innkeeper asked no questions – and with his reputation as a former prize-fighter preceding him, no one dared ask anything about the guests upstairs either. It had taken them three days in the coach to reach London, only stopping along the way to pick up their belongings in Stratford, and to rest and water the horses from time to time. They'd barely slept during the whole gruelling journey, too shaken about as the coach rattled along, its wooden frame in constant danger of being broken to pieces by the rough highway. Holed up in the Bunch of Grapes Inn, they'd spent the first two days simply eating, sleeping and recovering their strengths. Now Jack was becoming restless, tired of being cooped up in the cramped little room. His friends and Jess, however, seemed to be faring far better.

Tossing a bone into the air, Yori clapped and tried to seize three knuckles in one swipe.

'Oops, bad luck!' Jess giggled as Yori fumbled the bones. She gathered the pieces and took her turn. 'Let me show you how it's done.'

Yori watched eagerly as the bones rattled across the boards and Jess began catching them with practised ease. Jack smiled to himself at seeing his sister's growing friendship with Yori and in particular her enjoyment at playing knucklebones again. He was reminded of all the happy times they'd shared in their father's cottage, those memories so much brighter and more hopeful than the reality they now faced. Fugitives, not only from the law but from Sir Henry's wrath. Jack gazed despondently out of the tiny attic window at the murky and unending skyline of London. How England had changed in seven years! His home was no longer recognizable to him. In fact, as a foreign samurai, he no longer felt England *was* his home any more.

'So Kazuki followed us halfway round the world to kill you and regain his honour?' said Akiko, amazed. She sat cross-legged upon the bed, whittling a slender branch from a yew tree to make a new bow.

Jack nodded. 'Sensei Yamada once told me, revenge is self-defeating. It will eat away at you until there is nothing left. I guess there was nothing left of Kazuki apart from revenge.'

Akiko put down her half-finished bow. 'Do you think he's still alive?'

Jack sat down next to her and shrugged. 'I doubt it. The wound was pretty deep. Besides, Sir Henry said he'd exterminated *another* rat. I'm guessing he shot Kazuki as well as the *kunoichi* – and it was probably for the best. It would have put Kazuki out of his misery.'

Yori glanced up from the game of knucklebones. 'As Confucius said, before you embark on a journey of revenge, dig two graves.'

'Well, let's hope those two graves are for Kazuki and the *kunoichi*, then!' said Akiko, returning her attention to the bow.

There was a double knock at the door, the lock was turned and Signor Horatio entered with Rose. She could now walk unaided and the colour was back in her cheeks, her gunshot wound healing fast thanks to a combination of Yori's herbal medicine and healing mantras.

'Good news!' said Signor Horatio, beaming at Jack. 'I've found the *Hosiander*. She is still docked at Somers Quay.'

'That's wonderful news!' cried Jack, jumping up from the bed. 'Where's she bound for?'

Signor Horatio now turned his smile upon Akiko and Yori. 'The Far East. Captain Spilbergen informs me that he's casting off in the next day or so, as soon as all the supplies are stowed. He says we're *all* welcome aboard.'

Akiko let out a long, contented sigh and fell back on her pillow. 'Yori, we're going home!'

Closing his eyes, Yori put his hands together in silent prayer. At seeing their euphoric reactions, Jack experienced a bittersweet pang in his heart. As much as he was pleased for his friends, he was also disappointed that their time in England had been so fraught and full of danger. It was *not* how he'd imagined his homecoming would be.

'This is so exciting!' said Jess, clapping her hands in

delight. 'I've always had to stay at home, listening to Father's tales of adventure. Now *I* get to sail round the world, just like my brother.' She looked at Jack. 'Will we cross the Atlantic or the Indian Ocean? Will we see dolphins? Whales? *Penguins?* Will we visit the Spice Islands? The Golden Pavilion at Kyoto perhaps? Yori's been telling me the temple's painted in pure gold!'

Jack grinned at his sister's enthusiasm. He'd felt exactly the same way when he embarked on his first voyage with his father. He nodded in answer to Jess's outpouring of questions and she almost burst with joy.

Jack turned to Rose and Signor Horatio. 'Are you coming with us too?'

Rose gently shook her head, then looked at Signor Horatio and smiled. 'No, we have other plans, don't we?'

Signor Horatio proudly put his arm round Rose. 'We do, *signorina*. We're travelling back to my homeland,' he announced. 'I'm going to show Rose the delights and marvels of Rome, Milan, Florence, Verona, N–'

'And Venice!' Rose interrupted, planting a kiss on Signor Horatio's cheek. 'That's where we're getting married.'

Signor Horatio blinked in apparent shock, then laughed. '*Certo!* Anything for my Rose!'

'Then it's settled,' said Jack, glad to hear such happy news for a change. 'We leave aboard the *Hosiander*. But there's one thing I must do first.'

'Are you sure this is worth the risk?' whispered Akiko, as they crouched in the darkness of the rear garden of Sir Henry's London residence. Yori kept guard while Jack tried to jemmy open the mansion's back door. The Strand was quiet at this late hour, except for nightwatchmen with their sticks and lanterns patrolling the broad paved streets (the more disreputable characters preferring to lurk in the narrow lanes and shadowy alleys of the inner city).

'If we're to sail safely and swiftly back to Japan, I *have* to recover my father's *rutter*,' replied Jack, forcing his knife into the gap between the door frame and the lock. 'Without it, I'm half the pilot my father was – *damn this door!*' He swore as the knife slipped and sliced across his finger. He put the cut to his mouth. 'We should have brought Rose and her cutpurse skills along.'

'Let me try,' said Akiko, taking the knife from Jack. She gently inserted the blade into the lock recess, then tapped the hilt and the door popped smoothly open.

Jack stared at her in astonishment. 'You've obviously done that before! And you were hard on Rose to start with for being a thief!'

'Well, we're not *technically* stealing anything,' said Akiko, a mischievous smile upon her lips. She handed him back his knife. 'Only retrieving what is rightfully yours.'

Leaving her expert burglary skills a mystery, Jack sheathed his knife and crept inside. Akiko made to follow, but Jack shook his head. 'Best if I go. I know where I hid the *rutter*. It'll be quicker and quieter if I go alone.'

Akiko crouched back down. 'All right, but if you're gone longer than a few minutes, I'll come and find you.'

'Watch out for any servants!' hissed Yori, his eyes flitting round the gloom of the garden. 'I think I saw candlelight on the second floor.'

'Don't worry,' replied Jack, shooting his friend a wink. 'I'll be back before you can say *arigato gozaimasu*!'

He entered the garden room of the mansion, the waning moon giving him just enough light to see by. Spotting a door, he went over and prised it open. The hallway was shrouded in darkness, no sight or sound of activity. He knew he had to find the library, where he'd hidden the *rutter* the last time they'd been there. From what he remembered of the building's layout, it was down the corridor and round the corner to the left. Silently he stole through the mansion. The double doors to the banqueting chamber had been left partly open, the grand room now empty of revelling guests and bare of decoration. Jack was so tense that his heartbeat seemed to echo round the empty space as he passed. At the end of the hallway, he cautiously peeked his head round the corner. This corridor was deserted too: a relief, but no surprise considering the time of night. From what he recalled of their frantic flight from Sir Toby during the first banquet, the library was the second door on the left. He tiptoed over and, praying it wasn't locked, pushed the door. With the faintest of squeaks, it creaked open.

The library was as quiet as the grave, with only the dying embers of a fire in the grate. Jack stole inside and eased the door shut behind him. By the moonlight shining through the leaded window, Jack could make out the lines of leather-bound books upon the shelves. He went over to the nearest bookcase and reached up for the *rutter* . . .

It wasn't there!

He ran his finger over the shelf again, but no, the logbook's black oilskin cover was nowhere to be seen. Was he mistaken?

Jack looked a third time, then began searching the other shelves, panic welling up in him. *Has someone taken it? Or perhaps someone's moved it?* he thought. Or perhaps he hadn't remembered properly and, in the rush of hiding it from Sir Toby, he had put the *rutter* on a different shelf.

'Is *this* what you're looking for?'

His heart leaping into his mouth, Jack spun round and saw Sir Henry. He reclined in the armchair by the fire, the *rutter* in one hand, a loaded flintlock pistol in the other. Hidden by the shadows, he'd been so still and silent that Jack hadn't noticed him at first.

'That's my father's!' said Jack firmly. 'Give it back to me.'

Sir Henry shook his head. 'Tut tut, young man – what right have you to demand anything in *my* house? This book was in *my* library. In *my* house. So that makes it *mine* now.'

Jack moved to seize the *rutter*, but Sir Henry held up the pistol and put his finger to the trigger. 'Not so fast, young Fletcher.'

'You *won't* shoot me,' challenged Jack, his bravado disguising his doubt. 'You need me to sail your trading fleet to the Japans.'

Pursing his lower lip thoughtfully, Sir Henry regarded the logbook. 'But now that I have this "bible to the seas", I no longer have any need of *you*.' He set the precious *rutter* aside and glared at Jack, his face grave and bone-white in the pale moonlight. 'You were supposed to be my golden goose, the key to restoring my lost fortune. But you had to ruin everything by snooping round Lupus Hall and finding your good-for-nothing sister! Then you brought those plague doctors to my door, or whatever those devils were. As soon as I realized the house was under attack, I summoned the local militia — although a fat lot of good those bumbling idiots were! Lupus Hall is burnt to the ground, and all because of *you*! Now, Jack Fletcher, you'll pay for that debt with your life.'

Jack tensed, preparing to spring out of the way of the oncoming bullet. But Sir Henry's finger didn't pull the trigger.

'Well? What are you waiting for?' said Jack, his heart pounding in his chest. 'If you're going to shoot me, then go ahead and do it!'

'No, I'm not going to shoot you,' Sir Henry replied with a sly grin. 'That would spoil my prize Persian rug . . . and be far too *quick* for my liking.'

He rose from his armchair, keeping the pistol's barrel pointed at Jack's chest.

'Constables!' he cried, summoning four armed men into the library. 'Arrest this boy and his accomplices — who I wager are outside — for breaking into my house and stealing *my* property.'

THREE TIDES

The sun rose red like a bloodshot eye above the River Thames, a cold autumnal mist hanging low over its waters. Only the clink of sailing lines and the squawk of seagulls disturbed the peace of the waking dawn. There was a chill in the air that cut to the bone, hinting at the impending winter. Ships, moored at the myriad wharfs and jetties, shifted and creaked with the incoming tide. Sailors and dockhands shook off the heavy cloak of sleep and set to work, as the bells of the city churches tolled in mournful unison. London was stirring and a new day beckoned.

But for Jack and his friends it would be their last.

They stood upon a wooden plank spanning the gap between two of the jetties at Somers Quay. Nooses had been tied round their necks, the ropes slung over a scaffold and tethered to a pair of workhorses. A small, curious crowd had gathered to watch the early-morning execution, their interest piqued at the sight of the two foreigners and their dishevelled English friend being hanged on the gallows that was normally set aside for pirates. As the docks gradually came to life, more and more people joined the throng. In the middle of the front

334

row stood Sir Henry, dressed in his finest suit and ruff, a gold-topped walking stick in one hand, a fancy rapier on his hip and a haughty sneer upon his fat lips.

'Well . . .' gulped Yori, wobbling on the unsteady plank, 'at least I got to see the Tower of London.'

The oppressive drum-towered castle loomed behind them and Jack glanced sideways at Yori, astonished his friend could muster any humour at such a time. Following their arrest, and on Sir Henry's insistence, the three of them had been escorted across the city and thrown into the infamous Tower, a prison offering no hope of escape. For a day and a night, they'd been holed up in the pit: no light, no food, no water. Their trial had been brief and its outcome a foregone conclusion. The sentence: death by hanging.

'*Forever bound to one another*,' whispered Akiko with a tender look at Jack. Her eyes were pools of both sorrow and eternal love.

Jack desperately wanted to reach out, to hold Akiko one last time, to feel her gentle touch upon him . . . but their hands had been cuffed behind their backs. '*Forever bound to one another*,' he replied, the five words expressing everything he wanted to say and more – his lifelong promise to her and his deep regret at bringing her and Yori to England . . . his unending apology for their present fate; his hopes for their future and his sadness at their loss. But, above all else, his love for her.

A court official pushed his way through the swelling crowd.

'S-s-sorry, I'm late,' he mumbled to Sir Henry, who shot the diminutive and balding man a fierce glare. The court official busied himself with a piece of parchment, shakily unrolling it before taking up his position at the edge of the quay.

'Jack Fletcher, Akiko D–' the bumbling official squinted at the parchment – 'Dāte and Yori Sanada, you have been charged and tried for horse theft, burglary, larceny and arson. You have been formerly tried and sentenced for disturbing the peace, for wilful destruction of property, for brawling in a public place and for violent robbery; the punishment for which you then escaped and went on the run through His Majesty's kingdom.' The crowd fell silent at such a disgraceful list of offences. 'Considering the severity of your crimes and their repeated nature,' the official went on, 'the Court finds you guilty of *all* charges and has decided that you should be hanged by your necks till your bodies are dead and three tides have covered them.' Neatly rolling up the parchment, he then stepped back from the quay.

Now Sir Henry came forward and took his place. He eyed Jack with the utmost contempt. 'It is my duty, as servant of the King and the Court, to pronounce your execution . . .'

Deaf to the man's proclamations, Jack frantically pulled at the manacles round his wrists. If he could get a hand free, then he might just be able to . . . But it was futile. The iron cuffs were too tight, his efforts only shredding his skin. He'd have to chop his own hand off to remove them. He scanned the crowd for a friendly face. By now, Signor Horatio, Rose and Jess must have realized that something had gone terribly wrong with their attempt to recover the *rutter.* But they wouldn't know where to find them. *And what can they do even if they come?* he thought. To attempt a rescue would be suicidal. Jack just prayed that the three of them had seen sense and were already aboard a ship bound for Italy.

The atmosphere round the quay grew tense with excitement as Sir Henry raised his arm to give the hangman the command. Akiko and Yori held their heads high, facing their demise with the honour and dignity befitting samurai. Jack tried to muster up the same bold, defiant spirit, but the sense of injustice at their fate cut too deep. To rub salt into the wound, from his precarious position on the plank, Jack could spy the *Hosiander* among the countless vessels docked at the quay. Their last hope of escape was but a short dash from where they now stood awaiting death.

Sir Henry glowered at Jack and stood poised to signal the hangman. 'May the Lord have mercy upon your souls –'

Suddenly there was a commotion in the crowd.

'MAKE WAY! PARDON! MAKE WAY!' shouted a footman, barging through the bemused onlookers.

The crowd parted and a unit of guards followed hot on the footman's heels, escorting a man and two young women. Now Jack's despair deepened to unimaginable depths. To his horror, he saw the three being held in the guards' custody were Signor Horatio, Rose . . . and Jess! This was the final twist of the knife. Jess and his two loyal friends were to face the same cruel punishment.

Then an elderly silver-haired man wearing a formal chain of office and a slim rapier on his hip stepped forward from the unit of guards. 'Cut them down!' he ordered. It was none other than Lord Robert Percival.

One of the guardsmen dashed over and sliced through the ropes with his sword. Jack, Akiko and Yori teetered on the plank, Yori almost toppling headfirst into the water. Signor Horatio caught him and guided him safely to the quayside, before returning for Jack and Akiko.

'What is the meaning of this?' roared Sir Henry. 'These criminals have been formally tried and sentenced to be hanged until three tides have passed!'

Lord Percival held up a vellum scroll bearing a large red seal. 'I have in my hand a Royal Pardon for all three prisoners from King James himself.'

Sir Henry blustered. 'Let me see that!' He snatched the scroll out of Lord Percival's hand and broke the seal. His indignant expression turned first to befuddlement, then to astonishment, and finally to outrage. 'I don't believe it! No one in their right mind would pardon these rogues!'

A collective gasp went up from the crowd. Lord Percival stared hard at Sir Henry. 'Watch what you say, sir. Are you calling His Majesty the King *mad*?'

Sir Henry swallowed. 'N-n-no . . .' he stammered, 'that's not what I meant at all — just that this pardon might be a forgery.'

Lord Percival's hand rested lightly on the hilt of his rapier. 'Then if you aren't questioning the King's sanity, are you questioning my integrity, sir?'

Inclining his head in deference, Sir Henry replied quickly, 'Of course not, my lord.'

'Good,' said Lord Percival, taking back the scroll. 'Now, guards, arrest this man.'

'*What?*' cried Sir Henry, as he was seized roughly by both arms. 'You *can't* arrest me! I've done nothing wrong.'

Lord Percival peered down his arched nose at him. 'No

338

wrong, you say? The kidnapping and extortion aside, Sir Henry Wilkes, you're hereby charged with failing to pay your debts. It has been decided that you should be held in Fleet Prison until such debts are repaid, in full.'

Sir Henry's face blanched. 'But I owe thousands upon thousands of pounds!' he exclaimed, as the guards started dragging him away.

'Then you'll be in prison, sir, for a *very* long time,' replied Lord Percival with a wry smile.

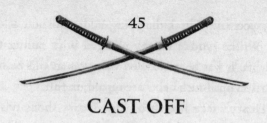

45

CAST OFF

'King James wishes you good fortune on your voyage,' said Lord Percival, handing Jack his precious *rutter*. They were standing on the quayside the following morning. It was a wholly different day from the one before. The dawn sun was warm, the sky blue and cloudless, and the air fresh and crisp, a steady westerly breeze blowing. London gleamed like a jewel in the autumnal light, the gothic tower of St Paul's a beacon above the shining roofs of the city. A regal bevy of swans glided over the waters of the Thames and countless ferries weaved in and out of one another like damselflies. The dockside was hectic and noisy, yet the bustle had a reassuring rhythm to its chaos – and no victims hung from the pirate gallows overlooking Somers Quay.

Gratefully welcoming the return of the logbook, Jack was then given an envelope with an official red wax seal.

'As His emissary to the Japans,' explained Lord Percival, 'you are asked by King James to deliver this letter of goodwill to the Emperor and he trusts that a mutually beneficial trading agreement can be brokered.'

'I'll do my utmost to fulfil His Majesty's request,' said

Jack, respectfully taking the letter and stowing it safely in his pack with the *rutter*. As part of the deal for securing their pardon, Jack was to act as the official royal envoy to the Japans. The promise of a lucrative trade agreement between those islands and England had helped Lord Percival convince the King of Jack and his friends' merit. But much of the credit for their last-minute pardon belonged to Rose, whose idea it had been in the first place to approach Lord and Lady Percival for help. Signor Horatio, being a knighted gentleman, had been able to make a direct approach to the lord who in turn had then secured an audience with His Majesty.

'Once again we must thank you and Lady Catherine for your kind graces and timely intervention,' said Jack, inclining his head stiffly, his neck still sore from the noose's burn.

'We offer you our deepest gratitude too,' said Akiko, bowing low with Yori.

'Consider it a good deed returned,' Lord Percival replied heartily. 'If it wasn't for you and your friends, I'd likely still be tied half-naked to a tree, and my darling Lady Catherine here would be without a head!' At this, she curtseyed her gratitude. 'Saving you from the gallows was the least I could do.' An arch smile crossed his lips. 'Just don't fall foul of the law again. The King won't pardon you twice!'

Akiko laughed. 'You can be assured, my lord, that we've no intention of getting into further trouble upon these shores.'

Yori raised an eyebrow and murmured wistfully, 'The only problem is – trouble seems to find *us*!'

Patting his friend amiably on the back, Jack said, 'It's lucky, then, that we watch one another's backs.'

341

'JACK!' called Captain Spilbergen from the quarterdeck of the *Hosiander*. 'We're casting off.'

Lord Percival shook Jack's hand, then bid farewell to the others. 'Forgive me, I too must attend to the King's business. I bid you safe passage.'

As they watched him and Lady Catherine depart, Jess turned to Rose and Signor Horatio. 'So, dear friends . . . this is goodbye, then?'

Rose nodded and pulled Jess into her arms. Jess began to cry and tears welled up in Rose's eyes too. Jack also shed a tear at the thought of leaving Rose, the girl who'd given him his first kiss, who'd guided them through the perils of London and all the way to Stratford . . . and who had ultimately saved his sister's life.

'The witch was right,' sniffed Rose, drying her eyes.

'About what?' asked Jack.

'Her prophecy,' Rose explained. '*One will live, Two will love, Three will cry, and Four will die.*'

First she nodded at Akiko. 'You lived after being drowned on the ducking stool.'

Then she turned her gaze affectionately upon Signor Horatio. 'We two fell in love.' As Signor Horatio kissed Rose on the cheek, Jack's eyes met Akiko's. Rose and Horatio weren't the only two to find love.

Wiping away Jess's tears for her, Rose went on: 'And at least three of us are crying.'

'And four died,' said Yori ominously, giving them all a grave look.

'I'm just glad that that part of the prophecy turned out to be the ninja plague doctors rather than us!' said Jack with a morbid laugh.

After Jess had finished hugging Rose goodbye, Akiko stepped forward. 'I know we haven't always seen eye-to-eye, Rose, but I was wrong to judge you too hastily. In our time together you've demonstrated loyalty, honour and courage – the virtues of a true samurai. As a token of my respect for you, please accept this small gift.' And, bowing, Akiko humbly offered Rose her golden *kanzashi*.

'Why . . . thank you,' said Rose, for once seemingly lost for words. Admiring the *sakura* flower engraved at the end, she added, 'It's beautiful.'

Akiko shared a conspiratorial smile with her. 'It's also deadly . . . just like *you*!'

'Signor Horatio had best keep on my good side, then!' Rose laughed and slid the sharpened hairpin into her mane of flame-red hair. 'I've only this pomander for you,' she said, and she presented Akiko with a strongly scented carved wooden ball on a red ribbon. 'The perfume will keep away the bad smell of the sailors!'

'It's not stolen, is it?' asked Akiko, sniffing the spiced rose aroma appreciatively.

Rose laughed, a mischievous twinkle in her eye. 'Of course not! I made it myself. On your example, I've finally seen the error of my ways.'

'Then it's all the more valuable,' said Akiko, hanging the pomander round her neck.

Next Yori bowed his respects and gave Signor Horatio and Rose a pair of matching *origami* paper cranes. 'For peace,' he explained.

Finally it was Jack's turn. 'Signor Horatio, you're a loyal friend, a fine gentleman and a true sword master. I know my guardian, Masamoto Takeshi, will be fascinated to learn the fencing skills you've taught me. The way of the rapier is another world to the way of the *katana*.'

'*Certo, signor!* That's what makes it such a fine weapon.' Then Signor Horatio unsheathed his slender steel rapier and handed it to Jack. 'Take it. You now have the best of both worlds.'

'I can't accept this,' said Jack, taken aback at such a generous gift.

Signor Horatio clasped Jack's shoulder. 'I can't think of a better student to wield such a blade . . . apart from Akiko, of course.' He then produced another rapier with a finely crafted handguard, which he presented to Akiko, who bowed deeply in appreciation.

As Signor Horatio stepped away, Rose came forward. 'I'm afraid I don't have anything for you, Jack . . .' she said demurely, 'except this –' and she planted her lips on his cheek. In that moment, the memory of a young red-haired girl kissing him beneath Moorgate awoke in Jack's mind. He smiled and gave his childhood friend a fond hug.

'*Are you coming or what?*' yelled a sailor from the *Hosiander*'s main deck, breaking up the tender moment.

After a final flurry of goodbyes, Jack, Akiko, Yori and Jess grabbed their packs and hurried up the gangplank. As the *Hosiander* cast off, they bid a final farewell to Rose and Signor Horatio down on the quay. Then, with the ship easing out of port, they ran to the stern. Their two friends still stood arm in arm at the far end of the quay, all the time waving, until the ship rounded a bend in the river and they disappeared from view.

★

Leaning on the stern gunwale, Jack gazed at the wake of the ship as it ploughed through the sea and at the thin line of land fast disappearing behind the darkening horizon. After three days' good sailing, the *Hosiander* had left the Thames Estuary, passed through the Strait of Dover and along the English Channel, and was now heading for the open ocean.

'I hope you're not too sad to be leaving your home so soon after arriving,' said Akiko, who leant beside him with Jess and Yori. Her long black hair rippled in the breeze.

Jack sighed, his face forlorn. 'I thought it was home, but after so many years away it didn't feel like home any more. England's become a foreign country to me.' He looked at Jess with a tender smile. 'But I found who I was looking for. That's all that *really* matters.' He wrapped an arm round his sister and drew her to him. She buried her head in his chest, and Jack experienced the warmth in his heart that only family could kindle.

'I'm just sorry I dragged you two all the way here,' continued Jack, giving Akiko and Yori an apologetic look. 'You must think England is such a dreadful place.'

'Not at all!' said Yori with surprising enthusiasm. 'Your country is full of wonders and riches.'

Jack frowned in astonishment. 'But from the moment we set foot on English soil, we were insulted, attacked, unjustly imprisoned, hunted down, accused of witchcraft, drowned or otherwise shot at, imprisoned again, and almost hanged from the gallows!'

'All that's certainly true,' said Yori, his hand gently massaging the purple bruise round his neck. 'But we've also seen London's magnificent bridge, browsed the market stalls at Cheapside, visited the cottage you grew up in, performed at the famous Globe Theatre –'

'We've attended a real English banquet *and* a masked ball,' joined in Akiko with equal zeal, 'travelled on horseback through glorious countryside, met some wonderful people and made some true friends, as well as –' she stroked the slim sword on her hip – 'been taught how to wield a rapier.'

'We even saw the Tower of London!' Yori exclaimed.

'Yes,' Akiko agreed drily, 'although I'd prefer it to have been from the *outside*!'

Yori laughed. 'You see, Jack, Sensei Yamada told me it's the journey not the destination that matters, but I've discovered it's *who* you share that journey with that is most important. And we shared it with *you*.'

Jack gazed at his friends with affection, heartened by their genuine passion for his country. Like his own experiences of Japan, there had been bad times, terrible places and cruel people. But equally there'd been much to delight in. And, with true friends at his side, he realized it didn't matter what life threw at him. One can always stand the rain knowing that the sun still shines behind the clouds.

'I'm getting cold,' said Jess, a shiver running through her. The night was almost upon them and England was but a slender shadow against the twilit sky.

'Let's go back to our cabins,' Yori suggested. 'I think I've mastered knucklebones now.'

'*Really?*' said Jess. 'That sounds like a challenge to me.'

The two of them headed down the ladder to below deck, leaving Jack and Akiko alone. Akiko nestled up to Jack, the chill wind making her kimono flutter like a sail. 'I'm glad you're coming back to Japan with me,' she said softly. 'If I'm honest with you, I couldn't live in England. But I couldn't live without you either.'

Jack gazed into her eyes, peering deep into her soul. 'And I would die without you by my side.'

Closing their eyes, they kissed as the first stars twinkled in the heavens above their heads.

All of a sudden, Akiko went rigid, her whole body seeming to freeze as if in crippling pain.

'Akiko! What's wrong?' asked Jack. But Akiko could only let out a feeble moan as she slumped against the ship's rail. Then a shadow from behind materialized into a hooded ninja.

'It looks like she'll die with you by her side instead!' rasped the assassin, laughing at his own joke.

'What have you done to her?' demanded Jack.

'*Dim Mak*, of course –' The ninja broke into a coughing fit. It was so bad that he had to pull back his hood for air.

'Kazuki!' gasped Jack, stunned to see his enemy alive and aboard their ship. But he barely recognized his old rival. Kazuki's face was pale and sweaty, his eyes watery and bloodshot, his skin peppered with oozing spots and his neck swollen with black buboes.

'A curse on your filthy country!' spluttered Kazuki, spitting up bile. 'I was right . . . your kind are a *pestilence*!'

With stark horror, Jack realized Kazuki had contracted the plague. He must have got it from his infected wound or the plague doctor's clothes he'd been wearing, or a combination of both. However he'd caught it, his rival was now a walking corpse.

Kazuki drew a *tantō* from his *obi* with a trembling hand. 'I've been w-w-waiting . . . until you t-t-two were alone,' he stuttered. 'Three . . . long . . . days . . . but now I will have my revenge!'

Kazuki lunged at Jack with the knife. The attack was desperate, fierce and wild. Jack nimbly dodged the blade, jumping aside to avoid any possible contact with the plague-ridden Kazuki. He then swept Kazuki's legs from under him. Having put all his strength into the strike, Kazuki fell forward and crashed into the gunwale. He lost his balance and tumbled over the rail.

As his enemy plunged headfirst into the churning wake, Jack dropped to his knees and cradled Akiko in his arms. Her breathing was rapid, her face purple and strained, her body shuddering. Jack shouted at the top of his voice for help. A moment later, he heard the soft pad of feet on the deck and Yori was at his side.

'What happened?' he asked, kneeling down and examining Akiko's stiffened form in the darkness.

'*Dim Mak!*' replied Jack as he held her gently, knowing from bitter experience the crushing pain that she would be experiencing in her heart. 'Kazuki did it.'

Without need for further explanation, Yori struck a series of pressure points on her back and released Akiko from the death grip. Her face immediately relaxed, her breathing eased and she stopped trembling. 'I'm all right . . .' she panted, giving Jack a reassuring smile. 'The pain's going . . .'

Leaving Akiko in Yori's good care, Jack peered over the gunwale for Kazuki. His rival was floundering in the wake, fast being left behind by the ship. Out of mercy, Jack threw Kazuki a line.

'Grab the rope!' he shouted.

But, even though the line was within easy reach, Kazuki let it glide past. As the *Hosiander* sailed away, he stopped swimming and slipped silently beneath the waves.

46

THE RETURN OF THE WARRIOR

The fan-sailed fishing boat eased through the emerald-green waters into a sheltered cove. Encircled by lush green cedar trees along its towering clifftops, the cove harboured a beach of pure golden sand within its inner bay.

'Welcome to Toba!' said Jack to his sister, who stood with him on the bow of the fishing vessel. 'The place where our father and I first set eyes upon Japan and –' he pointed to an exquisite temple of red pillars at the top of the headland, its entrance dominated by a huge standing stone – 'where I first saw Akiko.'

'*Utsukushī!*' breathed Jess, gasping at its beauty.

'Excellent, Jess,' praised Yori, joining them on the prow with Akiko. 'You're now speaking as fluently as a samurai!'

'*Arigato gozaimasu,*' she replied with a bow.

Jack grinned. After more than a year at sea and under Yori's daily tuition, Jess had quickly picked up the language and her Japanese was now almost better than his own. Alongside her linguistic skills, Jess had also been tutored by Akiko in Japanese etiquette and fashions. She now wore a silk kimono of pink *sakura* flowers, one of several robes

Akiko had helped purchase in the port of Nagasaki before their onward journey north to Toba. Jack too had exchanged his English doublet and hose for a samurai's *haori* and *hakama*, the two swords on his hip ensuring all recognized his status as a *hatamoto* in the service of Takatomi, the Regent of Japan.

As the boat approached the beach, Jack was surprised to see a lone figure standing upon the sand. They'd sailed to the secluded cove, rather than the main harbour of Toba, as they wanted to avoid a scene. The arrival of a foreigner on their shores — let alone two — would cause a serious commotion in the little fishing port. Not that Jack expected trouble. Rather, he anticipated a crowd so large that it might completely overwhelm them. Everyone would be fascinated to see Jess, a girl with golden blonde hair.

But someone clearly *had* anticipated their plans. Dressed in a crisp white kimono and equally pristine white *hakama*, the samurai waited and watched as the fishing boat pulled up at the beach's little wooden jetty. Before the boat had even docked, Jack jumped from the prow and headed purposefully down the narrow pier. Striding up to the samurai, his hand resting upon the hilt of his *katana*, he looked straight into the man's amber eyes and scarred face. Then with a deep bow Jack said in Japanese, 'You honour us with your presence, Masamoto-sama.'

Smiling, his guardian inclined his head, then bowed too, holding it as a mark of respect and affection for the young samurai. 'And you honour me with your return, Jack-san.'

In the rays of the evening sun the standing stone glowed fire-red. Jack sat against it, feeling the warmth of the rock and listening to the distant wash of the waves in the cove below. Their return to Toba and Akiko's home had been all he'd hoped for. Akiko's mother, Hiroko, had joyfully welcomed them with open arms, her delight at seeing her daughter once more reviving life into her lined face like the blooming of a flower. Akiko's little brother Jiro, older and taller, had nonetheless been as excited as the first time he'd met Jack, and throughout the entire welcome meal was entranced by Jess's blonde hair. Masamoto-sama had been his typical restrained and formal self, but even he couldn't hide his eagerness upon seeing a rapier and securing Jack's promise to teach him the Western way of the sword.

However, once the meal drew to a close and thoughts turned to bed, Jack desired a moment alone. To contemplate. So he'd strolled up to the headland, the temple's tranquillity making it the perfect place to think of his father. Jack missed him with as much pain in his heart as the love he held for him. But were it not for his father, Jack would *never* have come to Japan. He would *never* have trained as a samurai. He would *never* have met his dear friends Yori and Akiko.

For all that he'd lost, he'd also gained.

A light crunch of footsteps upon the gravel path interrupted his thoughts.

'May I join you?' asked Akiko softly, appearing from behind the standing stone.

Jack smiled and nodded. 'You never need ask.'

Akiko settled down next to him and together they watched the sun setting over the mountains and the last rays of light dancing over the rippling waters of the cove.

'Masamoto once told me that true victory lies in

forgiveness and understanding,' said Jack, his mind drifting back to the night Akiko had almost been killed by Kazuki. 'I now know what he means. I can understand Kazuki's hatred for me – for any *gaijin*, for that matter. After all, he'd lost his mother to a disease contracted from a foreign priest. In his eyes, I was that disease. But only now that Kazuki is gone can I find it in my heart to forgive him.'

Akiko took his hand. 'I know you tried to save him. But he was beyond saving. It was perhaps for the best Kazuki drowned himself.'

Jack nodded. 'Better that than a drawn-out death from the plague. I hope, for his soul's sake, that he has found peace at last.'

'And what about you?' asked Akiko, turning to him in the growing dusk. 'Have you found peace?'

Jack gazed thoughtfully at the darkening sky, searching his heart and soul, but Akiko seemed to already know the answer. She produced a Daruma Doll, the one Jack had wished upon and given her for safekeeping when he first left on his journey to find his sister. The round wooden doll had one eye painted, the other still blank . . . waiting until that time when his wish was fulfilled. Akiko handed him a small inked brush. 'You do it,' she encouraged.

With a dab of black ink, Jack painted in the other eye. He set the Daruma Doll upon a flat stone between them, then wrapped his arm round Akiko. As the ruby-red sun sank behind the mountains, Akiko drew closer and rested her head upon his shoulder. In that moment Jack knew he was truly home.

The warrior had returned.

JAPANESE GLOSSARY

Bushido

Bushido, meaning the 'Way of the Warrior', is a Japanese code of conduct similar to the concept of chivalry. Samurai warriors were meant to adhere to the seven moral principles in their martial arts training and in their day-to-day lives.

Virtue 1: *Gi* – Rectitude
Gi is the ability to make the right decision with moral confidence and to be fair and equal towards all people no matter what colour, race, gender or age.

Virtue 2: *Yu* – Courage
Yu is the ability to handle any situation with valour and confidence.

仁

礼

真

名誉

忠義

Virtue 3: *Jin* – Benevolence

Jin is a combination of compassion and generosity. This virtue works together with *Gi* and discourages samurai from using their skills arrogantly or for domination.

Virtue 4: *Rei* – Respect

Rei is a matter of courtesy and proper behaviour towards others. This virtue means to have respect for all.

Virtue 5: *Makoto* – Honesty

Makoto is about being honest to oneself as much as to others. It means acting in ways that are morally right and always doing things to the best of your ability.

Virtue 6: *Meiyo* – Honour

Meiyo is sought with a positive attitude in mind, but will only follow with correct behaviour. Success is an honourable goal to strive for.

Virtue 7: *Chungi* – Loyalty

Chungi is the foundation of all the virtues; without dedication and loyalty to the task at hand and to one another, one cannot hope to achieve the desired outcome.

A Short Guide to Pronouncing Japanese Words

Vowels are pronounced in the following way:
'a' as the 'a' in 'at'
'e' as the 'e' in 'bet'
'i' as the 'i' in 'police'
'o' as the 'o' in 'dot'
'u' as the 'u' in 'put'
'ai' as in 'eye'
'ii' as in 'week'
'ā' as in 'far'
'ō' as in 'go'
'ū' as in 'blue'

Consonants are pronounced in the same way as English:
'g' is hard as in 'get'
'j' is soft as in 'jelly'
'ch' as in 'church'
'z' as in 'zoo'
'ts' as in 'itself'

Each syllable is pronounced separately:
A-ki-ko
Ya-ma-to
Ma-sa-mo-to
Ka-zu-ki

arigatō gozaimasu	thank you very much
bushido	the Way of the Warrior – the samurai code
Butokuden	Hall of the Virtues of War
Daimyo	Japanese feudal lord

daishō	the pair of swords, *wakizashi* and *katana*, that are the traditional weapons of the samurai
Dim Mak	the Death Touch
gaijin	a foreigner, outsider (derogatory term)
hakama	wide-legged Japanese trousers
hamon	the visual pattern on a sword as a result of tempering the blade
haori	a jacket
hashi	chopsticks
hatamoto	honorary rank in the direct service of the Shogun or Regent
kagemusha	a shadow warrior
kamon	family crest
Kanojo o tebanasu!	Let her go!
kanzashi	a hairpin
katame waza	grappling techniques
katana	a long sword
kenjutsu	the Art of the Sword
ki	energy flow or life force (Chinese: *chi* or *qi*)
kiai-jutsu	the art of the *kiai* (shout)
kimono	traditional Japanese clothing
kissaki	the tip of the sword
kunoichi	a female ninja
kyusho	a pressure point
manriki	a short chain weapon with two steel weights on the ends
mempō	protective metal mask covering part or all of the face
Nam-myoho-renge-kyo	Buddhist chant
Nikyo	a wrist lock (second technique, or second teaching)

ninja	a Japanese assassin
ninjatō	a ninja sword
ninjutsu	the Art of Stealth
Niten Ichi Ryū	the 'One School of Two Heavens'
obi	a belt
ryumon ki	dragon's gate point
sakura	the cherry-blossom tree
samurai	a Japanese warrior
saya	a scabbard
sensei	a teacher
seoi-nage	shoulder throw
shakujō	a Buddhist ringed staff
shinobi	another name for a ninja, literally a 'stealer in'
shinobi shōzoku	the clothing of a ninja
Shisha no Nemuri	the Sleep of the Dead
shuriken	a metal throwing star
taijutsu	the Art of the Body (hand-to-hand combat)
tantō	a short knife
Tasukete! Abunai!	Help me! Danger!
tsuba	hand guard
ukemi	falling techniques
waki-gamae	a fighting stance in *kenjutsu*
wakizashi	a short sword
wako	Japanese pirates
ya	arrow
yubitsume	a Japanese ritual to atone for offences by means of cutting off one's own little finger (literally 'finger shortening')
yumi	a bow
yūrei	Japanese ghost

Japanese names usually consist of a family name (surname) followed by a given name, unlike names in the Western world, where the given name comes before the family name. In feudal Japan, names reflected a person's social status and spiritual beliefs. When addressing someone, *san* is added to that person's family name (or given names in less formal situations) as a sign of courtesy, in the same way that we use Mr or Mrs, for example, in English; for higher-status people, *sama* is used. In Japan, *sensei* is usually added after a person's name if they are a teacher, although in the Young Samurai books a traditional English word order has been retained. Boys and girls are usually addressed using the suffixes *kun* and *chan* respectively.

ACKNOWLEDGEMENTS

This final book in the Young Samurai series was the hardest of my life to write. Not only did I have to ensure the writing was at its very best in order to meet the expectations of my long-patient readers, but I was dealing with a personal family crisis that resulted in depression and my being unable to write for almost a year. So this story has literally been forged in a furnace of fire and tears.

The Return of the Warrior was only possible because of the support and love of my friends and close family. I wish to express my eternal gratitude to them . . .

My hypnotherapist Alex Vrettos, the man who performed a miracle and got me writing again; Mary, your healing powers are a gift; my acupuncturist Jeremy Marshall (is there any point on my body you haven't stuck with a pin?!); Paweena Promkot (Toto), for reviving me with your East–West therapy; Sara Davison for setting me up for a better, brighter and happier future; and my solicitor Robert Williams, for your calm guidance and compassion through a most challenging time.

My agent Charlie Viney, I will always treasure our

friendship over and above our excellent working relationship; my publishers for their understanding and flexibility in delivering this book, in particular Tig Wallace and Wendy Shakespeare; my accountants Dawn, Denise and Heidi, for not only providing numbers but listening and caring; and Trevor Wilson, Camilla Kenyon, Lisa Thompson and all the team at Authors Abroad for their support and understanding.

All my friends; only when you are truly in need do you discover who your true friends are. I am blessed to have you all in my life: the HGC – Dan, Dax, Larry, Siggy, Riz, Kul and Andy; Farah, Dotty, Becky, Cat, Debs, Stepanka and Nicky; Geoff (and Lucy), Charlie and Matt; Mark and Kate Dyson (and my god-daughter Lulu!); my neighbour and comrade-in-arms David Leppenwell; Brian and Kate Corr; Thomas Corr for your early advice; Emma Gibbins; Helen Caithness; Russell and Jackie Holdaway; Rob Rose for our cinema-therapy sessions; Sarah Hitt; Lisa and Simon Martin; Rob and Robbie Cooper; Nick Coward; Philippa Luscombe; Rob Dunkerley and Oli Bishop; and B, you have a heart of gold – thank you for being my burst of sunshine!

My neighbours and friends in the village who offered their support and helped me through: Jan and Scott Holt for their kindness and prayers; my dear neighbour Jan; Russell and Lucy Driver; Andy Hitt; Rachel Felton; Will and Caroline Kemp for their prayers too; Naomi and Ian McBain; Dr Thomson, Dr Graham and Dr Cook for their care; Chris at the greengrocer's; my Hurst Colt football friends Scott, Christian, Mike, Kieran and Neil; Sarah McCaffery for being there always for the boys; Colin and Heather; my counsellors, Beverly Nolan, Jaki Watkins and Dorothy

Orchard; Philip Carter for your friendship and counsel; and Cynthia Davies, my rescuer on the street.

My Uncle Brian and Cherrill for your unwavering support; and my godparents Ann and Andrew for your thoughts and prayers.

My soul protector Alessia for carrying me through the darkest times from near and afar. My two guardian angels Karen and Hayley for saving me again and again – I cannot thank you two enough.

My mum and dad, who were there with me every step of the way along this hard path. Now we can smile again, there is only light ahead . . .

And my two wonderful boys, Zach and Leo, you kept the fire burning in me. I love you with all my heart and always will.

Finally, *arigatō gozaimasu* to all my readers, librarians, teachers and booksellers. You have waited a long time for this book. Your patience and continued support are appreciated.

Thank you,
Chris

Any fans can keep in touch with me and the progress of the Young Samurai series on my Facebook page, or via the website at *www.youngsamurai.com*

MEET CHRIS

What was your inspiration for the Young Samurai books?
I've always dreamed of being a samurai. That period in history was such an exciting time and the samurai were the greatest warriors to have lived. The Young Samurai books are a way of living that dream!

Do you plot in advance or let the story develop as you write?
I always plot out the entire story before starting the writing process. I use this plot as a 'rough guide', since often the story will diverge in different directions as the characters take hold and live a life of their own. Somehow the book always ends up where I'd planned it to go. When I first came up with the idea for *Young Samurai: The Way of the Warrior*, I knew the end of the third book and the ninth book!

If music be the food of love, what do you think writing is?
The elixir of learning! Writing stretches the mind, taking it beyond its usual boundaries, and it allows one to embark on fantastic journeys of the imagination.

What hobbies do you have and how do they influence your work?
My main hobby is martial arts, so clearly my knowledge of samurai and ninja skills forms an important part of my writing. In particular, it allows me to describe fight scenes in true detail, so that the reader really believes they're participating in the fight and taking the punches!

Do you ever encounter writer's block and, if so, how do you overcome it?
I have regular little blocks that I overcome with a run or a walk or a cookie! But once I suffered a month-long block due to creative exhaustion. The solution: two weeks in South Africa with no computer or mobile phone, and just a bunch of giraffes, lions and cheetahs for company! Now I use hypnotherapy – this is a fast route to my subconscious!

Did you ever take any writing classes or specific instructions to learn the craft?

No, but I did read Stephen King's book *On Writing*. This is a brilliant guide to the art of writing and I recommend it to any aspiring author.

What are the best and worst aspects of writing for a living?

The hardest part is always starting – the fear of the blank white page and the knowledge that I have to write 70,000 words or more by a deadline. But, once I get going, the writing flows. The most enjoyable part of the process is discovering where the characters will take the story. I may be the author, but they are writing it – and they often surprise me!

Who would win in a fight, a samurai or a ninja?

That very question is answered in Book 3: *The Way of the Dragon*. The result of the fight may surprise you!

What's the best writing advice you have been given?

Simple: write the book you would want to read.

If you weren't a writer, what would you be?

I would love to be an explorer like my friend Steve Backshall. It's great visiting different countries and cultures. The amazing thing is that as an author I can go exploring as research for my next book series.

If someone were to enter a bookshop, how would you persuade them to try your new novel over someone else's?

I'd stand right next to them with my samurai sword and gently persuade them that their life depended upon it!

YOUNG SAMURAI

BLACK-BELT NINJAS &
BLOCKBUSTER ACTION

 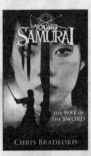  

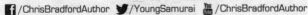

THE SOUL PROPHECY

'DEATH IS ONLY THE BEGINNING'

COMING NEXT FROM

CHRIS BRADFORD